SEWER SKEWERS

COOKING WITH DISASTER
BOOK 2

DAKOTA KROUT

MOUNTAINDALE
PRESS

ACKNOWLEDGMENTS

I see you've survived the Bove. That's a good start.

Look! You are at book 2! There's all the proof I need that my amazingly supportive wife is awesome at marketing and building relationships with people.

Thank you all for being a part of this amazing adventure with me. Especially you, Aaron Michael Ritchey. My son was named after him, because of how amazing this guy is.

May your future be delicious.

PROLOGUE

"Say that again?" Richard Crave wasn't sure he'd heard the Shadow Killer's real name correctly. "I thought you said your name was-"

"Nacho," the too-young kid told him with a wry grin. The Shadow Killer clearly *wasn't* a kid, but Crave felt just *so* much older than him. This Nacho character was in his early twenties and had just graduated from the University of Missouri–Kansas City, so Crave could be forgiven for considering him to be young. He hadn't been expecting the serious killer's nickname to be so childish. He had read the reports himself: the youthful assassin had the ethics of a starving rabies-riddled badger with an addiction to adrenaline.

He lived like he had nothing to live for at all.

Crave had been expecting nothing but dark looks and clipped words when he invited Nacho to talk in his guildhall, which he'd built over the Chicken Coop of Chaos Dungeon. Finding that dungeon—thanks to Paul 'the Dungeon Rat' Rizzo —had made all the difference during the earliest days of the apocalypse. Crave winced internally as he thought about his recently passed guild member. Poor sucker. Both Rizzo and Red Suzy Blacke had stumbled onto a Tier *two* monster way down in the Stone Cold Eve Staustin, a dungeon filled with swarming creatures that tried to wrestle you to the ground.

As far as they could tell, some dungeons were just flat-out impossible. Some were easy, like the Chaos Coop, which was why Crave felt so lucky. In the first days of the Juxtaposition, he and twelve other players had formed a party. They had killed *hundreds* of the chicken-bats infesting the place, and the party had turned into a guild as soon as they found a guild charter as a reward for defeating the boss monster.

The Chaos Coop had a kitchen, but Crave couldn't stand the taste of the Putrid Mana, so they'd smashed it up and turned it into a master bedroom; then eaten Store food for a long time. That had taken care of their Satiation levels just fine, until Crave and his people hit level ten.

Then the price of food tripled, and everything changed.

That was the very reason why Crave had reached out to the Shadow Killer. Crave was pretty sure that this Nacho was just as tired of throwing his credits away on overpriced buffet food that tasted like the leftovers at a nursing home. Crave might have found a solution.

Now, Crave and Nacho were relaxing in his guildhall, drinking Epic ale—hooch with a maxed-out rarity—from Store tankards. They sat across from each other at a rough-hewn feasting table, because the Patrons loved their whole medieval fantasy game setting a bit too much. No electricity. No internal combustion engines. No gunpowder.

Crave didn't question the physics that had forced these circumstances into existence. He just played the game, and in his mind… he played it well.

Six months of sweating and grinding. In that time, he'd built the guildhall, drawn a thousand people to him, and gotten a taste of every transaction, thanks to his guild tax. That had also included the special bonus for gaining a thousand members, which had been substantial—a quarter million credits right off the bat. Everything combined meant that he was sitting on half a million credits. Crave was buying Epic meals at sixty credits a pop, and he had no intention to reduce his spending.

The Guild Master only ate once a day to avoid the Starvation debuff. As far as he was concerned, his dungeoneering days were behind him. From now on, he was going to focus on the things that made him successful: riding out the rest of this 'game' by being a politician, convincing people to join him, and then living off their taxes. He would never lose his power or position, because he had a service to provide to his followers— his Patron, Fourtuna, had given him a boon.

This 'Nacho' fool was dressed in black and red assassin leathers, with a loose cloak over his shoulders. Crave had let him come in with his short swords, one curved for slicing, the other slender and straight for thrusting. Also of note was a short bow with a small quiver. Even so, the weapons were hardly worrisome. If the Shadow Killer went for Crave, he'd have to deal with Hogan and Whitney; both stood in a nearby entryway. If the heavies were too slow, Crave also had his magic feather. A single swipe across Nacho's cheek, and the Assassin would be asleep in seconds.

The strange kid pointed at Hogan and Whitney. "Goon One and Goon Two. I asked around. People like you just fine, but those two are escapees from a prison... at best. Why'd you take them in, Crave? Out of the goodness of your heart? Or were they like puppies that got dropped on your doorstep in a basket?"

"Not the second, that's for sure." Crave chuckled at the imagery this young Assassin could evoke.

"That makes good sense. Those are big goons. You'd need big baskets."

Crave snorted into his Epic ale. "Hogan and Whitney were with me from the beginning. We arrived in the AKC as just strangers on the freeway. I was on I-70 when it hit. Me and my wife… no. I don't like to talk about what happened before the Juxtaposition. It's just easier, you know?"

Nacho glanced down, and Crave glimpsed a hint of his inner pain slipping through the indifferent mask that he typically wore. "Yeah. Memories are stupid. I've heard people calling this the Alternate Kansas City. I guess that makes sense."

"Yeah. Good ol' AKC." Crave recognized that expression in Nacho's dark eyes, the look of someone who'd lost people and would never be the same again. He didn't want this meeting to turn sour, so he changed subjects. "Nacho… you've gotta tell me about your name."

Nacho shrugged and spit out a prepared speech, as though he'd told the story hundreds of times. "Not much to tell. I grew up Eli Naches, named after the river, or that's what my… that's what I was told while growing up. Eventually, Naches became Nacho. It fits me fine."

"It is fine. I like it, even." Crave was listening very carefully. It seemed this Shadow Killer had come from a less-than-ideal background. Perhaps that explained his moral flexibility? Crave didn't have that excuse; he came across his own immorality honestly—by just living life and seeking power over others in this world. Hoping to find out if the kid was another blessed individual—someone like himself—Crave gently probed, "I thought the Patrons might've named you Nacho."

The Assassin rolled his eyes in sheer annoyance. "If the Patrons ever talked to me, I'd have a thing or two to say to them. For one, the version of pizza they offer in the Store is about as bad as the countless deaths they caused to the peoples of the Earth. Another thing: I get that they didn't want us to drive around in our SUVs and shoot monsters with rocket launchers. But *no* electricity? That was low."

"I've talked to my Patron," Crave quietly admitted to the youngster. "It's never a pleasant experience. Or maybe I have a bad Patron, I don't know. But Fourtuna *knows* he has almost unlimited power, and that doesn't make him very nice. I guess if you're basically a god, you don't need to be nice."

"I wouldn't mind some of that." Nacho raised his tankard. "To growing so powerful that we don't need to be nice."

They *clanked* their drinks and let the golden fluid quench their thirst and blur their memories of a better time.

"Let's talk business. I'm pretty sure if you wanted me dead, you wouldn't have invited me into your hall. You'd have sent a Rogue or an Assassin to come after me. Likely, the woman with the bow. Not that she'd have been able to take me down, but still..." The young man considered the remaining contents of his mug, snapping his fingers as he tried to remember. "What was her name? Black Suzy? Scarlet Sue? Something Suzy something."

"Red Suzy Blacke," Crave answered with a heavy sigh. "She and Rizzo didn't make it. We lost them a few weeks ago."

"Ah... so *that's* why I'm here." Nacho shook his head and positioned himself for jumping into a fight. "You didn't send someone to kill me, even though I've poached credits from your hunting parties. I don't think you'd poison me with your fancy-schmancy beer. You want me to join your guild? I'm not exactly what you'd call a 'joiner'. I've only had two friends in my entire life, and they're both dead. Why would I give up my independence when I'm *already* the best at what I do?"

Crave set his tankard down and pointed at Nacho. "Right there. That's one reason. You *don't* need us. Yes, we agree that memories are stupid, and it's best not to talk about the world before, but I'm gonna go back on that a little. I was the Vice President of Sales for Big-Brand Sporting Apparel. I've done hundreds of interviews, if not thousands. It always comes down to two questions: what I can do for you... and what you can do for me."

"Well, that's very transactional." Nacho swished the Epic beer around in his mouth. "I can steal away credits for you. I wait for everyone to hit the big monsters, then swoop in and take the final hit of the beastie and hijack all the cash. But that's not why I'm here, is it? You want me to start killing people?"

"Not yet," Crave admitted quietly, suddenly feeling that

their meeting wasn't as private as he needed. "But that's where we're heading, and it's gonna be either humans or CrossHumans... you know what I'm talking about."

"To our impending need for cannibalism!" Nacho lifted his cup again, but this time his words were as sour as common-rank Store beer. "Shouldn't we be eating CrossHuman jerky with this?"

Crave didn't know what to make of the CrossHumans. They came through portals, had cross-shaped pupils, but were more interested in hunting regular round-pupil humans than monsters. The most dangerous of them, Arriod, had a katana that did some bad, bad things to human bodies.

"CrossHuman jerky wouldn't contain Putrid Mana, would it?" Crave shook his head. Putrid Mana was what had infected all of the animals and turned them into monsters. At Tier zero, it had tainted the flavor of any animal meat with a rancid after-taste—it wouldn't kill anyone, but it was hard to choke it down. However, if a person tried to eat monster meat from a Tier higher? It would definitely make their guts go loose, as in melting right out of them.

"The Putrid Mana is problematic," Nacho agreed easily. Everyone knew about it by now, so it wasn't exactly a secret. "Cannibalism is *also* kind of an issue, wouldn't you agree? Hard to be friends with people when they're eyeing your tender loins, and not in a fun way."

Crave laughed despite himself. "Look... *we* are going to be able to eat Store food for a little longer. I'm eating Store food, Epic flavors, for sixty credits a meal. It's worth it; let me show you."

The Guild Master purchased the Epic pork pot stickers from the Store. They appeared in one of his storage slots, and a moment later he placed the steaming appetizer down on the table. The six dumplings, a full portion, materialized on a red-and-yellow plastic Juxtaposition tray. The pot stickers came with one sauce bowl, but Crave bought another so they wouldn't have to share.

Nacho glanced at the dumplings hungrily. "Funny. You know, I stopped eating for pleasure a long time ago. On days I don't use my skills—which I admit are rare—I just slurp down whatever Store slop I can eat fast. Their chili mac is nice because it goes down easy. Slimy, yet satisfying, if you know what I mean. It's handy to eat during Active Combat. I've been trying out other meals, but it's hard to eat and fight at the same time, you know?"

"I do." Crave finally saw it—the leverage he needed. This guy was on the edge and lonely, and had been alone for six months now, which was why he was so talkative. Somehow, even with his reputation of being a brutal killer and thief, he hadn't lost his sense of humor. It was odd and seemed almost out of character, but to be fair, less than six months ago, the kid had been a simple recent College graduate. "Here. Have some of the pot stickers before they get cold."

Nacho scooped one up, dipped it in sauce, and took a bite. He let out a long, happy sigh. "That sauce is like the pot sticker sauce they sold at Costco. They were so good... I miss Costco so much. The Store is fine; it's convenient, but something about walking through those massive Costco shelves always used to put my mind at ease."

"I understand perfectly. It was the promise of plenty." The Guild Master couldn't help but chuckle.

The Shadow Killer ate three more of the treats in silence. Crave watched closely as he savored his own. Each pot sticker cost ten credits, and the simple meal was a veritable goldmine of steamed pork goodness.

Nacho finished, sipped his beer, and sat back. "Look, Crave, you've got food, money, and beds. Wow... just thought of that. I could have a bed. I might not be a joiner, but you're making this look pretty sweet. I prefer killing monsters, but I kill other players if I have even a hint of a reason. That said, you still haven't told me why you came after me. Am I talking too much? I feel like I'm talking too much."

The earnest self-consciousness made Crave laugh; he hadn't

thought he'd like the Shadow Killer so much. "You're fine. You've just been out there alone for a long time. I would imagine nights are hard."

"Long enough. I stopped being scared, and that helped. You get used to the cold, the noises, the monsters. Now I'm just waiting to kill or to be killed." Nacho paused uncomfortably and gazed down at the tray as if he was reliving all the interminable nights of the winter he'd had to endure alone because of the friends he'd lost. The Assassin abruptly stood. "Sorry, sitting too long makes me nervous, and I was nervous to begin with. It sounds like you want me to come and kill people for you so you can eat them and save a few credits in the Store. Weird. Dark. Not sure I'm your guy, Crave."

Crave stood and went around to the other side of the table. He gently raised a hand to stop Nacho's pacing. "*Easy*, Nacho. I don't have any fleshed-out plans for now. But I *am* trying to plan ahead. When we're Tier two or Tier three... let me tell you what I'm envisioning?"

"You get a few more words before I leave, but none if you touch me again." Nacho had stopped moving, and Crave realized that the agitated strides had been making his heart race. Even when this kid was just pacing around, he moved like a panther. Crave knew for a fact that Nacho rarely used his bow and arrow to bring down his kills. He almost always appeared out of the shadows even on the brightest of days, completely noiselessly, and murdered in a flash of blades and black armor. He most likely had the same Assassin skills that Crave had—Midnight Blend. Ninja Hush. Shadow Speed.

He just used them so much *better* than anyone else.

"Let me tell you my thoughts... call it intuition, if you like, but the minute I heard about you, the Shadow Killer, the thieving Assassin, I got this sense that you would do *amazing* things. You are the *epitome* of dope."

"I'm... dope?" Nacho clearly wasn't sure what to do with the information. "Great. Thanks. Solid boomer complement, dude."

"I'm being serious." Crave nodded sagely, keeping his body language non-threatening. "You are pure excellence. I don't know about others, Nacho. But I do know that you're not dangerous to me."

Nacho grinned a near-feral smile. "But you might be dangerous to *me*, right? It would be kinda ironic if, in the end, joining up with you is what gets me killed."

"I'll do everything I can to keep you safe," Crave stated as truthfully as possible. Nacho was a powerful Assassin, a force to be reckoned with. More than that, he was a *scalpel*. Crave already had his blunt tools: Hogan and Whitney, both of whom had the subtlety of bulldozers.

No, Nacho was special. Crave could feel it; the two of them were going to change the face of the AKC forever. All the other guilds would fall to them—Kala's Sunrise Brigade, the new Midnight Fist, and the Credit Machine; a guild who was earning a few too many credits a bit too fast. Crave wanted to either eliminate or merge with the Credit Machine, else they were going to be a problem.

There were the CrossHumans to consider as well, but nobody had a chance against them until Crave managed to unite Humanity as a whole.

At least he wouldn't be bored.

The two stared at each other, and Crave's nose twitched. He had caught the scent of someone who was wavering, and he knew exactly how to close this sale. Nacho was waiting for a little concession, just a tiny little thing that only he would get.

"I never properly introduced myself." Crave decided that making himself more approachable, a friend, was all the kid needed. He gave the kid one of the smallest secrets that he carried, his real name. "My full name is Richard Crave. It's nice to meet you, and I hope we can work together."

Nacho's smile seemed forced, as though he hadn't worn the expression in a long time. "Guess I'm joining up, Richard Crave. Where do I sign? I hope you know I'm giving you a lot of trust. Don't make me regret it."

"You can trust me," Crave promised the young man as he pulled out a document, only managing to keep his hands from shaking with excitement thanks to long years of practice at getting suckers to sign their lives away. "Now, how about something fried and tangy to celebrate?"

CHAPTER ONE

Eli 'Nacho' Naches stood blinking, trying to figure out how to process the fact that he was standing in a Costco, deep under the crust of what he'd thought was another world. He held a bag of nacho cheese Doritos in his hand and was so tired from their travel to the Bove's Lair that he had just daydreamed the first time he had met Crave... from the Guild Master's point of view.

Back in the Probability Vision, Crave had made some joke about eating pork while they could and had promised to keep Nacho safe. Lies on all counts. The only pork they ate after that moment was *long* pork.

The strange, intrusive dream was so out of nowhere that it just *had* to be a vision from his Patron, Kronos. But why? On that note, he still couldn't believe that he was standing in an actual *Costco*. When he had lived on campus, only two had been located in the Kansas City area, and this one wasn't in the right place to line up with old Earth. Then again, there was no doubt that the Patrons could do whatever they wanted with the geography.

Nacho turned to discuss the strange vision with his friends, wincing as he came face to face with Reuben and his leather 'Helm of Helming'. The big guy adored that helmet, and nothing they said would convince him otherwise. It didn't remotely match the chainmail they'd looted from the Deep Buggy Darkness in the same delve. The man's gear was a mess; he'd picked up some silver greaves that he'd strapped over his camo pants, and like Nacho, he still wore the same combat boots that had been packed for them.

Reuben chomped on the chips with gusto, one after another, popping open a new bag when he finished the first. "They're so *good*! No Putrid Mana, no Store weirdness. Just the wonder, the *majesty*... of Doritos. Bless you, Frito-Lay, a subsidiary of PepsiCo."

"What a beautiful prayer for a marketing major." Brie stood nearby, resplendent in a matched set of silver sabatons, chainmail, and winged silver helmet. Her massive hammer, the Splatter Mallet, rested casually on her shoulder. Taye, their archer on loan from the guild, was waving around a burning Oilbark torch which he was using as a poor-quality light source. His friends' presence helped Nacho shake off the last vestiges of the oddity that had passed through his mind, and he forced himself to take stock of their surroundings.

The entrance of the Costco was dimly lit by a couple of hooded lanterns they'd brought in. Two main aisles ran the length of the warehouse—one on the left, the other on the right. Through the shelves, the old food court and cash registers were visible on the left side. The low light was going to be an issue, but in his mind's eye, Nacho could practically see the place bustling with people as though they'd never left the world behind. As strangely picturesque as it seemed, the vision quickly faded into the dark reality that he was living now.

"You okay, Nacho?" Taye was more than a little concerned. Their resident archer was a tall, lanky kid whose friendly demeanor tended to put strangers and friends alike at ease, though he kept glancing around the eerily undisturbed warehouse with visible apprehension. Previously, he had been a junior in high school, but he was now one of the most capable players in the Chips Guild. He held his torch high to increase visibility while he clutched his bow in his other hand.

The bow was new, something called the Pull-Smart Compound Bow. Taye could magically increase the tension, which resulted in his Fitness bonuses being added to some wickedly cool arrows he kept in his quiver. The kid had also upgraded his armor to magical leather and chainmail, which was good. They *needed* Taye to stay safe. He was the youngest person that they had located in the entire world thus far, and it was important to everyone involved that he outlived all of them.

"I'm good." Nacho wasn't even sure if he was lying or not. "Just got lost pondering what life used to be, and how I've been living a lie and didn't know for *years*."

"It only *feels* like that Nacho. It hasn't been all *that* long." Kristie wandered up just then, joining the conversation and drawing the Cook's trained eyes with her approach and the light she was emitting. She'd picked up a magic item, Bracelets of Brightness, which she could focus like powerful flashlights or turn off completely.

Kristie was a Warlock who had an excellent ranged attack called Sorcery Strike. Like Taye, she could kill from a mid-range distance. Up close, another attack of hers was more complicated: Death Blossom. The Skill allowed her to erupt in an explosion of magical energy that wiped out everything in a fifteen-foot radius, flinging out a bunch of pink magic missiles in every direction.

The only real issue was that the spell hit friends and foes alike.

Like her hair, Kristie's magic was pink. Being a Warlock, she got her powers directly from a Patron; in this case, Caelius Apicius, who seemed to have some kind of connection with Nacho's cookbook grimoire. Kristie gaped around in wonder as she came closer. "I know you told us to expect this, but... an actual Costco? Tell me I'm not dreaming."

"You're not even close to asleep, dear." Abby thundered into the open area in her new plate mail. The middle-aged woman carried a Staff of Iron Power in one hand, a sturdy length of wood with big iron rings embedded in either side. With her magical armor, she could move like a tank while bashing things to death with her big stick like a monk. Abby was the shield that complimented Taye's and Kristie's projectile talents. She was also just like her armor: loud and unbending. Her severe steel-gray hair matched her personality perfectly. "I think we cleared every monster up until this point. No more baby Boves. Sad, but delicious."

The older woman went silent as something roared in challenge to her noisemaking, deeper within the Costco, which caused her to cock her head and gauge the area. "Quiet down; we'll get to *you* later!" She jerked out a satisfied nod as silence greeted her retort, then turned to the mismatched group of adventurers with a maternal smile. "That's back in the paper products, dearies."

Reuben had tucked one gauntlet under each armpit to free up his hands for chip-munching, and he wiped them clean on his camo pants as he chuckled. "*There's* a woman who knows her local wholesale club. Or… is it a warehouse club?"

Brie wasn't in the mood to joke around, but she *was* ready to start fighting. She took a few eager steps forward, eagerly adjusting the hammer on her shoulder. "Whatever that monster is, it sounds big… do we have any idea of what we might be up against?"

Nacho was as mystified as the rest of them, his previous timeline self never even having come close to discovering this place. "Costco monsters? Let's go over what they *don't* have at Costco: rotten free samples, surly checkout clerks, someone selling hot dogs and soda for a dollar and fifty-*one* cents-"

"Yeah, this place was the best. Fun fact," Reuben perked up and cheerfully threw in some random knowledge from his marketing education, "Costco hasn't raised the price on that deal since they started their business back in nineteen eighty-four. The food court is actually a loss leader for their company.

Or 'was,' I suppose. I think they'll hold that record forever now."

"That's great information that doesn't help us at all, thanks," Brie grumbled at her husband as she stood in the middle of the aisle, gripping her hammer and clearly fighting to hold herself back from charging ahead of the others. "The store is crawling, so glove up."

"'Glove up'," Reuben agreed instantly, trying to put a spin on her words. "While that's nice, it can't be *my* tagline. I've finally settled on 'blood and cheese'. Just suits us all perfectly, you know?"

It was a blatant reference to the Ring of Cheese, which allowed him to absorb three times his Health Points in damage. Each time he got hit, the resulting odor was utterly pungent. Brie gave him a little smile, arching an eyebrow appreciatively. "I like it. If you have to have a battle cry, might as well confuse your enemies. Maybe it'll make it easier to finish them off."

"Hold on, let's see if we can sketch out a plan." Nacho paused to consider their options. It had taken a full day of jogging to reach the Costco from Armor Mountain, and Taye's group had spent a good chunk of time exploring and killing monsters before progressing all the way down to their current location. The Costco definitely had to be explored, whatever was howling back there needed a good bashing, and they had some upgrading and stat work to do. Taking all of that into account, they were just asking to be ambushed if they strolled in without a specific plan of attack. "I've mixed up a new food gel I want you to try, to see if we can keep hunger up in combat."

Brie grabbed a small container, downed it, checked her stats, then shook her head at the cook regretfully. "No dice. Might as well be drinking water, except it didn't count toward Thirst either."

"Abyss. Why can't I get this to work?" The Juxtaposition was being finicky on what constituted an actual meal, versus a snack that did little to replenish their Hunger points.

"It would be better to wait until the morning, after we level up, to take on the Costco. This mission was solely to scout the entrance and verify that everything was still open and where it was supposed to be, so… mission accomplished." Nacho closed the half-empty Doritos bag with an air of finality. "Let's fall back to the barracks. We'll come back after we do some leveling, and we'll keep some volunteers here in the meantime to make sure no one swoops in on our territory. We definitely want to pillage this place. This is some *quality* gear, and I'm dying to know if the refrigerators and freezers kept anything fresh."

"Unlikely." Taye scoffed at the thought. "If there was any electricity here, the emergency lights would still probably be flickering."

Reuben slipped on the gauntlets and threw an arm around Taye. "This is why I love this guy. What a smarty-pants!"

Nacho didn't disagree with Reuben. Still, he figured if the Patrons had given them the same planet, only covered with an extra layer of rock and dirt, flora and fauna, they might have also put certain areas into deep freeze in a dungeony way—no electricity required.

Several members of the Chips Guild volunteered to stay and keep watch, but they agreed to remain at the top of the second spiral staircase. It was a perfectly adequate place to keep a lookout: if the unknown beast in the paper products section decided to emerge into the main area, the volunteers could send a runner to retrieve Nacho and the heavy hitters from the guild. Abby also offered to stay, since she was tank enough to keep the beasties at bay beyond backup being beckoned.

By sheer weight of numbers, the Chips Guild should be fine.

That strategy allowed Nacho, Reuben, Brie, Taye, and Kristie—the expanded Dinner Party—to fall back to the barracks. The cook got a fire started while the rest of them unpacked and laid out their sleeping bags on the bunk beds. The one-room building had clearly been designed for convenience rather than comfort, hence the nickname of 'the barracks'. They'd built two log cabins for forays just like this.

The first one, which they'd dubbed the 'Barracks', had been constructed on the banks of the Muddy River about a quarter mile from the entrance to the Bove's Lair—officially called the 'Bove's Lair Costco and Scary Shelves Dungeon'.

As for the second cabin, it had been designated 'Heartbreak Ridge' and was located halfway back to Armor Mountain. While it wasn't useful for their upcoming dungeon dive, it had turned out to be great for breaking up the long trip on their way out.

Seeing as it was break time and he was possibly the only surviving cook in the entire world, no one complained when Nacho decided to make dinner. He'd brought in leftover Oscreech meat—a cross between an ostrich and an eagle. In all reality, the thing was more emu than ostrich, and more monstrous than either. To add some weight to the concoction, he bought upgraded noodles and combined everything to make Oscreech noodle soup.

The perfect meal on a cold, snowy evening.

While he was engaged in Active cooking, Reuben passed around the chip bag. "Would you look at that? I've eaten a half-portion of chips. Interesting… the System says your fitness gel doesn't count as enough 'food' to be a portion, but eating enough Doritos constitutes half a meal."

"Game logic." Brie threw her husband a grin as she used his most-beloved saying against him. The failed fitness gel had been her idea; she'd had to eat chicken and biscuits during combat, and the fact of the matter was that rapid breathing and biscuits didn't go well together. Before the Juxtaposition, she'd run plenty of five-Ks and ten-Ks, and her go-to for rapid energy gain had been a fitness gel she could drink on the run; the viscous liquid was much easier to ingest during exercise than actually eating.

Too bad the Juxtaposition could care less about making things easy on people.

While Nacho cooked, everyone else chatted about the various goods they hoped to find in Costco. They were full of excitement, making some pretty big leaps of faith solely based on the Doritos. Nacho knew all too well that farther in, all of the products could have been turned into monsters. Demon refried beans bursting out of their cans. Undead rotisserie chickens that wanted to put *them* under warming lamps.

The cook had previously stored some plastic dishes in a cupboard, along with some of his other cooking supplies in preparation for excursions such as this. It was incredible to him how many variations on the same tool were required for him to do his job properly. As Nacho ladled his steaming soup into the bowls, he kept an eye on the newest tagalongs they had picked up. It was likely that Taye and Kristie needed to eat badly. They'd been fighting for hours, and surviving Active Combat meant using their Skills. Survival always came with a price.

Body Players—Fighters, Rangers, Berserkers, and the like— had Skills mainly based on their Hunger Points. It was a simple system: use a Skill, get hungry. Get too hungry, and a player's health regeneration would go negative. For Mind Players— sorcerers of all kinds—Skills used Thirst Points as well as Mana. If anyone ran out of water, Mana regen went negative as well. They could regenerate Mana in the same fashion that they could regenerate Health Points, but if they hit zero Mana, they fell unconscious and were almost certain to die if their Thirst was also negative.

Hunger and Thirst Points had to be taken care of the old-fashioned way.

Most of the players hadn't been in the game long enough to *only* eat when they used their Skills. They were still in the habit of eating multiple times a day—which just wasn't something necessary in the Juxtaposition. A player was only *required* to eat once every twenty-four hours. If they missed a day, they'd earn the Starvation Debuff, their Health Regen would turn negative, and once they ran out of Health… they died.

Frankly, running out of almost any resource pool nearly guaranteed death, so it was better to keep them filled as much as possible.

For the first time, Nacho was able to hold out hope that there *might* be some way for a Satiation Player like himself to get nutrients into people that had fallen unconscious. He wasn't sure, as the very *existence* of this type of class was new to him, despite his Probability Vision. He'd spent three years in the game, and while there had been rumors of cooks, brewers, and farmers... he'd never met a real one. He had chalked it up to wishful thinking by the end.

His thoughts turned to the Costco, and his mind nearly shut down from the sheer number of questions that streamed through. He'd never known anyone who'd found the fabled remnants of Earth, which the Patrons had evidently dubbed the UnderFun. Nacho couldn't *believe* they were still on the same planet. Sure, adding an extra mile of crust would increase the mass and surface area of the planet, which would cause all kinds of destruction, but it was pretty clear the Patrons didn't much care about the sciences. Biology, chemistry, and physics were all just toys to the Patrons. They'd given a billion people on the planet new bodies. What was a little tinkering with astrophysics compared to that?

After their meal, along with some boiled water, Nacho and the gang got down to business leveling and doing their stats work. Brie in particular wasn't happy. "You know, Nacho, I have to say, I'm super surprised that you want us to increase our actual levels. You've been pushing Skill increases so much that I thought upgrading our character class was a pipe dream."

"Let's just do it before he changes his mind." Reuben looked as though he was a flinch away from clapping a hand over his wife's mouth. "Just rip the bandage off fast enough that he can't stop us!"

CHAPTER TWO

Nacho sat with Brie, Reuben, Taye, and Kristie on simple wooden benches they pulled close to the fire. Abby had helped shape the benches by hacking them out of the many trees that Bove had thrown to the ground around his lair. Out of everyone on Armor Mountain, Abby, Old Bill, and Young Bill had the most practical crafting skills. As a point in fact, before the Juxtaposition, Abby had spent ten years in the Kansas City area buying houses, fixing them up, and then selling them. She had actually started her new life here with the Skill 'Home Improvement'.

The cook was glad Abby had stayed behind to organize the guild's members; she was both smart and very capable. She'd done well enough in the Evaluation World that she could've become an Assassin. Instead, she'd bought a Warrior class with three extra combat skills—one of which was Enhanced Aim. That wasn't a projectile skill, but one that applied to hand-to-hand weapons. It granted her incredible accuracy in hitting monsters where they were the most vulnerable. Along with Enhanced Aim, she had acquired Bad Bash, which added percentage points of damage to her strikes, not unlike Brie's

Combat Dash. Lastly, she had selected 'Slippery Block', which reduced the damage she took from being hit when she attempted to avoid it.

Nacho hadn't even realized *how* capable she was at first, since she'd leveled her class instead of her Skills, like most people on Armor Mountain. There had been a lot to cover in the past three months, and personnel had only been one of the aspects. They still didn't have the castle walls Nacho wanted, and some people still slept in tents—though they had upgraded those to the Epic expedition tents that came with an internal wood-burning stove. Throw in some common coal, and it became a heating system that would last all night and keep the tent's occupants toasty warm.

Snow continued to fall outside the Barracks, and Nacho realized that he'd been staring at it and zoning out. Meanwhile, Taye had bought a couple more arrows from the store and was slipping them into his quiver. "I'm still regretting the credits we spent on our character levels. But you know, we did our character classes first just to get the extra Health Points and more Mana. Both are tied to our stats, so I don't believe that it was a complete waste."

Kristie sat drinking wine out of a glass, or rather a clear Juxtaposition plastic cup with the word 'Wine' printed across the front. She admitted it was terrible, but she loved her tradition of wine after dinner, so she put up with it. "I wish we would've done our Skills first. Just seeing how impressive you guys are highlights how much better of an idea that is."

Brie joined Kristie in the wine, but Reuben couldn't be bothered. Even Epic booze wasn't good, though the Epic *root* beer, by contrast, was *amazing*. *Well* worth two credits, according to him, and it also worked to top off his Thirst Points. Alcohol did nothing to help a player in any way; an effect Reuben touted as 'the only thing that hasn't ever changed'.

"Let's get to it," Nacho called out to the others. "Tonight is going to be special for me. I'll finally be hitting level five. It's been a long wait, but I'm hoping it'll be worth it."

"I'm looking forward to not having to slow down for you anymore. Not gonna lie, it's strange to be able to jog faster than you can sprint. I like it, but I guess that's gone now, right?" Reuben snapped his fingers as he dredged up his knowledge of Nacho's level-up bonuses. "Your Build Type is insane. Your growth speed is going to shoot like a rocket into the outer space of awesome."

Brie quirked an eyebrow at the odd idiom, as well as at what Reuben was implying. "Not sure I'm understanding. What is he doing that's so special?"

"You know how we've gotten faster, stronger, and able to deal more damage, while Nacho stayed exactly as he was before we got here? Well-" Reuben's explanation was cut off by the annoyed cook.

"*Feces*, just wait, and you'll see in a minute. No need to illuminate all of my weaknesses when I'm fixing them." Nacho wavered between standing and sitting. "Not sure what position I want to be in for this. I remember that adding points to my Fitness was painful. Now, *all* of my stats are going to jump at the same time. Pain is to be expected… you know what? I'm gonna lay down."

Taye fiddled with an arrow while he waited for the show. "I can't believe you chose the Balance, Delayed Option. I mean, you *really* committed to being a Satiation Player."

"It wasn't just the Common Cook thing." Nacho did some quick stretches—not that being more limber would help with the pain. "I just knew the power of the Build Type. More than that, I trusted Brie and Reuben completely. For anyone else, this combination would have been a death sentence. No way to earn credits as the monsters got stronger, and easy prey for other humans. Now I get to see a return on that trust."

"You're making me blush!" Reuben toasted him with a red-and-yellow bottle that would dissolve into liquid in a few hours. Unless they clearly told the Juxtaposition that they wanted to keep it, the packaging always vanished. The apocalypse was the ultimate in recycling.

Nacho gritted his teeth as he firmed up his will. "Here's me, spending sixteen hundred credits and totally *not* panicking about it or thinking about all the ways the sizeable amount of amount of money could improve the quality of life for everyone else in the guild-"

"You're *stall~ling*," Reuben called out in a sing-song tone.

"How bad do you think upgrading his entire body at the same time is gonna hurt?" Kirstie covered her eyes but peeked out through her fingers in spite of herself. "It's bad enough when we get three total points per level, but five in each at the same time? I can't watch... but I *must!*"

Nacho let out a strangled yell and spent the one thousand and six hundred credits to buy eight hundred experience points, raising his Common Cook class to level five. He applied the points as fast as they came in and stifled a groan as a deep burning started under his skin, as though his blood was beginning to boil. He remembered that he had wanted to lay down, so he quickly dropped into a prone position. "If I pass out, don't let me swallow my tongue or throw myself into the fire. Okay? The pain has started—*oooh*—the burning is bad."

"They make a cream for that." Reuben chuckled at his aching friend, remembering his own characteristic increases. "You should contact all previous partners."

"The joint pain was the worst part for me." Brie sat down next to Nacho, then motioned for Reuben to stop talking. "Just remember that you get stronger on the other side. I don't *think* leveling up can kill you."

"Yeah... but I'm jumping five points in *every* stat all at once. I get to have the pain in my flesh and mind at the same time. Whee!" Nacho huddled on the floor, clenched his fists, and ground his teeth together as fire filled every one of his veins. To take his mind off it, the Juxtaposition was there to give him the good news.

.   .   .

Congratulations, Player! You're going to be taking a crazy ride to level five, and you chose Balanced, Delayed. This is going to <u>Hurt</u> with a capital 'h' and an underline! However, when it's done, you'll be better, faster, and stronger... all so you can chop those onions faster! What a waste that you chose the Common Cook class. Good for you, sticking to your inscrutable goals. Keep riding the pain train, Nacho! Choo-choo!

Nacho felt his fingernails digging bloody furrows in his palms while the internal fire grew worse. The joint pain hit, searing like his vertebrae were being pried apart with a flathead screwdriver. Chisels went for his ankles, knees, hips, and elbows. He was an entire hardware store of pain. Time lost all meaning, but suddenly it was over, and the memory started fading too fast to be natural. "How long was I down?"

"That took... like, forever." Reuben patted his leg, then grimaced as the comforting hand came away sweaty. "Yuck. You need a shower, dude."

Taye and Kristie had left them at some point. Nacho grimaced, cautiously pushing himself up into a seated position. "How bad was it?"

"Bad. I hope it isn't like that for us." Brie handed him a glass of water, and he drained it. "At one point, you literally sang the alphabet song. But backwards, and perfectly. Also *in tune,* as if the music was playing backward in your mind. I thought we were going to need to find an Exorcist class."

"That would be my brain getting rewired and rebooting, then running a self-test." Nacho mentally went over his body with a fine-tooth comb. He felt perfectly fine now, and he was far more in tune with his body, like he had been during the Probability Vision. To confirm everything, he pulled up his full Stat Sheet.

Eli 'Nacho' Naches
Class: Common Cook
Level: 5

Experience Points: 1300 to Level 6!
Current Credits: 134 (3916 total Dinner Party pool)

Build Type: Balanced, Delayed
Body:

- *Fitness: 15*
- *Metabolic efficiency: 15*

Mind:

- *Mental energy: 15*
- *Circuit: 15*

Satiation:

- *Hunger: 100*
- *Thirst: 100*

Total Health Points: 40
Bonus Physical Damage: 7.5%
Health Regen: 15% Health Regen/minute
Total Mana Pool: 32.5
Bonus Spell Damage: 7.5%
Mana Pool Regen: 15% Mana Regen/minute

Skill Slots (3/4)

- *Small Blades (Passive) Level 9: 18% bonus damage on all knife attacks*

  No Mana, Hydration, or Metabolic Cost

- *Ingredient Processing (Active) Level 9: Remove Putrid Mana from monsters up to Level 11*

$$Mana\ Cost = 5\%$$
$$Hydration\ Cost = 5\%$$
$$Metabolic\ Cost = 5\%$$

- *Cooking Magic (Active) Level 9: Create food that enhances a single stat by 45% of maximum*

$$Mana\ Cost = 5\%$$
$$Hydration\ Cost = 5\%$$
$$Metabolic\ Cost = 5\%$$

- *Open slot*

There was his current level, the Common Cook, sitting pretty at level five. All of his Skills had been at level nine for a while now, so he was honestly excited to finally be able to process Tier one, level one monsters. Fighting Tier one monsters remained a deadly proposition, since they couldn't determine which level a Tier one creature might be until they had already killed it. Since none of their party had risen above Tier zero, there was a good chance that any damage they *did* manage to inflict would be completely mitigated, even if a creature was only Tier one, level zero—also known more commonly as 'level ten'.

If they accidentally tangled with a peak Tier one—level nineteen—that was when their scream meter would hit zero, and dying was guaranteed.

Fighting up a Tier was *almost* always a death sentence, and the only reason they had beaten the Bove was its lack of experience. It had been used to *killing*, not fighting. It had reacted to pain with terror; when it hadn't won instantly, the confusion had been enough to seal its death warrant.

"Well," he took a deep breath and forced a grin. "Thanks to my Balanced, Delayed Build Type, *all* my Stats are now at fifteen! I have more Health Points to play around with, and my

Mana Pool is deeper. Not sure how much that's going to help me in the kitchen, but there are definite fringe benefits."

"Speaking of fringe, you ripped a hole in your pants while... writhing." Brie pointed out, drawing his attention to the tear along the seam that went from ankle to knee on his left leg.

"Drat, I liked these." He sighed down at his Store-bought hoodie and jeans. "I need some armor. Tomorrow, when we hit the Scary Shelves, I'll try to avoid combat and just process meat, but you know how that normally turns out."

"You get hit," Reuben agreed solemnly. "Like... every time. You're a danger magnet. Probably because you smell like home cookin'."

"What a lovely thing to say," Nacho deadpanned as he glanced around. "Where did Taye and Kristie go?"

"They couldn't handle the sweating and singing." Brie threw another piece of wood on the fire and dusted off her hands. "I guess it's my turn now. Let's get on with my levels."

Nacho rose and went through a far more advanced stretching routine than he had been able to manage previously. He couldn't help enjoying the feel of the improvements in *everything* he did. Now that the pain was gone, he felt stronger, both physical and mentally. His mind was clearer than it had been in a long time, and the magical potency of his new and improved Mana Pool also felt *fantastic*.

"Okay. We won't judge you *too* harshly for singing," Reuben promised her as he settled in to watch.

"I'm not going to sing," their Berserker stated with force behind the declaration. Perhaps even a hint of a threat. "Remember we only go up a few points at a time. Nothing like this crazy man."

"Probably correct," Nacho agreed with her to keep the bickering to a minimum. "It shouldn't be anywhere near as intense for you. But you never know."

Since Brie had a Build Type of 'Balanced, Instant', she got three Stat Points for every level, and they were applied to her

Stats evenly in a round-robin type of fashion. The other Build Type was 'Self-Applied', and while a player was given two points for every level, they got to choose where to put those. That basic option just wasn't worth it, as they would be forever weaker than their peers in everything outside of their specialization.

Brie frowned as she perused a screen only she could see. "I hate that this is costing us so many credits, but I love spending money."

"Yeah!" Reuben had never been on board with that issue. "Credits are meant to be spent! If we hoard them, we'll die because we're too weak!"

Nacho could appreciate frugality, but he agreed with his Healer. They had enough to buy her and Reuben enough experience to get them both to level five. Their Chips Guild coffers were healthy, and the credits kept on rolling in. Brie's eyes glowed as she begrudgingly spent the requisite credits. "Okay. Here goes nothing. Ooh, *there's* the burning."

She held onto Reuben's hands and grimaced, sweat sliding down her face. Her elbows glowed like lightbulbs under her skin, her other joints covered by her armor. After a long moment, she blinked in surprise. "That wasn't... too bad. Did I sing?"

"No." Reuben actually sounded slightly disappointed. "I wanted to hear more of your beautiful voice. Oh, well."

"Guess I'll just need to whisper into your ear tonight," Brie smugly informed him, making him shiver as a slow grin spread across his lips. "You're up next, and *you* can sing all you want. Let's take a peek at my Stat Sheet."

Since the three of them were in the same party, they could see each other's stats if they each allowed that function. They had *considered* sharing with the larger group—Taye, Kristie, and Abby—to start building a lot more trust, and so they could keep track of each other better, but it was very personal information. Certainly not something to do lightly.

Brie gave Nacho a view of her Stat Sheet, offering him the whole thing.

Brie McCurdy
Class: Berserker
Level: 5
Experience Points: 1300 to Level 6!
Current Credits: 223 (2316 total Dinner Party pool)

Build Type: Balanced, Instant
Body:

- *Fitness: 14*
- *Metabolic Efficiency: 14*

Mind:

- *Mental Energy: 14*
- *Circuit: 13*

Satiation:

- *Hunger: 100*
- *Thirst: 100*

Total Health Points: 38
Bonus Physical Damage: 7%
Health Regen: 14% Health Regen/minute
Total Mana Pool: 46
Bonus Spell Damage: 7%
Mana Pool Regen: 14% Mana Regen/minute

Skill Slots (3/4)

- *Athletic Endurance (Passive) Level 9: 18% reduction to hunger loss penalties when using physical skills*

No Mana, Hydration, or Metabolic Cost

- *Combat Dash (Active) Level 9: 18% Damage on Dash Attacks, 10-meter dash*

$$Mana\ Cost = 0\%$$
$$Hydration\ Cost = 0\%$$
$$Metabolic\ Cost = 10\%$$

- *Defensive Whirl (Active) Level 9: Spin toward your enemy, auto-blocking up to 5 strikes*

$$Mana\ Cost = 0\%$$
$$Hydration\ Cost = 0\%$$
$$Metabolic\ Cost = 15\%$$

- *Open slot*

Nacho was incredibly grateful for his Balanced, Delayed Build Type. Though they both were at the same level, his stats sat at fifteen across the board, while Brie was at fourteen for three of her stats, and at thirteen for her Circuit. He was also grateful that both Reuben and Brie had agreed to select a Build Type of Balanced, Instant. They received their points at every level, so they were able to fight to keep the rest of the team alive.

Even with all the issues it would bring, Nacho couldn't help but get excited at the prospect of getting them all to Tier one, because most of his team had maxed out all of their Skills at level nine. Since Skills couldn't be brought to the next Tier until a player had achieved Tier one with their level, they were stunted in the amount of damage bonuses they could achieve, as well as in their ability to inflict secondary effects like debuffs.

Brie's abilities were going to be especially interesting once she Tiered up. Nacho wanted to analyze some of the hardcore damage she would be capable of as she expanded out her levels more—and with her Athletic Endurance ability, eighteen percent off of her Hunger cost would truly help out.

Reuben took a seat on the nearest bench. "My turn, my turn! That didn't look too bad, but I'm going to sing. Any requests?"

"Don't sing!" Nacho and Brie shouted at the same time.

"Sorry, we aren't taking any requests today. Awa~ay we go!" Reuben's eyes flashed as he spent his credits. The ebullient man *didn't* end up singing as his joints and skin glowed. Instead, he grunted and tried to force out words, but didn't manage a single bar in the few minutes required for the leveling to be completed. "I was wrong. Couldn't sing. Hurt too much. Glad that's over."

His companions nodded in wordless empathy as they all looked over his Stat Sheet, skipping the build stats, as Reuben's was *exactly* the same as Brie's thanks to their identical distribution.

Reuben Colby
Class: Healer
Level: 5

Skill Slots (3/4)

- *Healing Hugs (Active) Level 8: 40 Health Points Restored Upon Hugging*

> *Mana Cost = 10%*
> *Hydration Cost = 5%*
> *Metabolic Cost = 0%*

- *Positive Vibes (Active) Level 9: Weapon blessing: (applies to whole party, lasts 5 minutes) Adds 18% physical damage*

> *Mana Cost = 5%*
> *Hydration Cost = 10%*
> *Metabolic Cost = 0%*

- *Marketing (Active) Level 9: Able to lure creatures to a location. Impacts up to Level:10*

$$Mana\ Cost = 5\%$$
$$Hydration\ Cost = 5\%$$
$$Metabolic\ Cost = 5\%$$

- *Open slot*

Nacho found it funny that Reuben's stats matched Brie's, even though they were both level five in their respective classes. The Healer was taller, bigger, and had more muscle mass, but the structure of the game ensured that everyone was equal when it came to their Stats. The more you leveled, the more powerful you became, and that held true for every single player. Even so, not everyone could express those stats in the same way. It took training and dedicated practice to get the most out of any increase, and Brie had that in spades. With that thought in mind, he muttered, "As always, practice makes better."

They'd made the choice to stop leveling Reuben's Healing Hug at level eight, as no one in their guild currently had anything higher than forty Health Points—even now, only Nacho did. It didn't make sense for Reuben to be able to replenish more Health than what people could possibly use.

Nacho grunted in frustration as he remembered the fact that most of the Chips Guild players had gone with the Self-Applied Build Type. Thanks to his advice, when they realized that leveling their Skills allowed them to do more damage and provided a larger benefit than just upping their Fitness, *most* of them had slowed down on advancing their character classes. He had been greatly relieved, as continuing down that path would have led to early starvation.

Reuben had insisted that, since they had to stop leveling his Healing Hug, they could upgrade his Marketing Skill instead. To everyone's surprise except Reuben's, it actually had come in handy. Not only had it proved useful in convincing more people to join the Chips Guild, but he'd also been able to use it on monsters, to some extent.

"Halfway to Tier one," Reuben cheered happily as Nacho hurried to the door, cracked it open, and called out into the snowy darkness.

"Hey, Taye and Kristie. We're done with the upgrading. Mine was concerning, sure. Brie and Reuben were less so. Even with all that, you shouldn't wander out into the woods at night with only two people."

Taye and Kristie shuffled back inside. The archer, always working, stomped snow off his boots. "We did a quick run of the perimeter. Quiet night so far. We also checked in on Abby. Nothing else has come roaring out of Costco. They *did* clear out a shelf of the chips, and they're eating as many as they can cram down."

"It'll make the night go a lot faster," Reuben played off his jealousy with a smile. Now that the work of the night was over, Nacho felt restless. He wanted to see what was waiting for him in the UnderFun.

Had he really lived three years with his old neighborhood just under his feet? It was starting to seem like it. They had so much exploring to do, and for the first time in a long time, he was looking forward to exploring... just for fun.

CHAPTER THREE

The next morning, Nacho and his friends didn't need breakfast —but the people that were used to three squares a day started complaining almost as soon as they were preparing to start out. Unfortunately for them, the cook wasn't about to bend on the requirements.

"You eat when you need to eat. Eating whenever we want is completely unsustainable. You need to get used to this world faster, and using the annoying restrictions to benefit ourselves will help." Even though he had chastised them, he'd prepared some battle snacks for his friends for later. They also had access to the Store, and they weren't above sneaking in their own food.

Today, he was trying out soup. Broth hadn't been cutting it when he needed to replenish Hunger, and it counted only as regular water in terms of fixing Thirst, making it a waste of ingredients. If he wanted to make a meal that could restore his group, the Patrons demanded at least three ingredients be involved. Broth, salt, and pepper was scathingly rejected, so Nacho had added in the classic noodles and chicken.

As they walked, he continued thinking up new recipes and 'correct' meals that he could concoct to give people edible fuel while they were fighting. If only he could make smoothies… but how did you make a smoothie without a blender? High level knife skills…? He could try that.

He was still researching, but he had the feeling that chicken noodle soup might hold the solution. It would be easy to slurp down the noodles, but they'd have to chew the chunks of chicken unless he worked to get them *exceptionally* small. Nacho had filled some Juxtaposition jars with soup, and had also whipped up a batch of what Brie had affectionately dubbed 'pocket pancakes'. The flat quick breads worked, but it was hard to eat a dry, thigh-temperature pancake while breathing heavily and fighting.

Nacho's brand-new waffle iron was back in his kitchen at the guild hall, but as long as he kept his prepared food in his Storage Slots, it didn't spoil. Or at the very least, it didn't make them sick. Altogether, that made using a Storage Slot for a huge batch of chicken and waffles… *less* of a waste of space.

The Colonel's Chicken and Breakfast cookbook had turned out to be an *amazing* purchase. Not only did it contain a ton of poultry recipes, but it likewise boasted a variety of breakfast options. Colonel White Beard's waffles—which included a required ingredient of bacon grease—were extra tasty, especially when they were paired with fried chicken.

The cook was shaken from his culinary musings by reaching Abby and some other members of his guild that he didn't know on sight, who had found a nice cave hidden away a few yards down from the murky glass doors of the Costco.

Snapping into his leadership role, Nacho instructed the rest of the nearby Chips to stand watch in case anyone came from above. It would be just their luck to be derailed by Crave or some other random guild busting in. Unlike the previous timeline Nacho had experienced, the dungeon-sniffer Paul Rizzo was still alive. He had a talent, or a boon, that allowed him to quickly find dungeons and magic items. The Bove's Lair wasn't near the Chaos Coop; in fact multiple days of travel were required to reach one from the other, so Nacho figured Crave and his crew were hitting dungeons closer to home.

If he was captured by Crave again, now that the Guild Master had experience, they would definitely force him to empty his Storage Slots. Too bad for them; now that he had boosted his Skills and levels to their current extent, he wasn't ever going to be captured again. Not by Crave, not by anyone. He had too much to lose, too much to cook, and—if this really was the Costco of his dreams—they were going to become the best-outfitted guild in the entire AKC.

The Dinner Party planned to raid Costco with the addition of Taye, Kristie, and Abby. Taye and his friends were trying to come up with a name for their adjoining party, but so far they hadn't had much luck. Nacho kept pushing for 'The Modern Dinner Party', but for some reason, his team was in agreement that it wasn't a good name. Arching a brow, he informed them, "Then until y'all find something better, I'm keeping it the way it was."

They finally stood in front of the glass doors, peering through the smeared mud. Nacho reached and touched the rock wall framing the doors, just to feel the roughness of man-made concrete. Around even *that*, the Patrons had encased the Costco in solid, more natural rock. Since that was the case, the real question was: what else had been hidden in the UnderFun besides the Costco? There must be cars, gas stations, literally a whole civilization buried, and they only needed to smash apart the rocks around them to find it.

"They have a *dizzying* amount of power." The Patrons must've chosen what they wanted to keep out in the open, and what they wanted to bury. Nacho decided it was time to lay out the marching orders. "Brie, Abby, you'll go in first, then Reuben, who is somehow both our Healer and tank."

"I'd call myself a Paladin, if that wasn't an actual class." The big guy waved his magical ring around. "Alright. Blood and cheese, everyone!"

"That catchphrase doesn't work in this situation." Nacho

reached over and adjusted Reuben's leather helmet to sit correctly. "I feel like that should be reserved for when the three of us are together and alone, otherwise it just doesn't make sense. How about, 'Here comes the big cheese'? I'll be in the back with our Archer and our Warlock; I brought snacks in case anyone gets hungry."

"My warcry, my choice," Reuben replied obstinately. "Blood. And. *Cheese.*"

"I like snacks!" Abby held out a hand right away.

"I have snacks for when you're hungry from using Skills, not from being bored," Nacho amended with a sigh. "These new players… also, to be totally upfront, you're probably not going to like my cold, slimy soup."

"Oh no… you made soup? A *new* recipe?" Brie made a face and shook her head apologetically at the other new members. "Nacho learning a new recipe is just asking for us to start spending money on Store food. It's more natural for swine to drink from wine glasses than it is for him to be in charge of making food."

The Berserker and Warrior grimly entered through the glass doors, leaving the affronted cook to be aghast all on his lonesome. Even so, Nacho held a lantern aloft and was trying to use its light to determine whether they were suddenly serious due to the threat of monsters… or his cooking. The group cautiously started down the left-side aisle, picking their way between the racks of useless electronics and bins of clothes. Abby picked up a pair of jeans with an excited coo. "Looks like once we clear the dungeon, we'll have a place for people to do some shopping."

Brie stood watchfully in her chainmail, hammer held high and ready to drop on anything that popped out of the stacks. "I'm pretty sure Old Bill bought all of his clothes from Costco, so he'll be happy."

"What's wrong with getting all of your clothes at Costco?" Reuben stopped and pouted at her in confusion. "That's what *I* do."

"It's what you *did*," Brie responded evenly. "But now you're married."

"Married *and* hunting at Costco for clothes even after the world ended," Reuben pointed out correctly. "They clearly were doing *something* right if even Armageddon couldn't keep the store closed permanently."

Satisfied that nothing was going to ambush them from the central aisles, they marched onward, going quiet as they moved into more open areas where the central display area still offered Christmas decorations. Back on November eleventh, the day of the Juxtaposition, the winter holiday had been careening at them like a freight train. Nacho felt almost grateful they'd had the Juxtaposition just to avoid the rampant holiday consumerism. "Now I'm thinking like Old Bill... that would've been something the old curmudgeon would've said."

The bakery goods on the left were still present and untouched. That brought them to the meat section, the contents of which had dissolved into decayed slime long ago. Much of the deli section would also likely be inedible, but thanks to the stable temperature so far down into the earth, perhaps some of the cheeses wouldn't be too bad.

The dairy and freezer section were on the other side of the store, down the right-side aisle, which also held the baking section, spices, processed food, chips, and canned goods. The familiar food—free of Putrid Mana—was going to be the true treasure and an excellent trade good. They had to hold their breath as they walked past cases full of rotten meat and the refrigerated room where the fruit and vegetables were kept. It wasn't as bad as the stench of Putrid Mana, but it still smelled revolting.

It was at that moment that they heard rumbling from the back of the store; the same sound they'd heard the day before, but louder and angrier. Reuben turned and grimaced at Nacho. "Well, *that* doesn't sound good."

"Sounds like something that needs a good bashing." Abby twirled her Staff of Iron Power with a concerningly bright grin.

"Or smashing," Brie agreed as she pumped her two-handed hammer. "Let's get to it."

"But first, a quick snack and a word from our sponsors!" Reuben interjected, his joke earning a pair of withering glares.

"Not hungry, bucko," Abby crowed at him. "Not for food. I *am* craving sudden and brutal violence, however!!"

"Not sure Nacho can make that up in his kitchen." Reuben chuckled weakly at the eye rolls as the modern Amazonians returned their attention to the monstrous sounds in the distance.

"Let's just go and kill whatever's growling." Brie rested her hammer on the ground and took in their location. They had stopped right next to the shriveled and inedible rotisserie chickens, a great landmark if ever there was one. "If we get separated, meet up back here."

"Hold up. Reuben's right. We don't need the Hunger Points, but don't forget that my Cooking Magic gives us Stat bonuses." Nacho's reminder gave the others pause, and they reluctantly accepted the yellow-and-red Juxtaposition plastic containers full of waffles and chicken tenders he'd made from Oscreeches. "Can't do waffles without chicken tenders. Well, you *can*... but then you don't get a forty-five percent bonus to a stat. Get ready to have almost fifty percent more fun!"

Nacho ate his chicken tender first, followed by the soggy waffle as a kind of dessert. The last bite had barely hit his tongue when the System threw him a message:

Hey, Cookie, the waffles and chicken were cooked with love and magic and murder in mind. Would you like to increase one of your stats by 45% of max?

Yes / No

Nacho chose to update his Fitness, figuring they'd be fighting monsters in the Costco, and he needed to be ready with his knives just in case. Reuben ate with his usual gusto, as did Brie and Abby. Taye needed to force himself to eat the cold and poorly-made meal, but being a gamer, he wasn't about to turn his back on upping his Stats. With additional strength came bonus damage.

Kristie seemed to have a nervous stomach, judging by the way she held her limp waffle and soggy nuggy. "I understand that this will help me have more Mana. I *know* this is true. Bigger pool, more spells… but how can I eat before I fight?"

"Like this." Reuben wrapped his waffle around a tender and stuck half of it in his mouth. He ate noisily and swallowed even louder, pausing to gargle the meat slurry before getting it all the way down.

"And *that*, my friends…" Brie covered her face to hide her pained expression, "is my 'til-death-do-us-part husband."

Abby elbowed her and winked. "You must be very proud."

"You have *no* idea." Brie finished off her meal with a distinct lack of fanfare, her muscles swelling slightly as she applied Nacho's cooking goodness to her Fitness. Instead of fourteen, she would be swinging her hammer with a Fitness of twenty, which gave her a serious boost to damage. Adding in her Combat Dash and Reuben's Positive Vibes, along with her double-damage Splatter Mallet, she'd be hammering out thirty-two points of bone-crushing destruction with each swing.

Another consideration was that she had nearly doubled her previous Health Points.

Kristie took on a determined grimace, chomping into the waffle and Oscreech tender to get the benefits. She winced and exhaled a shaky breath. "Instead of a Mental Energy of thirteen, I have a nineteen—you were right, I would much rather have a boosted Mana pool. Doesn't hurt *me* that I'll be doing a whole lot more damage. Go me."

Meals eaten, Nacho and the raiding party got to work, creeping to the edge of the wall. To the right were the freezers, to the left were boxes of beer and a variety of hard seltzer waters. Just beyond the alcohol, big pallets of soda products and paper plates remained stacked across the way—and their eyes all moved at the same time.

Something had shifted behind the toilet paper.

Reuben pointed with a shaking finger. "A lot of people are going to be happy about all that ultra-soft. Better than scraping with your fingers and then buying extra soap like we have to do."

"Dude… there's toilet paper in the Store. I know that even the good stuff is pretty thin, but that was way too much information." Nacho winced at the mental image his friend had just scarred him with.

"Are they always this… *this*?" Kristie's eyes were begging Taye to say no, but luck was not on her side.

The kid responded with a hard nod as he readied his bow. "Yep."

Kristie groaned under her breath and swept her Bracelets of Brightness over the shelves, revealing the creature that had been attempting to get the drop on them. Something long and pink slammed down onto the ground, and at first Nacho thought it was a worm crossed with an anaconda until he ran his eyes along its hairless length to find black, greasy fur bristling through a space in the shelves.

A pink hand with long claws clutched the edge of the shelves: a rat's hand. A *very* big rat. What they thought had been the entire monster was only the massive rodent's neon pink tail. Nacho tried to evaluate the gigantic rat with his System View, but the shelves blocked the way. Before he could shift to find a better view, the enormous rat hand shook the shelves, rocking them back and forth.

A pack of forks fell to the floor and exploded in a shower of rattling plastic. Something else ran along the upper shelves, making the shelves creak and sway even more dangerously.

Nacho didn't know where to look—at the giant rat, fifteen feet tall at least, or the hidden creatures scurrying around the top of the shelves. Whatever those things were, they had long limbs but were far too furry for Nacho to easily place them.

One creature scurried down, grabbed the box of plasticware, and went scampering back up the shelves.

Hoping to identify at least one beast they were about to fight, the cook tried to catch a System View of the long-limbed creature, but it moved so quickly in the shifting light that he wasn't able to zero in on it. Kristie, on the other hand, knew *exactly* what it was. "That thing is definitely a spider, and there are more on the shelves. *Lots* of spiders. I'm freaking out here; we need to back away"

"Just kill them with magic," Nacho suggested calmly. "Then I'll boil them up. Scalded spider leg with a browned butter sauce."

"I will *never* eat spider." Kristie hissed at him, her fear seemingly forgotten.

"You'll never eat a spider if you *know* it's a spider." Reuben chuckled at her ashen face, "Don't worry. Nacho doesn't have any insect recipes. Yet."

Brie exhaled some of her frustration. "Rat boy isn't coming out to play, so I'm gonna go hit him with my hammer."

"Wait. I don't like the idea. We have no idea what Tier this monster is. With your Fitness boosted as high as it is, I know you could probably hit anything Tier one, but if it's that strong, the rest of us could have some real problems." Nacho's reasoning was *barely* enough to get the Berserker to hold back. "We need information more than we need minced mice."

More scurrying from above made them realize that they were starting to become surrounded. The longer they stood there, the more of those spider things were likely coming in for the party. As far as Nacho could see, the arachnoid monsters were keeping to the paper products. That was fine, but the team needed a way to draw out the bad guys for evaluation.

Nacho only saw one way forward: an information-collecting retreat. "Brie, why don't you dash over there, hit the mondo-rat with your hammer, then dash back?"

"Thought you'd never ask." The Berserker needed no

further encouragement, shooting forward like one of Taye's arrows.

"Let's put a smile on those faces." Reuben held up a gauntlet and activated his Skill just before she got beyond his range. Instantly, the entire group was glowing a subtle golden color as his Positive Vibes took hold of them. Now their weapons would do an additional eighteen percentage points of damage. That wouldn't help Kristie, since the vibes only applied to physical damage, but Taye's arrows had likely just become the best weapon for this situation. Nacho had no idea why he hadn't thought of that first, but it was too late now.

Brie's running speed, even in chainmail, sabatons, and helm, was almost too fast for a basic human to track. She swept around the giant rat with contemptuous ease and brought her hammer down on its tail, earning a shriek as it whirled around and stomped into view.

The System was ready with a special message for them.

Hey, player, welcome to Active Combat! Wow! This is your first battle in the UnderFun—actually, this is the KC Costco UnderFun, because there are a whole slew of different UnderFuns just waiting to be discovered! You're gonna love the monsters we have around here! You know the drill. No Store access and no Health Regen. Oh! You're toting around Mind Players? No Mana Regen either. Good luck!

Their enemy was in full view by the time he blinked the notification away, fifteen feet of behemoth rat. Nacho finally could use the System View, and he was... *unhappy* with the result.

Ratty Sam
  Effective Tier/Level:??
  HP:?

. . .

"Tier one!" Nacho shouted as soon as he made the connection. "This is bad; we need to go!"

Brie spun into her Defensive Whirl as the rat attacked, and Nacho noted with a glower that she had ignored the plan. She wasn't dashing back to them, instead choosing to engage the creature. The huge rat tried to smack her with a length of wood covered by various things that had been nailed to it—cans of water, lengths of rotten pork tenderloin, milk jugs, and other objects the giant rat must've collected throughout the warehouse.

It was the first sample platter at a Costco that Nacho hadn't wanted to try.

The rat monster clearly had also gotten into the honey, because various items had adhered to a sweet crust covering its fur—napkins, paper cups, old eggshells from at least one five-dozen egg pack, and multiple entire rolls of paper towels. Taye called out, only half joking, "I wonder if all that stuff will act as armor?"

Watch out for that weapon!" Reuben let out a laugh as he became the first to understand the pun at work. "It's Sam's *club*! In Costco! The Patrons really *can* combine anything!"

None of the others could answer—they were saving their breath to scream at the sight of at least twenty human-headed spiders, each with the exact same haircut, pouring down the shelves.

CHAPTER FOUR

Nacho didn't know if Brie had done any damage to the rat or not. It was obviously a peak Tier one monster, leaving them little opportunity to actually cause it any harm. If it was close to level nineteen, they were going to find out exactly how fast they were able to run away.

The cook hoped, for all their sakes, that the newly-upgraded Berserker working in tandem with the others would result in breaking through the greasy rat's defenses without getting caught by Sam's club. It didn't take long for him to realize it was a futile hope, as the others needed to focus on the fight with the spiders descending in a sea of furry legs.

Atop their squat bodies were monstrous human heads, complete with fiendish fangs. All the human portions seemed strangely familiar, and Nacho wouldn't be surprised if they had been grown from the employees that had been working the day of the apocalypse. He had seen more disturbing things.

Nacho summoned his HungerCry Knives, hesitant to fight but knowing that these beasts weren't a real opponent to him. If he killed any of the creepy-crawlies, he wouldn't get credits... but he didn't need to care about that anymore. His grip tightened, and he moved forward with intent to kill. Surviving was the most important thing, and if falling back wasn't possible, he'd feel terrible if something happened to one of his people due to his hesitating about earning the maximum number of credits.

Overnight Stalking Spiders
  Effective Tier/Level: ?
  HP: ?

Nacho was glad they were Tier zero, but the names seemed to follow his original idea that they were made from recycled employees. His suspicion was further confirmed when he heard the things whispering, "Hungry. Sleepy. *Customers.*"

"Twenty-eight Health Points each, which means I don't have enough arrows!" Taye shouted after he had opened fire with his arrows. Using Fast Quiver allowed him to send three arrows and hit three separate spiders in his first volley. "I've never heard of a creature that hates customers-"

"Clearly you've never had to work in customer service. Sometimes I forget how young you are." Reuben's sniping was with words, but they were aimed as well as Taye's arrows and eased the tension on the group even though everyone knew the situation wasn't in their favor. The Healer stormed forward, his fists crunching exoskeletons; each successful hit inflicted fourteen points of damage. A right, then a left, a splash of green blood, and the first arachnid monster curled into a pile of twitching limbs and limp hair.

Other spiders took the opportunity to retaliate, and soon the limburger stink of the Ring of Cheese filled the air. Nacho leapt into action as his friend cried out, a knife flashing dangerously in each hand.

The Hunger cleaver dropped like a guillotine as the Cry chef's knife sliced a beautifully deadly pattern through the spiders. He punched the knife into a pliant body under the chin of a half-shaved head and chopped into an oversized tattoo. This wasn't the first time he'd fought a spider monster, but it *was* the first time he'd had a potent weapon that he could use in battle. If it could even be *called* a battle: his Small Blades Skill was turning out to be the perfect complement to the HungerCry Knives. In the amount of time it usually took to land a single blow, he didn't get in *one* attack... he got *four.*

In the kitchen, the blades halved his chopping time. On the battlefield, the Skill translated into dicing up Stalker Spiders. Stab and chop, chop and stab; the results were very satisfying, even if it was turning his stomach to kill creatures with a human face that showed pain.

Congratulations! You have killed an Overnight Stalking Spider!
   Tier 0 Standard Creature = 0 Credits
   Stupendous job!

"I changed my mind. That is deeply satisfying, and I could keep it up all day!" A spider leapt onto him from behind, while another was stopped in its tracks as he turned and bisected it with a blade that practically left afterimages with the attack.

Even with as fast as they were able to take down individual spiders, both he and Reuben started to take buckets of damage from the arachnids' venom. The Healer took a bad bite to the leg and shouted, "I think I know why there's so many of them! *They unionized*! They don't care how many they lose, so long as they are the only survivor at the end!"

"No wonder we're getting nibbled to death!" Nacho called back in a horrified voice.

Health remaining: 53/68!
   Health remaining: 46/68!

. . .

Nacho's Health Points continued to tick down until he was under forty. All benefits from his Cooking Magic had been used up and were being put to the test. A half-dozen strikes later, a handful of spiders were dead, but the fact that he needed to be healed didn't go unnoticed.

Reuben tackled him into a bear hug right there on the floor, and they went sliding through the green ichor and spider chunks together. Taye and Kristie teamed up to rescue them, the archer using one arrow to take sixteen health from a spider before Kristie blasted it with a pink missile of colorful destruction. Thanks to Reuben's Positive Vibes and the chicken and waffles, her Sorcery Strike blasts were able to reduce the damaged creatures to pink-hued paste in no time.

By arrow and by strike, Taye and Kristie were ending the threat of the spiders almost as quickly as they had arrived. For each one they killed, the Nacho heard a light *cha-ching* as the Chips Guild received ten percent of the credits in taxes. That made him happy, something solely needed right then, as he was trapped underneath a sweaty guy who smelled like cheese fermenting inside a gym sock.

As Nacho was back to full Health, he reminded himself that the discomfort was worth it. He turned his head just in time to see Abby spin her staff and slam it into Ratty Sam. A flash of silver light flooded the space as her skills added some tasty damage, or so he thought. Brie dropped back, breathing hard. She looked pale and *hungry*. "She needs some of my soup… Abby too."

Ratty Sam attempted to slam his club into Abby's side, but she was able to slip her ironbound staff between herself and the monster's weapon in the nick of time. The Warrior's Slippery Block talent wasn't as expensive as Brie's skill, but it also didn't completely block the attack: she got sent flying.

"I reached back for an arrow, but my quiver's empty!" Taye called helplessly.

"Time for Death Blossom!" Nacho bellowed his order, making his entire team flinch.

"Are you sure?" Kristie's voice was almost lost in the skittering of spider legs as they closed in from all sides. "You know that hits everyone in range, right?"

"I can take it!" Reuben roared as he puffed himself up as large as possible. "Everyone behind me, it's time to get smelly. Blood and cheese!"

The humans lined up behind Reuben, as close to him as they could manage. Nacho's stomach turned at the thought of his friend burning from the magic, so he tried to close his nostrils against the incoming stink of cheese and flesh. A moment later, Kristie was standing in front of the team as they huddled together in the hopes of minimizing the damage they would take.

She had a water bottle in her hand in preparation of using the majority of her Thirst points, and Nacho nodded in appreciation of her forethought. She needed to keep her resources in check, and it showed that she was getting used to her role.

"*Death Blossom!*" The swarm of spiders leapt onto Kristie, and she erupted in a fuchsia explosion as countless tiny hot pink magic missiles fired off from her skin in every direction. The spells crackled through the spiders, singing off hairs, turning tattoos into brands, and cauterizing the heads and legs of the weakest spiders.

The micro-missiles pelted Reuben's back like hail, and his limburger scent increased to sidewalk feta cheese growing in a sewer. Nacho couldn't stop himself from gagging. The fluorescent pink barrage also hit Ratty Sam, who was utterly unharmed by the damage—at Tier one, any damage required a minimum threshold, and twelve points per bolt wasn't going to cut it.

Most of the already wounded spiders curled up into shriveled husks as the searing projectiles tore through them, leaving only three remaining.

Kristie fell to her knees. Her Death Blossom had hit every

target in a fifteen-foot radius unless it was blocked, but it was also very expensive. The Warlock had continued hurling wave after wave of energy blasts, at three points of Mana and ten percent of her Thirst each, for a massive total cost of fifty Thirst Points and fifteen Mana. She'd dealt with the Thirst by chugging the water bottle, but she remained dangerously low on Mana, and all Regens were disabled until the battle was over.

Taye scrambled forward, pulling arrows out of corpses and firing them into the last few spiders, likely too hungry to use his Skills. His arrows were dealing heavy damage, but without the sniper-damage or Skills like Fast Quiver, taking the monster spiders out quickly was going to be nearly impossible.

Meanwhile, Reuben rose to his feet, having collapsed onto the cook. Nacho sucked in some non-cheesy air and stowed the HungerCry Knives in his storage before standing up and summoning jars of monster noodle soup. He shoved the containers into Reuben's hands, telling him, "Go heal Brie and Abby, then make them eat the soup. I'll help Taye and Kristie."

"Soup's on, Body Players!" Reuben sped over to where the pair of women were trading blows with Ratty Sam. Brie was distracted by her husband and took a club right in the chest, but she spun with it as blood flew from her mouth, landing a wicked blow on the rat's toes. "Ooh, *those* piggies aren't going to market. I'm coming, Brie!"

Taye let out a yelp and stumbled as two of the last spiders scurried onto his legs and tore mouthfuls out of him. Hunger and Cry whistled in Nacho's hands as he became a blur of stabbing. He took out both spiders in no time flat, and as a reward for surviving, Nacho tossed Taye a pocket pancake. From there, the cook raced over and slapped a fresh water bottle into Kristie's hands.

Satisfied they wouldn't die in the next few moments, he turned just in time to watch Brie deliver her final blow to Ratty Sam.

In a beautiful display of both Defensive Whirl and Combat Dash, she brushed aside Sam's club, then backhanded her hammer into the rodent's enormous face… where it bounced off and nearly rebounded out of her hands and onto her face.

The giant rat reeled back and glared at her, then looked around and noticed that it was the final monster on the field. It hissed a feral warning that promised future suffering, then jumped straight up, grabbed a shelf, and vanished into the stacks.

Congratulations, player! Active Combat is over! What an outcome! Ratty Sam had a complicated relationship with the Spiders. The rat would knock over a shelf, and the Overnight Stalkers would clean it up while complaining the entire time. Sadly, none of the management answered any concerns, due to being dead, which led to an oversized swarm as the spiders had no obstacles to becoming unionized workers.

Now there's no one to keep this place clean, and that's on you. May your future be delicious!

Brie was breathing hard and chewing angrily, a stray noodle dribbling down her chin. "All that, and I couldn't even *hurt* that thing. Also, Nacho, the soup was jelly. It was jelly soup. Drinking that nearly made me suffocate."

Nacho winced as he realized where the cooled recipe had gone wrong. "That would be the congealed fat. I told Reuben to shake up the jar."

His supposed friend crossed his arms in an 'X' over his chest. "False."

"No?" The cook paused and immediately understood what had happened. "I *meant* to tell Reuben to shake the jar. How were the noodles?"

"I was *already* chewing the soup, Nacho. The noodles just meant more chewing." Brie squeezed her eyes shut as she tried to temper her… temper, and give usable feedback. "The meat got stuck in my throat and made me nearly hurl-"

"That's-"

She pointed at her husband threateningly, cutting off anything he might have been about to say. "No jokes, Reuben. I don't know for *sure* where you were going with that, and for your sake, you should keep it that way."

Taye didn't join in the after-fighting verbal beatdown, as he was too busy gathering arrows. Kristie was looking better, but she'd drained all the water they'd brought; the main drawback of keeping a Mind Player going through combat. Body Players needed food. Mind Players needed water. Nacho, as a Satiation Player, needed both. He'd fought against the Spiders, but his real job started when the fighting stopped.

In fact, it was time for Ingredient Processing. He'd have to hurry—the spiders wouldn't last very long. "Throw me a bottle of the green stuff, Reuben."

Nacho caught the Pellegrino, twisted off the cap, and let the bubbly Italian spring water flow. It was delicious and would help him keep his Thirst levels up. Combine that with a few pocket pancakes, and he was ready to get to his main job.

From his backpack, he retrieved huge containers of salt and pepper for his go-to recipe, also known as the simplest recipe available: meat, salt, pepper.

The System let him know he was in the thick of it:

Hey, player! During ingredient processing, you cannot access the Store, and both your Health and your Mana Regens have been paused. You have two ingredients in hand and have acquired a third, which is full of Putrid Mana. Yuck! Since you're not cooking, you wanna process your newly acquired spider meat?

Yes / No

Nacho chose 'yes', and a new message appeared all in red.

· · ·

Here's a warning for you, cookie. This monster contains human meat. Are you sure you wanna go down this route?
Yes / No

He slapped 'no' like it had wronged him and let out a huge sigh. He'd dealt with a fair share of insects, thanks to the Chips Guild being built above an insect dungeon: the Deep Buggy Darkness. He could work around exoskeletons, legs, and all sorts of other issues, but... cutting off the human head *would* be a bit much even for him. The fact that the System seemed to indicate an issue using anything even remotely human was actually a good excuse not to cut them up, but the vague warning had him truly concerned. "Most likely, if I used human meat, I'd get a hidden debuff of some kind, and the recipes I got in the future would be... limited. No need to risk it."

While he watched the spiders slowly break down into bubbling pools of nasty, the others went scavenging and found plenty of usable food. Everything in the freezer and refrigerator sections was lost to rot, but they unearthed stacks of brand-name coffee, cinnamon, a variety of canned foods, breakfast cereals, and glorious vacuum-sealed snacks.

It wasn't long before the last of the spiders had fully liquified like bananas on a hot counter.

Congratulations! You made a wise choice, and you deserve some credit for it, even if it was the boring route! Here's an additional 144 credits for sticking to your class and being a class act—that can take some real guts. Good luck being delicious!

The god-like Patrons sometimes threw gifts around, and Nacho learned not to question it. He'd pocket those credits and be grateful for them. Not a second later, Reuben called from one aisle. "We've struck Wheat Thins! I repeat, we have struck Wheat Thins! *Ahh!*"

From there, the only sound coming from Reuben's aisle was the crinkling of plastic and the crunching of tiny, delicious squares. Ignoring the rapturous munching in the depths of the shelves, Brie trudged over to the cook, seeming troubled about something behind her, if the fact that she kept checking over her shoulder was any indication. "Ahh, Nacho? You might want to come and look at this. I found... well... I don't know what I found."

Nacho wiped the blood off his hands with actual wet wipes, then noticed that the Costco didn't end at a wall like he'd expected. Beyond the floorspace where they'd fought Ratty Sam stood an entire series of shelves holding standard goods... if Costco had been around during medieval France.

CHAPTER FIVE

The cook had no idea how he hadn't noticed until it was pointed out, but the Costco just kept going past the boundary where the normal cinderblock walls should've ended. Another series of shelves lurked in the semidarkness, full of various objects any knight might use on a quest for the Holy Grail. They walked to the first rack, which extended up to a ceiling that lacked wires, lights, or industrial supports; just simple rough-hewn stone.

The minute they left the Costco proper, the Juxtaposition sent them a message.

Welcome, Players, to the Bonus Shelves. Beyond this transitory area is the Ye Olde Scary Shelves Dungeon, where fiends lurk. The bonus shelves are just that: shelves of happy bonuses! There's a little treasure trove in the KC Costco UnderFun for you all. Congrats on killing the Bove. You certainly seem to be going places and causing us some worry. We didn't think you'd get this far this fast. Go, you! Race toward an early death!

. . .

"Did you get the-"

Brie answered before he could finish the question. "Yeah, I just saw that. The fact that the Patrons are worried about us has me worried… kinda feels like we might have a target on our backs."

Nacho couldn't help but frown as he inspected the first of the bonus shelves. There, in plain sight, were stacks of swords in cardboard boxes. Yep. Sword in a box. At first, he thought they were plastic, but they turned out to be actual steel broadswords encased in the bright yellow and red Juxtaposition packaging.

Behind him, Taye was still going around collecting arrows, while Abby and Kristie had exited the store to go back and check on the rest of the guild members. Nacho was glad they hadn't included the whole gang in the fight. Even at level nine, the spiders would've definitely killed some of the weaker members of his guild. Reuben came ambling up with his hand buried in a big plastic bag of Wheat Thins, his open-mouth munching interrupting Nacho's ruminations. "What's ya guys find?"

Brie unboxed one of the swords and gave it a practice swing. "Huh. This is… what are we supposed to do with this?"

Nacho took a handful of Wheat Thins and started crunching happily as he thought.

Kirkland Imported Signature Sword
Includes: A point for stabbing. Two relatively sharp sides for chopping into the flesh of your enemies (enemies not included). A cross guard, so you don't lose a hand. A handle wrapped in cow leather to improve the smell of your hands. A pommel made of recycled plastic. Sheath sold separately.

"'Kiss' swords." Reuben nodded as he thought over the name of the weapon. "Keep it super simple swords."

"Good point. That most likely means that none of them are magical," Nacho muttered as he glanced over all the boxes.

"Which makes sense. But there are hundreds of them. Let's get the guild in here to clean out the lot and make sure that every single member of the Chips has a sharp edge."

"Not so fast." Brie pointed upward, drawing his attention to the fact that there weren't just swords, but also Kirkland Signature maces, flails, polearms, and battle axes. Deeper in on larger shelves lay suits of armor with every piece packaged separately. Breastplates, chainmail shirts, and all the various accessories were present, though the descriptions for the armor were neither helpful nor funny. "Make sure they all have a decent weapon *and armor*, is what we should say."

Brie found Reuben a great helmet that would match his chainmail and gauntlets perfectly. The Healer lifted it with a slight hint of disgust and shook his head. "Nope. My current head protection is at ten. This metal bucket would *give* me ten, but I don't need that much metal sitting on my noggin. My leather Helm of Helming is perfect for both comfort and functionality."

"Only as long as you're Tier zero." Nacho tried to wheedle a deal out of his best friend as he touched another packaged helmet on the shelf. "Once we all advance to level ten, or Tier one, level zero, we're going to need to find new items. Well... you two will. I can upgrade the HungerCry Knives."

"I'll lose my gauntlets? Say it's not so!" Reuben pantomimed wiping away a tear, then dramatically clutched his hands together, crushing the top of the bag of crackers. "Whatever shall I do, when I can find fist-weapons wherever I decide to go for a stroll?"

Nacho and Brie rolled their eyes, and the trio continued on down the helmet aisle. Each package seemed to be reminding Nacho that he needed to invest in some protection to help him to avoid some of the damage he normally experienced in combat. He'd always found himself stabbing things when the situation turned dire, which tended to result in getting smacked around like he was a front-line fighter. If they kept up this pace, all too soon, he'd take a hit that he couldn't afford.

The truth was, Nacho was *great* at killing. He'd spent three years of his life fighting in the Probability Vision for what he thought was his life. Now that he had better skills and weaponry —the HungerCry Knives and his Small Blades ability—he could do *hefty* damage. In fact, thanks to the synergy of those in conjunction with his Build Type giving him additional stat points in bulk, he could deal nearly as much damage as Brie with her hammer.

The main difference was that Brie could release that damage in a single payload—one big smash—therefore meeting the minimum threshold for damaging low-level Tier one monsters. For Nacho, it was spread out among four attacks, and the low amounts of damage were practically *slivers* for the monsters if he was fighting up a Tier.

Reuben found a shelf of shields zip-tied to big yellow-and-red cardboard backs. He removed one, and a bunch of others clattered to the ground in a hurricane of noise that set the rest of them on their toes, weapons ready. "Sorry, guys… never took the training on how to properly stow medieval armor and weaponry."

They held their position silently for a long moment, but nothing came racing from the darkness to punish them for Reuben's mistake. Satisfied that they were all clear, Nacho nodded and slowly moved away from the pile of shields with his lantern raised. At the very end of the shelves of shields, they found a new row of freezers, with huge blocks of ice visible behind the glass doors.

Behind the strange freezers was the edge of the Bonus Shelves. They stood on the edge of a vast cavern, and the cook noticed that stairs had been cut into the side of the sheer cliff. The Patrons must've carved this whole place out of the bedrock, because it wasn't a natural cavern—all of the cuts were perfect ninety-degree angles. The floor was just barely visible about five hundred feet below, but the cavern below was filled with shelving units as far as the eye could see.

"Those must be the Scary Shelves," Brie reminded them as

they all shook themselves out of their awed astonishment. "This time, the Patrons found the perfect name. It's kind of eerie that all of them are empty, don't you think?"

"Empty? You're sure…?" Nacho stepped away from the edge, deciding that they could explore the deeper area once they'd bought more power. A *lot* more, if the named rat was any indication of what they'd be facing below. "I wasn't sure if we should press our luck by going down the steps, but that settles it for me."

Reuben pointed out something that Nacho hadn't considered. "You know, I would've expected to see the street, or pipes down there. Something, you know, from our world. But that's all Patron dungeon, and it messes with my head a little."

"Guys." Taye's voice echoed from where he had stopped at the freezer doors. "I think I found something over here."

Reuben and his friends turned from the ledge and joined their exultant young teammate. Behind one door of the frosty glass hung a full Archer's set of impressive chain and leather armor done up in browns and greens. Arm and finger guards, an embellished bow, and finally a fancy quiver with well-made arrows in the same color scheme sat on the shelf behind it.

Reuben slapped the teen's arm in excitement. "Looks like you hit the jackpot, Taye! Those are some awesome arrows. Uhh, why aren't you yanking open those doors?"

"That'd be…" Taye squinted at Reuben like he was a crazy man. "…because this is the Juxtaposition? I might open the doors, which might be trapped, and the Patrons would be all like: Congratulations! You opened the freezer, so we'll freeze you."

Reuben pointed at him as he grinned back at his now-leery friends. "Loving this guy! He gets it!"

"Isn't he great? I want to be like Taye when I grow up." Nacho took a moment to use his System View on the loot inside the Freezer.

．　．　．

Tier One *Robbin' Hoodie Archer Pack:*
  Includes:

- *Fashionable wrist guard and finger guard done in green and black. They aren't magical, but they are effective. +10% to your skill check when pickpocketing.*
- *Chain and Leather Armor of No-Arrows Allowed.*
- *Great Bow of Strength Detection.*
- *Quiver of Doubling.*
- *Assorted Arrows of Mass Destruction, or AMD's (Not to be confused with your so-called microchips, which aren't chips at all. They tasted terrible. We tried some Intel chips with French onion dip, and they weren't bad. Not great, but not bad.)*

Nacho gave Taye a slow but encouraging nod as he looked over the door itself. "We should be okay to open up the case, but there *is* some bad news. You're not going to be able to use any of that stuff until you're Tier one."

"Figures," Taye grumbled as he eyed the gear longingly. "I've been dying for some magic arrows. I was thinking of buying some exploding arrows from the Store, but they're *so* expensive—you have to buy them by the individual shaft."

Nacho checked the Store and winced; he couldn't blame their archer for not spending two hundred credits on a single arrow. Taye tilted his head as he looked over the gear once more. "What would happen if I tried to use Tier one weapons? Would they explode?"

Nacho touched the doors to the freezer and felt the cold on the other side. "They *might*. That's the problem; the result is practically random. Most of the time, if you use cross-Tier items, they work, but you can't use their magic until you hit that Tier. That's the best-case scenario. Unfortunately, they might explode instead, like you said. Worst case? Kills you instantly and leaves your team with some kind of snotty retort and a body to bury."

"There *has* to be a story there, right?" Brie tossed the loaded question his way, and Nacho suddenly felt the need to remind them again, very gently, that he would like to keep his boon and past hidden from the general populace.

"A *small* story." Nacho stated softly, "I knew a guy with a Tier two shield, and it turned into cardboard just as he went to block a hit. He died almost instantly, and the position got overrun. The Patrons sent us a message that said 'he made a mistake, he was using a shield too powerful, and they were revoking his cool magic shield privileges'. Short answer? Just *don't*."

"Wow… people already found gear that good? I feel like I'm behind the curve now." Taye didn't move to open the freezer door; instead, he simply continued eyeing the door, thinking and rubbing his chin. "It's an interesting game mechanic. Tying magical items to Tiers allows you to retire overly powerful items and entice your players to level faster so they can use the next overpowered stuff they find."

"I *like* my hammer." Brie was too serious, nearing surly. "What if I want to use the Splatter Mallet after I level?"

"You *can*… but it won't be magical anymore." Nacho put his hand on the handle. Since Taye had suggested the freezers might be trapped, he was feeling paranoid. Then again, was it really paranoia if the Patrons were actually out to get them? "When you Tier up, there's an option to attempt to upgrade your gear available for purchase in the Store, but buying a new item is usually safer and, um, better overall."

"Well, I'll need to find a Tier one hammer, then." Brie swung the Splatter Mallet back and forth a few times. "Should I just break the glass?"

Nacho shook his head, took a breath, and yanked open the door while diving back in a tumbling roll. Nothing came out except a wave of cold air. It actually smelled good in there, sterile and clean. Taye crept forward to remove the items, nearly caressing the arrows he couldn't use. The cook regained his feet and patted the archer on the back. "We'll just have to work harder to get you to Tier one. How much were the Spiders worth, anyway?"

Brie rolled her eyes as she was reminded about her failed fight. "Reuben mentioned the Spiders were worth twenty each, but I think Taye and Kristie got most of those."

"I'll have you know I killed six," Reuben defensively argued, finally deciding to rejoin the conversation, now that the Wheat Thins had been reduced to crumbs.

"All progress is good progress." Nacho shook his head as he contemplated their day thus far. "Yep. We've got to grind more, and all of this standard gear will help us a *ton*. Once we get the rest of the guild outfitted and running the dungeons more often, the taxes will come rolling in. Then we build walls around Armor Mountain, find a nice cottage for this newly married couple I know, and then we *pour* our credits into our levels."

"It's us." Reuben raised a hand, pointing the other at his wife, then himself as he grinned at Brie. "We're the newly married couple."

"Yes, dear," Brie grumbled good-naturedly as Nacho lifted the lantern and went to inspect the next compartment of the freezer. This one displayed a full suit of armor, excellent stuff, but he just *knew* it was going to be Tier one. He swept his System View over the cold, heavy metal anyway.

Tier 1 *Saturday Knight Armor:*
Includes:

- *Super Stiff Sabatons*
- *Thick Thigh Guards*
- *A Curious Cuirass*
- *Disco Pauldrons*
- *Helmet of Dancing Majesty*

Reuben's glove came down on Nacho's neck. "We were just talking about you getting armor, but it's pretty clear that's going to be for a Body Player. I'll tell you right now, I'm calling dibs on this set. It's custom-made for me."

Nacho ducked away from the gauntlet. "Unless, when *I* grab it, it changes like the MurderSong Blades did. We'll wait and see with this one… it feels too magical to make any plans without knowing for sure. Maybe we can offer a competition in the guild? First person to level ten gets the armor."

"Or we could auction off the items." Brie frowned as a nervous look crossed her face. "We have to make it clear we're not stealing credits from the guild coffers."

"It's fine, guys." Taye interrupted the worried musings. "Most of the people trust you. Not the Bills, and maybe not the people they hang out with, but everyone else does. You're always risking your necks for the rest of us, so you should be getting a few extra benefits."

They moved over to the last case, and there were bags and bags… of frozen potstickers. Most of the bags were the basic brand, but there was one that looked *wickedly* different. It was a bag of 'Firefly' Potstickers, and the front label boasted a sketch of potstickers with little firefly wings attached to them.

Finally, the vision that Nacho had seen upon entering the dungeon made sense. The conversation with Crave in the Probability Vision was all forced into his head to make him realize that there was something new he needed to be on the lookout for. He'd bet his last credit that this bag was a gift from Kronos. Nacho felt a smile cross his face as he eyed the Tier one food just *waiting* for him to be able to cook it.

It seemed his Patron was still watching out for them after all.

CHAPTER SIX

Nacho and his friends retreated to the Barracks in high spirits, where they enjoyed an excellent lunch of basic potstickers, complete with sweet sauce. The cook was so excited that he bought a pan specific to making dumplings, which once more made him question why *everything* required a specific method of cooking. An additional issue cropped up, as he had not realized how difficult working with three pans in the fireplace was going to be. Mainly because it was hard to get the heat to evenly cover each pan and keep it at the requisite temperature.

However, the effort was worth it. He didn't *need* to eat, but even so, he stuffed himself with the taste of home. The fact was, they couldn't leave the items in the freezers, as there was no way to know when that ice would melt in the Bonus Shelves, or if something would come creeping up from the Scary Shelves to refill it. That meant the next few meals would be dumplings, and hopefully they would all get sick of them for good... because when these ran out, there were likely no more left on Earth.

Just to be sure that the bag contained what it said it did, they opened it to inspect the Tier one dumplings and got a happy surprise. It also contained a recipe to make this particular item from scratch, but strangely enough, it was limited to once a week. That was amazing for multiple reasons, but particularly because—even though he could not cook them yet—the Firefly Potstickers were more than just food. They were also utility magic items. Inside the bag were ten little dumplings with little firefly wings folded shut on their backs.

Moments after the group opened the bag, they awoke and buzzed out. After lightly screaming and ineffectually attacking the Tier one food with his Tier zero knife, the cook stared in awe as their doughy bodies began to glow and light the place up.

Slowly getting the hang of them, Nacho soon found that so long as he held the bag they came out of, he could direct the lights wherever he wanted them. He wasn't sure how long they would last, but he could easily test it out, especially since he could make new ones as needed. There was a good chance that over time, they would slowly cook from the inside out, and when they were fully prepared, they would need to be eaten. Until then, he kept them in a Storage Slot so that he could do away with his need for a lantern the next time they were in a dungeon or dark location where using fire would be a bad idea.

For the rest of the day, they planned out how to transfer everything in the KC Costco UnderFun back to Armor Mountain. Traveling between the dungeon and the guild required a full day of walking for a low-level human. In total, the distance was approximately eighteen miles. The halfway point was their newly built cabin on Heartbreak Ridge, but the fact of the matter was that even though emptying out the armor and weapons would be a huge benefit to the guild, it would also be an enormous hassle.

Beyond the utilitarian weapons, they had found quite a few items that would go a long way toward improving their guild's quality of life as well. The most exciting to Nacho was the mattresses, which they'd found stacked in a back room, along with other mass-produced furniture. For other people, like the

Bills, who only cared about personal luxuries, there was the entire shop full of food and… just so *much* beer. That was one thing that Nacho knew was more specific to Kansas or other more southern states: beer and drinks with a low amount of alcohol content were classified as soft drinks and could be sold in stores.

He was sure if they had started in another state, they would never have been able to collect something like this unless they found someone with an actual Brewer class. "Matter of fact… might not be such a good idea to introduce all of that booze to a bunch of people going through the end of the world. We do need clear minds if we are going to survive this thing."

While Nacho let his stomach digest the solid brick of potstickers in his gut, he opened the interface to his guild.

Chips Guild Stat Sheet

- *Total Guild Credits: 13,803 credits*
- *Total Number of Members: 271*
- *Guild Master: Eli 'Nacho' Naches*
- *Alternate Guild Master: Daniel Chronour*
- *Third Alternate: Reuben Colby*

The full list could be expanded to include all two hundred and seventy-one names. At first glance, it appeared as though they had a ton of credits. Short-term, *absolutely* they did, and more were coming in all the time from the taxes levied on all monster murders and transactions. Even Nacho's preparation of ingredients was taxed and added to the overall guild funds.

Unfortunately, building a civilization after an extinction-level event was an expensive affair. The guild credits were almost exclusively used to pay for walls, housing for people on Armor Mountain, and other important utilities. That included things like a cistern and a series of waterworks, such as showers for improved hygiene. A well would be next, and they'd have to figure out how to pipe the water up to the top of the mountain. On top of sorting out these necessities, they were going to have to camouflage not only the pipe, but every major improvement that they put in place.

Being on top of the mountain was a huge benefit, as they could build up walls to limit how much of the burgeoning town was visible from below, but if Nacho had learned anything from guild siege warfare in his past life, the most important thing was *not* making sure that everything was camouflaged from outsiders. It was that people on the *inside* had to be restricted to a need-to-know basis.

It was far too easy for bored civilians to start spewing guild secrets as a form of bragging or a way to pass the time. Back when Nacho had been an Assassin, that was one of the best ways to learn an Elite's schedule so he could claim the bounty on their head: just find the most annoyed, bored, refusing-to-work sucker and pay them the slightest amount of attention.

He had never failed even a single time to gather the information that he needed.

As they relaxed after a hard day, Nacho tried to account for all of the impressive gear they had managed to collect. Taye had stored the Tier one Robbin' Hoodie Archer Pack in one of his Storage Slots. The thing that was most surprising was that everyone had agreed that Nacho should get the heavy armor if it worked for him. He would have preferred to auction it off or offer it as a reward for the first person who reached level ten, but he had been outvoted by his team.

As a matter of fact, Taye had smugly agreed to let the Robbin' Hoodie stuff go to the first Archer who could use it without issue. There were a few other Archers in their ranks, and it would give them all incentive to grind harder… but everyone knew that he was the *best* Archer, and the highest level. There was little doubt that he was going to get that gear at the end of the day.

Finding such impressive stuff in the dungeon, which they should never have been able to access so early, had lit a fire under everyone's rear. They all wanted to upgrade not only themselves, but also the tools that they had. The motivation stemmed both from the desire to keep themselves alive, as well as the innate need to make their enemies deader, faster.

Nacho, Reuben, and Taye stuck close to the fire in the cabin, either trying to unwind after such a dangerous visit to the dungeon or preparing food for the reinforcements that wanted to try their hand at delving. This worked out just fine for the cook, as his path to improvement involved practicing ever-more-impressive meals and perfectly processing difficult ingredients. Having willing test subjects likewise sped things along nicely.

Brie, Abby, and Kristie decided to return to the Scary Shelves, accompanied by more than a dozen other guild members. Seeing as there was a peak Tier one monster lurking somewhere in its depths, they'd agreed to move slowly, but they planned to begin emptying out the bonus shelves first. Nacho's magic-imbued food traveled along with them as snacks in case they needed power-ups, and he was scrambling to replace the loss of so many resources that had been stacked in his Storage Slots.

That gave him plenty to do around the fire, and he would likely be working into the late evening to resupply the enhanced food stores and pocket pancakes.

A cool breeze from outside seemed to sweep right through the rustic cabin they had slapped together, and Nacho frowned as the heat of his pans rapidly dropped. A glance outside informed him that it wasn't actively snowing, but dark, threatening clouds were looming overhead. He tossed another log into the flames as the remnants of his team pulled their seats closer to the fireplace. "I hate to spend the credits, but do you guys think we need a wheeled cart? We can hook it up to people and have them pull it, which... makes me even more reluctant to buy it, since no one is going to want to be the mule."

"I'll be your beast of burden," Reuben volunteered after a rapid inhalation and affecting a self-sacrificing tone.

Taye raised an eyebrow questioningly. "Why not just buy

horses? I saw them in the Store, and they're relatively cheap. I think I saw that they were around thirty credits?"

"I wouldn't buy a horse without buying a full info pack on horses and carts. I think you can connect horses to carts using... tackle? Cart tackle? Let me check the Store..." Nacho squeezed an eye shut. "That doesn't sound right... there it is. See? The Patrons love to dupe us into buying stuff we think will work without a problem. Then when we get it, we have to dump a ton more credits into buying an info pack to actually use it. Then, of course, there is the main issue of buying any animal: eventually, they will fill with Putrid Mana and turn into monsters."

"I think Matt and Maggie were horse people." Taye pushed forward stubbornly. "They just joined us, and they had a ranch on the outskirts of Kansas City where they boarded horses. If they had horse skills, that would help, right?"

Nacho knocked around the coals to rekindle the flames. "It would have to be specifically using carts and horses. Just saddles and ribbons wouldn't help, and I think you are purposefully ignoring the issue of the horses becoming monsters."

"Ribbons...? Did you mean 'reins'?" Reuben bought an Epic root beer from the Store and took a sip of the cold, fizzy beverage with a satisfied sigh. "I've never heard them described as 'ribbons' before. It's cute."

"Clearly there's a *reason* I didn't buy horses. To put an end to this, let me ask you, Taye: What happens when the horse goes feral because we don't have anyone that can tame it? Sure, we can get another horse, but after putting in however much time it will take to train the beast, do you really think they will be open to putting it down and starting over?"

Nacho paused his verbal thinking to flip the final pancake onto a plate, then stood up, feeling restless. "Even small expenses build up quickly. We need more walls on Armor Mountains. The gear in the Costco is *fine*, and it will put us in a really good position as a guild, but walls are our first priority. After that, we *need* to get to Tier one. Horses would be neat, and a cavalry would be nice. But the fact is: we live on a *mountain*. How would we get the horses on the mountain?"

"True. It's too steep. They'd fall, and wouldn't be able to giddyup." Reuben tipped his bottle of root beer back and winked at Taye. "We need to make a road in and out. Don't worry, Taye, he gets like this sometimes. Watch this... hey, Nacho! We need a plan! What's the best way for us to survive the winter and upcoming disaster, whatever it may be?"

"The winter?" Nacho stopped pacing and stared at the wall, his eyes unfocused. Reuben pointed at the stunned man and failed to hold back his laughter, setting off Taye as the cook started to rapidly mutter. "Walls. Carts. Levels—a house for you and Brie. Clear the Deep Buggy Darkness so the termites can't destroy whatever is built on top of the mountain again."

"Wait... again?" Taye stopped laughing suddenly, but luckily Reuben chose that moment to interject.

"Dude, you're sleeping on a shelf in your kitchen," the big guy pointed out easily. "Wouldn't hurt you to have a house of your own."

"I like my shelf!" Nacho protested distractedly, waving his friend away. "Besides, it is most efficient for me to sleep next to the stove so I can get to work right when I wake up."

"You're addicted to work." Reuben shook his head sadly. "It *works* for me, but still, there are other people that can... wait, never mind. No one else can cook. But! You can take some rest days and let people eat canned food now. Oh... if we combine Costco food with my Marketing Skill, we can lure new people in to join our Guild, and we make more credits! See how this all sounds? A little crazy, right? Why don't you take the rest of the evening off?"

Almost as if his words had summoned them, at that moment, a crowd of people emerged from the entrance to the Bove Lair and trudged toward their cabin. Reuben looked relieved as Brie came into credit transfer range; he had been trying to downplay how nervous he had been for her safety.

"'Lure' makes it sound so tawdry..." The Healer thought

for a minute. "Entice? Yeah, we can *entice* people to join our Guild. That's definitely the better word. We'll have actual, real, made-in-China American chips, and they'll come sprinting out of the woods like feral cats."

Brie rejoined them as soon as she entered the cabin and began to regale them with the stories of what her group had found down in the depths. She had come back several *hundred* credits richer from killing Pizza Cockroaches. According to her, they were triangular and dripped with cheese and olives. The reason they hadn't found the slice-shaped insectoids on their first excursion was that the monsters still followed the instincts of their base form and had been hiding under the first few rows of shelves. They'd been high Tier zero monsters and *surprisingly* hard to kill, but the large group had handily taken care of the huge swarm.

As she talked animatedly, Reuben began muttering about how he was never letting himself sit out of a combat run again. Frankly, Nacho had been surprised that he hadn't gone with her, but he had chalked it up to the Healer being completely wiped out. When she finished her story, both Nacho and Reuben had the same question: Had there been pepperonis on the roaches, and did anyone try to eat the monsters?

The answer was 'yes' on the topping, and 'no' on the eating, due to the Putrid Mana. Nacho didn't know if he was relieved or disappointed. No one had died; that was the important part. They were all richer; also good. Yet, he couldn't stifle the disappointment that he had failed to harvest pepperoni and pizza monsters. He was almost certain that he could get rid of the cockroach bit and just warm up the rest of it to make a proper American breakfast. Abyss, he could leave the cockroach in, and it would still be genuine New York style pizza!

The cook spent the evening speaking with various guild members about their Skills, explained what they should upgrade, and offered some strategies on maximizing their respective classes. It was a good public relations moment for Nacho, according to Reuben, but he only cared about making sure that his guild members didn't get caught up in the trap of low-performing Skills. Apparently, helping people get stronger and giving them a better chance at surviving long-term was something that earned a person a lot of good will. Who knew?

The night passed all too quickly, and as the sun crested the horizon hours later, The Dinner Party left for Armor Mountain. Taye, Kristie, and Abby—now properly known as Generic Party One due to failing to agree on a party name—would stay with the other volunteer guild members and continuously delve into the Scary Shelves to see if they could flush out any more monsters, as well as to learn how far those Scary Shelves went.

Nacho reminded them to be careful, and to run screaming if necessary. It seemed like everyone took his warning to heart, so he reluctantly began the journey back to his Guild encampment. The travel day passed with only a few encounters, mostly nasty monster animals that were put down with relative ease. Mutated rabbits were still rabbits, after all.

When they reached the halfway point of Heartbreak Ridge, Nacho grilled Wight-Tailed Deer steaks from a fresh kill over a fire for lunch. Nacho cut out the rot, processed out the Putrid Mana, and used Active Cooking to grill the steaks to perfection. "Ahh... Very Fine Venison is still one of my favorite and most flexible recipes. It's about as hard to mess up as it gets."

"Yet it goes down like chewing wood, every time." Reuben informed him as he gnawed on a fully-cooked chunk. "Ever heard of medium? Does everything have to be well-done?"

"I take it as a compliment," Nacho stated without looking up from his work. "The food is saying, 'well done'!"

"False," Brie countered without hesitation. "You're still just a really bad cook."

"Practice makes better." Nacho shrugged as he let their insults flow off of him. "You tell me how to make it better, and I'll try to make it happen."

The sun was just setting when Nacho and his friends finally climbed the rope ladder up the eastern limestone slope of Armor Mountain.

Walking along the main path felt good, like coming home. With the northern wall finished, the mountain gave off a feeling that this place was becoming an actual citadel. A substantial number of the guild members were still living in tents, but stone houses were starting to pop up more frequently as they earned plenty of credits in the bug dungeon below. Of course, Old Bill had to be a cantankerous old coot and had slapped together a shack made of random cast-off material instead.

"I'll burn that down and make him live like a human as soon as we have everything else upgraded," Nacho promised himself, having to tear his eyes away from the annoying little structure. He had visions of putting together a true medieval city of little multi-room buildings protected by strong walls, as well as a central citadel they'd build on top of their guildhall. It was a very 'Beowulf' mead hall at the moment, which was neat, but not entirely practical.

Mayor Dan hurried out of the hall to greet him, along with his wife, who was known as Iron Becky. Dan had picked up a leather-working Skill that allowed him to create coats from the monsters they killed, which meant the guild was outfitted well for the winter with fur-lined garments. It was a practical way to save on credits, not to mention the fact that Store clothes never fit quite right.

Dan and Becky were both fifty-four years old, and they'd barely made the cut to participate in the Juxtaposition. The older couple weren't exactly excited to be fighting monsters for a living, so they managed a lot of the guild activities in Nacho's stead. Becky had impressive defensive ice abilities—walls and shields—but she used her counseling Skill more than anything. The guild had even put credits toward improving it, as the higher her counseling level, the more rapidly she could help people through a hard time.

Not only was it impressive, but it was necessary to have a town full of people with excellent mental health. He knew for a fact that most population centers would be rife with people going native, acting feral, and a few already turning cannibalistic in some instances. He hoped that by keeping his people healthy in mind as well as body, they would be able to avoid that horror show within their walls.

It was too cold to chat outside for any length of time when there were better options available, so Dan and Becky ushered them into the guildhall. Nacho took a breath to look around at the large number of people who were setting out bedrolls for the night. Some people lived in the large space full-time, while others just needed a night or two out of their tents to have some human contact.

The guildhall was pretty crowded, so Nacho led his friends and the older couple back into his kitchen and put on some water for tea. He let the others have the chairs and pulled over a stool for himself, as he knew that he wouldn't be doing much sitting. Being a Common Cook meant keeping people fed, and that meant moving quickly from counter to stove and back again.

"What's the news, Dan?" Brie inquired as the cook started placing freshly cut biscuits into a few prepared cast iron skillets. When an awkward silence filled the room, Nacho turned to fully participate in whatever was coming next.

Mayor Dan gestured to his wife, shaking his head. "Beck knows more than I do."

Becky locked eyes with Nacho, the Guild Leader and person in charge of everyone on the mountain. "My news is… bad. Let's talk about finding a *Costco,* of all things. My stars, I can't believe our house just might be back where we left it. If only we had a shovel, we-"

"Might not work that way." Nacho explained how geography had been adjusted, resulting in the store that they had found being a combination of the modern building, a medieval storefront, and a sunken warehouse that could easily have been part of some alien home world.

Reuben quickly filled them in on the plan, as far as bringing their bonus treasures back to Armor Mountain and outfitting their guild members. After hearing all of their progress, Iron

Becky let out a long, slow breath. "Well, that's a huge relief. Especially considering my news. We had a run-in with some... unfriendlies. A few of our people were killed."

Between her tone of voice and the tear tracks she had clearly tried to wash away before meeting with them, Nacho knew they'd more than lost people. They had lost people that had truly meant something to this lovely woman that had been working so hard to keep the town functioning.

"Tell us everything."

CHAPTER SEVEN

Nacho made sure his oven was at temperature, nodding as he felt the radiating heat. With a practiced motion, he slid three skillets in to get the first round of biscuits going. He then poured everyone coffee or tea, trying not to note the fact that it cost two credits a mug for the Epic stuff. The cook made a conscious effort to throw off the unease of spending money on such frivolous items: it *should* be a justified expense. He hoped that the comfort it could provide would help to offset the emotional toll this conversation was going to take on all of them.

Reuben added a handful of sugar, which he took out of his pocket and added directly to his cup. Nacho didn't bother asking why it wasn't packaged; he wasn't sure he wanted the answer.

The cook settled in on his stool as Becky started explaining between sips of coffee. "We lost Maggie to a sneak attack by Crave. Technically his Archer, that terrible Suzy woman, but they don't do anything without him ordering it, I'm sure of it. The Martinezes were out with a hunting party, and they drifted south. A little *too* far south, it seems. They were tracking a herd of Wight-Tailed Deer when they were ambushed."

Silence fell in the kitchen, and Dan took over the story a moment later. "We think they were just attacking us for the credits. That's what Matt thinks, at least. The arrows started flying, and the guy with the mace charged in. There was a skirmish, and most of our people were able to run. Crave's killers chased them, but Matt and the others found the main party. When they realized they were outnumbered, Suzy and the others fell back."

"Red Suzy Blacke," Reuben growled as he recalled the arrows he had needed to pull out of his rear the last time they had come near each other. "She tried to make me *Swiss* cheese."

The mayoral couple looked confused at the non sequitur.

Nacho knew better than to attempt to engage his friend in conversation when he was acting like this, so he started speaking his thoughts aloud. "This sounds far less accidental than you might think... I'd even go so far as to say it was *meticulously* planned. Frankly, an accidental ambush would have been better; if we need to start a war with Crave, *all* of us are going to lose. We *just* found good reasons that can be used to draw people to Armor Mountain and the guild."

"Yeah!" Reuben's forcibly cheerful agreement was unnecessary, and Nacho started to think that he was playing up his silliness to hide his discomfiture. "Wheat Thins. We'll win the Guild Wars with Wheat Thins! Or nachos. Not the person, but the deliciousness?"

"We need to up our defensive capabilities." Nacho found himself planning aloud, the ideas in his head pouring out into the open in a surprisingly cohesive manner. "As much as I want to get in there and crack some heads, we *can't* focus on Crave. We need to build up our eastern walls. We have a great strategic position here, but if we're going to attract as many people as we intend, we'll need to do some city planning. No more letting people build houses anywhere they have been squatting. If we get, let's say... five thousand people up here, we'll need water, shelter, and toilets for everyone. In fact, there's a special half-price toilet option in the Store—no, let's stay on task."

"Housing should be pretty straightforward, right?" Brie offered her thoughts as she mentally divided the place up as though it were going to be hosting a whole slew of various track and field events. "If we put up houses along the main street, we also have the western cliffs that are currently empty. We can do stacked homes up there: part wall, part apartment complex. Perhaps we can make housing available more rapidly to people that start working directly for the guild? We need volunteers to bring the Costco supplies here, and this could be a way to incentivize it."

"Smart." Nacho agreed with her plan instantly, holding up a thumb in acknowledgement. "How are people taking the deaths?"

"Matt is doing... as well as can be expected," Becky stated haltingly, her face contorting slightly. "We talked, and I have to tell you, my counseling Skill is almost terrifying to me. The fact that I can help people through various stages of grief so rapidly and get them on the path to healing? It is probably the most unnatural thing that I have experienced in this world. That said, a new project might be the perfect thing for him to truly heal and be able to move forward with his life."

Dan joined in on the conversation once more. "I'll talk with him, but I don't think you'll have any trouble finding people to do the Costco run. Especially if you follow through on that housing opportunity."

Nacho rolled his eyes and scoffed lightly. "I shouldn't think it'd be hard. Frankly, even *without* the housing, I think that the option of getting priority access to those snacks would draw people in. This is going to be huge for us. Also, someone find out what Matt likes to eat, and I'll cook up something special for him. It sucks to lose people, but at least now we know how Crave is playing this game. I'm... kind of surprised, to be honest. I didn't think he'd be so openly brutal. I figured he'd make his moves and go into hiding before finally popping out into the open and trying to make it look like he is some kind of legitimate businessman. Ya know, a kindly old dude who's just trying to help people out but is restricted by the people influencing him."

"The people around him *are* probably influencing him," Brie growled while moving her hands to draw out a curvy feminine figure in the air. "I can't imagine he has many positive influences."

"Can't argue with that. I know *I'm* being influenced toward being a better person, thanks to all of you." Nacho tapped on the table before nonchalantly walking to the oven and pulling out the perfectly browned biscuits. The fact that he did it without even thinking should have been shocking to him, but his mind was miles away. "What were you going to say before I interrupted you?"

"Two things... I *don't* agree that people will be as excited as you think they will to be hooked up to large wagons as if they are draft horses. Definitely lead with the house as payment for the work." Reuben grinned at whatever mental image he was creating. "Secondly, I was going to say that I *do* agree with you about the situation. We don't need to—and definitely shouldn't —go to war with Crave. We can beat him by growing our guild until it is large enough that it is unmistakably clear that if they start something, we will come down on them like a landslide. Speaking of people we shouldn't seek out for combat, let's add Kala and your old buddy Myron to that list."

Nacho felt his stomach turn in disgust. "*Myron*. Ugh... that guy needs to be put down for everyone's sake-"

"Which is *why* I am adding them to the 'don't seek out for fighting' list. Otherwise, you might get drawn into an ambush. It seems like something that you'd do; chasing down an old rival for no *real* reason." Reuben nodded along with himself as though he were offering sage advice, and the cook didn't miss the fact that the stress on 'real' meant that the healer had been listening far closer than expected when he'd asked them not to share the details of his boon.

"Well, *thanks* for the vote of confidence." Nacho grimaced at his friend and continued, "You're also right. If we become the biggest beast in the land, and if we're well known for being able to feed people that hit Tier one, they'll join us just because they don't want to starve to death. On that note, we're probably eventually going to outgrow Armor Mountain. For now, I agree that we can keep houses down on the ground, as long as we have more walls. But make sure to let everyone know that eventually all houses will be replaced with larger complexes. *No* individual owns the space on top of the mountain—that belongs to the guild. If they want a permanent house, that will mean living in the Foothills. Less safe, but more private."

"Bill will definitely do that. I swear that man has a death wish. I can help set up some planning, since I have *some* experience with people like him," Dan said with a sad smile. "I'm glad we're not going on the warpath against other humans. It would seem… insane to me, and to anyone else. That would undoubtedly be the fastest path toward a vote of 'no confidence', since we already have enough trouble fighting the monsters."

"We still have the CrossHumans to deal with. I don't want my own people to be my enemy." Nacho couldn't guarantee he had *really* seen Arriod walking around, but who else could it have been? Someone that looked and sounded exactly like him? This early in the Juxtaposition? It just seemed so… improbable. If the man was really the human-hunting monster he had known in his last life, Nacho had no idea what had made the alien leave them alone. Perhaps it was because Arriod only had a normal sword at the time, and not the katana designed to help him take his gruesome game to its maximum limits.

Or perhaps he would never get it in the first place?

That hope made Nacho feel better; a *lot* better. It wasn't clear where that sword had come from, but most agreed that it was from the CrossWorld and had entered through the portal with the CrossHuman. Nacho figured that they'd have to go through a portal themselves at some stage, something he'd not had to do in his Probability Vision. If he could get that katana first, that might change the endgame even more than the ways things had already been changed.

His biscuits had fluffed up wonderfully, so he painted on some honey-butter to top them off, but he opted not to add in cooking Magic to make them useful. These were for comfort only, not to remind people that they always needed to be ready to fight. Everyone got a taste of his home cooking, spoke a little more, then slowly began to filter out of the kitchen. Dan and Becky left first, followed swiftly by Brie and Reuben, and Nacho privately decided that this would be the final night the newly married couple would need to spend in a tent.

As for the cook, he was just happy to be back in his near-modern kitchen. He pulled his bedroll out and whistled as he set it on the top shelf to keep his head near his oven. Once he was tucked away in his sleeping bag, his pillow comfortably under his head, he fell asleep instantly—as though he had no troubles in the whole wide world.

Nacho woke with a start, shaking off the last vestiges of a nightmare involving CrossHumans, zombies, and a Guild Master nibbling on his fingers and cracking them open for the marrow. "I hope that dream was because I only just now learned about the loss of one of my guild members. *Bleh.*"

They were bound to lose others, but *he* was the one that they were relying on to keep casualties to a minimum. He had never expected that kind of responsibility, and now it seemed that the stress was messing with his head.

Someone knocked on his serving window, nearly making him scream but *actually* making him fall out of the top shelf. He couldn't break his fall, as he was completely wrapped up in his sleeping bag, though he managed to twist around enough to land on his backside first. After picking himself up and rubbing his sore tush, he padded across the floor, knuckling the sleep out of his eyes.

He opened the door to find a bevy of fresh faces that he just *barely* recognized. Carl, a random player that had recently joined the guild, winced as he noticed the sorry state the cook was in. "Sorry to bother you, Guild Leader Nacho. We were wondering if you were open for breakfast? I thought I smelled fresh bread. Are… are those biscuits for anyone?"

"You can have those if you want them, otherwise I will get started on breakfast right away." He waved the dozen or so adventurers into the kitchen with a smile. Since he was in a good mood, all things considered, Nacho decided to get his fryer going and serve them more biscuits with some crispy Oscreech tenders. He knew some leftover meat was hanging in his icebox room. It was easy to keep cold in winter like this, but his kitchen was going to have some issues come summer without any further updates.

The strangest thing was that the difficulty was all about the sheer tidal wave of credits he had to spend on ice for his icebox. He could buy dry ice in blocks, but that might be too expensive. Or, it might work better. He was a cook, not an engineer. It could even be that because they were living in a magical place, with magical bodies, Epic-ranked dry ice just might last indefinitely. Unlikely, but maybe. "Then again, I bet it would all turn into carbon dioxide, build up in the freezer, then suffocate me as soon as I opened the door. *That* sounds like something the Patrons would do."

While he chopped the thick Oscreech thighs into tenders, getting double the yield because of the HungerCry Knives, he placed his industrial-sized waffle iron on the stove. It was four-foot by four-foot, so he heated it by using all the burners at maximum heat. It worked amazingly well to help him feed hundreds of people quickly, but it was truly Colonel White Beard's recipe that did most of the heavy lifting.

The sudden breakfast rush brought him another fifty credits, so he was sitting pretty at over two *thousand* credits among the three of his immediate party members. Brie and Reuben finally entered the area, sniffing hungrily, and Nacho already had their coffee waiting. "Finally convinced yourselves to leave the bed? I *should* charge you double. You both got to sleep in while I had to get the guild on its feet. But… we're fifty credits richer."

"Eh, so charge us double," Reuben good-naturedly teased him. "Zero times two is still zero."

Nacho rolled his eyes and handed them Juxtaposition trays with the last of his chicken and waffles. He knew that the fresh ones were a hundred times better than the leftovers, but he didn't need the torrent of comparisons that were soon pouring out of Reuben's mouth.

As his friend chattered on about how much he missed store-bought bread, Nacho's thoughts returned to Crave. He couldn't help wondering what the man was *thinking*. Had he really been the one to send Red Suzy out on a rampage? Nacho hoped not, but in all honesty, his old Guild Master was probably just fine with it. Crave had been willing to murder The Dinner Party outside the Bove's Lair, had captured Nacho to feed his guild, and likely had a bounty on the cook's head for killing off two of his trusted minions.

If the Bove hadn't been there to inadvertently help them out, The Dinner Party would have been slain the last time. That firmed his resolve in an instant. No matter what their relationship may have been like in another life…

In this world, they were enemies.

CHAPTER EIGHT

After breakfast, the trio left the guild hall through the door from Nacho's kitchen and went straight down the south side of town. They passed another collection of tents on their walk to the southern edge of the limestone cliffs, where they stopped to peer over and wince at the hundred foot drop to the trees below. It was a bit of a trek, but it was time to delve deeper into the Dark Buggy Darkness.

Nacho put his hands on his hips and swayed side to side to loosen up, preparing for the descent. "We have about a square mile of livable space up here, spanning from the northern wall to the southern edge, and from the eastern limestone slope to the western cliffs."

Reuben wasn't in his chainmail, instead opting for jeans and a thick coat from Costco, but he still wore his combat boots... as well as his leather Helm of Helming. Just like the rest of the team, he kept his armor and weapons in Storage Slots for ease of travel. "Fun fact—not sure where I picked this up—but a square mile is equivalent to four hundred and eighty-four football fields, or two-point-five million cows packed together."

"Ugh." Brie was also dressed in Costco casual. "You can translate miles into anything *except* kilometers, can't you?"

"Forty-four thousand, six hundred and a half humpback whales," Reuben stated helpfully.

"Moving on," Brie stated sternly, rolling her eyes as Nacho and Reuben fist-bumped. "Thankfully, you put the guildhall in a good, defensible location. I think we should also plan to put in a marketplace on Main Street. We could build houses above the market stalls and save on square footage, which would also help protect the merchants against thieves. Walls and housing are going to be our biggest cost and necessity."

Nacho could only sigh in light frustration at the incomprehensible number of credits they needed to accumulate. "It's just too bad that you can't store other people in your Storage Slots."

"I would sleep so good in there," Reuben adamantly agreed. "I just *know* it."

"Eh... not me." The cook itched his nose as he thought about being trapped in storage at the mercy of another person. "Yep. Definitely too creepy to put any real thought into, Reuben. Where do you two want your house?"

Brie clearly had given the concept some thought, though she hadn't planned out everything. "Being right against the wall would give us the best view; we're not ready to build the wall yet, and it probably doesn't make much sense to only build a single home. Guild members will be paying a credit per square foot of house. If we share walls, we get discounts. Believe me, I've read up on all of this. The best plan is to build a neighborhood off the southern end of the guildhall. Oh, and put in a cobblestone street, so it's not so muddy this spring."

Nacho felt his heart drop as he realized why he was *really* holding back on starting the project. "If we start building houses and streets... *everyone* is going to have an opinion. We need to figure out what to do about the eastern slope before we do anything, even announcing the project. Even then, there will be much... discussion. By that, of course, I mean complaining."

The Healer agreed easily, both of them sharing a shudder at

the thought of trying to appease hundreds of opinionated people. "You know what they say: Opinions are like elbows. Almost everyone has at least one, it's pointed, and it can hurt when it's thrown around."

Nacho had heard a different quote, but decided not to share it in polite company. As if summoned to fight him due to his thoughts on *nice* people, the Bills came ambling over. Both were wearing thick leather coats with Wasp Bear-fur collars and cuffs. Old Bill had killed the Wasp Bear, and the cook had to admit that the black and yellow fur looked fashionable when paired with black leather.

The hard-edged man plucked off his Kansas City Royals cap and waved at them. "I heard that, Reuben. I also heard about you finding that Costco. You know, before all this fantasy game nonsense, I bought *all* my clothes from Costco."

"Figures," Brie grumbled softly.

Nacho muttered in reply, "Still don't see what's wrong with that."

"I bet you already know the truth of the matter." Young Bill's coat was open enough to reveal a flannel button-up. "It's not fair if you use guild money to build your house, or even a bunch of houses. We need to vote or something. I vote for walls. We need walls first. The tents are cold, but if people don't like it, they can build their own houses, like we did. Also, I told you to call me 'Scrubz'. I was weak and joined in. I want to have a reminder of that."

"It's not *up* to a vote. It's whatever is going to keep the most people safe, and the final say is Nacho's to make, *Scrubz*." Brie squared off with both men, not backing down an inch as their glares intensified. "Before you get all worked up, we have money regularly coming in, and we are actively gathering more for these projects. Even now, Taye, Kristie, and Abby are in a dungeon earning credits for the guild, because *they* believe in what we're doing."

That was true. Nacho was constantly being spammed with notifications of a slow trickle of incoming credits. In fact, during breakfast, a pair of players that had gotten an early start from Heartbreak Ridge turned up in Nacho's kitchen. They had informed the trio around mouthfuls of breakfast that Taye and the gang had come across more Pizza Roaches, as well as something called a Weiner Wolf.

Reuben had laughed at the news and quipped, 'It looks like they're going to be fighting monsters based on the Costco food court for a bit'.

Nacho shook off the memory, focusing on Young Bill—no, *Scrubz*—who had lost a little bit of his scowl. Reuben turned on the charm and raised his hands in a soothing gesture. "We were just about to walk over to the eastern limestone, and we'd love your input, Bills. Double Bill, double the fun. That's what I say, anyway. As you know, the northern wall helped resolve our main security issue, but let's go take a gander at the eastern slope."

"Gander… do I have recipes that would work on goose?" Nacho muttered to himself as the five of them walked past tents to reach that section of their town. The air was cold, but the smell of the various fires made it seem warmer somehow. At the edge of the eastern slope, the rock was only twenty feet high: a major problem. The Bove had scrambled up the slope and battered right through the wall. If *that* monster could breach their defenses, others could as well. How soon? Impossible to tell.

Old Bill grimaced as he eyed the open area. "We spent fifteen *thousand* credits on that northern wall, and that basically cleaned us out. We needed it; you're right about that. But an *eastern* wall? Why? How many people are gonna try and scramble up twenty feet of limestone to get to us? We have guards."

"Exactly." Brie motioned at him with a 'and that's my point' open-palmed gesture. "Our public works projects have kept us safe, and now I'd like to focus on quality of life. You know, at some point, even *you* are going to want to upgrade your shack."

"Our shack is fine!" Scrubz' retort came out far more

heated than anyone else had expected. It seemed that when he was around Old Bill, the younger one thought he could get away with being a little more of a pain in the butt. Oddly enough, it evened out, since Old Bill became less of a curmudgeon because the next generation of bitterness had spoken.

Brie didn't back down. "It *is* fine. For *now*. But the Store is a good place to buy buildings. Most everything else is terrible, but the guildhall has worked out very well, as has the north wall. Back to our mutual problem: we need walls, and we need housing. More than that, we need to put credits toward upgrading people's Skills, and to level them up. That's the most important thing we can do."

"*Our* taxes shouldn't go to *other* people's levels and Skills," Old Bill grumbled darkly. "This might be a new world, but I'm a red-blooded American. You work hard, you should be able to keep what you earn."

Nacho kept quiet. This was exactly one of the discussions he'd rather not be having. At least they got a discount for being a guild—ten percent off buildings, building supplies, and various other Store items. Reuben saw the conversation going off the rails and decided to intercede. "Let's not go down that rabbit hole. At this stage, we need to get the most bang for our buck. Ideally, we'd build an eastern wall along with some housing and line it with a nice cobblestone street. The guild has about twenty thousand credits to spend, and this is an important upgrade."

As the Guild Leader, Nacho saw the logic of not building a freestanding house for Reuben and Brie; that would empty their meager savings. If they bought housing for a bunch of people instead, they could use guild money—then an idea hit Nacho. "You mentioned this last night, but what if we create a wall that *is* housing? We put a little street out front, which would work well, since the Store is offering a sale for double square footage for streets. Buy one section of cobblestone, get another section free."

Old Bill scratched his grizzled beard. "You know... that's

not a bad idea. If you can snap the neck of two chickens with one motion, why use two motions to snap those necks?"

Scrubz decided that he hadn't complained quite enough, but he could see that the argument wasn't going his way. That meant it was time to steer things how he wanted them to go. "The north wall is five thousand feet long and three feet wide, twenty feet high. For twenty grand, we couldn't do the entire east side, but... we could get started. Maybe make the rooms twenty-five square feet each?"

"Not that it matters in this case, but how tall do you think ceilings are in your typical house?" Nacho tossed out the question and wasn't expecting the vitriol it earned him.

Old Bill practically spat the answer. "A boy your age should know that. Nine feet tall."

"A *boy* my age. Interesting." Nacho tossed around the idea of slipping some poison into the old man's fried chicken the next time he came in for waffles. Arsenic was cheap from the Store, just one credit for the ingredient. "Moving on... we could game the system. We pay for apartments. Two apartments stacked on top of one another, and boom. We earned a wall in return. We can't do the apartments on the north wall, because I'd imagine we'll be facing actual siege equipment at some point. But that's not the case on the east side, thanks to the twenty-foot slope."

Reuben's face glowed as ideas began to flow. "Gaming the System? Is there *any* better phrase in the English language?"

"Free pizza is canceled." Old Bill's scowl lessened as they flinched away. "Love that phrase. Can usually make any teen wince, just like that. Now, I don't agree with Nacho and Brie on much, but I like the sound of this."

Nacho surveyed the eastern edge of the Armor Mountain with a critical eye. "Let's simplify the math. If we do square rooms, twenty-five feet times twenty-five feet is six hundred and twenty-five square feet per apartment. We can use arrow slits on the eastern side of the apartments and windows on the western side, along with a door. Ten apartments will cost us six thousand, two hundred and fifty credits. Stone walls a foot thick will give us two hundred and seventy feet of wall. But we're only paying for the square footage, and we can stack another ten apartments on top of them."

Old Bill pointed to a small grove. "We'll need to clear those trees, but that'll be easy enough, and we could use the wood. Can't burn it right away—too green—but we can add it to a wood pile we've started on the south side of the guildhall. Meantime, we got the southern sun warming us up."

Nacho remembered another little cheat. "If we put a little alley between apartments, five feet or less, the System would give us a discount for any section of wall there. We could do something with that… maybe we can have more windows, so they're less boxy."

Reuben crossed his arms. "This makes me think of my terrible Minecraft houses. We could put little fountains in the courtyard that don't work, and we can figure out water at the same time, for—you know—showers and toilets."

Brie kicked a rock down the slope and refused to look at her husband. "We agreed not to dwell on toilets."

"Not going to dwell," Nacho hastily agreed. Suffice it to say that no one was happy with the current bathroom situation. This late in the year, everything was either dried-out, soggy, or pine needles. After coffee, it was almost always straight to the Store for the other most common daily purchase. For those that could afford it, that meant Epic toilet paper.

When buying buildings in the Store, there were several design applications, and Nacho was able to share the view with Reuben and Brie. That function was only so easy because they were in the same party. Including Old Bill and Scrubz was initially harder, but Nacho took the time to find the parameters to include them—only possible because they were guild members.

The five of them came up with a square design, basically a one-bedroom apartment with a bathroom and no kitchen. Setting the apartments to six hundred and twenty-five square feet was easier to orchestrate, and stacking the apartments would give them at least eighteen feet of wall, though probably closer to twenty feet, all told. They opted to make the roofs flat, though they'd need to account for adequate drainage. Ladders in the front would let people climb up to the higher apartments, as stairs were not an option due to space requirements.

They spent some extra money on an archway and gate farther down the eastern cliffs, not wanting the entrance to have a straight shot to the kitchen. That was a basic premise of medieval sieges. A stronghold had to make it difficult for enemy troops, both when they were outside the walls as well as if they managed to get in.

Dividing twenty thousand by six hundred and twenty-five gave them thirty-two apartments, though with all the extras the team wanted, they couldn't afford all of them in one go. They finally agreed on twenty homes, which became forty apartments.

Nacho felt like a wizard as he waved his arms and directed reality to be altered in front of him, creating ten stacked apartments on one side of the gate and ten more on the other. He grinned when he noted that putting a five-foot alley between the houses *did* give them a discount. He had been worried that particular feature wouldn't be the same in this life.

The system only charged them twenty-five credits for a wall a foot thick, ten feet high, and five feet wide. The System must have been feeling especially generous, because pavement on the alleys was added for free. Nacho included the option to allow minor changes by the resident at their own expense, such as purchasing custom stone floors or tiles in the apartments if they wanted.

Before finalizing the purchase, the five of them double-checked all of their math. If each apartment was twenty-seven feet long, including the two feet of wall on either side, and they built twenty apartments, that meant they would gain five hundred and forty feet of protective space in all. However, adding in the eighteen small roads gave them another ninety feet.

The guild balance bought a twenty-foot gate, assisted by a few direct donations from Nacho's current team, and then they were out of money to do more. All told, it was only a tenth of what they needed, but they had forty new homes complete with plumbing for guild members, including one very happy newly married couple.

Nacho gritted his teeth and added seven hundred feet of cobblestone road, five feet wide, in front of the twenty apartments which connected to Main Street and took them to the front gates. Thanks to the discount, it only cost one thousand, seven hundred and fifty credits. He decided to dub it the 'eastern road', which wasn't very creative, but it was very accurate. The new homes became the 'Great Wall Apartments'.

Standing back, he appraised his work. The apartments looked like row houses in a big city, but those little alleys made all the difference, breaking up the monotony of the apartments fairly well. Like with his guildhall, creating something from nothing was satisfying. He took a deep breath and nodded appreciatively.

In a very real sense, the work of rebuilding their demolished civilization had just begun.

CHAPTER NINE

Building the first forty living spaces had caused an uproar, as everyone demanded one for themselves. Nacho lobbed that negotiation off on Mayor Dan and walked away, informing him that the only people that could earn one needed to work for the guild by clearing out the altered Costco. "I need to talk to Matt; do you know where he is?"

Mayor Dan, looking harried, informed the Guild Leader, "I enlisted Matt Martinez to help plan some farming in the soil to the south. He's pretty busy, and-"

"Thanks, and good luck with all this!" Nacho took that excuse and left at a run, ruminating over when he would finally get to go and earn credits for himself again.

It didn't take too long to find his quarry, as Matt was eager to work. He was the only person in the area that was moving at full speed and putting their full effort into everything that they did. It was clear that this was a man looking for any excuse to keep his mind busy. Nacho walked up to him, "Hello, Mr. Martinez. My name is Nacho, and I am the Guild Leader. I was wondering if I could interest you in doing some more... *useful* work for us than clearing land for a farm, especially when we do not have a farmer. Sorry to say, but as it currently stands, there's no point in this."

"That's what I kept saying, but they said the work needed to be done. I'm not about to pass up a chance to make my way in life with my own hands. Call me Matt. What can I do for you?" It turned out that Mayor Dan had already explained a little about what Nacho was hoping for, and the man was happy to be on board with the project. The Guild Leader promised to prioritize purchasing a Wagoneer's Info Pack for him so he could do his research and a little wagon shopping. Relieved at his enthusiasm, Nacho left it to the industrious man to figure out a way to pull their Costco treasures back to the guild, and they shook hands before parting ways.

Nacho felt increasing pressure to get that project finished as soon as possible, which made him freeze in place and groan when he realized a very important fact he had overlooked: all of the roads were gone. Even before they could get wagons moving, they were going to need to chop down trees to make the game path wide enough for the wooden carts. The 'road' would be dirt, and that dirt would turn to mud when the spring rains came. "Why did I ever agree to be put in charge? Tricksey peopleses, convincing me to take all the stresses."

He chuckled at his silliness; something about talking like a certain character that was always searching for his 'precious' just felt good in this situation. It was nice not to be on the verge of starvation, death, and destruction at all times. Letting the smile settle onto his face, he turned his mind back to his current predicament.

Moving the Costco stuff while it was still winter was impor-tant—the dirt would remain frozen into a good road—but equally critical would be transporting the supplies before other guilds or random bandits heard about the treasures. Nacho didn't want the hassle of fighting off other humans while moving cargo.

There was a lot to do, and the days were full. Everyone was able to create their own routine, and soon days turned into weeks as they all worked together on gathering credits. For Nacho, that meant spending worlds of time in the kitchen, processing Putrid Mana out of meat, cooking, and selling his finished meals, though he was pouring most of his earnings back into the guild coffers. He wanted to build as many of the Great Wall apartments as he could afford, as quickly as possible before the worst of the winter storms settled in.

At the same time, The Dinner Party continued to venture out and level themselves up until all three of them had achieved level nine. Everyone in the guild had their eye on the Saturday Knight Armor and the Robbin' Hoodie Archer Pack that had been pulled from the bowels of the earth, and all interested members had agreed to a race to see who hit Tier one first and could use them. Nacho and his direct Associates had a massive advantage in this regard.

The original idea of auctioning them off to the highest bidder had met with far too much resistance, since no one could really afford to pay what they were worth, and no one wanted to break the sets up, as they would lose the vast majority of their efficiency. The remaining option was a direct race to Tier up, and Nacho currently led the pack, thanks to his ability to constantly earn credits as other people lost credits by paying him for food.

As for the Robbin' Hoodie set, another archer was breathing down Taye's neck. Gabe would often go out to hunt with Brie and Reuben and delve deeper into the Deep Buggy Darkness for monsters and credits, and so far, they hadn't run into anything Tier one. Taye was utterly *unamused* by this fact, and for the first time was forced to push himself harder. Nacho approved of this message: there was no such thing as a free lunch in the Juxtaposition.

Even Scrubz was contributing, having discovered another dungeon north of Armor Mountain; a place called the Perdition Staircase. It was a so-far unending series of stairs, each set going down deeper into the earth. The upper levels were infested by monster mice, which were low tier with a high credit value. This discovery brought a surge of hope to the guild: a new dungeon meant they could go on slaughtering raids in the upper levels without fear of running into anything especially dangerous. It was a great find, and Scrubz strutted around making sure everyone knew exactly how great it was that *he* had discovered and shared it.

Old Bill was very proud of his surrogate son. Those two were as tight as ever, even with Scrubz, rich from his find, moving from the cardboard shack into one of the eastern wall apartments. The only way to get one currently was to buy it at twice the cost of making it—so that a full new section of wall could be built—or working with the guild in certain laborious jobs.

Along with clearing the new dungeon, Gabe the Archer had proved that the hunting grounds around Armor Mountain were especially worthwhile to prowl. Some of the smaller animals, like rabbits, badgers, and squirrels, were growing more powerful and turning into all sorts of creatures that were rich in credits as well as meat.

Along those lines, the Scary Shelves had turned out to be a goldmine of high-level Tier zero and low-level Tier one monsters. The rat that had nearly taken out The Dinner Party had been caught and killed when a shelf holding workout weights had been pushed over on it, trapping it long enough for the damage dealers to expose its brain to the open air. With that threat out of the way, the common monsters in the UnderFun had been practically enjoyable to hunt, even for low-leveled humans.

The credits continued to roll in as a full month passed. Under Matt's supervision, the first wagons from the Costco rolled in with a massive stockpile of the lost creature comforts from their home world. The wagons themselves were a wonder to behold, and it was instantly clear to everyone why anyone working on the teams was being granted an apartment merely for their efforts.

Horses would have turned into monsters, and any lingering skepticism on that front was cleared when they used the small woodland creatures as proof. That meant that *humans* were the only viable option for pulling the wagons, but no one wanted to be strapped to a wagon and unable to defend themselves in the event of an attack. Matt had requested a specific design from the Store instead, and it had been accepted. Everyone that assisted in moving the wagons stood on a short treadmill platform that spun massive tank-tracks instead of wheels. They had a handle to hold onto, but it was only a marvel of coordination as well as Matt's expertise that using the contraptions became possible.

If someone went too fast on one side, the wagons would start to turn. They quickly learned that all the walkers needed to be at about the same height as their opposing counterpart, and they had to push on the treadmill with military precision in order to make the behemoth wagons function properly. When the teams returned from their first foray, they were already showing signs of *highly* developed leg muscles, and Nacho had no doubt that would become more prominent as they made the trip over and again.

The guild set up a block and tackle pulley system to haul up the supplies on big plastic pallets bought cheap from the Store. All of Armor Mountain was buzzing with the changes, and a continuous stream of new people came pouring in.

Reuben used his Marketing Skills to the max, posting signs on the game trails about Armor Mountain and the Chips Guild, offering the creature comforts of old Earth as a generous bonus to people that joined up.

The hired help worked tirelessly at collecting credits, and in fact, the first wagonful of luxury items alone funded the completion of the entire remainder of the planned Great Wall apartments. In total, they managed to squeeze in three hundred and thirty apartments across the eastern limestone cliffs, making Armor Mountain both more intimidating from the outside, as well as a place that radiated prosperity and safety from the inside.

Though people came for the goods, access to the digestible exploits of a world-class chef was what sealed the deal.

The term 'world-class chef' was Reuben's idea, as Nacho preferred to think of himself as a middling fry cook. A glorified sponge getting laughed at by a crab was something to aim for. When people compared his cooking to fancy fast food, he took it as the ultimate compliment. He'd broken down and bought *Jimmy Cholesterol's Fast Food for Everyone*. Tacos, nachos, hamburgers, hot dogs, and pizza—he had access to it all. The only truly tangible benefit to the end of the world? Fried food was no longer the evil it had been.

It could've been the Great Wall, or it could've been Nacho's Chicago dogs, but the Chips Guild doubled their numbers even as the number of tents decreased and most guild members moved into wall apartments. Beds and furniture were bought, people discussed decorating tips, the chimneys puffed cheerful clouds of smoke, and flower gardens and bushes were planned for spring.

The truth of the matter was that not everyone was cut out for dungeoneering. Those same people would only ever be able to progress *slowly*, thanks to the variety of work they did. That was fine for the time being, so long as a benevolent leader provided them with safety and shelter, as well as being surrounded by plenty of other people willing to fight and advance, but there was a clear divide in wealth and personal power that only grew larger by the day.

The Bills complained about anyone who wasn't actively slaughtering monsters. The term 'freeloader' was tossed around too often, when the reality was that everyone found work. Charity just wasn't an option, beyond the small family units that managed to survive together. A single person not contributing meaningfully to the community could easily create a disaster. Luckily, it was clear to Nacho that everyone had an income, specifically because no one had starved to death yet. Seeing as that particular demise took less than two days in total to come to fruition... well, the answer was that any issues with people trying to *actually* freeload would resolve themselves all too quickly.

As for Nacho, he worked tirelessly. It called to mind something Grandpa Colby once said to him and Reuben: Be careful of what you're good at, because if you're good at something, you'll 'get' to do a lot of it.

During all waking hours, Nacho was either processing ingredients, cooking, or eating. He had to keep his Hunger levels maximized in case someone brought in a Wasp Bear, or a Goat Cheese, which they were encountering more often as the winter progressed. A herd had come within range, and Goat Cheese reproduced *quickly*. It was the only way they could survive, since all predators, including humans, could smell them from a mile away. They were white with creamy, greasy skin— more cheese than wool, without a doubt. A thin layer of slime covered them like fresh mozzarella, and their cheddar-yellow horns could deal a great deal of damage when they rammed into a hunter.

Underneath their fragrant cream-cheesy skin was layers of meat and fat, which made for great eating. Before they made their appearance, Nacho had never eaten goat in his life, but now he was constantly using the goat meat for the fast food recipes in the Jimmy Cholesterol cookbook. He'd bought a huge meat grinder to make hamburger, and... he hit his breaking point of waiting around after four weeks.

Nacho *needed* to get out of his kitchen. After spending an entire month without them, his number one destination was to visit Brie and Reuben. The cook put up a sign outside his pickup window that said the kitchen was closed, and people would simply have to deal with it. They could still buy food from the Store to regain Hunger Points and to stave off any

Starvation Debuffs, so nobody would die while they waited for him to return.

Even with the occasional storm, winters had always been fairly mild in Kansas City, and this year was no different. Spring was already in the air, and he breathed in the fresh scent of the buds on the trees and admired the flowers planted along the Eastern Road. The people inhabiting the Great Wall Apartments were using their alleys for all kinds of interesting things. Gardens growing, functioning fountains which burbled up Tier zero water from a magical source… all sorts of changes had occurred to make the dwellings feel alive. For a price, they could even upgrade their fountains, which had led to an amusing spectacle of people alternating on trying to spend just a *little* more than their neighbors and have a *slightly* more beautiful alley.

Nacho waved to some familiar faces as he passed, and had to wait for a short while as a returning treadmill wagon guided by Matt Martinez passed through the front gate. It was moving so slowly that Nacho eventually decided to climb over the wall down one of the multiple rope ladders. He looked back at Matt —a big man with a big belly, who looked like he should always be angry. The truth was, he smiled as much as he looked furious.

Either angry or laughing, that was Matt. He would likely never be in charge of horses again, but he had mentioned privately that people on the Treadmill Caravan often acted exactly like horses did, beyond the fact that they would shout colorful threats at him instead of bucking or trying to bite. He was in his comfort zone and getting better at managing both people and logistics every single day.

Matt noticed Nacho in kind, and it seemed that he had something that he wanted to say. The cook wanted to scream in frustration as the Caravan Master waved him over, motions becoming more urgent when it looked like Nacho would jump over the wall just to avoid whatever the conversation was.

Despite the fact that Nacho wanted a night off, no matter if

he was a Guild Leader, head cook, or chief bottle washer…
being the leader meant his own desires had to wait.

"How is it that being an assassin had better hours?" Nacho
grumbled under his breath as he reluctantly climbed back down
the rope ladder and hurried to catch up with the accelerating
wagon. "Maybe people were just better at realizing that
annoying me was a bad choice."

CHAPTER TEN

Nacho patted the rough hide armor of one of the big guys that pulled the wagons of their caravan. He chuckled as the man looked at him oddly, then started laughing outright after the increasingly confused worker accepted an apple that Nacho had been saving for this exact moment. Matt Martinez tossed the reins to shake the Guild Leader off and keep the wagon steady. From the expression on his frowning face, whatever he had to say, it probably wasn't going to be good.

The cook instantly tried to get out of the conversation. "Hey, Mr. Martinez, I'm taking the night off, but I'll have cinnamon fry-bread in the morning. My new fast food cookbook has a ton of tasty recipes that are terrible for you."

Matt furrowed his brow and waved Nacho closer. "I would imagine my cholesterol level is the least of my worries at the end of the world."

"End of one world, and the beginning of another," Nacho countered with a smile. "Can't be all bad; this new world has sugar on demand."

Matt went from scowling to grinning, though he clearly wasn't happy about it. "You have me there. I'm just glad that food works so differently here. I can basically eat what I want and not gain fat; my gut even *shrinks* a little every time I use a Skill."

"A wonderful and strange change," Nacho agreed as he slowly backed away, only stopping when he saw a slight tightening of the driver's eyes. "Having new bodies that work completely differently has been fascinating. I've known some Mind Players waste away to almost nothing because they only need to drink water to use their Skills. They eat only one portion of food a day to keep the Starvation Debuff away."

"Ha, yeah... hey, Nacho?" For a second, Nacho felt at ease with the small talk. Maybe Matt really had just wanted to shoot the breeze and then take his wagon to the south end? The mustached frown returned, and Nacho sighed. No such luck. "We *are* going to go after Crave, right? He and his people need to *suffer* for killing my Maggie."

Nacho froze as the horrible plea came out of the affable man's mouth. The Guild Leader didn't know how to respond. War with Crave seemed inevitable, but that wasn't the game that he wanted them to play. The only path was playing out this survival horror by facing off against the growing number of monsters and beating the CrossHumans. A war would only thin their forces. One less human in the AKC was one less human who could fight Arriod and his inhuman marauders.

But... he knew that Matt didn't want to hear that. He wanted Nacho to agree with him. Reuben had taught him that sometimes, it was best to tell people exactly what they wanted to hear, and he knew that this situation called for it. "I killed two of Crave's best goons and tricked him into giving me thousands of credits. Then he tried to kill us and steal our rewards from the Bove, and he failed. Crave and I have a long history. When he comes for us, and I do mean *when*... we'll put him down for good."

"Thanks." Matt's scowl turned into a strained smile. "That's what I needed to hear."

Nacho nodded at the man. When he turned around this

time, no one stopped him from walking away. Of course the widower wanted revenge. The cook knew about revenge, murder, and bloodshed better than just about anyone. During his Probability Vision, he'd been killed the first time out of revenge. The price for Kala the Death Knight's guild merging with Crave's had been his head. Nacho shook his head at the memory of how being *too* good at a job would create issues; it didn't matter if a person was an Assassin or a Common Cook.

Though he would admit that fewer people wanted to kill him off in this timeline, most just wanted him to work endlessly. It was all a complicated game, and Nacho needed a break. Tonight he was going to hang out with his friends, and he was abyss-well going to enjoy his night off.

Finally arriving at Brie and Reuben's little home after dodging dozens of guild members that were sniffing for any scraps he had, Nacho was invited inside and given the grand tour. Their front area was the living room with a couch, a table, and a little desk in front of the front window, which gave them a nice view of the slowly growing guild town. The other room was the bedroom, with natural light streaming in from two arrow slits, which had been covered with glass for now. Everything was… just perfect.

It was warm enough for them to sit on their alley patio, to the right of their door. They'd covered the alcove with a trellis of flowering vines, which would give them some nice shade in the summer, and some protection against a light rain.

"I am not moving. I am not cooking. I'm going to buy an Epic steak from the Store with french fries. I'm putting ketchup on *everything*, and none of you are going to say a word about it." Nacho settled into a cushioned chair as Reuben bought them both root beer and nodded silently. He felt like a million bucks, eating food from the highest selection of the rarity chart and slowly letting the tension drain from his neck. He tried not to think about how far his own cooking had to go, but he couldn't help but compare what he made versus how an Epic meal actually tasted. His was Common to Uncommon at *best*, even if it was tastier than the Common food that came from the Store.

Brie joined them before long, wearing a dress and heels with a cardigan thrown over her shoulders. Even though it had only been a couple of months since everything went tush over teakettle, it felt strange to see her *not* in armor. She looked nice, and for a second life, this felt almost normal. But Nacho's life hadn't been normal in years. Celestials, some of those months he'd lived twice, which was strange in and of itself.

He exhaled happily and popped a crisp fry into his mouth. Reuben lit a little fire in a pit, and before long, small, smokeless flames were crackling and boosting the atmosphere of the get-together. The Healer produced a strange object, a curved drinking horn, and wiggled it at Nacho. "Fun fact for you, friend. Did you know that some monsters drop items? Ah, right, of course you did. Brie got you that recipe. Well, *I* got this bad boy off an abominable snowman."

"You're joking," Nacho deadpanned as he stared at the horn. Nothing under 'Rare' ever dropped. "You got a drop? That's... like a one in five thousand chance, unless it's a boss or quest monster. What does it do?"

"I can add it to a stack of drinks in my Storage Slots, and it absorbs all the liquid into a single horn." Reuben sipped at the horn and let out a happy sigh. "Even better, it keeps the *perfect* temperature for whatever the drink is. Now I have perfectly chilled root beer forever. Oh! Guess what it's called?"

"A... drinking horn?"

"Nope!" Reuben chuckled as he pointed at a logo on the side. "It's a *Yeti* travel horn."

Nacho stared at him for a moment, shook his head firmly, and closed his eyes. "I hereby inform you that we are done talking for the night."

"Don't be like that!" Reuben laughed as he tried to convince the former Assassin to try the frosted root beer.

"*Okay.*" Brie savored a glass of wine, pretending to be relaxed, but from her shifty eyes, it was clear she wanted to talk business. "Nacho, we have five hundred and seventy-three people in our little guild. Reuben's signs are helping a *ridiculous* amount with our recruiting efforts."

Nacho closed his eyes as he futilely tried to ignore her. It didn't take long before he broke down in his desire to know more. "The *signs* again. What is he calling me? 'A world-class chef that provides old-world delicacies that will tempt your tastebuds'? You know that people are calling me 'Eli Naches'? Yes, I *know* it's my actual name—hold on—but I think you're only doing it because 'Chef Nacho' sounds like someone you should be buying food from at a gas station."

Reuben snapped his fingers. "Now *there's* a slogan! 'Better than gas station food'. Nacho, my friend, the wife and I have been talking… and we're wondering what your endgame with all this is."

"My endgame? That's easy. I'm going to save the world with omelets. Get an endless supply of eggs and force people to eat the same thing over and over until things are better," Nacho flippantly informed them. "I'm tentatively calling it: 'The Omelet Endgame'."

"Please be serious, Nacho. We just want to be a part of things," Brie gently requested, which only made him groan.

"Guys… *please*. This is my night off." Nacho leaned back and stared at the sky, stuffing a handful of fries into his face so that he had an excuse to stop speaking.

Brie wasn't having it. "A lot of the people joining us are hardcore players. That means they weren't just holing up and scraping by on only earning enough credits to buy food from the Store. These are go-getters, which means our numbers of fighters are up, and increasing every week. We currently have roughly four hundred people earning at least ten credits a day."

"Actually, with our work in the Deep Buggy Darkness, the Perdition Staircase, and the Scary Shelves, it's more like twenty credits a day." Reuben earned a sharp glance from his wife for the interruption. "Taye came back today with the latest cara-van. He found another dungeon off Heartbreak Ridge called 'the Stone Peck'. It's mostly demon pigeons. Don't worry; there are rock tarragon ptarmigans roosting there too, not just pigeons. They're just bigger and more mutated, which would be perfect for you if we could get you there."

"What rustic yet charming architecture," Nacho responded blithely, trying to indicate that he was not going to engage with their attempts at getting him interested in work at the moment.

"Come on, now!" Reuben brightened at whatever thought was going through his head. "Another bird dungeon! Remember those bird dungeons we tackled early on? Good times. Terrible food; worst pancakes ever. I can still smell the deer goo that you tried to cook. But great *memories*."

That made Nacho smile. "Reminiscing is nice and contributes to a normal evening."

The duo wasn't about to relent, and Brie poked him in the arm to make him stop whining about it. "Four thousand credits *a day*. That's what is being earned by our various teams right now. To *start* with, we get ten percent of that; four hundred credits goes into the guild coffers daily. On top of those taxes, we have all the inter-guild transactions, your work in the kitchen, and our superstars like Taye, who are bagging closer to a hundred credits a day on their own. I can't wait for him to get the Robbin' Hoodie Archer Pack."

"Is there a point here?" Nacho's face crumbled as he realized that he wasn't going to be able to get away from the topic, and he might *never* be able to do so.

Brie rolled her eyes. "Yeah, it's called celebrating! We have credits rolling in, we're hitting four dungeons, and I've talked with Bill, who has agreed to actively hunt for more dungeons. He's also following up on the leads you 'found in an information pack'."

"He wants to be called 'Scrubz'," Nacho reminded her.

"I don't care."

"There's plenty to celebrate. Think of all the replenishing resources the guild has access to these days." Reuben rattled off the names of the dungeons that he could remember. "The

Labyrinths of Lick, the Terrible Tunnels of the Big Beef, The Grease Pit, Pork Alley, The Amazing Maze of Maximum Mercilessness."

Nacho wrinkled his nose, shifted in his seat, and forced a smile. "Celebrating. I like the sound of that. We have our wall, our wagons, and at this point, I'm feeling good. Which is why I'm *taking the night off*."

"Exactly!" Reuben raised his bottle. "To us! To The Dinner Party and the Chips Guild!"

Brie raised her glass, and Nacho slowly followed. For a long moment, it *did* feel like they'd arrived.

As though it had been waiting for this exact second, the System message flashed in all of their eyes.

Greetings, All Players Everywhere on the Terran Starter World! This little message is especially for those lucky players in the Greater AKC Area!

It's been a pretty amazing start to this Juxtaposition, hasn't it? As the Patrons in charge of running this iteration of the Juxtaposition, we want to congratulate you on not dying! Some of you have actually become fairly powerful... and some of you are pathetic. We feel sorry for you. Most of us are betting against you.

Back to the main message: We'd planned to wait a year or two, or three —five, tops—before reaching out and offering artifacts and surprises for different regions. However, for those of you in the AKC, for those in guilds, and for those independent contractors, we have decided to advance a special item of incredible power for you to try to collect! It's a spear that any class can use, and beyond a few other interesting powers, it also carries a special option that allows you to damage creatures a Tier higher than your own! Base damage is thirty points, and it'll grow in power as you do!

We call it the Dragon Spear, and it will be a game-changer for you in the AKC. We're looking at you and your competition, Guild Leader Eli Naches.

Anyhoo, make your future delicious!

. . .

Nacho nearly dropped his root beer. "Tell me you saw that. Tell me I'm not crazy."

"I saw it." Reuben blinked owlishly at him with a frown covering his usual smile-spot. "Who cares? You were mentioned by name, Nacho. Is that a good thing? I mean... I can use it for marketing, and the name recognition alone will likely boost our membership in the next few days, but are you okay?"

"I... have no idea. But my heart is currently in my shoes. What does all of this mean?" Nacho was too stunned to know how he felt. He had gone so long suppressing his emotions or tossing them aside in favor of death and cruelty that his instinctual reaction was either to hide until this blew over, or to stab anyone that asked questions. Right now, both options were impossible. "I'm gonna look it up in the Store... yep, there's the item, but you have to search for it by name. It could have been in here the entire time. Check it out and see if you notice anything that I don't."

The Dragon Spear

Level/Tier: Growth

Price: More than you can afford (and yes, we know you can afford quite a bit; aren't you special.)

Rarity: Growth. The rarity chart does top off at Epic, but special items such as this one aren't categorized the same way. Something like this you can only gain from a quest agreed upon by the Patrons.

Base Description: Anyone, of any class, can pick up this spear and start killin'! The Dragon Spear laughs at levels and hates Tier differences. If you want to kill something that's just a little out of reach, this is the weapon for you!

Browse for more info?

Yes / No

. . .

Nacho knew that he wasn't the only one choosing the 'yes' option at that exact moment. *Everyone* would be checking on the weapons.

More info, you say?
  This Advanced Description We'll Do In Quick Verse
  Things are bad, and they can get much worse!
  Well, here you are
  Without a home or car.
  We know you feel fear,
  So here's a tasty spear.
  To stand in perpetual awe,
  Find the Ivory Talon.
  We know Dragons are cliché,
  But we love them anyway.
  In a Downtown UnderFun,
  You'll have a smile upon that day.
  Find that KC Cesspit!
  Go run, don't just sit!
  We want your future so delicious,
  But sometimes the recipe isn't nutritious.
  So we made this rhyme
  To waste your time
  While other people are already hard at work
  chasing the dragon.

If you want <u>real</u> information, place a wager. If you think you can win, bet a lot. If you lose, too bad! Winner takes all. The more precious the buy-in, the more starting information you'll get. Wanna place a bet?
  Yes / No

Reuben slumped with his head in his hands. "Yep, this changed from survival horror to an Epic fantasy scavenger hunt. We have people hooked up to treadmills to move our all-terrain wagons, and now we're faced with a poem leading us to an artifact and a betting system that is almost guaranteed to backfire."

"I *promise* you, it's still a post-apocalyptic survival horror," Nacho darkly informed his friend.

"What does this mean, Nacho?" Brie looked to her leader for support, concern growing higher as she read the confusion on his face. "For the guild, for us?"

The cook couldn't answer her. His brain had seized up for a moment. There were so many things he didn't quite get, and he only knew one thing for sure. "I'm thinking that the Patrons had to move up their timeline because of Kronos' Probability Vision boon. I'm cooking, and that's changing things… or… this could be our fault. We found the KC Costco UnderFun too early, and the System even warned us that things would start moving faster. Either way, we know the Patrons are watching us specifically. Crave knows it too."

"I have a theory." Reuben slowly started speaking in his 'super serious' voice. "Also a way to test it. It looks like, even though the message *seemed* to be sent to everyone, most of that was only sent to the AKC."

"They made that pretty clear, yes." Nacho truly had no idea where his best friend was going with this. "Why do you think it matters?"

"It matters," Reuben told both of them, "because this might be a Legendary weapon release for *other* areas as well. Different population centers, I mean. If someone finds *one*, they might want to collect the full set. This could start a massive war."

The implications of his hypothesis killed conversation as each mulled over the new information. Nacho cleared the plates and grumbled softly about his only night off getting canceled. Already Mayor Dan, Becky, and the Bills were visible at the far end of the stronghold, marching intently down the street directly toward Brie and Reuben's apartment. Trailing along behind them was level nine Taye, who must be truly concerned. Being part of the approaching group meant that he was slowing down instead of pushing for Tier one, just to be a part of the conversation.

"Should we get ready for an Epic quest, Nacho?" Reuben was already gleefully rubbing his hands together.

The question made the conversation they had just been having crystallize in his mind, and the guild leader firmly pressed his lips together. "*No*. No, we shouldn't. This might mean more power purely for the sake of power, to defend against other people and creatures with this weapon. But my plan is survival-"

"You've already told us that you want to win. We might not know the conditions after winning the first portion of the Juxtaposition, or of defeating the CrossHumans, but we do need power." The fact that Brie was the one arguing so strongly threw Nacho for a loop. "Does having the information that we just got mean that our plans need to change?"

The Guild Leader closed his eyes and considered it. Finally, he had his answer. "It doesn't change a thing. Not unless there's a *great* reason for it. Frankly... there's no justification to care about this weapon other than bragging rights."

"But think of what we could say-" Reuben tried to change his mind, but Nacho cut him off by shaking his head just as the others came within hearing distance.

"It doesn't matter. The best way to show off our success is to live well. Let's not jeopardize that for some shiny trinket."

CHAPTER ELEVEN

Days later, Nacho was hard at work deep frying taco shells when the door to his kitchen was thrown open. The sudden interruption caused a knife to blink into his hand, spun around, and whipped at the intruder in an instant. He palmed another and dropped into a fighting stance before finally taking in the consequences of his actions.

Reuben glanced down at the knife sticking out of his gut as the smell of rotting cheese filled the room. He calmly pulled it out and tossed it back without a word. The cook let out a long sigh of relief. If that had been anyone else, they'd have been seriously injured at minimum before their Health Regen kicked in. "Sign says knock before entering."

"Right." Reuben felt the hole in his shirt, wincing at his freshly cheesy scent. "Got it. No judgment. Ah... you good now?"

"Yup."

"Great. C'mon, all." Reuben lost most of his characteristic enthusiasm when he realized that there was no apology incoming, but it came back in full swing as a bunch of guys, including the Bills, carried a 'Cow Poke' into Nacho's kitchen. It wasn't even the whole monster, just the back quarter, but it took five of them to lug around the already partially tenderized hunk of meat. "Brie almost beat this guy into juice before we managed to pull it away from her. Where can we put it? Also, we were hoping for steak burritos."

"Sorry to disappoint." Nacho dove into the meat; any faster, and it would have been a flying tackle. His big apron, which was covered in grease and flour, now had the dubious honor of adding Putrid Mana-filled blood to the mix. "I went with the 'Jimmy Cholesterol' recipes, which offers bean burritos but refuses to steer toward steak burritos. It's complicated, but the easiest explanation is that the food is too healthy to count for the current recipe."

"I thought you got the *Guillermo Cuisine* cookbook?" Reuben was definitely disappointed, though he did chuckle. "You said '*steer* toward steak burritos'. Took me a moment."

"Nacho, where can we put this?" Old Bill erupted when it looked like their banter wouldn't be ending anytime soon. "It's heavy!"

"I literally didn't even realize you were still holding it." Nacho stepped away and cleaned his knives with a flourish, waving for them to clear the counter. He launched himself back at the meat as soon as they slammed the monstrous cow leg down. To the cook's great delight, they'd also already chopped off the spiked hoof and peeled back the hide. "There's a ton of protein on that leg. That bone is mega hacked up, though... how many of you were using axes?"

Old Bill took off his Royals cap to wipe the sweat off his brow, exposing plenty of blood splatter that didn't come exclusively from monsters. "Five of us, but we were getting nowhere until Brie whipped over and took him down. Only two question marks in the System View, so we're looking at a low-to-mid Tier one. Too much for us, but she managed... decently."

"Look man, I'm a Healer for a reason," Reuben interjected, noting that Nacho was too far in the zone with slicing to pay much attention. "My gal keeps me outta distress, and I keep her Health topped off when monster cows are in a bad *moo~ood*."

"Beasts like that are only too much for us until we get that spear." Scrubz joined the conversation with a scathing tone. "Who gets the spear?"

Nacho ignored them in favor of working while they chatted. There was only so much time remaining before the big hunk of bone-in steak fully converted into liquid Putrid Mana. He grabbed the Cry knife and distractedly muttered, "Frankly, I don't want us to bother going after it. It's just a *weapon*. Only one person can use it. Why bother putting *lots* of our lives at risk to get it?"

"Dadgum, Nacho. You're scary with that blade. You *sure* you're just a cook?" Scrubz's eyes hungrily watched the meat as it was professionally stripped away, missing the pause in slicing that his question caused. "Why wouldn't we go after it? I'd like it; who wouldn't? Sure, I'd have to probably buy a spear skill, but it would be worth the expense."

While he wasn't sure what class Scrubz was, let alone what weapons he preferred, Nacho wasn't about to make any decisions that would cause an argument in his kitchen. He left Reuben in charge of mediating with a pointed glance, and the Healer stepped in with exquisite timing. "Let's go on the quest first. You'll be with us when we delve into the UnderFun, don't worry. We'll need your dungeon-finding skills."

"There is no *good* reason to go, and I'm not going to send our best people away from here unless you can come up with a better reason than 'shiny stick that pokes real good'," Nacho insisted with a bit more heat than he typically used in conversation.

"Sure, Nacho. Sure, sure." The goofy cheese-scented man was using a tried-and-true technique: buttering people up with compliments when he didn't want to fight with them. "As for you, Scrub-z buddy... cool. Glad we're on the same page."

Nacho shook his head in annoyance and studied what remained of the Cow Poke. The limb had come from a massive cow with a razor-sharp spear for a face—kind of like a unicorn cow, if a cow didn't have a mouth. Even with this haunch alone, he could process a hundred pounds of meat if he hurried, thanks to his knives. The real problem was the fact that even if his knives could cut it up, the meat was too high level for him to process the Putrid Mana out.

The Cow Poke turned out to be a level fifteen monster, also known as Tier one, level five. Frankly, the fact that Brie could punch up levels so easily was still shocking to him, but that was not the issue at hand. The cook's Ingredient Processing Skill was already maxed out at level nine. He wasn't Tier one, and thus could only process monsters who were level eleven or lower.

To increase his Skill cap, he would have to raise his class to level ten. He had remained at level five since his last level-up, which meant an additional five levels would take eight thousand and one hundred Experience Points, also known as sixteen *thousand*, two hundred credits. Even if he could process a thousand credits out of the Cow Poke, that wouldn't make it worth doing.

A million thoughts flashed through his mind, but only four stood out enough to matter. One: he didn't want to miss out on processing the Cow Poke. Two: he'd had to turn away more and more Tier one monster meats due to his insufficient level. Three: the monsters in the area were getting stronger just as fast as he had remembered. If they didn't start breaking through to Tier one soon, all of his Hunters were going to die. Four: if he was *not* a Tier one cook at that point, he wouldn't be able to feed them… and the guild would rapidly begin spiraling into debt and cannibalism.

Nacho swallowed hard and made his choice. He reminded himself that pouring their resources into Brie made sense when they needed to prioritize combat, but he was better than anyone else when it came to the pure generation of credits. On a good day, between processing monsters and selling his meals, he was making a couple *thousand* credits between sunup and sundown.

His contributions had already allowed his friends to advance their classes all the way to level nine.

For *him* to achieve level ten, it would take all of their remaining savings, *and* he'd have to tap into the guild coffers. Steeling his resolve, Nacho explained to Reuben and the Bills about his situation and the number of credits he needed.

Old Bill rubbed his chin. "Well, blast it, boy. It'd be a right shame to lose out on the Cow Poke's meat, but that's a ton of credits. You want to use guild money, and I'm not all for it."

Nacho shrugged as if it didn't really matter to him. "Every second we stand here talking this over, I'm not processing the meat. Wait too long, and we should just forget about it."

The men began to clamor.

"That thing nearly killed me; I wanna eat it in revenge."

"Shut your face, Bill. That thing is delicious, I know it."

"I say we feast! Worry about credits later. That's a problem for future us."

The consensus was clear: they all wanted Nacho to upgrade his skill.

Reuben grinned, not even bothering to try to hide it from the stone-faced Bills. "Do it, boss. Besides, Brie got a big bonus for killing the cow."

"Ain't nothing compared to *sixteen thousand* credits, you tool," Scrubz grumbled in a low tone. "That's almost a row of *houses*, all so he can cook burritos?"

Nacho tried to take away some of the sting. "After this, I'll buy the Tier one Cantina Cuisine cookbook. Who knows? Maybe I'll be able to make things taste *great* instead of 'I can force myself to eat it'."

Old Bill closed his eyes, looking pained. "Just do it before that fight turns out to be a giant waste of time. We need you processing stuff we find, and I had my heart set on a steak burrito. I'll… I'll even throw in for that cookbook."

There was a long moment of shocked silence before each of the other men offered to chip in some credits for the cause as well. Scrubz begrudgingly agreed after a tense pause, though blood trickled out of his mouth from biting his tongue as he transferred Nacho the credits.

"Okay, then." Nacho motioned for the men to step outside. "Reuben and I can take it from here. Thanks for bringing in the Cow Poke. I'll get to work on it."

The other men left, but the Bills paused at the door, squinting at the two as if there was something nefarious going on. "When are we going to the UnderFun?"

"Guys. This needs to stop. I'm putting my foot down. There is no guild-run excursion that will be looking for this thing." Seeing that they weren't moving, Nacho had to get them out of his kitchen, so he pushed a little harder. "If anything changes, I will let you know. Besides, even if we wanted to go, there's no way that we could leave before the caravan returns with Abby and Kristie."

They'd cleared out most of the food products and clothes from the Costco, and they'd finally started bringing in the weapons and armor from the Bonus Shelves. The non-magical items could be utilized by practically anyone as soon as they arrived and were especially necessary for the unexpected droves of people coming in who were still using crude clubs and stick spears. Shockingly, there were *still* people who didn't really understand how the Juxtaposition worked. Some just needed to be pointed in the right direction, and giving them armor, swords, and shields was a good place to start.

"You guys need to go," Nacho prompted nervously as he felt time running out. "I can't work with this many people around. I get... nervous."

"Exhibit one." Reuben pulled his shirt taut, displaying the hole where Nacho's knife had gone right through it. "He's pretty serious about this."

"I'm almost Tier one," Scrubz demanded obstinately, fully showcasing his lack of social awareness. "I should get some credits-"

Old Bill could take the not-so-subtle hints that Nacho and Reuben were tossing about and pulled Young Bill along with him. "Come on, Scrubz. Let's get back out there. We'll get you up to Tier one, don't you worry. I'll stay in town to make sure things run smoothly, since Mayor Dan and his wife need to be held accountable. Else they're liable to do all sorts of crazy things."

"Like giving away stuff for free," Scrubz spat with a dark laugh. "*We* wouldn't be giving people swords and honey-roasted peanuts as a signing bonus. They should pay."

"They *should* pay," Old Bill scowled, his voice starting to fade as they walked away. "If you give people things for free, they don't appreciate it. Even now, I'm giving Nacho credits, but *I'm* going to get a steak burrito, and-"

Reuben shut the door that they had left open, cutting off the random complaints. "You need to get to work on that Cow Poke, or I'm never going to get a delicious burrito."

Nacho stabilized himself in his kitchen, easing to the floor to get ahead of the incoming bodily changes. "Okay, Reuben, say goodbye to our life savings. Tier one, here I come."

"That sounds unpleasant?" Reuben winced dramatically. "I hate seeing people hurt so much and being unable to do anything about it."

"Pain in this case is literally weakness leaving the body. Deal with it." Nacho rolled his eyes. "There's a thousand credits in processing that Cow Poke haunch alone, as well as a huge amount of steak. We can have a cookout tonight. A big going-away feast for the Dragon Spear strike team."

"'Dragon Spear Strike Team.' Has a nice ring to it. Hey, by hitting the next Tier, you'll win the armor." Reuben grinned as his eyes went distant, and he continued with a Cheshire grin. "I'm glad it's one of us."

"Yeah. I'm very curious to see what happens when *I* put it on." Nacho rolled his neck muscles to get relaxed. "It could turn into cooking utensils. I have no idea if I can even *use* armor like that."

Reuben looked infinitely uncomfortable. "I should get Brie.

I shouldn't be here alone. It's unnerving. Maybe… let me just go and get her?"

"No. We don't have time. I have to hurry and Tier up so I can salvage the Cow Poke." Nacho hoped the change would be over fast enough to keep the meat. From his experiences in the Probability Vision, sometimes leveling went quickly, and sometimes it took a while. When he had Tiered up as an Assassin, it had been super fast. As a cook? Well… he'd just have to hope for the best.

Nacho accessed the guild coffers and found the money that the Bills and the other men had donated. He transferred the credits over, then opened the Store, where he bought the cookbook for four hundred credits, and finally bought all the Experience Points needed to make the jump to Tier one, level zero. "Grab me one of those old biscuits over there. I might need something to bite down on."

"Not jerky?" Reuben quipped as he hurried to follow the instructions.

"Don't have a recipe for jerky. The biscuit'll do; those ones are at least three days old."

Reuben knocked it on a counter. "Not hard enough to damage the stone, but close. Yep. That'll work."

The Healer tossed Nacho the hockey puck pastry, and the cook transferred the credits. Before the points had even finished vanishing from his account, his blood started burning.

He was dying, or at least that was what it felt like. Everything was pain; then mercifully, he blacked out as his brain was rewired to function at a higher level. When he came back around, he was falling, so he tried to regain control of his body —only managing to stagger blindly around. Reuben was there to catch him, thank goodness. "How… when did I stand up? Maybe… shouldn't have left the oven open."

"Did more than *stand*, twinkle toes." Reuben told him with a strained tone. "You practically *danced* around the room."

He tried to figure out why this leveling process hurt so badly —*way* worse than the last time—and decided that it was because he was not only adding five extra points to his stats, but he was also hitting Tier one and forever altering his reconfiguring body. Unable to remain open a second longer, his eyes rolled back into his head.

Nacho woke up on his sleeping mat, which had been pulled from his kitchen-shelf bunk bed. Reuben wasn't in the room, and the cook wasn't sure what was going on for a minute.

Then a System message appeared to remind him of the big change.

Congratulations, Player! You've hit Tier 1, Level 0. This is colloquially known as level 10! Congratulations, you are at the starting point of not being useless! As a word of warning, Tier 0 food and Tier 0 water will no longer do anything for your Hunger and Thirst Points. At least you've been smart enough to get to Level 10, and you now know the basics of how the Starter World and the fabulous Juxtaposition work. You'll do fine.

Your body has been remodeled with Mana, and now you will be able to unconsciously block low amounts of damage. Pure damage mitigation working in your favor! This will extend to any clothes and armor you are wearing, within reason. Can't 'wear' a house, right? People have tried. Doesn't work.

Let's not forget your now-useless items! Take a quick look and see for yourself. As a Tier one awesome-person, you won't be able to use any of the effects of your Tier 0 magical items without attempting to spend credits to upgrade them. Caution: there are risks!

Whoops, spoke too soon! We see you have the HungerCry Knives! These are special items that are guaranteed to upgrade to Tier 1 items. Would you like to upgrade them to Tier 1 for 400 credits?

Yes / No

"Well, that was new." Nacho rose to his feet with a fluidity of body that he had previously achieved as an Assassin, but only when he had leveled all the way up to Tier *two*. He glanced around his kitchen and found that his eyes practically highlighted areas of interest, thanks to his massive increase in Fitness and Mental Energy. One such item was the haunch of Cow Poke meat lying in his big basin. "Reuben must've gotten help to move that much meat around. Or... abyss, it's bone and goo, so maybe he just waited and mopped up the mess."

He growled at the wasted opportunity, vowing to never get so far behind in levels and skills again. After spending all those credits, it was disappointing that he had missed out on such a haul right out of the gate. "Well, might as well make the best of the situation."

Nacho inspected the upgrade menu option for the HungerCry Knives and asked for more information.

The HungerCry Knives are special objects for many reasons, but also because they can be upgraded! Not all magic items are as cool; in fact, most have a specific planned obsolescence each Tier. Now, here's what your knives can do since you made them into fancy new Tier 1 versions!

- *Yield increase of +50% on all ingredients cut.*
- *Chopping speed increased by 2x.*
- *These knives can cut through the Mana barrier of monsters a Tier higher than you. Hey look, you have a Mana barrier now, too! I guess that means we should say that you can cut 'Entities' a Tier above you.*
- *NEW! When you impressively chop food of a lower Tier, there is a chance that you can increase the rarity of the ingredient! As you know by now, eating food of a higher rarity allows for food-based buffs to stack! (Minimum Uncommon rarity for stacking to occur)*

Now, here is where the real fun begins! Here is a list of advanced abilities you can choose to increase your knife-work mojo (You can choose only one):

. . .

Silent Cut (500 credits)—Chopping receives a 75% reduction in decibels generated. This is a good ability to have if you live in a small apartment and you like to chop up a nice midnight snack, but downstairs neighbor Earl is a super light sleeper and gets up at five for his yoga. Earl would love for you to buy this ability.

Bountiful Beauty (500 credits)—Improve your Increased Yield to 75%. That's a 25% bonus! Wow!

Fast Whacker (500 credits)—Triple your chop time instead of doubling it! What else would we have meant?

Kitchen WarCry (1000 credits)—We altered these blades from the MurderSong to the HungerCry because you're a Satiation Player. We also know that the kitchen isn't a safe place. There's literally fire in there. There are sharp knives everywhere, and we still haven't forgotten what you did to Hogan and Whitney. Sometimes, when we close our eyes, we still have flashbacks. Along those lines, we want you to be protected… so we're offering you this Tier 1 ability. Now you can fight like a samurai chef. With this skill, you'll double your damage to living entities. Each knife delivers ten points of damage instead of only five.

Knife Blind (1000 credits)—Use your knives with such skill that there is a 33% chance you can literally blind your opponents. If you are actively butchering meat or chopping onions, there is a 66% chance of blinding your opponents for thirty seconds.

Garlic Crusher (1000 credits)—Always have garlic on hand. Use this ability to produce unlimited garlic by using the blade-press maneuver to peel your garlic. This maneuver involves cutting off the ends of a clove of garlic and then pressing down to loosen the skin. Do this on a single clove and continue to produce garlic until you can slay every vampire in the world.

Forever Sharp (2000 credits)—The HungerCry knives, given that they're artifacts of unimaginably powerful quality, will never get dull. Not only that, but they are a good influence on the other blades in your kitchen. With the Forever Sharp ability, all other blades within the area of effect will be kept sharp through peer pressure alone—thanks to having the HungerCry knives nearby!

Nacho considered the list carefully. The Kitchen WarCry seemed to be the best option for him at present, but he wasn't sure if it was the best option for long-term success. In fact, just bringing the knives up a tier had already given him important information. When he was a better cook, he could double, maybe even *triple* the bonuses he was able to give people. No wonder this class was the most expensive and rarest of them all. Besides, a cook wasn't really *supposed* to be in battle, right?

Thankfully, the System gave him an option to select the upgrade on the HungerCry Knives later. Closing the menu, Nacho stood and placed his sleeping mat back on the top shelf.

He turned around and nearly jumped out of his skin, the knife in his hand practically leaping out and flashing through the unexpected person to stick in the wall behind them. That allowed him to calm down, though he was annoyed that he'd need to repair the wall later. Still, it was time to put his best foot forward.

His Patron had come to call.

CHAPTER TWELVE

Kronos gave Nacho a happy little salute, which was disconcertingly out of place when a god-like entity was the one performing the action. The Patron was a tall man who looked kind of like a beloved fictional chaos theory mathematician traumatized by dinosaurs, but with fuzzy sideburns. As before, he wore a white toga and golden sandals. His wild hair billowed out from beneath a New York Yankees baseball cap, turned around so the bill faced behind him.

Nacho wasn't sure what to say to that. For a second, he wasn't quite sure if this encounter was real or not. Kronos was just... suddenly there, blue eyes twinkling, mischievous smile a mile wide. To the cook's increasing confusion, the patron tapped a three-day-old biscuit on the counter. "I wasn't sure if your culinary skills would improve, and it looks like my fears were justified. Are people actually *paying* you for your cooking?"

"You know they are. They're forced to pay." Nacho was suddenly ungodly Thirsty—ironic, thanks to his current company. He used two credits to buy an Epic Tier zero sports drink, orange flavored. He slammed the whole bottle in one breath but didn't feel a thing. It was as though he had just sucked in a bellyful of air, and even though he was disappointed, he fully understood why. "Ah, *man*."

Nacho was in a Tier one body now. Buying an Epic Tier one Juxt-Ade—the Juxtaposition off-brand sports drink—would run him twenty credits. Drink prices had just gone from one credit… to *ten*. With the Rarity Chart in action, Epic drinks were one hundred percent more expensive. No longer an option unless he wanted to go bankrupt, in other words.

Kronos laughed at his sour expression. "Rookie mistake, Nacho. You can't make rookie mistakes any more. I have too much riding on you. If you mess up, *I* could lose everything. I bet everything I have on you. My power, my future. You're not a novice, so stop playing around. Start breaking things."

"*Me* mess up?" Nacho whirled the phrasing around to strike the Patron instead. "What in the name of… what is going on with you and the rest of the Patrons? Are you targeting me? Are *they*? This UnderFun opening situation is *messed* up."

"You went beyond the bounds of what was *probably* going to happen. Once again, that's why your buff was called 'Probability Vision', and not 'Future Sight'." Kronos took off his cap and waved it around. His hair seemed to grow even more frizzy while they stood there. Somehow, Nacho was bothered by the Patron being affected by small issues such as local humidity, but not his knife. "You found the UnderFun before anything even had a chance to grow in there. That *probably* wasn't going to happen for five entire *years*, if you'd let things be. The lower-level monsters were supposed to get more powerful. To get through them was going to require a full raid. We're talking Tier three pizza rats; stuff the current you can't hit at all with a spell or sword. You messed that up… and it's awesome."

"Five years? You're *happy* about the change?" Nacho's Thirst finally broke him down, and he bought a bottle of common Tier one water. He guzzled half of it before noticing it tasted like suburban pond water. "What happened with that Costco we found? What *really* changed?"

"For one, you killed the Bove. Fancy, fantastic work, that. You won't understand how much this matters, but an entire Pantheon of animal Patrons lost *all* their influence on this world because of that alone. Think of the biggest animal rights organization in North America, only if they had power to kill *people* instead of just animals." Kronos chuckled as he slid open the reinforced wooden door to Nacho's icebox room before continuing to speak.

"For another, the river had some flow troubles. The unexpected flooding wiped out some of the monsters and exposed the entrance. It was all rather... improbable. The other Patrons are... what's the word? *Ulcerous* with rage. They accelerated the timeline in the AKC, which is topping the leaderboard for the entire Starter World at this point. But the Starter *CrossWorld* still leads the betting. Those CrossHumans were *always* going to be ahead of you."

"Why?" Nacho didn't expect an answer to his throwaway question, so he flinched when Kronos slapped his cap back on and spun, speaking rapidly all of a sudden.

"Earth was behind in *all* the things. You should've spent more time—as a population—playing video games. I mean, come on; all that other stuff you were doing while you could've been gaming?"

Nacho couldn't help but try to defend himself. "Not me, though."

"Not you." Kronos walked around Nacho's kitchen, but it still didn't seem like he had a real body. It was more like it had been before—a hologram of light that phased through anything that was inconveniently placed.

The cook took a minute to flex his upgraded body and mind, noticing appreciatively that he was feeling better than ever. He should be—his stats had just rocketed up by five points each for a total increase of twenty in one go. He felt stronger, his mind clearer and more focused, and he could almost feel his Mana pool expanding beyond its previous limits as his Thirst Points increased and his Mana pool began to regenerate. He was dying to look at his stats, but talking with his Patron took precedence.

"Are the other Patrons gunning for us?" Nacho decided that was the most important thing to worry about. "Fourtuna, for instance? I know he gave Crave a boon, and he's talked with the guy, I think."

"Anyone that lost influence can't do a single thing. Everyone betting against you is gunning for you, and vice versa." Kronos grunted at the sight of the big puddle of meat in the sink. "Ugh, gross. Good luck cleaning that up. Mmm, actually.... as to Fourtuna... yeah, he's the worst. Fishy as they come. Now, no one can gun for anyone in *particular*. It's all very controlled, and very macro. Micromanagement isn't worth the effort, in the first place. I can't say much because of the rules, but I will say Fourtuna is a Patron for more than just your boy Crave. He has a lot of pawns. I just have *one*. You, Nacho. You're my guy. Just keep playing the game like you're playing it."

"Should I go after the Dragon Spear?" Nacho prayed he'd get the answer he wanted.

Kronos scowled at him like he had just asked if toilets were seats for fancy dinners. "Of *course* you need to get the Dragon Spear. It was put out there to level the playing field *against you*. We had to do something to at least *pretend* to offer balance because of the boon I gave you. The boon wasn't easy, mind you, and it brought me some much unwanted attention. But as long as things progress like I hope they will, we should both be good. For now. *Things* are watching this game closely, and I'm risking everything by coming here. I shouldn't be talking to you, but then Fourtuna shouldn't be talking to Crave. That gives me a little bit of leeway for sharing information with your sorry butt."

Nacho sipped the nauseating Tier one water to give himself a moment to think. "Anything you can tell me about the Dragon Spear?"

"You don't have a valid reason to care about it, at least not one your guild would accept. Not *today*. Can't have you changing your mind without a reputable source of outside information; it would make you look weak." Kronos paused for a drawn-out moment before waving his Yankees cap through the air. "You are correct to plan for the long term. It's not just about me and you, Nacho—it's not just about the credits I plan to make. *Worlds* die if you don't win. Fun thought to leave on."

The Patron started slowly dissolving the mess in Nacho's big sink. The liquified meat swirled around, then slowly formed back around the bone. In seconds, the huge haunch of Cow Poke meat had been restored. "Here's a little gift from me to you to celebrate your advancement to Tier one. Just remember that I'm in your corner, though it might not always feel like it. You should *always* be in my corner."

On that cryptic and slightly worrying note, the Patron vanished. The cook didn't pause to ruminate over the conversation; that would come later. He had a huge amount of Cow Poke meat to process and steak burritos to make. There was also probably enough meat to make the entire guild hamburgers, *real* hamburgers, from the Jimmy Cholesterol cookbook.

Now that he was a Tier one Common Cook, his skills were no longer capped to the previously low level. It only took nine hundred and twenty credits to upgrade his Ingredient Processing Skill from level nine to level thirteen so he could process the level fifteen Cow Poke meat.

As per usual, he was encapsulated by the power and flooded with warm, fuzzy feelings of fresh knowledge. After it ended, he crossed to the sink and touched the skinned meat. Before he could process so much as an ounce, the System flashed him a message.

Advanced Ingredient Processing – Tier 1!

You can now eliminate Putrid Mana from a distance. Yes, prep dinner from the other room! This is the standard boost to all Skills when you raise them to Tier 1: Skills at a distance! You can do some great stuff when you have some space. In most cases, that equals about fifteen feet, but not always. Gotta keep things interesting!

Ingredients, especially those at a lower Tier, are now easier to increase in rarity!

"Now *that's* interesting. I'll have to try that at some point; still gotta figure out how to increase the rarity of an ingredient in the first place, though. Let's start cookin'."

Reuben and Brie came charging into his kitchen through the side door just as scraps of meat started flying. The big guy let out a huge sigh of relief, both at the fact that Nacho was awake, as well as not getting a knife chucked at him for the surprise interruption. There was no way he could've known that Nacho had clearly heard them approaching well before they reached the entryway, his boosted characteristics bringing him ever further from human. "Glad you're upright! I was freaking out a little bit. I didn't want to come in here alone and find you still on the floor."

"That's why you came and got me?" Brie crossed to stand by Nacho, the look of worry on her face easing slightly as she observed his incredibly efficient and smooth movements. "Are you feeling well, Nacho? Reuben had me so worried."

"Yeah, I'm just fine." Nacho's reply was slightly more abrasive than he had been intending it to be; he just didn't like being the center of this kind of attention. "Actually, you guys can help me. I have got to process this meat as fast as possible. Once I drain out the Putrid Mana, it'll have the shelf life of an average hunk of meat. Take what I hand you and stack it somewhere the Putrid Mana can't drip on it."

Nacho didn't want to reveal that he'd talked with Kronos, not right then. There was too much information to work through before he shared it. First, the fact that Patrons were beholden to the system—needing to generate their own credits —seemed to be important information for the future. Were they actually just players that had reached incredibly high levels? Or was the System something else entirely?

Secondly, *worlds* were depending on him? How did that work? He wasn't sure he wanted to know.

There was something else that he *did* want to know, and as he finished the maximum amount of meat that he could process in one go, he finally couldn't hold back a moment longer.

Chugging his remaining water, he waited for Active Cooking to end so that he could purchase some food, as well as ingredients for the next steps. He pulled open his Stat Sheet to see how much more Mana he had available. Before, he had only been able to use his Ingredient Processing around eighteen times, which was where he had stopped in processing the Cow Poke to be safe, even if that amount might have changed now that he'd made such a big jump.

Eli 'Nacho' Naches
Class: Junior League Chef
Level (Aggregated Tier and level): 10
Experience Points: 14,400 to Level 11!
Current Credits: 0 (0 total Dinner Party pool)

Build Type: Balanced, Delayed
Body:

- *Fitness: 20*
- *Metabolic efficiency: 20*

Mind:

- *Mental energy: 20*
- *Circuit: 20*

Satiation:

- *Hunger: 100*

- *Thirst: 100*

Total Health Points: 50
Bonus Physical Damage: 10%
Health Regen: 20% Health Regen/minute
Total Mana Pool: 40
Bonus Spell Damage: 10%
Mana Pool Regen: 20% Mana Regen/minute

Skill Slots (3/4)

- *Small Blades (Passive) Level 9: 18% bonus damage on all knife attacks*

  No Mana, Hydration, or Metabolic Cost

- *Ingredient Processing (Active) Level 13: Remove Putrid Mana from monsters up to Level 15.*

Tier 1 Enhancement: Process ingredients from 15 feet away. Increased chance to upgrade Rarity of ingredients.

  Mana Cost = 5%
  Hydration Cost = 5%
  Metabolic Cost = 5%

- *Cooking Magic (Active) Level 9: Create food that enhances a single stat by 45% of maximum*

  Mana Cost = 5%
  Hydration Cost = 5%
  Metabolic Cost = 5%

- *Open slot*

"Nearly died just now. Whoops. Right... *amount* of Mana

doesn't matter for these abilities." Nacho wanted to grumble about that, but at least it had remained consistent. He had more Mana, but five percent of max Mana per shot was five percent. He still could only process ingredients nineteen times. If he tried for twenty rounds, he'd go unconscious. He wasn't sure if Active Cooking would end at that point, or if the Patrons would let him die because 'cooking was in progress', or if he'd be able to fall out of it and regenerate his Mana pool while knocked out.

Probably a coin toss, and it sounded like Kronos might not have the same power to intercede that he'd once had.

He also wasn't sure he liked his new class name. Junior League Chef? Sure, it was better than something like 'Kid Cook', but it still wasn't great. He had nearly forgotten how the Patrons liked to give different people different names as they increased their Class, both to insult as well as confuse people. He'd known one Assassin who'd earned 'Meanie Face' for their Tier one Class name because he took himself too seriously.

During his Probability Vision, Nacho had 'Lookin' Good Killer' for his Tier one Class name, and his Tier two Class name had been 'Shadow Killer'. Shaking off the memories, Nacho took a breath and returned to the task at hand.

He raised his cleaver from across the room, deciding to test out the distance prep. With a downward slash, five pounds of meat fell away, fully cleansed and ready for cooking. Reuben dove out of the way with a yelp. "Careful with that thing! *Wait!* You have a ranged attack now? That's awesome!"

"Not quite. This is just processing the meat." His recipe called for five pounds of steak, which was how he could get so much with each swing—because of his amazing knives, every time he hacked off a hunk, he got fifty percent more meat. Fifty pounds of animal muscle became seventy-five pounds of beef in no time. With each swing, he lost renewable personal resources, but it looked *way* more awesome to perfectly cleave meat from across the room and generate the equivalent of a glistening A5 marbled steak.

Nacho had purchased several five-gallon plastic bags from the Store, which were perfect for marinating meat at this quantity, no matter what his friends said about it. He had Reuben and Brie fill up the bags with the raining meat, expecting the Cow Poke to liquify at any second.

But Kronos must've given it a good dose of love. Nearly ten minutes later, Nacho was once more down to fifty percent of his Mana. He had processed another seventy-five pounds of meat he wanted to use for hamburgers. Luckily, his Jimmy Cholesterol recipe kept things simple. All he needed was a dash of salt and pepper per each pound of meat. Before starting back in, Nacho had set aside a small amount of the Tier one ingredients, since he didn't need that much, and he had to find a way to eat without breaking the bank.

Once he'd cut off a sizable hunk of the beef, he threw the pieces into his industrial-sized meat grinder, and Reuben started cranking. Brie collected the ground beef in a big metal pot, and after the cook successfully tempted them with the promise of a Tier one burger, his friends agreed to help him pat the hamburgers into shape. After using nineteen rounds of Ingredient Processing, Nacho only had a meager handful of Mana remaining. He was light-headed and a little dizzy, but as long as he didn't use any more Skills, he could keep right on cooking.

Kronos had been correct. He did need to celebrate hitting Tier one, and he wanted to try on the Saturday Knight Armor. Also, he wanted to talk with everyone about the Dragon Spear quest, once he figured out a logical reason for changing his stance.

Finally, even with Kronos restabilizing it, the Cow Poke haunch started to liquify. Nacho dropped the small remainder into his special drain with a satisfied noise; he'd cut most of the meat off. No longer was it a massive waste and disappointment. Unable to hide his excitement any longer, he turned to let his friends in on the fun. "Guess who I talked to after I leveled up? I'll give you a hint: he was glowing, and not in the 'looked full of health' way."

"Let me guess. A certain fan of a New York sporting team?" Reuben inquired with sparkling eyes.

Nacho nodded as a cockeyed grin appeared on his face. "Yep. Jets fan. They would've had a great year if the Juxtaposition hadn't hit."

"Doubtful." Reuben winced and shuddered at the thought. "They would have lost so hard to-"

"*Literally* doesn't exist anymore! Why do you two only care about sports now that they're gone?" Brie interrupted the inane conversation as she continued to help Nacho pat patties.

"Well…" Reuben thought hard for a moment, then brightened as he found his answer. "Now those sports are *fantasy games*, right? You know I enjoy that sort of thing. The idea of playing a video game now? That'd be like playing Sims, or a walking simulator on a treadmill. Just… normal life now. Boring. But baseball *isn't* something that can be real here. Throw a ball? A Tier two pterodactyl gets upset that something is in its flight path, swoops down, and kills us all."

"Right… how about I just tell you what went down?" Nacho outlined, in general terms, his conversation with Kronos. "We now know that Crave has help of the supernatural kind, which is far more direct intervention than I expected. But more importantly, we're ahead of schedule—by about five years, according to my Patron. That's rather surprising in and of itself."

Brie smacked a patty down and laid it on one of Nacho's grilling trays. "I don't know if that's good or not."

Nacho acknowledged her point but went on. "We also have to… okay, this is gonna make you look at me funky—it seems that if we *don't* win, a bunch of, um, other worlds will die? It's not just the Earth we're fighting for. It's everyone. Apparently. Interesting note, we're leading the world. Bleeding edge of improvement. I always knew Kansas City had a greatness that people would one day appreciate."

"You're not joking." Brie added another slab of slapped-together meat onto the pile. "I thought you might be joking."

"About the AKC?" Nacho questioned hopefully, knowing for a fact that he did not have any answers to any questions she might bring him.

"About all of it." Brie blew hair out of her face in annoyance.

"Nope." Nacho took a moment to let the pressure build to an uncomfortable level. "No joking at all, really. Kinda sucks how serious it all is."

Reuben cackled as Nacho tossed the burgers on the hot grill. "At least we get monster hamburgers. I bet I can get five hundred more people to join the guild if I can use these in advertising. As we've seen, more people working with us means faster progression. Let's just focus on doing what we can. By the way... is that burger showing as Rare?"

"Huh." One of the burgers was visibly glistening, and Nacho had no idea why. "Guess I need to just keep making these until I figure out the trick. As always, practice makes better."

CHAPTER THIRTEEN

The night before they left for the UnderFun, Nacho collected his prize for hitting Tier one. He'd managed to extract a total of six hundred additional credits from processing the Cow Poke, and he was going to be raking in a ton more by selling his food that night. That was level fifteen meat, which meant he could sell access to the feast for ninety credits a pop for three servings. The fee matched the Store's price for *Common* Tier one food, but thanks to his choice of ingredients and fresh flavor, the Store food couldn't match Nacho's *Uncommon* rarity cuisine.

With the money he earned from serving his food, Nacho planned to buy a mobile kitchen backpack, a special Satiation Player item he had found that would make cooking on the road much easier. Anything extra would go toward repaying what he saw as a debt to the guild.

He grilled up the slices of steak in his kitchen, and then had a team of helpers wrap the burritos. Grilling the hamburgers in the main hall on both of the fireplaces in the meantime created a mouthwatering scent that he knew would reach far beyond the borders of Armor Mountain. There were entire chafing dishes full of condiments, Epic lettuce, tomatoes, and pickles, but only a small number of grilled onions.

Most people had brought their own mustard, ketchup, and mayonnaise, ranging from Common to Epic, depending on their personal preference. Many of them shared, and while Nacho had planned on giving away the feast as a way to celebrate his Tier one fun... he couldn't. Not with his debt needing to be repaid. That wasn't a problem, however; in fact, most people *insisted* on paying the full price.

Once everything was cooked, the Guild Leader clanged his knives together, relishing in the first few points of Mana Regen. Draining a bottle of water, he was back to his full forty Mana in no time flat.

The building was *packed*. A lot of people were curious about the armor, while others wanted to talk about the Dragon Spear quest, and a minority were there to complain about whatever was on their mind.

"Music to my ears," Nacho muttered as he laid out the tray of steak burritos, which had turned out very well. He didn't want to leave people eating hamburgers without french fries, so he splurged on pre-cut sliced potatoes, which he threw in grease with salt and pepper. The fries turned out... not very good. He took them out of the grease too early, and so they were cold and chewy, not to mention rather tasteless. "Thought I'd followed the recipe from the book. Might've missed a step."

That was his only excuse, even though it didn't help with the dirty looks a few french fry connoisseurs sent his way. Frankly, he was too exhausted to care. Leveling, talking with Kronos, and then cooking all afternoon? No one got a second glance, and the worst offenders were 'politely' informed that they were on mandatory dishwashing duty that night. That thought made him smile, even if it was a bent out of shape and tired smile.

Unlike his last lifetime, punishment didn't have to be something terrible, twisted, or anything remotely torturous. Simply making people wash dishes for a few hours was enough to induce them to keep their complaints to themselves in the future.

A klaxon call that had no right existing in a world like this shattered the cheerful atmosphere.

Whoop! Whoop! The first weeks' worth of wagers have been placed on the Dragon Spear, and information has been granted! Did we not mention that the wagers are going to be public record? Ha, too late now! Here's who is in, and what they wagered!

Collective credit amount from various free agents that wanted information: 238,931 credits!

Guild Master Kala: one year of service! In return, she received a decent starting point and some basic information on monsters! As she is a Guild Master, her service comes with the service of her guild, whether she wants it or not!

Guild Master Crave: his <u>entire</u> guild as collateral! Wowzers! He was given the location to a private entrance, information on the monsters inside, as well as a starting point in the UnderFun to commence his scavenger hunt.

Several additional wagers were listed, but none of them were substantial enough to catch his eye. Most of the others were individuals who were throwing a few items against it to try their luck. Frankly… Nacho did not need to see any more than that.

"If we get it now, the cash prize is a nice little windfall, but the ability to *take* Crave's guild? Get Kala's working for us for a year? Even if we got nothing else, so long as Crave is bound by the rules of his own Guild Charter, he wouldn't be able to fight us anymore. This… this means… ugh, *fine*." Nacho grumpily heaved himself up from his seat and got everyone's attention, informing them sullenly that he would be taking The Dinner Party, Taye, and any additional volunteers out to look for the Dragon Spear starting the next day.

The best part was that they were not going to be putting in a wager of their own. They already had more information than anyone else would have started with and would be going to search for the UnderFun where they believed downtown Kansas City should be located.

Everyone reacted excitedly, many of them shouting that they wanted to come along or wishing him good luck. There was one standout: Old Bill loudly calling, "A warrior leader should look like a proper warrior! Are you going to put on the new armor you won or not?"

With almost everyone in the guild present and eating in the hall, a few people spreading the news that Nacho had hit Tier one turned into a tidal wave of cheering for him. The Saturday Knight Armor was lugged out, and he trudged over as the set pieces were placed on the table at the far end of the main room.

"Yeah!" another voice agreed. "Put on the armor! Let's see what you look like all fancied up!"

Colleen, Mayor Dan's daughter, sat at a table nearby, giving Nacho a thumbs up as he walked past. He smiled politely at her, and she smiled back. Cheeks warming slightly, he looked away first. Even if she was cute, Nacho wasn't sure he wanted to consider starting a relationship with anyone until he'd established the area a bit more.

"Okay, okay!" Nacho lifted the helmet and set it on his head, their jubilant mood forcing him to crack a smile.

He got a message from the System right away.

Stop right there, Scullery Scum!

The Saturday Knight Armor is for Warriors! Body Players only! No other type of player need apply. Your battles are in the kitchen. You whip the cream. You beat the eggs. You batter dough. You pound schnitzel. You show no mercy when it comes to your cuisine. Unhand it before-

Item Update!

The Saturday Knight is Armor is now the Sunday Brunch Armor! When you are battling breakfast and lunch, the only true victor is brunch!

Congratulations, Satiation Player!

Protect yourself and your friends from monsters as well as mediocre meals!

Would you like more info on your armor? We assume so. Just start equipping the pieces of your ensemble, and you'll discover how well each one will work.

"Woo... that was strange." Nacho's voice echoed oddly as he looked around the room.

Reuben gestured to his head, and Nacho had to wonder what the helmet looked like from the outside. "Uh... I wonder if anyone has a mirror so he can see himself? It used to be this pretty cool helmet, like with wings... you know, like... cool fantasy stuff. Now, it's... uh... how do I put this?"

"You have a pot on your head, Nacho," Old Bill shouted from another table. "Ha! Our fearless leader is a pot-head!"

"A saucepan?" Nacho's voice sounded odd to his ears, a strange feeling that he needed to get comfortable with.

"Not a saucepan, boy. If it was a *saucepan*, I would've said saucepan. It's a pot." Bill shouted down anyone that tried to counter his assessment. Nacho reached up and felt the handles, confirming what he had been told.

He was wearing a pot.

Pulling it off and setting it on the table earned him a message:

Helm of Boiling!

No, we don't mean boiling your brain—we're hoping to protect your gray matter. Here are a few things the Helm of Boiling can do:

- *You can expand this pot to various sizes:*

10 Quart
12 Quart

> *15 Quart*
> *20 Quart*
> *24 Quart*
> *30 Quart*

- *All water placed inside will boil instantly!*
- *While you wear it, the Helm of Boiling will act as a Tier 1 Helmet.*
- *Note: The Helm of Boiling has handles on the side. Be warned! A monster might grab the handles and try to rip your head off. Active Combat is not for the likes of you. Combat is hazardous to your health, in case you haven't noticed by now.*

"Well?" Scrubz shouted with aggravation filling his voice. "You can't leave us hanging; we all saw it change! What can it do?"

"I can boil water instantly!" Nacho triumphantly held the pot in the air so everyone could see it.

Most people laughed, but Old Bill nodded. "Might be nice to have that when you're camping. You're always boiling water for some reason or another."

"Are you kidding me? He just wasted an awesome set of armor so that he can *boil water*?" Scrubz argued with the elder Bill in public for the first time. As the conversation devolved, Nacho pulled on the gauntlets. This time, he could watch the resulting shift. They changed from metal gloves ready for combat into bright red oven mitts covered with little yellow smiley faces.

Gauntlets of Oven Taming!
   These lightweight gloves will allow you to hold things that are super-hot. The stain-resistant material will always look happy and clean, and they will not burn, no matter how hot the heat source. Grab anything from a hot skillet to a spatula you dropped into lava.

Note: We do not recommend you use any sort of molten rock for cooking. Lava is very dangerous and will melt your pans.

"Next item!" Nacho showed off his Gauntlets of Oven Taming. "Yes, people, I have the coolest oven mitts ever, though they're more gloves than oven mitts!"

"To oven mitts!" Reuben raised his Yeti horn full of root beer as people cheered, though there was no small amount of confusion filtering through the crowd. Nacho needed Reuben's help to strap on the breastplate, which immediately shifted from cool cuirass to weird wok.

Wok of Block!

This is the mullet of armor. As you know, the mullet is business in the front, party in the back. The Wok of Blocking is business when it's on your chest, party when you take it off. Withstand dragon fire, then whip up a nice stir fry using dragon meat.

This is what your new breast plate can do:

- *Protect your back and thorax.*
- *Nothing will stick to this surface, so you won't need <u>much</u> oil. You'll need some, because oil, like sesame oil or Korean chili oil (spiced with gochugaru) makes things delicious. But we're serious about this having a non-stick surface. Trust us. Easy cook. Easy clean. Undeniably the best wok you'll ever use both for armor and stir fry.*

Note: The Wok of Blocking may or may not protect you from dragon fire.

Additional Note: Dragon meat may or may not be poisonous even when free of Putrid Mana.

Final note: Dragon meat is really tasty. Try some.

. . .

"What does that chest armor do?" Iron Becky called, clearly slightly tipsy.

Nacho raised a fist and ran it over the shining surface. "Non-stick surface!"

People gave out a half-hearted cheer, watching sadly as two pauldrons that fit over his shoulders turned into pans that linked magically to the wok, almost as if they were all magnetized together.

Pauldrons of Frying
We'll cut to the chase. Fry up some breakfast, and then rush into battle with your shoulders and arms protected. Both frying pans are fully adjustable with non-stick surfaces.
The sizes are adjustable:
Expand the pans to various sizes:

- *8 Inch*
- *10 Inches*
- *12 Inches*
- *14 Inches*
- *15 Inches (for that extra inch of greasy goodness)*

If you need to turn your frying pans into a sautéuse, the rims are fully adjustable to up to three inches. That should be enough to sautéuse your life up!

Note: We're not sure what the word 'sautéuse' means, but you'll figure it out. If you want an eleven inch crepe pan, get rid of the rim entirely. Spreader and spatula sold separately. We definitely know what crepes are.

"Yay...!" Nacho weakly cheered as he unhooked both pauldrons and held them in the air. "More non-stick pans."

Colleen grinned and whispered to her mother. "He's like that guy on Christmas who gets excited over socks."

The minute Nacho picked up the sabatons, they vanished as

metal ridges appeared on his normal boots. That was all that happened. He liked how his boots looked, all decked out in metal, but he'd expected another saucy name for the armored shoes. When nothing else happened, and no further happy messages assaulted his senses, he felt a little disappointed.

He wrinkled his nose. "Looks like the sabatons just augmented my existing-?"

Gravy Boots
    Mystery item—Must be Level 20 to Unlock The Special Ability.

"What do your boots do?" The Healer questioned instantly. Nacho assumed that Reuben must've seen the lights flash in his eyes. "Do they turn into muffin pans? I miss muffins. I know, I know. They're breakfast cake. I like breakfast, and I like cake, so it's only natural that muffins would have my firm and unwavering support."

"I won't know until level... twenty? Yikes. But they aren't called sabatons anymore. They are Gravy Boots now." Nacho picked up the shield and smiled widely. The minute he touched it, the shield turned into a giant cast-iron skillet. His mouth immediately began to water. He could make some major biscuits in that pan, without a doubt.

Skillet of Turtling
    Is it armor for your back? Is it a shield? Is it a weapon of mass food construction? Yes, yes... and yes. The Skillet of Turtling is there for you when you need it, such as needing to fry up five dozen eggs or a barrel of boar bacon—if you want to enjoy battling in and out of the kitchen, then this is the skillet for you!
    As a weapon, the skillet does a base damage of 10 Health Points while protecting you like a shield should. Plus, it's as fireproof as the Gauntlets of Oven Taming!

Does not shrink for either battle or biscuits. Why should it? You have your Pauldrons of Frying that are fully customizable!

Nacho put on all the armor and slid the Skillet of Turtling on his back with the handle angled up so he could grab it. Somehow, it stuck back there because... magic. Possibly large magnets. "I feel a little like a superhero right now. Aren't there superheroes that use shields?"

"You are joking. Someone tell me he's joking." Reuben looked personally offended by the comment, so Nacho decided to stop messing around and get back to work.

The cook immediately practiced snatching the Skillet of Turtling off his back and swinging it like a club. He could see how it might work as a pretty hefty weapon. It also stuck automatically to the front of his Gauntlet of Oven Taming, so it really did act as a shield. The downside to that soon became clear: as soon as it was off his back and used for another purpose, there was nothing protecting his back from damage.

Not ideal when his main human opponent was an Assassin that was really good at backstabbing people. He slipped the enormous skillet back onto his back and looked around the room, pretending to feel all sorts of hoity-toity. "Well, now, how do I look?'

Brie hid her smirk behind her glass of wine. "You look like someone who opened a cupboard too fast and all the stuff fell out on him. If you were flat on the ground, I wouldn't be able to tell the difference."

"That's what I thought." Nacho directly ignored her comment. "I look awesome. Reuben will think so, for sure."

The oven gloves—still bright red with yellow smiley faces— was the only thing that felt *really* out of place. Reuben agreed with a double thumbs-up. "Absolutely, you do! Also, you're protected. That's the most important thing. I'm just glad you didn't get a gravy boat codpiece."

"It would really seal in the flavor." Nacho proudly quoted a fan-written line of dialogue attributed to a bat-inspired super-hero persona which he had read on the internet years ago.

"I hated that, thanks." Brie grimaced and had to firmly set her drink down.

Scrubz stood up and walked over, eyeing Nacho up and down. "You know how Brie goes into combat, and she's this avenging Valkyrie with her matching armor and big hammer? Well, you're like... the opposite of that."

Nacho slung on the belt with his HungerCry Knives in their sheaths on either side of his hips. "Is this better?"

Scrubz shrugged and snorted disparagingly. "You're a Satiation Player. You look like a Satiation Player. Is that bad? No, but you look as useless as you actually are-*eep*!"

Nacho had *flashed* across the space between them in an instant. Silent, near-flawless movement without a hint of wasted effort, all so perfectly choreographed that it was hard to keep track of him.

"There's a rule we used to follow in gaming." The knives he had just strapped on tapped on Scrubz's shoulders twice before he idly spun them in the air and slammed them back into their sheaths. "*Never* judge a player by their gear. The more ridiculous it looks, the better stats it probably has. If you see a dude running around in hot-pink bikini armor, you should run and hide. It's likely you can't even damage him, thanks to the powerful options it grants him. You see a cook wearing a kitchen, be very afraid."

"It's perfect camouflage!" Old Bill burst out with sheer exultation. "No one in their right mind would go after you first. That's good. We need you alive, Nacho. Those abyssal hamburgers you made tonight were the best I've had in a long time, and I mean even before the Juxtaposition."

Nacho accepted the compliment. If old Bill was right, then he was going to be hiding in plain sight as the cook of the group —and who killed the *cook* first? Not the monsters—they wouldn't care—but the thing he feared the most, the players, wouldn't either.

He'd be a target to capture, but never to kill.

With that reassuring thought in mind, Nacho took a deep breath and waved farewell to his guild, stepping back into the kitchen. It was time to get prepared to leave at first light. He'd find the Dragon Spear before anyone else, and he didn't mind looking ridiculous while doing it.

Success was all that mattered.

CHAPTER FOURTEEN

Bright and early the next morning, Nacho, Reuben, and Brie were tromping down the Bove Road—the new name for their burgeoning superhighway. The cook had been opposed to the title at first, because of how many lives had already been lost to that monster, but he eventually came around as increasing numbers of guild members explained that they wanted a reminder of their first big win in this world.

Taye was with them, still decked out in his old armor and wielding his old bow—for now. Last night a large group of people, including Gabe the Archer, came to The Dinner Party and told them that Taye should have the Robbin' Hoodie set items. They had good reasoning, which boiled down to the fact that Taye had been important to Armor Mountain since the very beginning. The Archer was touched beyond words at the gesture, and even now, he was quietly contemplative about the situation.

The young man walked a bit behind Nacho, Reuben, and Brie, along with about three dozen other guild members who had volunteered to come along to help. Many would be following the latest caravan of wagons back to Armor Mountain to make sure no one tried to raid what they looted from the subterranean Costco. Since Abby and Kristie would be going with Nacho, the caravan would need the extra protection.

To that point, there had been only a few bandit attacks, partly because Nacho required the guards to throw Juxtaposition tarps over the wagons. The tarps were particularly obnoxious—bright yellow, kind of water resistant but not actually waterproof, as well as being stamped with the official motto of the Juxtaposition 'May your future be delicious' in red across the front. The covers made spotting the wagons easy, but they also obscured the looted goods and made it impossible to tell the value of the contents.

Bills Old and Young were walking with the other guild members behind them. While the Bills had been civil last night, that civility had melted into thin air when the decision was made to give Taye the Robbin' Hoodie Archer Pack. Both thought it wasn't fair, even though Taye was three levels above the nearest archer—and frankly, Taye was the best of them.

Nacho planned on raising Taye, Reuben, and Brie all to Tier one before they found the UnderFun. Between Brie and Reuben, they had the melee combat covered for the time being, so they needed to focus on cultivating some missile support. Having a Tier one archer with Tier one magical archery equipment would only help them.

The lad in question wandered a bit behind them, which allowed Nacho to talk to his closest friends in privacy.

"Just making sure we're going to upgrade Brie next." Reuben tossed out the assertion as they tromped across the tracks the wagons had dug into the soft ground.

"I don't know about that, guys. Tiering up means I'll lose my hammer, and it already lets me hit higher than I should. Maybe we wait on boosting me?" Brie dramatically tossed the weapon into the air and caught it with a sound like a baseball hitting a glove. "What about your knives? Can you still use them?"

"They're... special. I can upgrade them, and I get to choose a new option for them, but I haven't decided what I want them to do yet." Nacho had to stop before he said too much in public. He wasn't decked out in his new armor, which was well on the ridiculous side for appearance. Until he needed it, he'd keep it in a Storage Slot. On a happy note, because it was a set item, it all fit in a single Slot. That had been a particularly nice benefit he had never been able to learn of in his past.

There was another reason he paused, though. He hadn't yet explained the embarrassingly large backpack he had brought along. While he might look odd, he was already in love with his mobile kitchen. Nacho had spent most of the night trying to figure out all the little options, but he was sure it would still surprise him in the future.

Inside the capacious backpack, he had discovered special compartments for his cutting board, a whole array of spices, and his cooking utensils. If that wasn't cool enough, it included a system of magically enhanced poles and canvas hardened into what felt like particle board covered with linoleum. With a flick of a few of the poles, he could turn the backpack into a table almost instantly. When it came to meal prep, nothing helped quite like a flat surface.

Nacho didn't keep his *Aria* in the backpack, of course. No, he used a whole Storage Slot for his precious kitchen-friendly grimoire instead. If anything happened to it, he would lose access to all of the recipes he'd gathered so far. The additions included three full cookbooks and his venison recipe. The book was the single most expensive item he owned at this point, and it would become worth more as time went on.

He adjusted a strap, and his entire pack swayed, nearly knocking him over and earning a laugh from Reuben. "That backpack is so big, it looks like you're a porter from an anime."

"Not wrong," Nacho agreed with only a hint of strain in his voice. "But it's magical. A little gift for Satiation Players, since we are so rare. I'm surprised, actually. It seems they like making it hard on people to do anything. Like, you know, *existing*. The Patrons generally don't make anything easy, but this backpack was only four hundred credits. I suppose it's not all that surprising, now that I think about it. You need at least fifteen points in Fitness to carry this thing, and twenty to carry it around easily like I'm pretending to do."

"What in the world are you doing *not* having that in a Storage Slot?" Brie tapped at the pack, wincing when there was no give at all. "How heavy is that?"

"The real question is: why are we walking so far ahead of everyone?" Reuben snapped his fingers. "Oh, *that's* right! Because you two are anti-social."

"No, we're not!" Brie defensively turned her attention to her husband. "Just for that, I'm not talking to anyone for the rest of the day."

"Proving. My. Point!" Reuben shoved a finger into the sky to mark his win.

"Keep the sweet talk in your apartment, lovebirds." Nacho finished his adjustments to his mobile kitchen. "We're not anti-social. We just don't want to walk with the Bills and other people. We're fine, just the three of us. We could wait for Taye, though. We all like Taye."

"We do like Taye," Reuben agreed easily. "Also... you should call Young Bill 'Scrubz'. He asked for it. It's polite."

"Taye is fine, but I worry about the Bills going full *mutiny* when we get close to the Dragon Spear." Brie scowled as she tied her hair back in a ponytail, ignoring her husband's drawn out sigh. "Bill only wants us to find it as a reminder that we 'forced' him into the guild. It's his way of maintaining his reasoning for disliking us. I'm not sure I want to play into that."

Reuben scratched his chin, and when he opened his mouth, Nacho knew immediately that the man's next words would not be anything that actually contributed to the conversation. "I don't think it's a mutiny when it's on land. Would the right word be rebellion? Or revolution?"

Nacho shrugged his shoulders in the sunshine, making his pack wobble precariously once more. "I think with a revolution, you need a drummer. Bare minimum."

"Understandable," Reuben agreed, the bizarre non sequitur making Brie mime hitting him with her hammer. The ground was a little soft from the rain, but it was dry, the sun was out, and the air was finally getting warmer. Spring's arrival meant that there was always a chance that the temperature might fall thirty degrees overnight, but that was a risk they needed to live with at this point.

"Speaking of people we *like*, that Colleen gal doesn't seem unhappy to sit near you at dinner." Reuben waggled his eyebrows obnoxiously.

"Don't see it," Nacho deflected instantly. "Not one little bit. You're looking for something that's not there."

Reuben hurried to follow after his wife, but he threw a sinister smile over his shoulder. "We'll see, Nacho. She hasn't decided if she's going to guard the caravan or go on the Dragon Spear quest with us. I hope she picks the UnderFun. Who knows? There might be love in the air."

"Screams," Nacho deadpanned, his eyes going hollow. "There will be screams in the air. It's like love, but with far less romance and much more... screaming."

"That can be fun in the right circumstances-"

"*Anyway*," Brie cut her husband off impatiently, "at what point should we decide to invest in upgrading me and Reuben? Neither one of us wants to lose our magic items, and it's scarily expensive."

"Necessary," Nacho pointed out with a shake of his head. "We can't have you stuck at level nine skills forever. We need you to be a *lot* more powerful—and there's also at least a *chance* you won't lose your magic items. It's a bad chance, but a chance nonetheless."

Brie saw right through him. "They're gone when we rank up. I get that. Let's just make sure to plan properly to have good weapons on hand when we get to that point. C'mon. Let's get some miles under our belt. If we beat the others to the Heart-break Ridge cabin, we can discuss our plans for leveling there with relative privacy."

All three of them agreed with that sentiment. Since he was with the best fighter and Healer in his guild, Nacho didn't worry about making too much noise with his big creaking backpack. The way he saw it, if they could draw in monsters, they could kill them and get credits.

That didn't happen.

They *did* spot an unkindness of Oscreeches flying overhead. The heavily muscled legs trailing behind them made Brie consider using the bow so they could have enormous drumsticks for dinner, but the giant emu-eagle crossovers were flying too high to make it worth taking the shot.

They covered a lot of ground, traveling through the morning. The day was bright, the trees bursting with new growth, and the grasses were greening up nicely. Everything smelled fresh and good. There were even some tulips coming up through the dirt, which reminded Nacho of an incoming unfortunate fact: the flowers would be changed by Putrid Mana, like everything else.

No one had really needed to fight many monster plants to this point, though that would change with the coming of Spring. The Juxtaposition had started the previous autumn, with things dying, and then winter had happened—not a lot of growth there—so Spring meant the onset of monstrous plant life.

Meandering toward the bottom of Heartbreak Ridge, they found that the latest Caravan had nearly caught up to them and was currently passing under a canopy of Oilbark trees whose roots spread across the uneven ground. Unlike the mostly dry tree that stood sentinel over the Deep Buggy Darkness, *these* Oilbarks were leaking ichor across the spongy soil, and the resulting goo had trapped the treads of their three wagons. Nacho looked again, "Wait… those treads shouldn't be stopped by a little oil?"

There was something else going on; that much was clear. The wagons had formed a triangle, or rather a makeshift fort. The humans that walked on the treadmills had been directed into the center to maintain their safety. Abby and Kristie, along with the other caravan guards, suddenly found themselves under attack by a large herd of smelly cheese-horned goats. Their pliant white flesh was a bit melted from the sun, dripping down onto their sharp hooves.

These Goat Cheeses were easily three times the size of the ones that Nacho had processed before. Upon reading the System View on them, he sucked in a harsh breath.

Extra-Sharp Goat Cheese
  Effective Tier/Level: ??
  HP: ?

These things were Tier one, but they couldn't be very high-level. There were a dozen in the herd, and they stormed forward as one. Kristie hurled her Sorcery Strike magic, while another Archer fired arrows, but it was Abby who did the heavy work.

She charged out front without hesitation, smashing her staff into goat after goat and doing some real damage to their feta cheese frames. A blunt crack of her staff on a cheddar horn sent it rolling across the ground. It wasn't made of cheddar cheese, more like a typical horn covered in cheddar cheese powder, so it was even more impressive a feat.

"Brie, we need to get over there and help them." Nacho dropped his pack, equipped his armor from his Storage Slot in an instant, then stored the pack in the now-empty slot. He turned and *blasted* toward the enemy, his twenty-points-in-every-characteristic shining through as he sped to join the battle.

Meanwhile, Kristie and the other guards had climbed onto the yellow and red tarps covering the wagons. Their aim had been to escape the goats, but enemies had appeared in the air as well. The low-level Archer next to Kristie fired an arrow at some kind of monster bird, only for gray-green tentacles to encircle the bow and try to pull it away. Kristie flung her pink missiles into the creature, and it went flying away with a furious squawking.

The monster bird was quickly joined by its other bird friends, and the flock swooped low for another run. Nacho thought he recognized them, a quick System View confirming his suspicion.

Robin Deadbreast
   Effective Tier/Level:??
   HP:?

These were high-level creatures, and their swooping assault explained why the wagons had been forced to stop there, in the muddy recesses of the Oilbark trees. The Robin Deadbreasts were exactly like normal robins, if normal robins were the size of rottweilers. Where their red breasts should've been dangled a nasty snarl of rotting tentacles. In that way, they were similar to Ghoul Deer, except the Robin Deadbreasts also had razor-sharp beaks and claws which could rend flesh in any number of grue-some ways.

Nacho ordinarily wouldn't have worried too much—these were creatures a coordinated attack could fend off near-indefi-nitely—except for the arrows bristling out of the tarps of the wagons. This little ambush wasn't planned by monster feta goats and undead squid birds. This was a premeditated direct attack on his guild.

Just as he was about to curse Crave out of sheer force of habit, he heard weaselly laughter and noticed Myron in the shadows of a nearby Oilbark Tree. He twirled a set of daggers menacingly, though Nacho was pretty sure those knives didn't have even half the magic his HungerCry Knives offered.

He was happy that he had managed to nerf the Assassin, but a serious question remained. Was this an attack by Kala and the Sunrise Brigade? Or was it just Myron acting alone? This fight might turn out to be a lot more consequential than Myron expected. If the weasel wasn't acting alone, and his people were being targeted by *two* outside guilds...

Nacho would finally have enough reason to decisively hunt both of them down and end the threats they represented without the risk of giving anyone in his guild anything to complain about.

CHAPTER FIFTEEN

Welcome to Active Combat! No Store access and no Regens!

At least a dozen of the goats and birds were actively attacking the caravan, which by itself meant that the fighters had their work cut out for them. Brie armored up in an instant, then Combat Dashed right past Nacho into a Goat Cheese—proving yet again that combat skills were more effective at traversing terrain than merely running quickly. Her hammer sent about five pounds of gooey feta cheese splashing off the bones of the monster, who bleated angrily and raised itself on its back legs.

Flashing front hooves did their best to get a piece of the Berserker as four other cheesy goats came stampeding in a thunder of rage. All five of the goats were sent sprawling as Brie whirled in a cyclone of chainmail and heavy weaponry.

"Looks like we've got some cheese-on-cheese action! Positive Vibes for everyone!" Reuben raised his glowing hands, and a moment later, his friends glowed the same hue as the buff took hold. He followed up his spell by storming into combat even as his chainmail shirt appeared on him. Oversized gauntlets started impacting goats, left, right, and sideways. "This might be the most fun I've had the entire time we've been stuck on this world! Death to goats! Blood and cheese!"

Nacho had lost track of Myron, but he knew that rogue was still somewhere out there, along with at least a few of the Sunrise Brigade's archers. Those arrows sticking in the wagons hadn't fired themselves. Still, it was more important to stave off the beasts than it was to hunt down the humans that weren't actively attacking. The Cook held his blades out to the sides as he dashed past all of the creatures—his torso so low to the ground that he would need to clean oily mud off his Wok of Blocking later. In mere seconds, he had come up behind the furthest of the creatures and began attacking.

"I'm gonna cook you after I win, so I get to taste victory *twice*." The sheer amount of power that he could put behind his strikes, combined with the heightened ability to slice through tough meat that his blades possessed, meant that his first full power attack *should* have left a gaping laceration on the goat that he chose as his target but it only sent the ungulate flying through the air with a small cut. Sure, it landed hard enough that it might have taken terrain damage, but that was insufficient in his eyes.

At that moment, it was hard to decipher who was the Berserker of their group: Brie or Nacho. The goat had barely hit the ground before the cook was on it again, both blades raised. He twisted for maximum impact damage, practically drooling as he stared into the goat's eyes. "I just *know* you're hiding something delicious under all that skin."

"Blood and cheese!" Reuben bellowed his warcry in reply once more. "For the Chips!"

Taye came into view, bow in hand, his arrows practically inserting themselves into enemies with how easy he made the shots look. Between projectiles, he sprinted to the wagons to get some cover, then started pulling back his string in *earnest*.

A Robin Deadbreast flew toward Nacho in a storm of writhing winged tentacles as the goat he had been attacking was struggling to its feet. Nacho reached back and snatched at the handle of his Skillet of Turtling, pulling it forward into a heavy surprise attack that stopped the bird's forward momentum. It was a mighty hit, and thanks to his enhanced strength and Reuben's Positive Vibes, he managed thirteen points of blunt damage against his feathered foe.

"Good. At least I can damage *these* things with my skillet." Nacho carefully checked the sky around him as the wounded bird chirped in pain and struggled away from him. The other birds were all distracted by easier targets, so he started targeting the goat once more. "I guess I shouldn't be too surprised, even if it is just a skillet, it is still a Tier one item. Right... back to work."

Reuben was having less luck with the goats. "I hit them, they get some extra stink, but I'm not doing any damage! They have ninety-three Health Points, and I'm only punching for thirteen. What's fifteen percent? How close am I to being able to deal damage that sticks?"

"One point off! Need to deal at least fourteen damage to the goats per hit for the pain to stick." Nacho slammed his big skillet onto his back, where it seemed to magnetize back into place. That was still a super cool effect to him, and he felt impressive doing it. He selected a container full of leftover hamburgers from his Storage Slots—extradimensional space was even better than a refrigerator—and shoved one of the patties into Reuben's hand.

Eating a hamburger during combat wasn't going to be easy for his friends. These were burgers that he had managed to raise to higher rarities, anywhere from Uncommon to Rare. That meant any stat bonuses they applied would stack. If they could choke down two burgers, they'd get a *ninety* percent bump in their stats, or a bump to two different stats, if they so chose.

The cook decided to take his own plan and put it into action. He shoved a burger in his mouth and chewed vigorously, gulping down the lukewarm leftover meat like a competitive eater. When prompted, Nacho doubled up on his Fitness, bringing his already inflated characteristics well into inhuman territory. At a Fitness of thirty-eight, he was suddenly capable of doing an extra nineteen percent in damage.

The boost resulted in high enough physical damage to beat a goat to death with his bare knuckles—much less his blades—if he so desired. Then again, mid-combat mathematics was not his specialty, so he was going to test it out with a practical application.

Nacho sped away after he frisbeed the container into Reuben's hands, then turned and swept around into a perfect over-the-shoulder swing with his Hunger Cleaver, landing a critical blow that separated monster head from monster body. Grinning exultantly, the cook grabbed his skillet shield with his off hand, and it connected flawlessly to his Gauntlets of Oven Taming.

A goat barreled toward him, seeking revenge for its fallen comrade, but Nacho deflected the attack—saving himself a world of hurt—by catching the blow on the shield. The cheesy horns butted against the iron with a loud *clang*, and the cook swung his cleaver as a perfect counter-attack. Because of its innate magic, he was able to pierce the tough cheesy skin of the beast, not once, but *twice*, thanks to his high-speed slashing. "Thank you, HungerCry! Now *die!*"

Damage dealt: 16! Your weapon base damage is only 5! You have a 19% damage bonus from Fitness, and 18% from Small Blades skill. Finally, 18% from Positive Vibes. You only actually dealt 8 damage, but your speedy knives hit twice. Did you put your full effort into that? Ooh, that's gotta stink as bad as your enemies do!

Good luck against this entire herd of Goat Cheese!

The knives penetrated the cheesy flesh only to leave inconsequential wounds, and Nacho's eyes narrowed in annoyance. The System, while wildly aggravating, had a point. He could keep the goats busy, and maybe even take down one or two, but as far as killing them fast enough to make a difference on his own? Death by a thousand cuts wasn't going to work, but then again... all the cook had to do was hold them off while his team took care of business.

Reuben was almost done gulping down a hamburger. Watching him chew while holding food in one big metal glove and punching with the other was a bit surreal. The brute wasn't doing any damage, though he was successfully protecting himself and giving himself the time he needed to ingest the buffed food.

Overhead, the Robin Deadbreasts wheeled above the battle-field, but Taye fired three arrows almost at the same time and managed to take the wounded one down. Shouting encourage-ment at her team, Kristie killed another in a flash of pink magic.

The goats started grouping up to take another run at the caravan, but before the monsters could charge, Abby joined Brie in scarfing down hamburgers from the package Nacho had tossed to Reuben.

The Healer and cook fell back simultaneously to stand behind the frontline fighters. Even though Nacho might've felt ridiculous with his skillet shield and his cleaver combo, it was keeping him safe. As he studied the monsters attacking his team, he suddenly realized something. "I could make a full Greek salad out of these things! Lean bird meat on top, goat cheese as an ingredient, and fresh vegetables that we find along the path-"

"*Dude!*" Reuben's shout shook Nacho out of what his power fantasies had devolved into. "Focus! Now is *not* the time to be planning our next meal."

Nacho took those words and turned them into action, swinging his cleaver out and managing to deal some damage on another goat by carving through its coat of feta and into the meat underneath.

. . .

Damage Dealt: 16/93.

Reuben followed up by punching the goat and was rewarded with the telltale crunch of bone breaking. That extra point of damage he was able to add after eating the hamburger had pushed his damage-dealing capabilities over the edge. "Yes! I'm useful in combat again!"

Another goat tried to ram Nacho, but his skillet-shield held. The stunned goat bounced off and right into Reuben, who fed it a gauntlet-knuckle sandwich. It tumbled away, struggling to its feet and running off before they could execute a coup de grâce, just as another wave of goats came hurtling at the formation.

Nacho blocked one Goat Cheese with his shield, but another kicked him right in his chest, which was only mitigated thanks to his Wok of Blocking. Its hooves didn't rip into his skin, but the blunt force trauma hurt exquisitely and sent him flying. He tried to roll with the force as he impacted the oily ground, but he couldn't manage to pop right back up.

As he slowly forced himself to his feet and got back into position, he checked what his notification had to say about the hit.

Damage taken: 33/50!

"That kick stole *two fifths* of my health? Through my *armor?*" Nacho shook his head in annoyed astonishment. While that didn't seem fair, these things were admittedly a lot stronger than he was, *and* he didn't have much that he could use as a comparison. He could count on two hands the number of times an enemy had managed to damage him back when he had been an Assassin. "Point taken: don't get hit."

Just as he decided that was going to be his strategy from this point forward, Nacho was rammed from the side. His Health

Points fell to twenty, dropped further still by a Robin Dead-breast flying over and raking its talons across his back. Since he was using the skillet as a shield, his back currently had zero protection. In less than two seconds, Nacho was down to ten Health Points and nearly unconscious from the searing pain. "Ow! *Ahh.*"

Reuben wasn't much better off. Two goats had trampled him to get to Brie and Abby, which—while understandable, because they likely smelled better than the Healer at this moment—was the wrong choice. This was proven at nearly the same moment that the thought crossed Nacho's mind.

Brie smashed in one skull with an overhead swing of her hammer. Bolstered by the magic of Nacho's hamburger, she was running rampant with her damage output. Combat Dash enabled her to bring the hammer down, and she decapitated the monster with a blinding flash of speed. "Tenderized and ready for the table."

"Ha!" Reuben coughed at what he thought was a joke, a spray of bloody spittle leaving his mouth. "She's finally on board with finding her own catchphrase."

"I think she was being literal." Nacho's shaky hand reached out, stopping just before he touched the shredded flesh on his back. "She actually means that she's trying to make it easier on me to process the meat. Ninety percent positive. Also, I could really use a heal."

"Yeah," Reuben grunted in reply, punching a goat in the face when it got too close. "Here's the blood…"

Brie had continued wrecking goats as the two men whimpered back and forth. With her hammer—which had a base damage of twenty—she was doing a full thirty-two points of damage when she combined the attack with Combat Dash. Without it, she was still doing twenty-seven points; almost a third of a goat's health with every strike.

Reuben wrapped his arms around himself and glowed as his Health skyrocketed. "…and there's the cheese."

Nacho only had eyes for Brie in that moment. He had never

seen someone manage to deal damage above their Tier so consistently, and she gave him hope for the future all by herself. The cook breathily whispered, "If nothing else, I made the right call in saving you guys."

Abby's Fitness had also been hamburgered up, and between that and her Bad Bash ability, she succeeded in crushing the spine of a goat. It happened to be one that both Nacho and Reuben had already hit, which made the Healer call, "I softened that one up for you!"

That pulled her attention over to the two men that were bleeding all over the place, causing her to snort and crack a smile as she got back to fighting. Slowly but surely, they were taking down the goats while Taye and Kristie helped ward off the Robin Deadbreasts, firing upon the monsters with the other Archers and spellcasters on their team. There were still so many monsters attacking that almost everything engaged in combat was taking damage, but currently all of the guild members could still fight.

Admittedly, some of them weren't exactly combat oriented. For instance, Matt Martinez—who was waving around a Costco Signature Sword—was taking clumsy swipes at the birds, but he was also smart enough to know that he wouldn't be able to do any damage to the Goat Cheeses. He, along with nearly everyone else in the Chips Guild, wouldn't be able to penetrate their rinds thanks to the Mana barrier that they naturally generated.

An arrow struck Nacho's neck at that moment, and he sucked in a breath, fully expecting to die. However, an odd rebounding effect occurred instead, and the arrow dropped to the ground next to his feet. It hadn't even left a mark on his skin. A wide-eyed glance at the ineffective projectile informed him that it was a Tier zero arrow with a damage of only five. "I'm… alive? Right… to affect my Health Points at all now, something needs to deal me at least seven and a half damage. Abyss… that was too close. Reuben. Please. Save me."

With only a measly ten health remaining, Nacho was truly

worried about getting finished off. He managed to fling his arms wide just as he found himself swept into a hug by his friend. It was as awkward as anything—maybe as awkward as trying to eat a hamburger during battle—but he sagged with relief as Mana flowed into him, closing his gaping wounds. In only a few seconds, the cook was completely restored and feeling good. Reuben let out a puff of air, staring at his friend and Guild Leader with wide eyes. "Too close, man."

"Agreed," was all Nacho could afford to gasp out.

Reuben wrapped his arms around himself to start fixing his own issues. From atop of the wagon, Kristie downed a Juxta-Ade and called out, "More birds flying in. I'm setting off a Death Blossom!"

Nacho thought that was an excellent idea, so long as it was far away from him. The arrow proved that they still needed to keep an eye out for the Sunrise Brigade, though. Myron was around, and Kala just might be watching as well. A Death Blossom had the potential to sizzle some of their hidden enemies out into the open, which was well worth the friendly fire risk, in his estimation. He called to the Warlock, "Do it on the other side of the wagon. Get the birds off our backs, and we can take it from here."

"Stop giving people permission to damage my caravan!" Matt called halfheartedly as several more Goats charged out of the underbrush to join combat. Nacho purposely ignored the complaint as he slammed his giant skillet back onto his back and ducked a Deadbreast's claws. With a thought, his backpack popped into existence: he was about to test his new Ingredient Processing ability. Between Brie and Abby, they'd managed to bash apart two-thirds of the Extra-Sharp Goat Cheeses, but there were still so *many* left.

It wasn't like the monsters were going to stop coming after them, so the cook figured that he might as well start prepping the after-battle victory meal right away and make the most out of all the fresh meat.

From the other side of the wagon came a blast of blinding

pink light as Kristie erupted into a supernova of rose-colored energy, blasting already wounded birds out of the sky and frying some that hadn't yet been damaged.

"I'd call that overpowered if it didn't make her practically useless after she used it." Nacho eyed the fallen monsters as he mused aloud. "I'll attempt the Deadbreasts if there's any meat left on their bones, but I want to get processing the Goat Cheeses while I still can."

If the sinking feeling in his gut had any validity to it, this was only going to be the first part of the battle. An attack from the Sunrise Brigade when the Chips were down could change the whole nature of the fight. It was time to act his role and get off the front line.

Nacho hauled his mobile kitchen back behind the end of a wagon and anchored it into the dirt. Pulling his *Aria* out of his Storage Slot, he set it on the ground and flung it open. A special page under 'Main Courses for the Messy Masses' section was his go to—a simple venison recipe. It had worked for all the ungulates he'd tried it with so far, but now he was planning to publicly use the advanced option that his Ingredient Processing Skill came with.

Prepping at a distance.

He swung his cleaver while activating the upgraded Skill. Across the battlefield, a dead goat's leg popped off its hip bone in a splash of blood and an exhalation of hot, cheesy air. He switched knives and with a flourish of his Cry knife, the hide peeled away, revealing fatty pink meat. Even so, the cut was jagged, and the meat had been impacted. There was plenty of room for improvement in his technique.

"I clearly need a lot of practice to get better with this." Nacho smiled as the new personal challenge took shape. "No time like the present."

CHAPTER SIXTEEN

Nacho ignored a steady stream of intrusive thoughts pressuring him to get back into combat while he sliced up a pound of the goat meat from just shy of fifteen feet away—remaining in the relative safety of the wagon's shadow. A satisfying *cha-ching* rang through his head as twenty-two credits came pouring in. The Goat Cheeses were level eleven, which seemed pretty low, given the fact that they had ninety-three Health Points. "These aren't cows… why are they so beefy?"

Crossbow bolts whizzed into the sky, arcing downward to drop one of the Goat Cheeses. A cloud of arrows simultaneously streaked into the air, dropping Robin Deadbreasts out of the sky like a feathery hailstorm. Brie didn't like that one bit. "Where did all those arrows come from? They were angled toward us!"

From the shadows of a tree emerged a knight in black armor, visor pulled down, holding a very familiar two-handed sword. It seemed that Kala had found her Death Knight armor, and Nacho cursed softly when he realized that he had forgotten that it allowed her to hide in the shadows like an Assassin.

Kala slew a Goat Cheese with a whirl of her blade and a

shockingly loud shout. The last goat remaining went down under Myron's knives as he appeared out of nowhere to ram the blades into its stinking rind. One by one, they began picking off the wounded monsters, both on the land and in the sky, taking the credits for themselves instead of allowing the Chips to finish off the beasts.

A throng of Sunrise Brigade guild members emerged from the trees on the other side of the road. Twenty players at the very least, all in armor, with their choice of bows, crossbows, swords, or axes. Those who didn't have weapons had hands glowing with power—mostly Warlocks, though there were likely Elementalists and Illusionists in the mix.

Nacho stayed hidden behind a wagon wheel, still slashing at his meat and gathering credits from the herd of dead goats with every usage of his Skills.

Reuben finished hugging Abby and drained a water bottle gripped in his big gauntlet to start the process of regaining his Mana. Brie was eating whatever Nacho had left her, chewing furiously as she prepared to fight against these opportunists. Kala struck a pose in the middle of the battlefield, sword dripping feta cheese, and looked around with a grim stare. In a challenging tone, she shouted, "Who's in charge here?"

Reuben held up his index finger as if to say, 'hold on. I'm drinking'.

Kala's eyelid twitched, and she pointed her sword at Brie. "I think I recognize you with the hammer. You were with the Satiation Player. Isn't that right?"

Brie likewise held up a 'hold on, I'm eating' finger. Hers was *not* the polite index finger that Reuben had used, and it was decidedly less diplomatic.

The System fired off a message that revealed that even *it* wasn't sure how things were about to play out.

Well, Player! Active Combat seems to be over, but it looks like your two guilds might rumble, like an old-timey street fight. You are on a road, which is kind of like a street, so we'll keep Active Combat and Active Cooking on. No Store and no Regens unless you agree that you aren't fighting, or a good amount of distance appears between the groups. We wanna see this play out.

That annoyed Nacho. The Juxtaposition was such a pain, and it wasn't the first time he'd seen the Patrons keep Active Combat up in hopes that people would murder each other. Myron's husky voice called into the stillness, "Where's the cook? He must be around, since something called Active Cooking is on. I figured he'd be back at Armor Mountain, making his usual slop for the masses?"

Kala turned his helmet to take in all the guards of the caravan. "I don't see Old Bill or Mayor Dan. Did you kill them?"

"Of course we didn't," Taye called out righteously. He wasn't *necessarily* pointing his bow at anyone, but he had an arrow held to the string. He maintained a ready position on top of the wagon, Kristie right next to him drinking some terrible grape Juxta-Ade. She'd be very thirsty after her Death Blossom attack had cleared the air—it took a full fifty Thirst Points for that particular magic attack.

"Fine, don't want to answer that one? Let's try this on for size." Kala slowly let her sword dip out of the air; a cynical portion of Nacho's mind told him that she likely couldn't keep it in the air any longer with her basic characteristics. "What's in the wagons?"

"If you actually wanted answers or a happy conversation, you probably should've asked *before* you started an ambush, riling beasts to attack us, and then stealing credits when it became obvious that we were winning." Nacho came clattering out in his full Sunday Brunch Armor, including the pot on his head. He bent down and hacked another hunk of meat off the goat, refusing to lose a single credit because of this dirtbag guild. The fact that it was intimidating as all get out to see him easily remove and toss around half of the animal at a time was just a small bonus. Hooray for inflated stats.

"We *didn't* shoot the arrows," Myron insisted, the claim ringing more hollow than an open cavern with a single bell in it.

Brie turned to pull an arrow out of the wagon and tossed it up to Taye. "Is this one of yours?"

"Not one of mine," the kid casually confirmed. "Also, some crossbow bolts are stuck in the wagon right here. Real hard to use those in a bow and shoot at myself. I'm assuming they're from the crossbow guy trying to hide in the leaves over there, wearing bright blue armor."

Crossbow Guy had some very nice armor, a mixture of leather and lacquer painted sky blue, and was hefting two cross-bows that he suddenly was trying to hide behind his back. The weapons seemed to have reloaded themselves—that was a neat trick. Nacho didn't see Kala's father, so this wasn't the entirety of her guild. Or had she sent others forces to sneak up behind them?

Taye had the same thought. "I don't know what you're planning, Kala, but we have people keeping an eye on the forests around us. The minute I see anyone, I'm shooting to kill."

Laughter rang from Kala's helmet. "Who are you, teenage archer? I'm not sure I remember you. I know those three... hammer girl, fashion disaster, and the cook."

"As *if* you don't remember Taye, the person who kept your sorry behind alive when you first got here. Also," Reuben plucked his travel horn out of a Storage Slot, noisily slurping on the frosty root beer and letting out a massive belch. The cheesy man sucked another mouthful of the liquid down before deigning to speak. "It's *Mr.* Fashion Disaster to you, Kala. Are we going to fight? We'd get more credits for killing humans than we would for killing Tier one smelly goats, which sucks, but I think we can take you."

For now, the cook kept cutting meat even if he was out of the Mana he needed to remove the Putrid Mana. No one took particular note of his butchery, though Myron slid out of another shadow to point and snicker. "We found the cook! No need to ask around anymore. Friend, you have the most bizarre armor I've ever seen. A pot? Is that a *skillet* on your back? I guess that's one way to haul around the tools of the trade, but…"

At that moment, Nacho seriously contemplated attempting to dice the unibrowed rogue with a little Advanced Ingredient Processing, but he wasn't going to be the one to draw first blood. He'd spent enough time killing people in the Probability Vision, and he'd sworn that he'd be a lot less bloodthirsty this time around. Still… that promise only went so far. 'Less blood-thirsty' was relative.

"Hello, Kala." Nacho loudly took over the conversation. "You started a guild. Judging by the armor and weapons you've acquired, you're doing fairly well. Good for you. We'll even *let* you keep the credits you stole from us. Consider it an offer of goodwill. Now, what do you want?"

"The *Dragon Spear* wouldn't be in any of those wagons, would it?" Kala's abrupt question hung in the air like a crystal ball, tantalizing the mind and filling both groups with tension.

The strained silence was instantly shattered as Nacho started to laugh. Through all of it, he kept processing meat, not even bothering to give the Death Knight his full attention. "There's no way to answer that question in a way you'll believe. Even so, I *will* tell the truth. We don't know where the Dragon Spear is. Frankly, you've been in the game long enough to know that the Juxtaposition is going to get *chatty* when someone finds the spear. That alone should be enough to prove that no, we don't have it. Even so, if you're wondering what's in our wagons, all I can say is that we'll *butcher* you if you try to force your way in to find out."

"Correction!" Reuben thundered, using those big lungs of his to maximum effect. "*You'll* try to fight us, *then* we'll go on the offensive and annihilate every last one of you. We're not gonna make the first move, but we're ready to defend what *we* have earned."

Brie Combat Dashed to stop within five feet of Kala, freezing in place with her hammer raised before anyone could react. She could have quite clearly brained her target if she'd wanted. It was quite the dramatic gesture, and it cemented the fact that if the Sunrise Brigade wanted to test them... their Guild Master was going to pay the price before anyone else did.

In the end, Kala and her people were far too reticent to enter into a battle with people and not monsters. It was more likely that the arrows and crossbow bolts they had fired from the safety of the trees were an attempt to intimidate the Chips Guild into simply rolling over, since, as far as Nacho could tell, no one in the Chips Guild had been killed. Still, the cook knew better than anyone that once a hunter managed to tenderize their prey, there was no way it was going to become tough meat again. A single show of weakness would have turned them into a target forever.

Nacho threw some salt and pepper in a few of his team members' faces to get them out of their current frame of mind. He had plenty of experience with combat situations, and he fully understood that once people realized how they were acting, there was a good chance they would practically become a different person. It didn't take long for the first of them to start sneezing, begin noticing the sharp weapons pointing and being pointed, then shift into shamefaced grimaces.

Reuben sipped his root beer, cool as a cucumber. "Kala, Myron, Crossbow Guy. I'd suggest y'all mosey on out of here."

Kala's big sword disappeared, and she raised the visor of her black helmet. "We'll go. But remember, we *helped* you with those Goat Cheeses... *and* the Robin Deadbreasts. Remember that. We will."

"Nothing like 'saving' us from *your* ambush." Brie's laughter could only be described as the textbook definition of sardonic. "All we'll remember is that you didn't jump in right away. You waited until we wounded most of them, then you poached credits from us. I'd say we'll remember your 'help' perfectly, and we'll make sure to 'help' you the same way in the future."

"Just stay out of our way. *We're* going to find that Dragon Spear, and next time, we won't play nice." Kala slammed her visor back down, but not before Nacho saw her face distort with rage. She turned and walked into a shadow, vanishing too swiftly for it to be natural. The rest awkwardly retreated back into the forest, and it wasn't clear where the other guild would go from there.

The System appeared incredibly disappointed in the outcome.

Aww. No big dance battle between the Chips Guild and the Sunrise Brigade? Just some saber rattling? Boo, boring. Anyway, Active Combat is over without anyone murdering each other. Have fun shopping and enjoy your Health and Mana Regen!

May your future be delicious!

"I cannot believe you used the word 'mosey' in a serious situation." Brie was whispering loudly into Reuben's ear. "You are *ridiculous*, and I love you."

Nacho kept processing meat for another fifteen minutes, needing to take several long breaks in order to regenerate Mana, eat, and drink as fast as he was able. He managed to wrest two hundred and forty-two credits from the goats before the remainder turned to an inedible gooey cheese-whiz Putrid Mana puddle.

Stretching his back to get the kinks out of bending for so long, he smiled at his now-full-health guild members. "Well, we have a feast to dig into. We could eat here, or we could take the wagons back to the cabin. We're definitely going to need someone to act as guards after that, though. I volunteer Bill— sorry, *Scrubz*—and the others that haven't shown up yet. I don't trust that Kala is going to just let this drop."

As the others cheerfully nodded their agreement, Brie

walked up to him and waved her hand toward an area no one was standing near. "Nacho, you and I need to talk."

"Some of my least favorite words in the world when they're put in that order," The cook grumbled, though he followed his friend without hesitation.

CHAPTER SEVENTEEN

Taye quickly organized the other guild members to dig the wagons out of the Oilbark mud. It wasn't clear what the plan was after the confrontation with the Sunrise Brigade. Still, Nacho wasn't going to waste time doing only one thing at a time. He motioned for Brie to follow him back to his mobile kitchen, unfolded a grill which fit over the flames that sprang up, and started roasting the Goat Cheese meat.

Right back into Active Cooking.

At least he had gained some of his Mana back, so he could add magic to his meals. He would've liked to use the cheesy feta of their hide, but he didn't have a recipe for any kind of sauce. Besides, the rich sauce might've been too much paired with the fatty goat meat… also, the dissolving hide smelled even more like sweat, and cheese with sweat in it wasn't likely to be well-received at dinner time.

Brie let out a deep sigh, settling back and crossing her arms as she watched her friend organize slabs of meat on the travel grill. "Nacho, I said we needed to talk, and we do, but not while you're cooking. I want your *full* attention."

"Good luck with that." Reuben blew on the first hunk of

grilled goat that Nacho distractedly handed out and took a bite. "Isn't there goat meat in gyros? We might need to invest in a middle eastern cookbook. These goats are *everywhere* right now."

"I was thinking the same thing," Nacho muttered as he eyed the wheelbarrow-load of meat he had managed to collect.

Brie sighed with frustration. "This is too important to be put off, and I feel like it's not asking a lot to have your full attention for a few minutes."

"You're correct, you deserve better." Nacho used tongs to turn the pieces of goat meat. "But please, let me multitask? If I don't do this now, I have to give up more of my time later. There are only so many hours in each day, and if I devote my full attention to only one thing at a time, I'm going to start getting so far behind that I'll never be able to catch up. Do you want to turn the wagons around?"

"Nope. Stop." Reuben snapped his fingers, making Nacho blink in surprise at the sudden shift in his otherwise playful tone. "Brie is upset, and I agree that you need to know why. Mainly so I can figure it out as well."

"Nice," Brie grumbled at her husband. "Listen, if the only reason he is going to hear what I have to say is because *you* tell him to pay attention, we're gonna have a whole *new* problem on our hands."

"I'm just trying to make a united front with you!" Reuben desperately waved his hands in front of himself and kicked Nacho.

"'Kay. Hold on." Nacho tried to pull thoughts together. He *was* really scattered, and the reason why was clear to him. He'd known the future, which had allowed him to put together a definite plan. Now that the outcomes had changed, so many options had appeared that he was having trouble deciding what to do next.

On the plus side, it was pretty clear what he needed to do at this moment: listen to Brie's concerns. Nacho wanted to give her his full attention, he truly did, but he couldn't help keeping about a fifth of his attention on the meat grilling and the rice bubbling off to the side. He was trying out his helmet pot for the first time to make the starchy accompaniment. Should he have washed it out first…? Nah, rhetorical question.

"This'll do." Brie stood next to his cooking table, still in full armor, leaning on her hammer while she held her helmet under her arm. "I understand that we need credits as fast as possible, and I *know* you only have so much time to process the meat… but next time, finish the fight before you start on that. You put *all* of us at risk, and that is unacceptable. I'm *glad* Kala and her guild were there to take out those last few goats. I was hungry and low on Health Points. Even though you don't get paid per kill, we could've used your help. We were overwhelmed. We almost lost people."

"I'm… I guess I didn't think about that. I'm still trying to get used to being in charge of people." Nacho rubbed at the back of his neck as her chastisement filtered through his own thoughts. "I see myself not as a fighter right now, but as a credit collector. I… it didn't even cross my mind that some of you were close to death. I could only think about how it's going to take over thirty-five thousand credits to get you and Reuben to Tier one. Every credit counts at this point, and if we don't need to buy the food… how is it, Reuben?"

"Stay on track, Dudemeister McCheesy." The big guy held up some of the grilled meat. "Super good, actually. But do some active listening. Repeat back what Brie said, and it will make the rest of the day less awkward for everyone involved. *I'm* involved, and I don't wanna be here."

Reuben was nearing expert levels in advanced interpersonal communication, claiming that it was the only reason he had been able to hold onto Brie for so long. Frankly, it was surprising he hadn't earned a Skill for it… but then again, what was marketing beyond making and keeping connections between people?

Nacho went to cross his arms, but remembered at the last second that it would make him look too defensive. Instead, he went to fold his hands, but then that might show him as weak, so he opted to put his hands on a pair of tongs and *clicked* them twice. That seemed okay. "Let me get this straight, Brie. You're saying I should wait until you guys are finished fighting and *then* start earning credits."

Brie's brow was still furrowed, and she shook her head. "Communication is key on the battlefield. We'll let you know how we're doing. You need to make sure that you *can* join the fight if we need you. How low were you on Hunger and Thirst while Kala was still threatening us? Did you have enough to be *active* in fighting?"

"I was... very low. Fair point. I will try to be a lot more communicative during a fight. I'm... still used to silence in a fight being my best bet, unless I'm attempting to throw off a target." Nacho lifted a finger, wanting to voice a bunch of details that may or may not have helped him. Instead, he closed his mouth and used the tongs in his hand to turn his steaks before allowing his thoughts to spill. "I hate that I don't get credits for fighting. In every fight, I'm in a rush to get to the meat before it spoils."

"A good start. Now we know where you're coming from." Reuben knocked on his wife's armored arm. "Your turn again."

"Our lives are more important than credits, Nacho. As for *you*, stop minimalizing this. This is a conversation between *two* people, and it needs to be said." Brie scowled and gently shoved Reuben away from her. She inhaled, then let the breath out slowly. "Nacho, I get that you feel like you're contributing by collecting the meat and the credits. We appreciate it. We do. Also, I have to say, rush-eating that hamburger was a lot easier than I would've thought. The bun was soggy, so it was better than pocket pancakes."

Nacho nodded solemnly as he took her advice to heart. "Biscuits are the worst. Too crumbly and dry to get down easily."

"Here's my proposal." Brie looked the cook dead in the eye. "You're the Guild Leader. You're in charge of long-term planning and keeping us alive. From now on, I'm in charge of the battlefield. During combat, you clear plans with me unless you *need* to make a move. That means you'll make sure *I* okay you starting on food gathering. Confirm that *I'm* fine with you rushing off to kill something on your own and leaving our flank unprotected."

Nacho's eyes lit up at that, even as Reuben looked concerned. "Done and done. You want battlefield command? I am all over that. Not going to lie, I have no idea how to position people in a way that is most effective. Clearly, I also had no idea that my actions were going to impact the team as well as morale to such an extent. If I need to override you for some reason, I promise I'll have a good reason for it."

"Good... enough."

The Berserker still looked troubled, and Nacho was aware enough to pick up on it. "What else is going on?"

"It's just..." It was Brie's turn to cross her arms, then drop them back to her sides instantly as she realized her own body language. That made Nacho smile; they were very similar people, and sometimes it was nice to see that in action. "Right after saying that I want battlefield control, I'm going to ask you a favor. I can't stand the idea that I'm going to be killing anyone. It was pretty clear that Kala and the Sunrise Brigade might've gone after our people if we hadn't shown up. I think when she saw what Abby and I could do, she backed off. If Kala had gone after me, I would've killed her without hesitation. If I need to do that, can I count on you to help me? Physically if you can be the one to hold the weapon, and emotionally if you can't?"

"I'm sorry to say that I have talked dozens of people through their first kill. I will be there for you." Nacho wasn't sure what else to say about that. He'd killed hundreds, if not closer to a thousand in his Probability Vision. It had gotten to the point that he had begun to see people only as walking credits. On the positive side, going back to the past seemed to have fixed most of the ingrained structural issues with his brain from living like that for so long.

He attributed his current ability to function in society to that simple fact.

Nacho tried to consider what she needed to hear, then decided on the truth. "You know that I was an Assassin. It got so bad that we were killing people just to feed ourselves. I want you to know, I'm *not* driven by credits. I'm just *extremely* motivated for survival, in a way that lets us sleep at night."

"Yay, cannibalism is back in the conversation." Reuben winced at his own joke when both of his best friends shot a glare at him. "Sorry."

Brie didn't respond, only returning to looking into Nacho's eyes as he continued forcing his internal struggles aside for the sake of honesty.

"If it comes down to it, I would far prefer to be the one driving the knife home. But if it has to be you, I know how to get you through it." He didn't blink, digging deep to find sympathy for the situation. All he had was *empathy*, having gone through it so many times already. How could he show sympathy to someone who was worried about a *sure thing*, when they didn't actually *know* what it would do to them? "We can only hope that we don't have to play the game like we did before. The Patrons love it when we fight among ourselves, and I don't want to give them the pleasure. At some point, once people are struggling to stay fed, they'll see how joining us will help them."

"You think we can just wait out all the other powerhouses?" Brie swallowed hard, trying not to let the sudden spark of hope shine through too much. It would make life that much worse if she eventually lost that hope. "Or do you think that we will get the Dragon Spear first, and we won't have to worry about them because we will be in control of them? Do you really think we can do that?"

"I *know* we can. Their choices will shortly be limited to starving to death, starting to eat other people, or coming to us for food and partnerships. Only the worst examples of humanity would willingly go down the darker route if there was another choice. We just have to make our guild more attractive than cannibalism; personally, I feel that's a pretty low bar."

"I'm going to go ahead and rejoin the conversation now. Feels like a good time to do it." Reuben scooped up more meat as Nacho set the steaks on trays for the other guildies to eat after the thick-thighed runners got back on the treadmills of the wagons. "Let's take it a day at a time. We need to figure out where we go from here, so what are you guys thinking? Back to Armor Mountain to make sure the Sunrise Brigade doesn't mess with the caravan? Or do we press on to Heartbreak Ridge?"

"That depends." Brie slowly started to relax, now that her concerns had all been addressed and there was a working plan in place. Even if it *was* pretty basic. "How important is the Dragon Spear? Is it more important than the wagons? Secondly, how sure are we that the Sunrise Brigade will come after us?"

"I think there is a real possibility that Kala isn't done with us, especially since chances are high that we'll be able to take control of her and her guild by proxy if we do get the spear. I don't think any of the people placing bets were expecting that knowledge to be made public, and I'm sure it has them more than a little bit nervous. Let's take the wagons up to the top of Heartbreak Ridge," Nacho decided while calmly checking on the rice. "We have more people with us than the entire Sunrise Brigade, and I think the wagons will be safe just due to sheer numbers. The rest of our strike team will meet us there, and then we hand pick the team to take along for our UnderFun adventure."

"As for my thoughts on the spear…" Reuben winced and nodded grimly. "Beyond the obvious win conditions, it's huge for marketing purposes. The first time the Patrons call out an actual item, let alone showcasing how important it is? If *we* have that, I think it will be the final tipping point for starting to absorb other guilds. The Chips Guild wins this spear, and suddenly we're the guild to join. Not that we'd take in Kala or Crave, obviously, but there have to be others that are less… you know, death culty. If someone else gets it, all of our other plans take longer. Long enough that people start dying, not to mention what they would do with Crave and Kala taking them under their wings."

Nacho fully agreed with the assessment. At this point, they genuinely needed the spear. Their biggest head start was the fact that Nacho was fairly certain that only the Chips Guild knew about the original Earth under their feet, and he wanted to keep it that way as long as possible.

The weary caravan guards finally trudged over for their post-battle meal. Nacho had burned the bottom of the rice, so only about half of the pot was edible, even though all of it tasted like sulfur. The System let him know that Active Cooking had ended, and they made fun of his merely-Common rice that didn't offer stacking bonuses. No mercy at all for the weary cook in their lives.

After they ate, they took the wagons up the hill to the Heartbreak Ridge cabin, happily arriving in time to avoid the clouds rolling in and the pounding rain that immediately followed. Matt used his own credits for an open-room pole shed with some cheap roofing to keep the rain off the caravan and protect the treadmills from getting slick. People stood in the shed, packed themselves into the cabin, or stayed under the eaves to get out of the rain. It was chilly, but warmer weather was definitely on its way.

Scrubz showed up before long with Iron Becky and Colleen, informing the group that he and his people had also encountered Kala. Wiping off his rain-soaked hair by the fire inside the big cabin, he finished his braggadocious narrative, "So anyways, I told Kala that we had gear and food from an actual Costco! We even gave her those salted chocolate caramels she told us she used to love so much. I made it clear that she didn't need to mess with us; she can have her guild with their terrible Store food, and we'd have our good eats with our cook. She made the wrong decision, but she was always welcome to come back. Did I convince her? Can't say I did, but I sure set her straight."

"You just... *told* her about old Earth hiding just under the surface? Are you out of your...?" Nacho stifled a scream of frustration, unsure if the man had done the right thing or intentionally sabotaged them. Either way, there was no going back. The decision had been made for them.

"I'm sorry for my part in today's debacle." Iron Becky sat nearest to the fire with a blanket over her shoulders. "I think encountering me didn't help the situation. Kala and I never saw things eye to eye."

"That's putting it, um, diplomatically." Colleen smiled at her mother warmly from her seat across from the older woman. "Nacho, we've all been talking, and we think we know the answer to the speed bumps we've been hitting. We need to get the wagons back to Armor Mountain. I suggest I act as the escort, along with my mom and a bunch of other people. If Kala does try anything, I pull out an illusion of Brie. I can do a pretty good Brie by now, and I think Kala is at least a little afraid of her."

Reuben grinned proudly, sneaking a glance at his wife. "Normally, I'd feel hurt that it wasn't me. But in this instance, I totally get it. Brie-zerker is one tough b-"

Brie raised her hand to stop him. "One tough *beauty*, thank you very much. You really think Colleen's illusion would do the trick?"

Colleen's fist glowed gold. A knock sounded on the door, and one of the other guild members opened the door. In walked a copy of Brie, complete with her chainmail, helm, and a blood-dripping hammer. There was a slight golden sheen to her, but that could easily be attributed to a skill of some kind. Overall, it was nearly impossible to tell the difference. "I can create sounds, and I can generate a single figure, though I have to be relatively close to the target. As long as I have enough to drink, I should be able to keep Brie walking around often enough to trick anyone watching."

"If they see Brie, they might expect that Reuben and Nacho are around as well. There will be a bunch of us traveling with the wagons." Iron Becky was nodding her approval as she thought through the germinating plan.

"I got something to say." Scrubz raised his chin defiantly. "Yeah, I'm gonna say it. I want the Dragon Spear. If I find it first, then I get it. Finders keepers."

Nacho's eyes darkened as he studied the man. Though he squirmed with slight discomfort at the stare, Scrubz clearly had no idea how many people Nacho had killed, or that he was willing to remove as many more as needed. The cook barely managed to keep those exact words to himself, but his actions showed his true thoughts. The former Assassin had gone totally still, and he could tell that his dead eyes were making the people around him uncomfortable.

He took a deep breath, and consciously exhaled slowly, forcing himself to release his menacing demeanor along with the dispelled breath. "All I can promise is that we'll do what's best for the guild. That decision especially will depend on what makes sense. I'm not saying you *won't* get the Dragon Spear in the end, but *logic* will dictate who gets what. We all have to work together, or we'll die alone… fighting over scraps."

Scrubz glanced away, deeply unsure of why his forehead was letting out so much cold sweat. Nacho could only shake his head and sigh. He hated not trusting the people around him, and the implications of the man's chosen name bothered him more than he wanted to admit.

The Downtown UnderFun was already proving to be dangerous, and they were nowhere near the entrance.

CHAPTER EIGHTEEN

Nacho basked in the noon sunshine outside the entrance to the Bove's Lair. He was enjoying the warmth, but observing the murky length of the Muddy River gave him pause. Spring rains had swollen its banks a mile wide at the narrowest point, and they'd probably have to try swimming across. "That water is going to be practically ice, there's no way we're going in it."

At Heartbreak Ridge, they'd divided into two groups. Iron Becky, along with Colleen and about a dozen other people, would escort the wagons back to Armor Mountain. Meanwhile, Nacho would be taking twenty people on the Dragon Spear quest. They left fifty sentinels at the Bove's Lair, guarding their Costco and grinding out credits from the Scary Shelves by taking out random Costco food court monsters.

The Chips Guild members were warned not to go too deep and to stick with Tier zero monsters. If they met a Tier one, they needed to run like they were starving and the biscuits and gravy were ready. No one from the Chips Guild had spotted any unfriendlies around the Bove's Lair, which was good.

"Ugh. At least the *location* of the Costco is still hidden." Nacho was fairly certain the Dragon Spear wouldn't be around the Costco. No, it would be farther east, but before anything else, they had to cross the Muddy River without drowning, and he just was not sure how to make that happen. Abyss, in Nacho's vision, there had been a guild that started a *business* ferrying people across the Muddy. It had taken dozens of people, with lots of practice, to accomplish it with minimal risk.

Kristie had finally come up for a name for her party, which included Taye and Abby: The Breakfast Club. It was a far better name for the three of them than 'Generic Party One', and the other two members seemed pleased with it. Given that Nacho had The Dinner Party, they had decided that with their powers combined, the twenty-person strike team would be called: The Brunch Force.

Six of Nacho's twenty companions were the best players in the Chips Guild, and the… others… included Scrubz and thirteen volunteers that were attempting to make a name for themselves on this mission.

Upon hearing the name of their raid group, Reuben had gone off the deep end into marketing waters, trying to figure out the best way to make the name stick long-term. "Like using the force, but more brunchy. It's a force to be reckoned with. It's a strike team that has both breakfast and lunch menu items? It's an elite task force, which may or may not include mimosas. The-"

Nacho hadn't been able to last any longer and had wandered off along the banks of the river as Reuben sank into a revenue generation loop. Others meandered over to their leader as well, thinking it was time to go.

"This is going to be terrible. We're all going to freeze." Brie was already pricing bathing suits. "Not sure I'm a fan of the yellow and red options for clothing, but it seems bikinis only come in Juxtaposition colors."

Scrubz had already stowed his armor and was in the process of taking off his flannel shirt.

"Ahh! No!" Nacho put his hands over his face. "Warn us before you start stripping, Scrubz!"

Brie inspected the flowing water more closely and then brought up a real concern. "Listen, I grew up swimming in Kansas reservoirs, which have the visibility of coffee. There is no way we're going to see any monsters that are down there—I'm assuming there are monsters, right? Catfish eat Putrid Mana from the bottom and grow to become the size of a minivan?"

"We're going to have to buy boats." Nacho started outlining his plan. "Two rafts. We'll ferry the people across in groups. I'd suggest rope, but we'd need a mile of it. We'll have to paddle up the river in rafts, against the current, because it's going to be flowing down. We also need to make sure we don't lose visibility of the Bove's Lair, as that gives us a rough idea of the geography underground.

"They should start a smoky fire," Scrubz suggested as he re-buttoned his flannel shirt. Armor would follow, though he didn't have much, and what he did have was questionable. He wore a short sword, and he'd bought a spear, evidently prepping for when he got the real deal. It wasn't clear what kind of Body Player Scrubz was, and he certainly wasn't telling anyone very much.

Scrubz motioned to the entrance of the Bove's Lair. "We'll be able to see the smoke from a distance—actually, we should at least spend the day walking upstream a bit just to look for a narrow part of the river. Or an island. If we found an island, we might be able to come up with a rope system to stretch across the river. Or maybe purchase some timbers. No, we'd want a steel cable. If we had that, we could do a pulley car."

Was this where Scrubz shined? Coming up with different solutions to engineering problems? Nacho shouldered his mobile kitchen. "Walking upstream is a great idea!"

One of the Bove's Lair guards promised to keep a smoky fire burning, at least during the day, while the adventurers got a sense of the land on the other side of the river. They hadn't been shy about keeping a fire lit in the winter, and so far, it hadn't brought any raiders.

Nacho led the Brunch Force upstream along a game trail. About a half a mile north, they found a long narrow strip of trees rising up on an island in the middle of the river. If they spent four hundred credits, they could buy two rubber rafts, which would carry six people apiece. One pair of oars that came with each one, fitted and locked into the oarlocks. Extra oars were fifty credits each.

Reuben's eyes glowed while he shopped. "Life vests are two hundred credits *each*. The Patrons really aren't all that excited to see us survive this."

Scrubz suggested they buy two extra pairs of oars, so others could help row, and they'd have some extra if they lost a pair.

After checking, Nacho saw that over thirty thousand credits had built up in the Chips Guild coffers. He teased his standard opponent a bit, "You okay with me using guild funds for the rafts, Scrubz?"

Scrubz shrugged and looked away. "It's a business expense. It's not like you'd buy these rafts if you were by yourself."

Nacho made the purchases without further comment, pulled them from his Storage Slot, and laid them out on the banks of the river. He would go in one boat with Reuben, Brie, and some of the lower-level guild members, while Taye and the rest of the Breakfast Club would go in another. Scrubz and some of the other newbies offered to ferry people back and forth.

Brie was on edge. "This is terrible. We're practically defenseless! For one, I can't run anywhere to use Combat Dash, and I'm not going to be able to do my Defensive Whirl in the middle of a raft. Another thing? My hammer is heavy, and I need two hands to swing it. What if I end up dropping it into the river? It'll be gone for good."

Hank, a thick middle-aged man with a beard, lifted his spear. "I got my spear, Brie. Hazel can use spells. If anything attacks us, we'll have your back."

Hazel was Hank's wife and a Warlock. Her main move was a magical purple shield, which she had told everyone in no uncertain terms was to keep her husband safe. They were a nice enough couple, but Nacho wouldn't exactly place his survival in their hands. He rubbed his neck, which suddenly felt very strained. "We'll just have to hope for the best."

Reuben stroked his wife's back reassuringly. "Don't worry, sweets. I'll be oaring in the back. You and Nacho will be oaring up front. With Hank, Hazel, and Chris the Katana Guy... we'll make sure nothing goes wrong."

Chris the Katana Guy was a short, quiet member of their guild who seemed very nice. He also had a katana. That was one hundred percent of the information Nacho knew about him.

"I love to oar!" Reuben yelled happily.

"For the last time, it's called rowing!" Brie was already slightly green. "You are not inspiring confidence, here!"

They all stored things they couldn't bear to lose in their Storage Slots and loaded up the raft with their other gear. The current wasn't too swift, and with Reuben working the back oars and Nacho and Brie rowing up front, they gradually made their way up the river. About halfway across, they let the current sweep them down until they reached the island. It was only about a hundred feet wide, so they carried the rafts through the sparse forest to the other side.

Breaking up the ride was nice, making it less intimidating to tackle the whole river. If anything went wrong, they had less distance to cross. Scrubz's and the Breakfast Club's raft followed them across the first section of river to the island, and then both rafts were making their way across the main channel. Nacho was relieved that they hadn't been attacked by any monsters, but the water was as transparent as split-pea soup. There could be anything under those turbid swells.

They didn't run into trouble until they pulled up onto the swampy banks on the eastern side of the river. As soon as the first oar touched the water twenty feet from the target bank, huge creatures splashed through the murky brown river toward them.

They slid through the liquid with only the tops of their

heads showing, but even that was far too much for comfort. Going by the long antennae and beady black eyes, along with bodies protected by gray-green exoskeletons, they seemed to resemble crayfish. Strangely enough, most of their back carapaces were covered in black fabric. As they swam closer, it became apparent that they were actually wearing clothes, which wasn't exactly the best idea for a monstrous crustacean.

Their pincers remained under the surface, likely dragging along behind them as they wiggled up the river. There were at least ten of the creatures, each of them a dozen feet long.

"Why are they wearing clothes?" Nacho shouted his confusion aloud while he rowed as fast as he could.

"I'm betting there's a pun involved." Reuben laughed with delight. "Can't wait to find out!"

Brie slammed her paddle into the water and pulled with all her might. "No banter! Just row! I do *not* want to fight these things on this boat!"

Nacho and his raft were close to the shore, but they weren't in the clear yet. Those giant crayfish were coming in fast, but a few seemed to be angling after the second raft, rather than the first. Taye was already on his knees, drawing an arrow back on his bow. Kristie's hands glowed pink in anticipation. Abby wasn't in her armor, but she had her staff ready to go. None of them looked at all happy.

The cook finally got a System View lock on one of the crayfish.

Formal Crawdad
  Effective Tier/Level:??
  HP:?

These were Tier one monsters, and since they were creatures of the water, they had a definite advantage.

"Formal Crawdads?" Reuben asked in wonder. "I'm not getting the pun yet."

Taye let an arrow fly, and the shaft struck with a mighty *thunk*. The crayfish rose up on its hind legs to reveal its body— six legs, two pincers, and one tuxedo. The black fabric they'd seen poking through the water was the back of a suit coat, and its front was what might've been a white shirt if the monster hadn't been wriggling around in mud. The crustacean's bizarre ensemble was finished off by a very smart bowtie.

The crayfish whistled out a shriek from its bottom-feeder mouth and waved its pincers threateningly.

Reuben laughed instead of screaming in fear, the only reasonable response to this absurd situation. "Oh, that's just bad."

Brie considered the muddy mess of the riverbank with a fair amount of apprehension. "I don't think I can Combat Dash across that. I also need my feet free to do my Defensive Whirl. How can I fight in that slop?"

Hank and Hazel reached the banks and waded out, along with Chris the Katana Guy. Hazel held both hands together, then slowly spread them apart to create a massive purple shield of magical energy. Once the barrier was stable, she hurled a big purple grenade, which detonated in a mishmash of muddy water, pieces of fabric, and small chunks of exoskeleton.

"They bleed blue, they like formal wear…" Reuben knew exactly what that meant. "They're blue-blooded crawdads!"

"I don't get it," Nacho freely admitted as Hank stepped forward with this spear, driving it into the face of one of the crayfish. Hazel continued to stand with the shield outstretched in front of her hands, sinking a second purple shield into the water to keep Hank and Chris the Katana Guy safe.

Arrows and pink missiles flew, striking another crawdad.

Scrubz was rowing as fast as he could, but it appeared that the raft wasn't going to make it to shore before the nearest monsters hit it.

"Time to get combat ready!" Reuben hit them all with Positive Vibes as Nacho shoved a hunk of leftover goat into Brie's hands.

Brie swallowed the fatty meat without chewing, choked, then started to chew furiously after a moment of mild panic. She vaulted over the side of the raft into knee-high water, snatching the Splatter Mallet out of one of her Storage Slots. Fixing her feet in place, she smashed a giant crayfish in the head-area with her hammer. A pincer attempted to snap her in half as she hit the monster, but she got the weapon up in time to prevent herself from being crushed. Despite the impressive block, she did earn a nasty gash on her arm which would require healing.

She hit the crayfish again, the mallet crunching through the exoskeleton and managing to kill it. "These things aren't that tough for being Tier one!"

They also weren't smart. Instead of continuing to go after Scrubz's boat, they reoriented as one and converged on Nacho's people as blue blood spilled freely into the river water.

Reuben grabbed the Dinner Party's raft and hauled it onto the mud of the bank. Nacho hopped out and tied it down so it wouldn't float away, followed by chucking some goat to Reuben.

Reuben chewed on the cold meat vigorously as he splashed back into the water to heal his wife with a hug.

Brie, Hank, Hazel, and Chris led the Formal Crawdads out of the shallows and onto the banks, where fighting shifted to their favor. Moments later, Scrubz's raft came sliding in next to Nacho's. Scrubz and his warriors piled off the boat along with Abby and her staff, falling on the monsters and felling them in seconds. Since Brie could kill one with only two swings of her hammer, they couldn't have more than sixty Health Points each.

"Looks like this is already practically over." Nacho called out to his favorite Berserker, "Hey, Brie, can I start processing ingredients?"

"Do it!" she yelled back. "Thanks for asking; it matters!"

Nacho whipped out his chef knife and casually strolled over to a dead Crawdad. He tried to remember if crayfish had actual meat anywhere. "People used to eat crayfish, right? Pretty sure there were crawdads in gumbo."

He cut off the tuxedo, then regarded the cracked shell of the beast. Blue blood dripped onto the sand, and he was mesmerized by it for a long moment. Finally, he stood up and tossed his hands in the air in confusion. "I have *no* idea how to cut this thing open, or where the meat is. Or if there *is* meat. Never been big into seafood."

"Yeah, you were always more of a Fruit Loops and grilled cheese sorta guy." Reuben kicked one of the crayfish, his boot bouncing off without leaving a mark or making the body shift. "Crayfish in tuxedos? I don't know... what that's about. I admit it, if there's a joke here, it's not in my wheelhouse. But I think I know why these things are in such good shape-?"

"I know that tone." Brie leaned on her hammer. "He~ere we go."

Reuben leaned toward Nacho with his eyebrows raised dramatically. "The Crawdads are so fit because... they train on *lob*stacle courses."

"Yeah, thanks for that." Nacho booted the monster until it was on its back but was greeted by more exoskeleton. "Hey, Reuben, do you have any idea how you would butcher a crawdad?"

Reuben wrinkled his nose. "Uh, no. I eat mammals and fowl. Crustaceans are basically water spiders."

Nacho consulted his *Aria*, but Colonel White Beard made it clear that he was limited to chicken and breakfast foods only. Just to test it out, he tried to activate his Ingredient Processing ability.

Hey, Cookie, what exactly are you cooking? I mean, if you don't know, we aren't gonna help you out. You still need to know what you want to do before you can just 'magic' it into working.

. . .

The cook sighed and searched for a relevant cookbook and information pack, shaking his head at the outrageous price of six hundred credits. Things weren't going to get any cheaper, but he wasn't sure he wanted to start cooking crustaceans or insects. "Why *are* there so many bug cookbooks? Why such a push for that?"

Scrubz walked over. "We going to have a seafood boil on the beach? I'm starving."

"Sorry, Scrubz, but I don't have any kind of recipe for that. No recipe means I can't cook it. I can't even process the ingredients, so we're still on regular rations tonight."

Scrubz looked disgusted, one hand resting on the short sword sheathed at his side. There was no sign of the spear. He must've thrown and lost it, but the short sword also looked used. The man shook his head. "I guess I'll have a pocket pancake I keep around for emergencies. At least give me some of that goat meat to go with it. Abyss, *just* when I think your cooking thing is worth it, you let me down."

Nacho gave him a hunk of leftovers, grumbling notwithstanding. Scrubz turned without another word and got back into his boat. Another big warrior that seemed to hang on Scrubz's every word got in the other raft, and the pair rowed back to get the rest of the Brunch Force.

"You're welcome for the pancake and the goat," Nacho muttered under his breath. "Who was that other guy?"

"That's Eduardo." Reuben slapped him on the back. "He's cool. You know what I've realized? Scrubz is a lot like these crayfish… just so *shell*fish."

Brie walked up to her husband and laid a hand on his arm with a tight smile. "We need to go before I accidentally kill you."

"Sweetest way to die, baby." Reuben winked and tipped his leather Helm of Helming at her. "Going out for a good cause, just because my wife says so."

"Now I need to find something to kill and grill, so people's tongues I can thrill." Nacho sighed as he found himself alone for the first time in a long while—which of course happened to be the exact moment that the plants near him started rustling. Knives twirling, he felt ready to take on whatever decided to show up.

An unexpectedly canine face burst through the underbrush, panting and shivering. The green dog hadn't grown much larger since the last time Nacho had seen it, but it seemed this creature was not meant to deal with winter on its own. It padded over slowly, then lay down at the human's feet with its paws over its eyes.

"Every time I see you, I need to remind you that I am not going to be the one to put you out of your misery." Nacho was extremely hesitant to allow this creature to continue to follow him and show up in random places, but short of killing it himself, he didn't know what else he could do about the situation. "Wait… you're here because I said we need something to eat, aren't you…"

Obviously, the dog didn't say anything. It just looked up at him with eyes full of expectation, its gaze clearly traveling back and forth from his knives to its own body as if begging the cook to slice and dice it.

Reaching down, he picked the little dog up by its scruff and dropped it in the river. It bobbed back to the surface with a plaintive yelp, its verdant body barely able to sink in at all. "Uh huh. That's about what I expected. Bye bye, vegetable dog."

He could feel its sad puppy eyes on him as it floated away down the river, but the cook refused to glance toward it a single time to see if it was still floating away. "There is no *way* that thing is safe or good for my health."

CHAPTER NINETEEN

"I have no idea why this thing only requires fifteen in Fitness to use. To move it at *all*, maybe?" Nacho was glad he had twenty points in Fitness; his mobile kitchen wasn't light, and he'd been hauling around the huge backpack for two days. Reuben refused to let him use his Storage Slot, pleading the fact that the Yeti travel horn he stored his root beer in was more important to keep safe than Nacho's heavy and unwieldy mobile kitchen.

Seventeen other people of the newly-formed Brunch Force followed behind his enormous backpack. Before today, there had been a near-endless stream of jokes, chatting, and playing around, even as everyone did their best to maintain focus. The vibe had changed, drastically and most likely permanently, when they stumbled across the first settlement that had been destroyed by monsters.

Every single day, Nacho wished he didn't know what human remains looked like. Even though the bones were picked clean by whatever nightmare scavengers haunted this section of the AKC… the cook had decided to keep some of the collected information to himself. To his discerning eye, there were clear teeth marks that could only ever come from people gnawing on people. As much as he didn't want to believe it had already begun, it was clear from the signs that cannibalism had started flaring up.

His close friends knew that something was up, but all Nacho had to say on the matter was that if there were any survivors, it was likely that they were desperate and dangerous now. He gave an order as Guild Leader not to trust any unknown people from that point forward and instructed them to continue moving.

The flat, treeless prairie was arguably a bad place to try to build a settlement. For one thing, monsters hunting from the air could locate the buildings with relative ease. Then again, it was all about luck. If Nacho, Brie, and Reuben hadn't been on Armor Mountain when the Bove attacked, history reminded him that the cow monster would've killed every last person that was sheltering there at the time.

Brie motioned the rest of the team onward. "Nacho, Reuben, you guys tell the others to go on, but I'm going to level up. From what I've seen, I don't want anyone to see me... you know... flop around on the ground and spit blood."

"What're you *actually* hiding?" Scrubz scowled and tried to stop, but he kept on walking with some of the other foul-tempered group members that he had gathered around himself when Reuben glared him down.

"Picking fights for no reason isn't something that people planning to *survive* should be doing, Scrubz." The Healer was surprisingly imposing when it came to his wife. "We've been together for the last several days out here in monster-infested territory, hunting for weapons. Even if she *were* hiding something, it would be something that she brought with her, and also none of your business."

The conversation ended at that point, as no one else felt like arguing for the sake of arguing. Nacho looked at his friend with open admiration; he was glad he had some good people on his side, but he knew that if he messed up too often, those people would not hesitate to do their best to get him ousted from his current position as Guild Leader. Unlike Taye and the Breakfast

Club, who worked without complaining in an attempt to become constantly stronger, there was a surprisingly huge number of people that just... wanted to pretend the world hadn't ended. They either wouldn't, or couldn't, adapt to the new reality of life.

Not without learning the hard way. Nacho had to hope it wouldn't come to that.

Taye itched his neck with an arrow. "Okay, so Brie will go up a Tier now, which is cool. I'd like to gain Tier one either tonight or tomorrow morning. I'm still a couple hundred credits short, but I was wondering if you could loan me the difference? I'll pay you back."

"I know you're good for it," Reuben waved him away, "but don't worry about it, man. I have no idea what hijinks the people back at Armor Mountain are up to, but the guild coffers are going crazy. We're getting a ton of credits."

Nacho patted Taye on the back. "We got you, Taye. Besides, I want to see what you can do with the Robbin' Hoodie Archer Pack."

"Okay, but I'd like to see Abby and Kristie leveled up as well." That was Taye, thinking about other people. His caveat earned an approving smile and nod from the others. "I'll make sure they get through it first, and then I'll get back to you."

With a buoyant grin, Taye hurried to catch up to his friends.

Yet again, Nacho was left alone. He realized that he was unsure what Reuben had meant about the guild coffers going crazy, so he checked out the Guild Tab on his Stat Sheet, only to be met with a blinking notification.

Congratulations, Master of the Chips! You signed up one hundred new guild members in under an hour! Also, your guild successfully cleared the Fearsome Forest, a quick above-ground garden adventure. Can we call it a dungeon if it's not underground? Does it matter? Probably not!

We have to applaud Gabe the Archer, William Merrick, John Grover,

Mike Hernandez, Daniel Graves, and Kyle Smith for excellence above and beyond!

You go, Chips Guild; we are very impressed and a little dismayed. That's good… right? To drive you to work harder, there are bonus prizes for reaching a thousand guild members first! Get out there and recruit!

Chips Guild Stat Sheet
> *Total Guild Credits: 38,375*
> *Total Number of Members: 816*
> *Guild Master: Eli 'Nacho' Naches*
> *Alternate Guild Master: Daniel Chronour*
> *Third Alternate: Reuben Colby*
> *Morale: Not everyone is happy. Sad face.*

Nacho was surprised at the newly increased number of members. Not too long ago, they'd passed six hundred people and had been closing in on seven hundred. But suddenly that number had jumped. Why? It was also concerning that his guild was getting so much Patron attention. This was something, as far as he recalled, that hadn't happened during the Probability Vision.

To be fair, he hadn't had his own guild his first time around, so he couldn't say for certain that it hadn't gone like this for key players. Still, Nacho figured that Crave would've told him. They had been close enough for the Guild Master to share a great many details with Nacho about Final Victory, and a minor complaint about the messages would have been voiced constantly if it had been happening.

"Are you looking at the guild bank right now?" Reuben nodded and grinned like the Cheshire Cat about to get some canned cat food. "There's better than thirty-eight thousand credits in the coffers. I know we can't use *all* of it to upgrade our A-Team to Tier one, but we can use a good chunk. Not for Taye; Archers are flighty."

"I know you're trying to joke, but don't. Not about him." Brie tripped her husband, though he caught himself after only a slight stumble. "Don't even *pretend* to speak poorly about Taye. I'd trade in a dozen Bills for a single Taye any day of the week. Besides, why *shouldn't* we use those credits to upgrade the best of the Brunch Force? In the end, they *are* our star employees."

"Agreed," Nacho stated instantly, eliciting a momentary silence as Brie tried to figure out why he was so on board with spending the money. "When the Bills complain—and they will —we'll see where they are with their levels and what they can do. Do we have any idea what Bill's class is, and what his Skills are?"

"Level nine curmudgeon. He has the 'Get Off My Lawn' yelling ability. He also has a 'Knows Too Much About Lawn-mowers' Skill." Reuben paused to take off his gauntlets and tuck them under his arms. "Or maybe *Scrubz*—remember the name, Nacho—split his consciousness and traveled through time to become Old Bill. Wait. Have we ever seen Old Bill and Scrubz in the same room at the same time?"

"Enough, *please*. Let's just Tier me up." Brie had stowed her armor in her Storage Slots, as well as her hammer, which left her in her fatigues and combat boots. "Reuben, catch me if I fall, and stop me if I get too close to a cliff or something. I…"

"What is it, love?" Reuben held out his arms to her, his eyes searching her face for the answer as to why she was getting all misty-eyed.

"I'm going to miss my hammer so much."

"Oh, for the love of… we'll buy you a *new* one!" Reuben promised in an unconvincing grumpy tone. Nacho was nodding along with Brie; he was also sad to see her lose the Splatter Mallet. It had turned out to be far more useful than his Splatter Millet, which he hadn't used at all. He did lug it around, because he figured they would eventually encounter some kaiju grains and he could go to town on making something he missed more than any other breakfast food: donuts.

Checking the Store, Nacho found a pretty decent magical

hammer for a thousand credits, but it would only offer a base damage of twelve. Brie's Splatter Mallet did *twenty* damage. It would cost at least eight thousand credits to replace the hammer with something of equal quality, and Nacho had to pause once he calculated the impact. "Hold on, Brie. Let's think this through. You're doing twenty base damage. All bonus percentages of damage are based on that base—your Fitness increase, your Combat Dash, and your hubby's Positive Vibes. At this point, you're doing thirty-two points of damage when you're fully loaded. We drop that by ten, and you're suddenly left doing sixteen measly points of damage."

"Yeah, I thought about that. Here's the thing," Brie countered instantly, and Nacho knew that he was about to be shown that he was out of his depth. "If I jack up my Combat Dash ability, I can be adding *thirty* percent extra damage at level fifteen."

Reuben saw where she was going and managed to do the mental math as Nacho slunk away from the direct confrontation. "Yeah, but I think you're using your current weapon as your calculator... thirty percent of twenty is six, thirty percent of *ten* is only three. You got a wicked hammer right away, so we'll have to replace that. I hate to say it, but at this point, I agree with Nacho that bringing you up to Tier one isn't worth it. Not if you can't use your hammer or have a better one ready to go."

"But... ah, abyss it. My math was off," Brie grumbled, motioning for them to move after the main group that had continued walking. "Let's forget this for now."

"Yeah, let's go catch up to Taye," Nacho agreed as they hurried along. "Sorry to kill your excitement, Brie."

"No, it's just... I had myself all psyched up for the change. If we can't do mine, then we can't do Reuben either, because he loses his gauntlets and his ring. This Tier system sucks." Brie squeezed her eyes shut and growled as she mentally conceded the delay, then took off running to work off the frustration.

"She likes to run. Me? I hate to run. But run we must."

Reuben grabbed his friend, and both of them sprinted to catch up. When they pulled Taye back to Tier up right away, he seemed overly confused.

"Me? Why me, and why now?" They sat him down on some old stones which seemed like a good size for chairs. Taye was sweating lightly, either from nerves or the heat. "I'm going to take your couple hundred and get to Tier one, but why before Brie?"

"It's all about the gear," Nacho explained simply. "You have an upgrade waiting. There's only good in you doing this, while *she'll* suddenly be less combat effective."

"Just spend the windfall before they figure out a way to convince you to stay Tier zero," Brie sighed in annoyance. The others looked at her questioningly, and she bobbed her shoulders. "I was looking forward to being stronger."

Funny enough, that stopped all other questions and concerns the younger man seemed to have. Taye spent the credits and sat waiting in his jeans, a t-shirt, and boots. "I don't feel anything. Wait… Oh, no! That… is it supposed to hurt this bad?"

Taye's eyes lit up like his skull had become a jack-o-lantern, glowing from the inside out; every bone was visible through his clothes and skin alike. Without warning, he dropped his bow, his quiver, everything, and went running off, shrieking with laughter.

"Grab him before he hurts himself!" Nacho bellowed as the Archer sped away.

"I got this!" Brie Combat Dashed to get in front of him, then grabbed the hysterical teen and held him while Reuben and Nacho raced up.

Taye's muscles spasmed hard, practically a seizure, and it took all of their collected efforts to pull him down. He fought them wildly for a minute before collapsing onto his back in the grass. His eyes stopped glowing a second later, and his phosphorescent bones faded as reason started to reappear in his gaze.

The kid blinked rapidly and scanned their faces as his eyes refocused. "How bad was it?"

"Not great." Reuben looked pained, but that might have been the blood leaking from his right nostril. "You've got a wicked right hook."

"*No~o~o.*" Taye covered his face with his hands. "I'm sorry. You know I'd never-"

"Not another word. You were unconscious and your body was getting upgraded. That's all the reasoning you need," Brie pointed out, then ignored anything else the young man tried to say.

"You know what would make me feel better? Put on that super cool armor you earned. I want to see how awesome you look in it." Reuben's wide smile was less friendly-looking this time, as blood dripped onto his teeth.

Taye gulped, nodded, and pulled out the first part of the Robbin' Hoodie Archer Pack of black and green armor. The entire leather set was embellished with a variety of chains, with a thick leather hood in place of a helm. It also came with fashionable wrist and finger guards done in green and black, though they weren't magical, just fancy.

As soon as the Archer had finished slipping on the various items, he smiled. "I'm getting a message... it has a hidden magical function! It's called 'Aura of No-Arrows Allowed'. Looks like I can't be hit by arrows—or crossbow bolts—at or below my Tier and level. Also, I take half damage from magical missile attacks. That's cool."

Nacho couldn't help but think of Red Suzy Blacke and smile. In an archer battle, Taye would win, no contest. Taye pulled a face. "Ugh. The Patrons are laying it on thick. Let's take a look at the bow."

He lifted a very fine carbon fiber compound bow, also done up in greens and blacks so it matched the armor. "I think I need to buy an info pack on magical compound bows so I can take care of this properly, but I can start using this right away. Just like my other bow, it detects my strength, but this bow doubles it, so I get double my strength bonuses when firing arrows."

"Then... if you eat my Cooking Magicked food?" Nacho pondered slowly.

Reuben brightened and excitedly supplied the answer. "Tons of damage fun! That's going to be devastating."

"It'll only do a percentage of the base damage of the weapon." Brie frowned as she motioned at his quiver. "Your arrows only do five damage. It's just not that much."

"Says you of little faith!" Reuben admonished his wife. "Keep going, Taye."

The kid wrinkled his brow. "With Eagle Aim, if I take my time on each shot, I can double that damage to ten. But I'm not doing thirty damage like Brie. I'd like that to change."

Reuben kept being encouraging, trying to make the kid feel better. "Yeah, but with Fast Quiver, you get triple the attacks, so if they're not Tier one, you're good."

"But we'll be fighting more and more Tier ones." Taye worriedly tapped on his new bow.

"Let's slow down and see what else we're working with." Nacho gestured at the rest of the gear. "Why don't we check out the quiver?"

Taye's eyes started glowing, and a ghost of a smile crossed his face. "The quiver doubles the arrows I put in it, including magical arrows. That's pretty nice. I find a flame arrow, and I put it in the quiver, and I get two flame arrows? Plus there's another cool mechanic to that; with every arrow I draw, there's only a twenty-five percent chance I'll fire the master arrow, which means it might break, or I might lose it forever. But that also means there's a seventy-five percent chance to fire the copy, which would work just as well as the original. If anything were to happen to a copy, a new copy is made."

"Not *exactly* endless ammo, but a much lower chance of you running out in a longer battle. That's pretty great!" Nacho was already excited enough by just that information. "Even so, it's like a lottery quiver—are you firing the real one or the fake? It's nice that it's not a fifty-fifty chance."

Reuben rubbed his hands together, then clapped them. "Great, *extra* arrows, we got it. Let's get on to the arrows themselves. Ever since we first saw this, I was curious about the 'Arrows of Mass Destruction'. Let's see what those AMD's can do."

Taye retrieved the impressive arrows from his Storage Slots —one nice thing about bundled items: they could be stored in a single Storage Slot. These arrows, like everything else, were black and green.

The young Archer slid them into the new quiver, one at a time, recounting their information aloud. "Two flame arrows, normal five damage, but bonuses to ice-based creatures. Two ice arrows, normal damage but bonuses on flame-based things. Two lighting arrows—no surprise here—wet things take bonus damage. Three explosive arrows for double damage in an area of effect, and… ooh. Two arrows that do triple damage."

"Is that all of them?" Brie questioned after the archer went quiet for a long moment.

"No… there's a single black arrow that does *quadruple* damage." Taye had a firm smile creasing his face at that moment, and no one could blame him. With the Quiver of Doubling, he'd have two arrows that could basically hit like Brie's hammer. "Now, for my stats. I didn't do Self-Applied—I did Balanced, Instant. Since I'm level ten, I have an eighteen Fitness, but if I eat Nacho's Uncommon chicken biscuit surprise, that gets jacked up to thirty-four. The bow doubles that to sixty-eight, so I'm doing an extra thirty-four percent damage."

Nacho was absolutely *loving* where this was headed. "Add Positive Vibes and that's another eighteen percent, so… abyssal math… let me get my paper. Mmkay… then you're doing an extra fifty-two percentage points of damage. That's eight points of damage with a single arrow, rounding up. Eagle Aim doubles that to sixteen. Fast Quiver makes that... twenty-four. Wow. This was the right call, for sure."

"What about the quad damage arrows?" Reuben turned his eyes to the sky to do the math. "That would be ten points of damage, rounding down. Or twenty-one points of damage, rounded up, if he uses Eagle Aim. Or *thirty* points of damage with Fast Quiver!"

Brie nodded in confirmation that she'd gotten the same result. "That's with his skills at level nine. What happens if we upgrade those skills to, say, level fifteen?"

"Five arrows with Fast Quiver. Quadruple damage with Eagle Aim. *Guys.*" Taye suddenly got emotional, and Nacho found himself wrapped in an exuberant hug. Reuben was pulled in as well, though Brie hurriedly backflipped out of range. "I was so worried I was going to be left behind as a ranged class."

"No, come on, we'd never-" Nacho started weakly.

Taye's voice cracked like a middle schooler winning the National Spelling Bee. "You guys, I can't thank you enough. You've made this so much more bearable. Before we found you, everyone looked at me like I had all the answers. I'm just a high school gamer, you know? I got a 'C' in physics, and then suddenly, all these adults were wondering what they should do, and *I* had to tell them? Now I have this bow, and it's all... just... thank you."

Reuben stepped closer into the hug, while Nacho extracted himself and tried not to get too emotionally invested. He had already chosen the people he would keep alive at all costs, and he wasn't open to expanding that list. Too much work. Still... he looked back as a couple of tears worked their way down the teen's face; a face that was just *barely* old enough to have made it to the apocalypse.

The Guild Leader cleared his throat and roughly grumbled, "Bah. Kids these days. Can't even give 'em nice things without them getting all excited about it."

CHAPTER TWENTY

That night, Nacho and the Brunch Force camped on the only dry grass they could find on the edge of a swamp. The prairie had become a morass of various streams and channels hidden by long grasses, although there was one stone path traversing the bog that was frequently submerged in black water.

Thanks to its putrid feel, lack of any redeeming qualities, and general miasma of rot, they all agreed that if there was a downtown Kansas City hiding underground, it would be around here. It was hard to tell for certain, since geography was impossible to guess when alien deities tossed a mile of dirt and rock on someone's hometown and messed up all the rivers.

Nacho figured they'd get close enough to find a dungeon entrance, then start their descent. Before then, they needed to survive in the unforgiving area for at least one night. The lack of trees and useful vegetation necessitated buying Store firewood, which gave off an unpleasant odor and was always smoky. It had an annoying way of always blowing right into the face of the person who hated it the most; in this case, that was Kristie.

Back in her old body, she'd had asthma, and she hated any

kind of smoke. Eventually the exasperated Warrior gave up and went to bed, earning a few chuckles at her expense when the smoke followed in a straight horizontal line into her tent, eliciting a scream of frustration.

Nacho kept at his grill, making sure that if nothing else, his group was well-fed and ready at any moment to take on the horrors of the night. Scrubz and the Cocktail Party—the name his group of complainers had taken on in retaliation when they heard that they were the only ones without an individual group name—assumed they'd be fighting some kind of alligators or crocodiles or dinosaurs, since they were traversing wetlands central.

Nothing had crawled out of the swamp yet, but Nacho had a sinking feeling that whatever appeared would be some kind of mosquito monster. It was spring, the nights didn't freeze, the days were warmer, and they were surrounded by a lot of stagnant water that was perfect for bug eggs. He also couldn't stop thinking about the ruined settlement where the stone buildings had been melted into lava. There had been murders for certain, but it didn't look like any survivors had escaped. Combining that with the melted and twisted stone? There was some kind of flame-aspected creature around and he was dreading the encounter.

"Dragon mosquitoes?" Nacho muttered softly to himself as he tried to think through the possibilities. "Wouldn't put it past the Patrons."

After Kristie went to bed, Brie wasn't far behind. She and Reuben left for their Store-bought tent, while Nacho figured he'd just flop down in the dirt near his mobile kitchen. He'd leave it out to cook people breakfast, which meant that he would need to be near the first people awake in the morning. Again, nobody necessarily needed to eat, but people *liked* to eat, and coffee was an absolute necessity.

Taye was gathering a following, but the kid was naturally resistant to gloating or bragging. It required a number of people pressuring him—Abby the hardest—before he reluctantly showed them all the stats of his Robbin' Hoodie armor. As soon as he spotted the Archer in his matched set, Scrubz spat out the comment Nacho had been waiting to hear. "Well now, golden boy... how much of *our* tax money did you use to get to Tier one?"

Taye attempted to speak, his face flushing, but Nacho cut him off. "Thirty-two hundred credits of *our* money paid for arrows that explode and another person that can keep all of the people on this trip *alive*. Stop complaining, unless you want everyone to stay the same level of weak so that we can all die together in a nice 'fair' way."

That caused Scrubz to clam up, but only for as long as it took to toss aside any shame that he was feeling. Not long, in other words. Just as he went red-faced and opened his mouth, Abby coughed and waved her hands from the stink of the logs burning. With Kristie in bed, the smoke was terrorizing the big woman something fierce. She looked the irascible guild member over and questioned, "I'm wondering, what *is* your class?"

Scrubz hissed, "Wouldn't you like to know. Stop distracting me; it's not fair that we're using our taxes to upgrade only a few players. We should *all-*"

"It matters because we don't know how best to help *you* level or gear up," Abby interjected, not finished with her point. "We don't know the best ways for you to contribute, which earns you extra credits, as well as our trust in your abilities."

Close to snarling, Scrubz leaned forward menacingly and ground out. "What does it matter? I am saying that I don't think it's *fair* that Taye-"

"Fair is where you eat cotton candy. It means *nothing* out here." Nacho stepped into the conversation, voice deadly dangerous and pitched for everyone in the camp to hear clearly. "You think that being *fair* is going to keep us alive? Will bringing a hundred people to level five allow us to kill a *single* Tier one monster? No! We're doing what needs to be done to keep your ungrateful rear alive, and you continually repay that with hostility and plotting."

Nacho drew closer, looming over the revolutionary with a warning gleam in his cold eyes. "Knock it off, or I'll boot you from the guild, no matter how useful you *claim* to be. Look around, Scrubz. Whatever destroyed that *entire town* back there might hit us tonight. Are you suggesting that Taye doing five damage with an arrow gives us the best chance at success? *Who* does that help, exactly?"

Scrubz didn't answer right away, completely put on the spot. After a moment of silent spluttering, he tried to change the subject. "I thought you were upgrading Brie? That would have made more sense."

"I thought so too," Taye muttered quietly, not meeting the eyes of anyone around him.

"We did the math while trying to find the best path to *surviving*. Until we can find her a replacement weapon, it isn't worth spending the credits. But, yes, once we do find one, we're going to be spending anything needed to get her there. Because *she's* a proven asset." Nacho tried to meet as many eyes as possible with that statement, wanting everyone to know that they were willing to spend guild money on any team member if they were close to leveling. "You know who we will *not* spend the credits on? People that set low personal standards for themselves and even then consistently fail to meet them."

"Is Scrubz having grand delusions of adequacy again?" Reuben called from his tent, getting a round of laughter for his efforts.

Nacho took over once more, wanting to drive the point home without driving the group toward sabotage or malicious compliance. "Look, we can't leave our credits gathering dust. We *need* to use them to optimize people's talents, which will keep people alive, as well as allowing us to make more credits faster. In this case, it made the most sense to invest in Taye. Brie is already doing a crazy amount of damage with her hammer. When you, or anyone else, shows us that we can rely on them—especially in combat—we will gladly put in the effort and investment to bring you up with us."

"How many damage points counts as a crazy amount?" Scrubz seemed relieved that he wasn't in the hot seat anymore.

"Let me look at the conversion chart!" Reuben took the opportunity to shout a joke over. "Looks like there's a stupid amount of *pounds* in a crazy amount of damage? Shoot, this is the wrong chart! Quick! Someone call the British!"

"Wait. I know this one. There's an *unbelievable* number of ounces in a stupid amount of pounds." Brie's dry amusement rose from their tent, even though Nacho had been expecting her to shush her husband instead. "I'm not telling you the exact numbers; there might be someone listening in."

As the situation devolved into poking fun and everyone started to relax, Scrubz seemed to be a little shamefaced, and the Cocktail Party didn't split off. Eduardo, a guild member Nacho hadn't interacted with yet who seemed to have taken the role of tank for Scrubz' party, was even in a good mood and started in on Scrubz with jokes of his own.

Nacho wasn't ready to be happy yet. He had trouble keeping in his darker emotions, and he decided that he needed a small walk to clear his head. Once he was far enough from the camp to feel alone, he tried to spit out his vitriol quietly. "They survived another day in the Juxtaposition. They should've just been *grateful* we even bothered to help them live up to this point."

By the time he wandered back, nice and calmed down, Scrubz had volunteered for a watch, as had some of the other insomniacs. Nacho didn't like that very much, and he felt glad he was sleeping out in the open so he could spring awake and into action if anything happened. Meanwhile his looking-on-the-bright side was telling him that Scrubz was taking his words to heart and was trying to prove his usefulness.

Somehow, the night passed quickly and peacefully. Nacho was soon up out of the damp grass, rolling up his mat and stowing away his sleeping bag. He started the coffee and break-fast first—Uncommon oatmeal, if his plan went the way he hoped it would. He put in the extra effort to pan-toast some raisins and nuts, splurged for Uncommon M&Ms, and tried to make the otherwise unappetizing meal as appealing as possible.

People complained at first about having simple oatmeal, but Nacho decided to remind them of the reality of the world they were in now. "I don't know why you don't understand that things don't need to taste good. It's *food*. This is to fuel your body and Skills, not your desires. With your Juxtaposition bodies, there's no difference between ice cream and fried chicken. It's all either quarter portion, half portion, or full portion. End of story. Suck it up or put the food down; I'll serve it again at lunch."

Between his glare and the surprisingly great taste, it didn't take long for Nacho to win over his customers. Soon they were all raving about the oatmeal, which was imbued with his Cooking Magic. Nacho made extra so the Brunch Force Delta —what they were secretly calling the most powerful and helpful members of the raid group—could store a few bowls of leftover oatmeal in their Storage Slots.

They finished breakfast, then went tromping across the muck-smeared stones of the path and pushing through the marshy grasses, ready for anything to attack them either from the ground or air. In the distance, to the east, smoke drifted into the sky, but they were too far away to smell it or see the source. Reuben asked about it quietly, but all Nacho could do was shrug. "It's probably another settlement. Humans, for the most part, clustered together. People are social animals after all."

As the march progressed, an order slowly continued to form. Brie and Abby took point, with Scrubz not far behind. He kept his short sword ready, as well as some cheap Costco armor. Reuben pointed out his new position near the front, whispering to Nacho, "He's been *suspiciously* quiet about his class and level. What's his deal? Do you think he's a spy or something?"

"Hope not," was all Nacho could say on the subject. He wore his Wok of Blocking and his Skillet of Turtling, since he was expecting an ambush at some point. Unfortunately, with the sun beating down and the humidity of the area, it was already too hot for all his armor. By mid-morning, the day was even more humid, but what really added to the discomfort was the boiling swamp water around them. They could only assume they'd stumbled across a hot spring, but with the Juxtaposition being magical, that may or may not have been the case.

It was another good hour of walking until they found a path leading up out of the marsh and across a ridge. Unfortunately, it was disconcertingly narrow and was bordered on both sides by boiling black water. Brie stopped and waited until everyone had gathered into a small crowd before waving into the distance and speaking quietly. "Do you guys hear that?"

Nacho listened carefully, but all he could hear was what could potentially be the sound of a waterfall. The group cautiously followed her lead to locate the sound until they encountered a circle of stones... with a spiral staircase in the center. Water rushed in a torrent down one side of the circling steps, and the other sides were *just* tall enough to hold the swamp water back. But, judging from the lapping waves... who knew for how much longer?

"Well, I think we'll want to check out this dungeon, right? Those steps are going to be slippery... and we're going to get wet." Scrubz pushed forward and peered down, holding up a hand and nodding after a long moment. "Yup. This is a dungeon, alright."

"What? No *way!*" Reuben quipped with an eye roll and a light punch at Scrubz's arm as Nacho, Brie, and the rest of the team all crowded around the staircase. The glistening walls were covered in moss, as well as long strands of various grasses. Water splashed onto the steps, but then kept on falling, with no indication of how deep the spiral staircase descended.

Taye cocked an ear. "Wait. There's something... do you guys hear that?"

"Yeah, Taye, that's what a waterfall sounds like." Scrubz spit into the black water, adding to the impending overflow.

"No... not that." The kid started rolling an arrow around his fingers as his eyes scanned the distance. Nacho picked up the sound next, as his senses were heightened to the highest level in the group. He could only assume that Taye had a bonus or a perception Skill, since he could hear the buzzing sounds that rapidly filled the air before the cook did. Overhead, a shadow passed over the grasses, blocking out the sun. The threat wasn't crocodiles coming out of the boiling water. "Airborne monsters!"

Nacho pulled his pot helmet and oven mitt gloves out of his Storage Slot, along with his Pauldrons of Frying. "We're about to be dive bombed, people! Eat your extra oatmeal and prepare for combat! We'll need to form a skirmish line to create a protected retreat for the people running down those stairs; we're not going to be able to fight all of these things."

"Who got extra oatmeal?" Scrubz called in confusion. No one answered.

The cook remembered rumors he'd heard in the Probability Vision about strange fiery monsters on the east side of the AKC, and nodded sharply at the fact that some of his knowledge was still ringing true. These had to be the same creatures that had destroyed the settlement they'd passed through, and he appreciated that. Otherwise, if his concerns about cannibalism had been accurate, he would have been forced to burn the place to the ground himself.

He shouted to their newly raised Tier one archer. "Taye, keep your ice arrows ready, but use explosive arrows first to take them out in clusters. I know it might feel like a waste, but it is probably for the best to use them up instead of trying to hold them for another situation."

"Positive Vibes, people!" Reuben had his gauntlets, helm, and chainmail on and in position. He was already slurping down his portion of leftover oatmeal from a Juxtaposition container, finishing and tossing the bowl to the side just as Nacho turned to him. Reuben raised his gloves, and they glowed with a brilliant sheen that was soon reflected by the others in the Brunch Force.

Scrubz started down the stairs, likely because he knew that

he wasn't getting any additional buffs. "I'll run recon in the dungeon to make sure we aren't fighting a battle on two fronts. You just hold off whatever those things are."

Somehow Reuben got the first look at the monsters, and he decided to share that information with the rest of the group. "Uh… what are 'Succ'n'blows'? They look like giant mosquitoes. Tier one, though they can't have that much health, right? They're about the size of poodles."

That was all the warning they got before the swarm hit them. It turned out that Succ'n'blows were giant mosquitoes that sucked in blood with one end and… released… fire from the other. They didn't seem terribly dangerous; more concerning was their numbers, all the way until one of them broke rank and flashed toward the group.

Nacho felt a proboscis hit his arm in the same instant—it was like having a skewer shoved into his flesh. Before he could chop into the bug monster with his cleaver, it had turned away and blasted off by letting out a squeak of flaming gas.

Health remaining: 42/50! You've been stabbed and cooked, which is ironic, given your class. Flame damage ignored, thanks to your armor, or that woulda been a critical hit against you!

"Seriously? They deal *one* point more damage than my Mana barrier can ignore?" Another Succ'n'blow *buzzed* past him, letting out a stream of fire, and Nacho took the flames on his skillet shield. The message had reminded him that at least *he* had some protection from the terrifying heat these things generated.

Taye fired an arrow above them, and the explosion threw pieces of bug across the swamp—though it also ignited a firestorm that rained down onto the grasses, setting a nearby hill aflame. Luckily, there was plenty of water around, or there would have been a chance that they'd be trapped by the fire for who knew how long.

One of the Succ'n'blows squeaked near Brie and hit her straight on with the swamp-gas flame, earning a scream of pain from the Berserker as she swung her hammer and squashed the bug into flaming goo.

"It's like fighting vampires stuffed full of napalm!" Reuben bellowed at the group as he grabbed Nacho, hugging a heal into him. "Don't kill them too close to your body, or they'll do damage when they go down!"

"We *get* it; just heal us!" Brie yelled as she used her Defensive Whirl to block five of the mosquito creatures at once, sending them tumbling to the ground from the unexpected resistance.

Reuben grumbled lightly as he healed her of the terrible burns that had appeared on her skin. "Spoken like a true DPS. Don't you know better than to run away from your Healer? I *will* chase you, and then we'll both die."

Abby was using her Slippery Block ability to its utmost potential, which also helped her to take less damage, so she worked hard to draw fire as the lower-level Cocktail Party followed Scrubz down the steps. The Succ'n'blows seemed to be instinctively drawn to the lower-leveled people, and they dove down the hole without hesitation, though the waterfall helped to dampen the damage their flames could cause. The mosquito creatures also had a harder time flying in enclosed spaces. Just like their mundane counterparts, they weren't good fliers by any stretch of the imagination.

Reuben grabbed Kristie and gave her a tight squeeze. She'd been impaled and burned, and the pressure helped keep the blood in as his spell cleaned up the damage. He called over to Nacho. "'Succ'n'blows' is pretty bad as a name. What about tootsquitos?"

Kristie panted in pain for a moment, then managed a joke as she was healed. "Skeeter Shooters?"

"Or what about Flatu-flighters?" Taye used another explosive arrow, and the air was filled with smoke, a red mist, and monster mosquito ichor. "I admit, I'm not as good with the jokes."

Brie swirled around, defending herself, but this battle turned out to be one of those times that her single strike attacks weren't that effective. It was Taye's arrows that were really doing the trick. With a base damage of ten, coupled with the buffs from breakfast, his new bow, and Reuben's Positive Vibes, the incendiary projectiles exploded in a fifteen-foot radius for fifteen points of damage. Taking advantage of every loophole he could, he tied that together with Eagle Aim to send the arrows to the perfect location so the damage was doubled.

With every draw, he was taking out *clouds* of the creatures. Nacho could literally see the credits rolling in. Kristie broke out from Reuben's healing embrace with a grunt. "You guys get below. I'll Death Blossom and jump!"

Reuben instantly refused. "I'm not going anywhere. I'm full of stink, so I've been taking some damage, but my Ring of Cheese is still absorbing it just fine. Nacho, get the others down there. I'll make sure Kristie doesn't get overwhelmed."

Nacho swung his skillet and banged a Succ'n'blow right in the proboscis.

Damage dealt: 15/30!

"Still got it," he muttered as the *clang* rang out. The mosquito monster released a surprised toot-flame, but he managed to fully dodge it at the last second. The flier buzzed angrily and was abruptly joined by a whole host of the noisy insectoid murder-swarm.

"Kristie's plan is good; time to take this meal to *go!*" Nacho tried to herd the others down the steps, but Brie paused to smash one of the mosquito creatures with her hammer, and

Abby had to kill another one with her ironbound staff before they would submit to leaving the field of battle.

Above them, the air *boomed* with a pink magical explosion. Any of the wounded Succ'n'blows were killed, as well as leaving behind a bunch more wounded. Most importantly, moments after the detonation of pink Warlock power, Nacho was relieved to see a very scorched, utterly stench-ridden Reuben half-carrying Kristie down the steps.

Taye had become a machine-gun of arrows, and Hazel was endlessly hurling exploding purple grenades into the air above the dungeon entrance. Between the two, they kept more of the mosquito monsters from coming down until the last of the team walked underneath the hot water tumbling from the entrance. Once they were obscured by the falling liquid , it seemed as though the Succ'n'blows couldn't see them anymore. Nacho scanned his group anxiously, finding all of them heaving for air with wild eyes. "That was too close."

"Why do you think they gave up?" Reuben voiced the question all of them were thinking. "Maybe it was because of the hot mist in the air?"

"You think Tier one monsters are going to be stopped because of a little *water*?" Scrubz spat, still wiping the foul fluid from his face. "Most likely, they can't enter the dungeon. A territory dispute or something."

Either way, soaking wet, wounded, hungry and thirsty from the use of Skills and Spells, Nacho and the Brunch Force descended about a hundred feet down the spiral staircase. The water continued to act like normal water and kept on pouring down into that deep, dark pit. Above the entrance, the Succ'n'blows swarmed around angrily, lines of fire erupting from their black bodies. They had filled the pit opening shortly after the team had descended further into the cistern, but the angry insects weren't flying any lower.

"Looks like the only way out is to wait until they get bored, or to clear the dungeon and hope there's a *new* way out." Nacho realized that Active Combat was over, and he paused for a few minutes to let his resources get topped off. It was only as he was squinting around in the gloom that he noticed another significant issue. "It's dark as the abyss in here."

Kristie had her Bracelets of Brightness, but few other people had light sources. Nacho knew that it was his time to shine, so he pulled out his Firefly Potstickers and let all ten of the winged potstickers fly into the air and illuminate the spiral staircase around him as he waited for the System to give them a 'Welcome to the Dungeon' message.

Instead, they were met only with silence, which Scrubz noticed and decided to comment on. "Maybe this *isn't* a dungeon. Maybe… this is just the long entrance to the UnderFun?"

With how deep those stairs seemed to go, Nacho could only hope that the curmudgeon-in-waiting might be right.

CHAPTER TWENTY-ONE

Nacho found their strange descent wildly concerning. Not only had they *not* been given a dungeon name, but the staircase seemed endless. Around and around they went, dashing from one side and easing down behind the sheet of mucky water until they were hidden from the buzzing menaces above. The monsters hadn't been willing to come closer, but there was no reason to tempt fate.

Each time they passed under the waterfall, the water seemed hotter, which shouldn't have been possible when the liquid was so far removed from its heat source. As an additional issue, the entirety of the boiling swamp seemed to be draining down into the staircase they found themselves in. The stream kept increasing in size, and soon rumblings that they were all going to drown were bouncing around the group.

"Can anyone think of something better?" Reuben tried to play games to keep them cheerful. "I still don't care for the name 'Succ'n'blow'. The Patrons could've done better. They could've gone with hemo-pyroes, flame-drains, or bloodblazers. Maybe one could be called FireToots McSquito. Nah... that sounds like a tween show."

Nacho was glad for the extra Fitness points his food provided, since his mobile kitchen was neither light nor easy to balance. Every time he ducked under a waterfall, he worried that the pounding deluge might send him careening down into the darkness below. His Firefly Potstickers appeared to be water-proof—the first test had been *exceedingly* concerning—and they had a helpful tendency of flying to illuminate wherever he was looking.

They'd eventually gone so far underground that the top of the staircase was only a pinprick of light far, far above. After a few tense moments of scouting in the darkness, Scrubz called up from below. "There it is! I see the bottom. There's a lot of water; ah man… this place is just going to be more swamp."

So abruptly that a few people slipped and had to be caught, the System provided them with the name of the dungeon.

Greetings Player!

Welcome to the Best Barbeque Tunnels! We hope you have an appetite for destruction, because you're about to get a bellyful of bad beasties! Prepare your eyes for the bloodbath of a lifetime! This is no shrimpy dungeon. It's a big, spicy sausage of tricks and tunnels. Feel free to pig out!

Bonus offer! Stay in Active Combat for one hour straight and win ten thousand credits! Stay in Active Combat for two hours, and everyone in your group will win ten thousand credits each, and the highest damage dealer will also win a Weapon of Weaponing! Maximize your training experience through continual, exhausting combat!

Have fun, and as always… may your future be delicious!

They gathered at the bottom of the hole, where they stood in stinking black water up to their knees. The central chamber was a cacophony thanks to the waterfall, as well as numerous smaller trickles leaking down into the bottom of the staircase pit. Brie frowned and yelled over the noise, "If I have to fight in this muck, my abilities aren't going to do us much good."

"Let's hope we can find some dry ground." Nacho shifted his pack around on his shoulders.

Reuben, ever the font of wisdom, released his question as a shout. "What's the difference between Kansas City barbeque and the rest of it? The sauce, right? I mean, everyone else is all about the dry rub or vinegar."

"That has nothing to do with the situation at hand!" Taye called back, only for Reuben to shake his head.

"You're missing the point. The ground isn't vinegary, it's *saucy*! That means we won't sink as fast!" No one could make sense of the advice, which seemed to make Reuben frustrated beyond belief. "It's a massive benefit! Why am I the only person that gets it?"

The Brunch Force soon left the main waterfall chamber and sloshed through a corridor into an open cavern where the water was a bit more shallow—only coming up to about mid-calf. Tunnels had been carved into the stone to the left and to the right. It was still loud in the cavern from the waterfall room, and the place stank of murky water and wet stone.

"Eduardo and I will run a little recon. You guys wait here." Scrubz scowled at the plethora of options and motioned his team member forward. The two left through the passage to the right, and Nacho watched them go with complicated emotions filling him.

Kristie had a dizzy smile on her face. "Back to the discussion. I think barbeque is just... barbeque. Doesn't matter where it's from. That means Reuben should stop trying to get us to understand this and let it go. Right, Nacho?"

The cook hooked his thumbs into the straps of his heavy backpack and decided to try to end whatever... *this* was. "I think she's right. It's just a consistency thing. We're just gonna be finding thick sauce, and the dungeon is gonna be heavy on the meat. Maybe extra-meaty, also known as healthy and hard to kill, monsters."

"You've been a cook for like two minutes, and you're forgetting I've known you your entire life," Reuben replied righteously. "Before you got here, I'd only ever seen you eat prepackaged meals or order from door dash. You can't tell me I don't know what I'm talking about, because you have no idea."

Everyone looked at Nacho, who shrugged helplessly. "He's not *wrong*."

"Oh, for celestial's sake." Brie cast around for anything she could use to get them off the topic. "There has to be a drain somewhere. The water is shallower in this room. Nacho, what did you think of the welcome message?"

"No, I think I'm starting to see what he's getting at. I would have to guess that we're going to be fighting giant shrimp, some kind of sausage creature, and pigs. That's in line with the message, like you were mentioning, Brie. I'd imagine there will be dry tunnels at some point. We should try to stay in Active Combat as long as possible, all of us, to get whatever bonuses we can manage. That means *highly* focusing on your specializations. Reuben won't fight, he'll *only* heal. He'll eventually run out Mana, so try not to get hit. Everyone else, make sure to listen to Brie when combat does start; we agreed that she's better at calling the shots than I am in that situation."

"Full ride scholarship with *lacrosse*," Reuben bragged on her behalf as he nudged Taye. "You even know what that sport is, kid?"

"No." The Archer's blunt answer took some of the wind out of Reuben's sails.

Before the Healer could educate Taye, Scrubz came sloshing back into the room with Eduardo, clapping his hands sardonically. "Thanks, boss. 'Try not to get wounded by the pig monsters'; great advice. Couldn't have thought that one up myself. Listen up: the tunnel to the right is a dead end. We'll want to go through the tunnel to the left. That's probably where the monsters are."

"I hope there *are* pigs." Reuben smacked his lips loudly. "Pigs means *bacon*. I haven't had bacon in a lo~ong time."

"Bacon would be too hard to eat during combat." Brie took off her helmet and tucked it under her arm. It was hot and humid in the tunnels, thanks to the previously boiling water. Nacho didn't want to get sidetracked into a bacon discussion, and apparently neither did Brie. "Scrubz, as an unbiased source, do you think we should try for the credits and the Weapon of Weaponry?"

The unknown-classed-grump nodded instantly. "Yeah. I mean, we're down here anyway. Two hours of Active Combat is going to be brutal, though."

"It is, and we don't *need* to do it," Nacho agreed, deciding to take control of the conversation. "Once we start, we'll cycle fresh warriors up to the front line and bring the tired ones back to catch their breath. We have to keep moving the entire time. We'll have an alpha team, led by Brie, who will engage the first line of monsters. The beta team, led by Abby, will charge forward once those initial monsters are killed. I'll keep everyone fed; I have a recipe for peanut butter balls I can cook up if we need them."

"You meant to tell me that *we're* gonna fight while you just... cook?" Scrubz must have been practicing his sneer, judging by how good he was getting at it.

"Brie hits things. You?" Nacho shot him with a finger gun, which turned into a 'who knows' gesture, then he pointed around the group. "Reuben heals. Taye shoots. I feed people so that they can use their skills for the required *two full hours* of combat. Get that chip off your shoulder. On that note, does anyone else have a healing ability?"

"Only our natural Regen," Taye stated with a wince, as everyone else made agreeing noises. "Which... won't be working."

"Correct. Got that, *Scrubz*?" Nacho got a few chuckles at that, and the tension dropped a notch. He knew that not getting a break to heal made this dungeon run all the more dangerous, and they needed to be ready for it. "If anyone gets too hurt and they don't get back to Reuben for Healing Hugs, they are *not* to continue into combat. The bonuses aren't worth anyone dying during this dungeon run. Agreed?"

Scrubz still kept his sword sheathed as though it was a weapon of last resort instead of an item he needed ready at all times down here. "Fine. Me and Eduardo will lead the gamma team. Alpha, beta, gamma, like the frat houses, right?"

Nacho winced, then reluctantly nodded. "That's... like the Greek alphabet, but, yes."

"Eduardo's going to chonk it up on gamma." Reuben's face glowed with a smile. "Now, that's a good tagline. Eduardo, how about you wear the Ring of Cheese if you're gonna take my role as a tank? Scrubz, you can wear my gauntlets if you want."

Reuben handed Eduardo the ring, but when the guy tried it on, he shook his head. "No, the System says it's yours, and you'd have to transfer it over to me permanently, and it wouldn't work for you anymore. Thanks for the offer, though."

Nacho had figured that would happen. There were some magic items that could be used by multiple people at once, but once a player claimed an item, it was almost always exclusively theirs until they gave it up forever or Tiered up and handed it off to someone else.

Scrubz tried the gauntlets, looking dejected when they didn't work. "I really hoped I could use these."

"It's okay, Scrubz. We'll find you a super cool item down here in the Barbeque Tunnels," Reuben promised with a manly arm slap. "Don't you worry one bit."

Ever insightful, Taye asked the question that had been plaguing Nacho. "What's the verdict? Are the Barbeque Tunnels part of the UnderFun?"

Nacho swished his leg through the water and let out a deep groan. "I don't think so, but I'm hoping they *lead* to the Under-Fun. We are deep, and this feels right. But we won't know until we run through 'em."

"So let's get running," Scrubz offered, making Nacho tense once more. Scrubz volunteering for work felt... unnatural.

Kristie's eyes glowed a light pink. "Hold up, Scrubz. I'm checking on potions that might give us Mana, since it's going to be an issue once we start. Us spellcasters can drink water and

Juxta-ade, or root beer if you're Reuben, but we won't have a way of regenerating our Mana."

Nacho knew what she would find and hid a grin as her eyes lit up when she found the item… then the shift into horror when she read the associated cost.

"Ouch!" The pink Warlock winced. "The Mana Potions are crazy expensive, but they're not a class item. Guys… it takes a thousand credits to restore *ten* points of Mana. I don't think we should buy them. I guess for this dungeon run, we'll have to rely on our Body Players."

Kristie and Hazel, as well as some of the other spellcasters of the group, had a mixture of relief and disappointment on their faces.

Brie didn't spare the shirkers a glance. She simply motioned everyone forward, taking the alpha team through the left tunnel. To everyone's relief they soon encountered a ledge that allowed them to escape the water. It was a good thing. Almost at the same time, Tier zero shrimp monsters came splashing up at them, a hefty number of them in this colony alone.

Nacho was up front, just behind the main row of fighters as the grind began.

Hey, Player, welcome to Active Combat! We'll run a timer on you, since the Barbeque Tunnels have their own special specialness. No Store access and no Regens. Better be packing a Healer! If you didn't buy the Potions of Mana Replenishment, it's too late now!

"Ignore the message; they're just messing with us," Nacho informed a crestfallen Kristie. He and Reuben scrambled onto the ledge, and Nacho dropped his pack. He raised his cleaver and his skillet slightly just in case any of the monsters thought that the cook would be an easier target. Abby and the beta team stood back, taking pot shots at monsters but letting Brie and the alpha team do most of the killing.

The shrimp monsters looked like classic shrimp, except that their legs were far longer, and they wore steel boots with spiked toes and hooked heels. Their antennae acted like whips.

A System View of them showed that they were referred to as 'Ironically Booted Shrimp', or IBS. In Nacho's mind, that took them off the menu. That practically shouted that they would make the team sick, no matter how he cooked them.

Brie used her Defensive Whirl and Combat Dash liberally, because these things were only Tier zero and she had two other teams to relieve her. With no Mana requirement, she could simply eat and be combat effective again in moments. Still, two hours of Active Combat was going to be a grind. While Brie smashed, one of the other guys Scrubz had suggested backed her up with his bow.

Nacho decided to take the opportunity to look the other party members over. It was hard to ignore them for so long, and it was important to have a good relationship when they were going to be in close contact for a long time. Alonzo was an older bald guy, a standard Warrior, who was proving without a doubt that he wasn't a very good shot, though he *was* pretty good with his mass-produced Costco-branded sword. Linda was a spell-caster that helped out the alpha team. She threw standard blue magic missiles when the occasional monster was tough to take down, but knowing that there was no way to regenerate the Mana she was using, she didn't cast too many of them.

That was the main drawback of that class archetype. Spell-casters could drink water to get their Thirst levels up, but with every spell, they were using precious Mana that couldn't be replenished until combat ended—at least without potions. Nacho winced and glared when a Warrior got slashed by a giant shrimp antennae. The man tottered back to Reuben, who healed him with a single hug.

Reuben had thirty-one Mana Points, and every heal would take away ten percent of his total Mana. That meant he could only take care of nine major wounds, and they were already down one with combat barely started. That was the bad news.

The good news? He was replenishing a whopping *forty* Health with each hug.

The sounds of the battle were fierce, so Nacho had to yell above the din. "Reuben, most of our people only have around thirty Health, and I hate saying this, but we're going to have to wait until they're seriously hurt to heal them. You only have a few heals left. We need to make them count."

"No Positive Vibes for these bros," Reuben sighed dramatically and seemed to be contemplating something. "Is this worth it? The bonus?"

"For the credits? Maybe not. But for this weapon…? *Maybe.* Depending on what it is. We've all seen how important base damage is. It's why Brie's not leveling yet. Buying something enchanted enough to replace it is gonna be rough." Nacho spotted the pink blur of a shrimp swimming through the water, and before he knew it, he'd slammed a cleaver into the creature's head as it launched itself out of the water. Twice. His whack-whack combo, thanks to the HungerCry knives magic, hit with eight damage each. "Feisty little guy, aren't you?"

Damage Dealt: 16/26!

Brie only had to hit them twice to fully end them, inadvertently showcasing how important Skills like Positive Vibes and Combat Dash were. Without them, she was only doing twenty-three points of damage, and that was mostly because of the extra ninety percent that was added to her Fitness from eating more of Nacho's upgraded oatmeal. Nacho was grateful that her total Health was at sixty-four because of the tweak to her Fitness, but was it going to be possible to keep this up for two hours? Even *he* was already having second thoughts.

When Abby and Taye led the beta team through to wipe out the last of the shrimp, they splashed onward to fight the next batch of baddies: Burnt Enders.

Abby headed the assault by bashing through cubed meat that was smoking and sending intermittent blasts of flame at them. Taye used an exploding arrow and got lucky enough to land it among a huge group that was attempting to attack, scattering shredded beef across the area.

Reuben focused on running triage, asking people how much Health they had—what their maximum was, and where they would be once Nacho's Cooking Magic wore off. A few people had lost half their Health, but a single reminder from Nacho was all it took to make Reuben hold off on healing them in case someone needed the help more than they did in the near future.

Meanwhile, Nacho checked through his store of leftovers—he already knew he was going to have to make the Peanut Butter Power Breakfast Ball recipe during combat. It wouldn't be cooking exactly; just mixing the ingredients and rolling them up. Essentially, he was going to combine partial preexisting portions to a higher efficiency. "Ugh… gonna have to buy some Store hand sanitizer. My hands are gross with the filthy—abyss, no Store access in combat. Good thing my hands are perfectly clean. Hear that, anyone that's listening in? *Perfectly clean.*"

Once the beta team had wiped out most of the Burnt Enders, the gamma team hurried forward to act as cleanup. Before long, they moved into the next room where they engaged the hardest of the monsters so far: big boar men with crimson necks, wearing overalls and wielding rusted cleavers. They had vicious tusks, and while they stood on their hind legs, they were definitely more pig than man.

Someone claimed they were called Pigbillies, sending Reuben into near-hysterical laughter as Nacho sloshed into the chamber to watch the gamma team fight.

Scrubz immediately threw his spear, opting to use that over pulling out his sword. He found a patch of dry ground and got into position, hurling kicks and punches with abandon. Nacho took the opportunity to scan the chamber, noting that this cave offered piles of dirt and sand for them to fight on. Scrubz and

SEWER SKEWERS

his Cocktail Party took advantage of the high ground right away, and it was lucky they did.

The Pigbillies were Tier one monsters with low Health, so they weren't *impossible* to hit, just difficult. Scrubz quickly found that he could do more damage with his kicks than his fists, so he stopped throwing punches and focused on his feet. He moved through a surprising variety of kicks—ax, front, roundhouse, and others Nacho didn't have proper names for.

The cook did have to laugh as one thing became abundantly clear: Scrubz was a Warrior, but he must've been majorly into martial arts in his prior life in order to earn passive Skills in punching and kicking. In essence… he was a Monk, and Nacho was dying to use this knowledge to tease him relentlessly as needed. When Scrubz's foot struck a boar man, it resulted in an explosion of golden light, and the pig guy's head crumpled like a ball of wet paper towels.

Hazel, seemingly more of a support than anything else, tossed her shields up to protect Hank and some others while they fought the Pigbillies.

In the meantime, Nacho found a relatively secluded corner of dirt in the cavern and set up his mobile kitchen, setting to work on his peanut butter balls as he kept one eye focused on the aggressive creatures. He couldn't believe that he was able to calmly open up his cookbook and go through the recipes in the middle of a battle sequence.

Everyone else would fight, and Nacho would cook. Scrubz hadn't been wrong about how this would go; he was just a jerk.

The cook went over the ingredients, pulling them out one by one as he prepared everything that he needed. The most important step to take to boost a dish into a higher Rarity was to use a better material for at *least* the main ingredient, he was almost sure of it. In this case, he chose his secret stash of Rare chocolate chips. They were usually his secret vice, and he would regularly sneak a handful when no one was looking. For the sake of survival, he decided he would share today.

The cavern echoed with spell explosions, people screaming

231

for the Healer, pigs squealing in either rage or pain—it was total chaos. Then there was Nacho, hunkered down in a far corner, humming a tune and mixing ingredients, then rolling them into perfectly shaped balls. He added in his Cooking Magic to give them all a forty-five percent bonus to their stats, almost instantly finding himself running into the Mana problem. His Cooking Magic required ten percent of his Mana, as well as ten percent of his Hunger and Thirst Points.

They had food and water, but just like everyone else, he couldn't restore his Mana. Brie and the alpha team sprinted in just as he finished a round, grabbed the peanut butter balls that were settling in place, and chewed almost the instant the food was past their teeth. Brie gave him a friendly pat as she moved past him. "Those are good, but you used another ingredient that's hard to eat during combat—peanut butter is dry and sticks in your throat."

"Noted." Nacho couldn't keep the exasperation out of his voice, but she only chuckled at him.

"I know you'll eventually figure something out." She strode back into the fray as the biggest of the boar men advanced with a giant machete-like butcher knife. "Looks like in the land of pigs, the butcher is king."

Brie Combat Dashed forward and slammed her hammer right into the pig man's face. A glance at the timer informed Nacho that it had already been thirty minutes of constant fighting.

"We have a *long* hour and a half remaining to clear the rewards." He got back to work, grimly promising his team, "I'll make sure we don't need to do it on an empty stomach."

CHAPTER TWENTY-TWO

Out of all the things they fought in the Barbeque Tunnels—Pigbillies, the Burnt Enders, and the Ironic Booted Shrimp—the Smoked Sausage golems turned out to be the absolute wurst.

The enormous man-shaped creatures had been graced with arms and legs resembling swollen hot dogs cooked in the microwave too long. Their heads were pinched closed with a steel casing clip, leaving them faceless but apparently able to navigate via magic. Those steel clips were also bound around their wrists and ankles, and the golems used them as bludgeoning weapons—it didn't matter whether they threw punches, kicks, or head-butts; those casing clips *hurt* when they landed.

It was like being attacked by Oktoberfest food armed with bashing bracelets. Even more frustrating was the fact that they were mid-level Tier one monsters, so only Brie, Abby, and Taye could hit them and leave damage behind. More than ever, Nacho felt the need to spend the guild's credits to level people's Skills and push them all to Tier one.

Cooking would be more expensive but easier overall, because then Nacho could cook for a single Tier all at once, and not need to split recipes between Tier ones and Tier zeros. The dichotomy had made meal prep a logistical nightmare, since food with Tier zero ingredients didn't help with a Tier one's Hunger Points, and the Tier zeros wouldn't get any additional benefit of eating Tier one ingredients; the only thing they would see was a higher price tag.

When they fought an oversized sausage golem that was level eighteen, Nacho was on his tenth and last round of peanut butter balls and completely out of Mana. Naturally, the boss sausage was a named monster: the Kill Basa.

It was eight hundred pounds of murderous meat shoved into a sausage casing. The only positive was that they fought him in a dry place, a platform where the swamp water ran by in channels on either side. The continually cloudy liquid poured off the edge of the platform in twin waterfalls, and a rusted metal ladder descended into darkness between the identical cascades of gushing water. It seemed they'd reached the end of the Barbeque Tunnels, but they hadn't hit the two-hour mark yet.

"Seems we sped through the dungeon too fast." Reuben had left his humor in the tunnel about twenty minutes ago, when exhaustion had settled into his bones. "Gotta... drag this out somehow."

On the platform, hooks at the ends of various chains dangled from the ceiling, giving the area a part butcher shop, part horror movie vibe. The Kill Basa had an uncanny way of slipping through the hooks without getting caught, but the attackers were having a significantly more difficult time maneuvering. Since so many of the fighters couldn't be active damage dealers, a few folks were on hacksaw duty, cutting through the links and clearing a path for their Tiered up members.

Scrubz led the chain-cutting crew—his idea—while Brie was a dynamo of Defensive Whirl and Combat Dash as she cut off the monster from squirming through every hole it could find in their formation. Abby's only job was only to smack around the giant hot dog with her Bad Bash, and she was forced to take a few hits. The reduced damage effect of her Slippery Block was the only reason she was still standing after the second hit, and Nacho could see that she was hesitant to get back in the mix.

Meanwhile, Taye stood back in his leathers, powered by Nacho's peanut butter balls. He fired his double-damage arrows, dealing *quad*-damage, thanks to slowing his aim and using Eagle Eye to pierce the sausage golem's pinched-off head over and over.

"Nacho! I'm getting *hungry*!" Brie called out with great concern in her voice.

"Ayy, I'm working here!" Nacho shouted in his best Italian accent. His Firefly Potstickers were winging around him, giving him plenty of light to finish his last batch of food. He rolled the last peanut butter ball and scraped his bowl, hoping that he could make at least one or two more. "Need a runner!"

"On it!" Reuben grabbed Nacho's balls and sped into the danger zone. He managed to dodge the first of the sausage golem's kicks, but took a casing clip to the face. There was already a stench around him that left the air stinking like a cheese factory in August, but he'd finally pushed the Ring of Cheese too far. Blood gushed down his face, and he staggered and fell to a knee. As he dropped, he shoved the bowl and sent it clattering across the stone floor.

Brie knelt, grabbed a peanut butter ball, and popped it into her mouth, trying not to spare too much concern for her damaged husband. If she lost focus, they *all* died.

As the Berserker gulped down the dry protein ball, Abby got hammered by the Kill Basa and went flying. Brie had just enough time to chew and swallow—she'd had her water bottle ready to help get the sticky treat down. Taking a fresh grip on her hammer, she went dashing past Abby as the fighter impacted the ground and bounced.

Another arrow struck the monster in its pinched head, staggering it. Taye shouted above the ruckus, "Hold up! The Kill Basa is down to twenty Health. We have five more minutes to the two-hour mark; we just have to keep this thing busy for just. *Five. Minutes.*"

"That's going to be tough; I want it dead." Reuben scurried out of the meat-eor of a foot as it tried to stomp on him. The monster strode over almost calmly, driving a casing-clipped fist into Abby, who tumbled dangerously close to the murky water running in a torrent down a stone channel against the wall. "Abby!"

Brie went racing in, but she didn't hit the boss. All of them knew that a single hit would take it out easily, but they had to wait. She did use her Defensive Whirl to block two of the thing's punches, making it hiss in frustration. At least… steam escaped from the places its casings joined together. It sounded like *frustrated* steam, even if the cook couldn't figure out a way to make that sound right in his head.

Nacho organized the troops from the rear, seeing that all of Brie's attention was on keeping the Kill Basa occupied. "Taye, save your arrows. Reuben, I don't know how bad you're hurt, but heal Abby if you're able. Everyone who has some Health to spare, take a turn in the ring with the Kill Basa!"

"I was totally thinking the boss would be named Frank N' Stein." Reuben was already on his feet, heading towards Abby, his retort coming out with near-no enthusiasm. "Meat and beer combo attacks. Best wurst case."

Nacho plucked his skillet shield off his back, knowing that it was time to get in the mix. He had done his job, and now it was time to cycle through. The sausage boss brought his steel clip down on the shield, and even with redirecting the force, Nacho took most of the blow and felt his arm crack. "Ahh! This thing is *nasty*!"

Damage taken: 29/50 health remains!

.   .   .

Nacho had given away every last bite of his magic food, so he didn't have any bonuses going for him. With a Fitness of twenty, he thankfully had fifty Health and the mentality needed to push through the pain. He could take one more blow before pulling back, but he was rare among his group.

Almost the entirety of the Brunch Force were still Tier zero players with only around thirty Health Points. Two Kill Basa blows *would* kill them, forcing them to retreat if they even got grazed. Abby popped back into combat in the next moment, healed up and whirling her ironbound staff. She prodded the Kill Basa with one end to get its attention, sending it stumbling back into the hooks. "Looks like you got a little *behind* in your work!"

She backed up when the thing raced after her, grabbing a dangling hook and using it to swing in an arc to evade its furious blows.

Hazel stepped to the front of the line and took a turn. As a spellcaster, she had stayed back for most of the combat through the tunnels, though she had tossed a few of her purple grenades to take out bunches of monsters at a time. She deployed her purple shield and hunkered down, and it crackled as she took repeated Kill Basa blows.

"Only a little longer!" Taye called out as Hank rushed forward with a yell, only to take a casing clip to the face and drop right under the boss's feet.

"*Hank!*" Hazel screamed, charging in with no shields to protect her. She joined her husband on the floor, and Nacho plowed forward, skillet held high. He could only do a little over ten damage with the oversized frying pan, but that didn't matter. He couldn't pierce the thing's thick sausage casing skin, and happily, he didn't *need* to hurt it. Nacho just needed to draw the Kill Basa's attention, and slamming ten pounds of metal into its version of a kneecap did the trick.

Scrubz joined him and threw a roundhouse kick, only to have his foot rebound from the impact. "Kind of like working the heavy bag."

Neither did any damage, but it gave others enough time to pull Hank and Hazel away, dragging them behind the line just in time for Nacho to get creamed again. He took a casing clip to his pot helmet, flipping into the air and flying through dozens of chains while the hooks tried to tear him to shreds.

"Do it now! End it!" Taye bellowed the excellent news. "We're all clear! We've spent two hours in Active Combat; take that thing down!"

Brie dashed between Nacho and Scrubz with a triumphant Berserker's yell to bring her hammer down into the belly of the monster. The torso casing burst, arms and legs went flying, and pieces of the stuffed central hot dog went everywhere. The entire party had to actively dodge the massive explosion of raw sausage, and after the last scraps splattered to the ground, Brie was left standing alone, huffing and puffing. "At the end there… I wasn't afraid of the Kill Basa getting me. I thought I was going to choke to death on peanut butter."

Silence filled the chamber for a long moment, then everyone started to laugh and collapse to the ground.

Congratulations, Player!

Active Combat is over! You get to shop, and you get your Regens back. We can almost hear the Mana and Health being replenished—kinda like the sound of a fairy getting her wings waxed.

Congratulations +1 bonus! You have completed the Barbeque Tunnels! Nice job taking out the Kill Basa! Everyone that was present gets ten thousand credits!

Congratulations +2 bonus! Special Bonus Complete! Barbeque bonuses means there's something for everyone! Everyone in this temporary party gets the credits, but only one person has earned the Weapon of Weaponry! Calculating the damage dealt and assigning a special reward to that player!

Reuben was busy healing his broken nose and bruised face, but it was taking a moment and making his voice sound a little off.

"It's quite the payday, and we all get a nice chunk of change. I was thinking we'd have to back off and divide the cash among the twenty of us. That was probably the longest two hours of my life."

Nacho agreed, though like everything with the Patrons, he was cautiously optimistic; in this case, more cautious than optimistic. One person being assigned a weapon did not mean that it was going to be worth having, or even usable by that person. It could be that the weapon would do nothing at all, or provide no bonuses. The Patrons sometimes raised players' hopes just to dash them.

The sound of a slot machine hitting a jackpot filled their ears as the *cha-ching* of the money hitting their accounts rang out. Every one of them was instantly nine thousand credits richer.

"*Taxes*? We had to pay *taxes* on a bonus?" Scrubz shouted in frustration, mirrored by the grumbling of his small faction. "What's the weapon? We can't decide who gets it until we know what it is!"

The Patrons certainly weren't going to answer that when there was so much delicious tension building.

"Guys. We just stopped fighting. Let's not get all worked up." Reuben found a steel casing and lifted it up. "Hey, these are magical... they're Sausage Clips of Striking? Oh, nice! A Tier one item! They help with punching. Scrubz, how about I take the Sausage Clips of Striking and give you my Gauntlets of Monster Destruction? After that exhibition, I'm assuming you're some kind of warrior monk?"

"I'm... something like that." Scrubz hadn't hidden the look of disgust on his face. "You're just trying to buy me off. What if *I* want the Weapon of Weaponry? What if one of my people do?"

"*Our* people, Scrubz. We're all in this together." Nacho squeezed his eyes shut, trying to sort through his emotions without going wild. He'd taken a nasty hit, and that was messing with him, but he needed to keep things calm.

Taking a deep breath before speaking again, Nacho found himself interrupted by Hank, who was leaning heavily on his wife. "Y'all are crazy. Brie is going to get the weapon, or Abby is. They were the ones who took the lead over and over again. The rest of us only got put at risk when we *needed* to do it."

That was true, and it ended the argument with no further complaints. Even though the Gamma Team took their fair share of lumps in the Barbeque Tunnels, the Alpha and Beta teams had undeniably done all of the heavy lifting.

Hazel also had something to say about the situation, and though she looked woozy and determined, the pain in her eyes was fading by the second. Perfect regeneration when not in combat meant she was healing nicely. "Brie should get the new weapon so she can level up to Tier one and donate her Tier zero hammer to someone else. That would give us another *two* actually-combat-effective people instead of just one."

"I agree with this assessment." Abby shook her staff, then screamed at the ceiling. "Hey, you Patron potato heads! Give Brie the Weapon of Weaponry!"

Other people joined in the shouting, and soon they were all shouting and chanting Brie's name. Scrubz relented and waved down the crowd before things took an ugly turn. "Fine! Brie gets the weapon!"

"Okay, let's-" Nacho paused as a hand grabbed him. He looked over at Brie, who was shaking her head. "Listen up, everyone. Next person that interrupts me gets stabbed. Enough of this."

"Sorry, Nacho. I had a good reason." Brie's eyelids fluttered and her face lost all expression. "If I'm gonna get the weapon, I want it to be Tier one. That means I have to be Tier one... so I'm going to pay for the upgrade. Level ten, here I come, and everyone else better look away."

Every single person locked their eyes on her, curious to observe what Tiering up would look like. Brie's head drooped, and she whispered softly, "You've gotta be... abyss, I hate all of you."

CHAPTER TWENTY-THREE

Only a few people had ever seen someone reach Tier one, and it was always a spectacular display. Brie didn't end up screaming in pain or doing anything too wild. She tied her hands over her mouth, and that blocked almost everything. Even so, she winced at the pain, grunting a few times as her joints lit up, and turned pink with embarrassment as she was blasted a few feet off the ground when her Mana barrier sprang into existence.

It looked like a wild, flaming aura spreading across her skin that faded into her body an instant later. Somehow, everyone still knew that it was *right there* waiting to block anything they could throw at her. After officially reaching the higher tier, Brie stood and raised her hand as the System informed them that yes, they had been correct in their assumption. She had dealt the most damage while clearing the dungeon.

A long black wooden handle with a beautiful gold inlay appeared, the rest of the weapon materializing as golden particles coalesced… and finally revealing itself as a lacrosse stick. The hoop appeared to be made of actual gold, while the netting was a black metal mesh. An odd embossed face with a mustache and monocle decorated the top of the hoop, giving the impression that anything put in the net was going into the figure's mouth.

"They gave me a message that I could literally have anything I wanted as a weapon. I chose what I'm the absolute best at, so I got a lacrosse stick." She carelessly let her hammer drop to the ground as she whipped the stick through the air admiringly.

"Milley!" Reuben called softly, hand outstretched to the cast-aside mallet.

Brie pulled a ball of glowing white energy out of thin air and tossed it up, catching the orb of radiance in her net and flinging the ball into the wall. It exploded on impact, filling the platform with dust and bits of shrapnel. "Before you ask, I can't just throw any kind of ball. It has to be one of these, and they aren't cheap."

"Then why did you waste one on showing off?" Scrubz called out as he grabbed the fallen hammer and started dragging it to the large crowd to find it a new owner.

"I can buy a ten pack for four hundred. They're expensive, but the explosions do the same damage as me hitting the target directly." The Tier one Berserker ignored the annoyed retort of her obnoxious party member, "Now, I *finally* have a ranged weapon. I'm up from twenty to thirty, and that's just the base damage of Mr. Lacrosse Stick. That's the... they named it."

"I bet it was you, and now you're just having buyers' regret." Scrubz's attitude finally seemed to get to her, and she turned and brandished her new weapon at him.

"Sorry, Scrubz. I can't hear your negativity." She twirled her stick and slammed the end down in an impressive display of control. "I'm going ahead. Stay fresh, cheese bags."

"You *did* it!" Reuben had tossed Scrubz his Gauntlets of Monster Destruction aside as he tried to clean off the casing clips that were covered with raw Kill Basa sausage innards. He had gone completely still mid-task, and now he was staring at his wife and clapping his hands in overdone excitement. "You made your catchphrase!"

"No, I was trying to casually insult you guys-" she tried to say, only for Nacho to join in on Reuben's side.

"He has a point; that was pretty smooth. 'Stay fresh, cheese bags'? I love it." The cook shot her a reassuring grin, then had a great idea. "You know, I'd have to spend some credits to upgrade my Ingredient Processing, but then I could process this monster, though he's basically sausage already. I'm getting Mana back, and I should be able to carve out a breakfast for dinner. Anyone up for biscuits and gravy?"

"Eating a monster... made of animated processed meat." Abby hammered Nacho on the back. "Great idea! We could all use a minute to gather ourselves while you do that. I don't know about the rest of them, but I'd like a good ol' fashioned ponder on how we're all going to spend that money."

"You guys are ridiculous. Fine, you *want* me to call you 'cheese bags' long term? Fine. *Fine.*" Brie swept her new Weapon of Weaponry through the air. "I don't want to eat up here, so let's at least get down the ladder first."

"Hmm." Reuben watched her move, tapping the now-nearly-clean clips together as he thought. "Something tells me it *isn't* fine, but that's way too good of a phrase to give up. I'll work on her. If I could convince her to marry me, I feel like something like this should be easy."

"Ah, yes, pleading and cajoling: the Reuben special. Have at it." Waving his best friend off encouragingly, Nacho took a peek at the defeated boss, finding that the Kill Basa was a level nineteen monster. He shook his head at the discovery; even the Bove would have only been ground beef in front of this thing. "We... probably should have died fighting this, if I'm being honest."

The only reason they hadn't that he could think of was that their main damage dealer had been carrying a boost of ninety percent to her base stats. That put her at least on par, if not higher, than a standard person at Tier *two* while she had been fighting the massive golem. The power scaling was incredible, even more so because they were managing so wonderfully against higher tier creatures. Nacho swore to himself as he realized he would have to bring his Ingredient Processing skill up to Tier one, level seven and succeed in processing the abomination.

One thousand, two hundred, and forty credits out of his bonus was easier to spend with the knowledge that he'd earn some of those credits back after he processed the meat. It was a race against his own Mana Regen, as well as his skills in actively processing the sausage before it turned to goo. With everything prepared, he dove in.

Nacho set up his kitchen near the back entrance where they'd come in and quickly got to chopping. Working as fast and efficiently as possible, he still only got through ten rounds of Ingredient Processing before the rest disintegrated. He couldn't feel too disappointed, however, due to the fact that it earned him back three hundred and eighty credits, as well as about fifty pounds of raw sausage. He stuck it away in a Storage Slot—the ultimate in food storage. He *could* stow the meat while it still contained Putrid Mana, but that didn't slow its degradation. He'd opened his slots before only to be met with pungent black goo, and he had learned his lesson by now.

Most of the party was okay when it came to their hunger, seeing as they hadn't been too active throughout the entire slog. Those who needed to top off were given some rations, and soon everyone was ready to descend the ladder. Eduardo was the final winner of Brie's old hammer, and they were all glad to have another person ready for frontline fighting duty, even if it was a little strange to see the weapon in someone else's hands. The fighter especially seemed happy to be able to deal some real damage, and he held his new tool as though someone was going to try to take it from him.

There was some discussion around Reuben upgrading his class to enable him to use the Sausage Clips of Striking, and eventually the Healer took the initiative and spent his own money to make it happen. Nobody blamed him: they were a Tier one magic item, after all. As soon as he could equip them, they shrank to fit but otherwise didn't change in appearance.

They weren't cool vambraces, and they didn't even look like bracelets. No, they were unmistakably hot dog bangles.

Reuben *loved* the fact that they remained the same. Between his janky new weapon and his bizarrely-shaped leather Helm of Helming that had decided to upgrade itself to stay with the Healer, he certainly wasn't going to get any prizes for fashion. "Even the Ring of Cheese is still usable! I hit the jackpot!"

Brie, his counterpart in all things, was the complete opposite. She wanted black and gold armor to match her lacrosse stick, but for the time being, she'd have to live with the fact that her new weapon clashed with her silver Sabatons of Lower Half Protection, her glittering chainmail, and her helmet. It was a greatly displeasing discrepancy for her, and it took all her willpower not to bite someone's head off when they brought up the fact that the armor wouldn't even work for her anymore.

Once everyone in the Brunch Force was healed up, Brie led the way down the ladder, sans armor, which she had handed off to someone else. Scrubz waited patiently as the others descended, wearing the gauntlets Reuben had tossed to him after equipping his new bangles. Nacho cocked an eyebrow at the man as he waited for the cook to start climbing. "You ever going to tell us about your class and skills?"

The tax-hating-yet-somehow-charismatic reformed complainer shrugged. "Maybe. But I don't want anyone using that information against me, so I'm going to be careful who I share it with."

"Here's the deal." Nacho decided to be forthright with the guy. "We've been together for four months. No one's gunning for you, Scrubz. We're working together, and frankly Reuben didn't have to give you the gauntlets. We've liked seeing your progress, and we want to facilitate that. Gonna be hard to do if you won't trust us enough to open up even this much."

It seemed uncharacteristically shy, but Scrubz smiled. "Maybe you're right. Eduardo is going to kill it with that hammer. What 'it' is, I don't know, but I figure he's going to kill 'it' dead for sure. So that's cool. You go first. I've got your back."

"I'd like to have yours." Nacho paused before reaching for the ladder. "If your plan was to murder-hobo your way through the Juxtaposition, you're in the wrong guild. You know that, right?"

Scrubz let out a laugh that didn't sound very happy. "I know. If we really thought you people were gonna get us killed, me and Old Bill would've left a long time ago. We believe in what you're doing. It's just... we're not going to follow along blindly, and we're going to call out anyone that we think is doing anything unfair. Now, let's just get down the ladder and see if we can find a way into the UnderFun before someone thinks we're up here fighting."

"Gotta hope for the *Downtown* UnderFun," Nacho corrected as he carefully laid on his belly and eased himself over the edge. His first foot found the top rung—it seemed to be made from rough metal rebar pounded into the rock. The mist from the water falling made them slick, but the rough swirls in the metal still allowed him to get some good traction.

Nacho started down, the water falling on either side of him. The downpour was wet and definitely smelled like garbage water, but the torrent wasn't hitting him directly. That would've torn him right off the ladder, so he was thankful. His big mobile kitchen backpack *creaked* behind and slightly above him, and he was glad for the cover. Especially since his mobile kitchen was waterproof. The bulky bag unexpectedly allowed him to just enjoy the view and the peace of the moment.

The drop was unnerving; it was a good five hundred feet down the ladder to the ground below. People were going slow, being careful not to fall, which made the descent even harder for anyone that hadn't invested in Fitness. Nacho eventually forced himself to stop looking below and just focus on moving down one rung at a time. He certainly wasn't going to look *up*. Scrubz was above him, and the view wasn't flattering. "Gonna need him to invest in multiple pairs of underwear. Flipping one inside out when it gets dirty doesn't work when you use it for four months straight... nah, I bet he'll think it's a pointless expense."

The deeper Nacho climbed, the more water splashed down on him. A few times, he was forced to grit his teeth and hang on for dear life when a breeze reoriented the streams of water. When he finally got close to the ground, Reuben hustled forward and helped him off, holding up his backpack so he wouldn't catch on anything. They moved back from the ladder and the waterfalls as Scrubz came off the rungs, the final member of the Brunch Force to reach the bottom.

Nacho's Firefly Potstickers buzzed overhead, granting them light. They were standing on soaked asphalt, definitely a modern Earth road with white lines in the middle and yellow on the edges. On either side ran sidewalks, gutters, and drains—the waterfalls above were running directly into Kansas City's old drainage system. Reuben shook his head at the thought, "A river draining into a sewer, turning into a river, then a sewer. How far does it go? Maybe *everything* is sewers and rivers, all the way up, and all the way down."

"How about you keep your cuckoo-banana-pants philosophy to yourself, huh?" Scrubz growled as they started traveling down a shattered tunnel. The walls were full of hunks of concrete, exposed rebar, and literal tons of crumbled bricks. It must've been one of the underpass tunnels of the freeway. Nacho didn't recognize which one, but he knew for a fact that they'd never been closer to the Downtown UnderFun.

Pausing for a moment, Nacho took off his mobile kitchen to rest his shoulders. "Once I hit level fifteen, my Fitness will increase again, and that backpack will feel like a feather."

"Until then, we appreciate you keeping all complaints to yourself." Brie slapped him on the arm, nearly sending him staggering to the floor. He glanced at the massive smile on her face, then to the reason it existed: the lacrosse stick she had access to once more. "Taye, Abby, and Kristie are running recon. We think we might be close to the UnderFun."

It wasn't five minutes before the scouts came hurrying back out of the tunnel, Taye looking anxious and overwhelmed. "I found it...! Sorry, *we* found it. But it's strange. I mean, I knew we were deep. First the spiral staircase, the downward slope in the Barbeque Tunnels, and then that ladder. But... maybe you should just come and look for yourselves."

Nacho hurriedly shouldered his mobile kitchen and shuffled forward, Reuben and Brie flanking him. While he'd assumed that the tunnel was created from debris, it turned out it was at least somewhat natural. He traced the damp stone as he walked across the asphalt and wondered at the power of the Patrons. This was an especially odd mixture of rock and building.

Kristie's bracelets, Chris's katana, one of the guys in Scrubz's group that seemed to be covered in bioluminescent algae, and Nacho's Firefly Potstickers lit their way as they walked down the paved street. The asphalt ended in a precise line as if cut by the world's biggest circular saw, right at the edge of a rounded archway that had clearly been fashioned by the Patrons.

Nacho was treated to a view of the Downtown UnderFun that made his jaw drop. Torchlight flickered in some of the buildings of what had been Kansas City. Yes, there were buildings, but only about the first six or seven floors. The tops were lost in rock. It wasn't the entire downtown, just the buildings around the convention center. Nacho immediately recognized the Marriott and some familiar shops. To his right, in the distance, rose the yellowish façade of city hall and the court building.

"That must be what's left of the Power and Light district." Brie gestured toward a few of the streetlights that burned with an eerie green fire. It wasn't electricity, but rather a magical fire. Cars were scattered around the streets. There were buses and fallen streetcars as well, but no bodies. It was a stark reminder that every single person on Earth had been snatched up and either put in a waiting area to age in—babies, kids, and elderly people—or were sent directly to the Evaluation World.

Shadowy monsters with the gait of dogs haunted the streets. Their slinking forms sent a chill down Nacho's back. How many dogs had been in Kansas City during the Juxtaposition? Dogs? Cats? Rats? *All* of them were in the process of being altered by the Putrid Mana. A few birds—maybe bats—flitted through the air, disappearing into the broken windows of the buildings.

A beat later, the System had a message for them.

Welcome, Players, to the Downtown UnderFun. Technically, this is the Downtown Kansas City UnderFun, or the DKCU. We know why you're here, and we have to warn you that the DKCU isn't just one dungeon. It's many, many dungeons. Each one has pluses (treasure, bonus credits, ancient artifacts, and a cool post-apocalyptic feel), as well as minuses (monsters, death, screaming, sorrow).

Have fun exploring what's left of Kansas City!

Good luck on your quest for the Dragon Spear! You're in first place, but you're not alone—other guilds are on their way! In fact, they're right behind you! AHH! Right there!

Made ya look.

Nacho couldn't help but be disappointed at the message. It was true that other guilds would be on their way. If nothing else, Crave and Kala had been given some kind of information that they'd use to make their way here. Even if they hadn't gotten good information, they'd check the Bove's Lair, maybe find their tracks, and they'd come. He hadn't *seen* anyone following them, but both guilds had acquired stealth players, and he immediately began kicking himself for leaving behind a very visible trail.

Myron could move unseen, and Crave himself had Assassin abilities. It was naïve to think they wouldn't be using them. Reuben brought him back to the present by breathing out a single word, before waxing eloquent as though his marketing

Skill had taken over. "*Wow.* It's a giant underground cavern filled with the leftovers of our world."

Scrubz strolled up and laughed, though the sound didn't relay amusement. It was almost maniacal. "Anyone else having a slight breakdown moment? I mean, we were on Earth the entire time, and I *still* didn't see this coming. It's crazy."

"'Crazy' is a good word to describe all this," Reuben agreed easily. "Not one dungeon, but a ton? We're going to have a lot of ground to cover... I'd imagine we should split up. But first, we need to spend our credits, level, and rest up."

"Then a sausage party!" Nacho's cheerful words garnered only silence and strange looks. "Why are you all looking at me like that? We have a ton of sausage to cook up from the Kill Basa."

"You know what you said, Nacho." Reuben stage-whispered, breaking the awkward silence with laughter that the others joined in on to tease the cook.

Nacho let a smile play across his lips as he surveyed the area. He could see a trail leading down the debris to a hotel's courtyard, a Residence Inn, if he wasn't mistaken. It would likely still have a grill area, rooms to sleep in, and there might still be snacks in the lobby. Half the structure was buried in stone, and Nacho was curious to see what some of those rooms looked like. Were they completely invaded with stone, or was the rock simply layered onto the roof? "Let's head down there and take stock of things."

"Glad I Tiered up." Reuben jangled his new bracelets. "I want to see what kind of damage I can do with my new magic items."

Brie pulled her husband close, giving him a compliment as well as something to think about. "My sweet love... I'm okay with you looking like a homeless warrior at Tier zero. Even Tier one. But by the time you hit Tier two, you're going to get a complete makeover. You can't be trusted to dress yourself."

"Oh, come on! I don't think-" He started, only for her to cut off the complaint with a kiss.

She smiled and tapped his Helm of Helming. "Just think of marketing yourself properly, so that your wife doesn't need to go looking off-brand to find what she wants."

With a wink, Brie turned and sauntered off, leaving Reuben actively reconsidering his current attire.

CHAPTER TWENTY-FOUR

The Dinner Party portion of the Brunch Force raid group led the others down a trail of rubble that connected the entrance to the DKCU to the nearest street, which was as specific as they could be. Currently, it seemed that any street signs which had once stood in the area had now been intentionally ripped out. Luckily, the trio had spent so much time downtown that they had a good understanding of where they were at, even with the Patron's alterations.

Walking through the underground city was surreal. Even though shadows were darting through alleys, howls came from the distance, and blood-curdling screams erupted from the sluiceway, none of the monsters attacked them as they covered the distance to the hotel that was their target. As the ambient sounds reached a crescendo, Nacho made a startling realization.

He couldn't *wait* to explore this place.

The cook was unconsciously sharpening his knives on each other in preparation for finding new and improved ingredients to make extravagant meals with. Swiping his arm across his mouth, Nacho cleared away the accumulated drool and hoped that no one had seen his instinctive reaction. It wasn't long before they were standing in front of the Residence Inn's glass doors, and as expected, the lobby was dark.

Reuben walked forward and waved his hands in front of the sliding glass door. "I never thought I'd see a Marriott that looked so dungeon-y. No electricity, no happy skeleton behind the desk to buzz me in. You'd think the Marriott corporation would throw us a bone here. I mean, it's *just* the end of the world; are you really gonna let that impact the bottom line?"

While everyone stood around being nervous, not sure if they should make a choice, Brie was more decisive. She strode forward and smashed in the glass of the door with Mr. Lacrosse Stick, then crunched across the glass with her weapon raised and ready to strike at any sharp teeth that appeared from the shadowy corners of the lobby. "No 'welcome to the dungeon' messages... hello? Anyone there? ...Any *thing* there?"

A few of the Firefly Potstickers buzzed in with her at Nacho's direction, showing proof positive that nothing was in the area to answer Brie's call. Nacho was certain that he wasn't the only one that thought that was a good thing.

Light filtered in from the central courtyard through the elegant glass windows, granting the enhanced humans all of the visibility they needed in order to secure the area. *Most* of the Brunch Force was still cautious as they shuffled inside, though Reuben casually strolled into the little pantry area and tossed Nacho a granola bar. "Here. A treat from the before-fore times."

Looking at the yellow and green packaging seemed surreal, but that didn't bother the cook. "Reuben, we can't even *pretend* that people aren't going to be doing that in a few years for real, so let's try and delay destroying the vocabulary of the human race until it decays on its own."

Eduardo bashed open the cash register with the Splatter Mallet, and Scrubz pulled out the money and flung it into the room. "Paper money seems so pathetic now. It's about as useful as the gold we find in dungeons. Only one currency that matters anymore, and that's credits. I *knew* that having a centralized currency was going to be a sign that the world was getting destroyed."

"See how they just started smashing things that are literally irreplaceable? That's exactly what I was just talking about. It's not going to take long at all before all traces of humanity are as gone as we originally thought they were." Nacho shoved open a door and walked into the courtyard as Reuben chuckled and egged on the vandalism.

The cook took into account the grill, the counter space, and the outdoor living room furniture, and instantly knew this was going to be the base that they ran strike teams from. Even if the propane wouldn't ignite for game logic reasons, he'd buy some cheap charcoal from the Store. "Wait, the cheap stuff will ruin the grill... oh well. Better than ruining my mobile kitchen. Best get to it."

Nacho crossed to the grill and unpacked his gear. Once he had organized his workstation to his satisfaction, he purchased and lit the charcoal, then expanded his Pauldrons of Frying to their full fifteen inches, all while making his dinner plan in his head. It was important to have a standard operating procedure in place, otherwise he wouldn't be able to quickly adapt to new and changing circumstances down here.

Once his pans were hot, he'd pull out the Kill Basa sausage and start on the gravy. In the meantime, he set up various stations in his kitchen but slowly ground to a halt and sat down on the mass-produced furniture before long. Nacho couldn't focus on anything long enough to really get it finished.

His mind was *racing*; flipping between pondering his credit situation and what he needed to upgrade, and he was *dying* to take a long break to peruse his Stat Sheet and make the choices he had been putting off. He wanted to bring the entire Brunch Force up to Tier one so they could start looking for the Dragon Spear as a useful fighting force. "Now I'm thinking we should put guards at the entrance to warn us when some other humans or—celestials forbid—CrossHumans show up."

He didn't want another guild waltzing through the

Barbecue Tunnels now that his Brunch Force had cleared it. To be fair, the monsters would *eventually* re-spawn, but there seemed to be no rhyme or reason to the actual time it would take. In fact, he was almost certain that the more that he wanted the respawn to occur, the slower the Patrons would be to act on it.

Reuben walked over and surveyed Nacho's kitchen chaos, noting the near-constipated expression on his friend's face. "You okay over there?"

"No. Yes." Nacho grinned sheepishly, lifting his face from his clenched fists to meet Reuben's eyes. "Trying to figure out what to start first. I've accidentally kind of started everything at once."

"Pobody's Nerfect." Reuben set his gear down and dropped into a wicker chair at the table. "You know I'm better at all the metagaming, so why don't you let me help you with whatever's going on. Is it your build order that's got you down? While you cook, we can do a little shopping. How about it?"

"I could go for a little retail therapy," Brie enthused as she sat down next to her husband. "Also, I hate to say that I agree with Scrubz… but we all lost a thousand credits to the guild tax, and I think we should refund those credits back to the Brunch Force. We need all the help we can get down here. If we can use the credits, we can earn more, faster."

"My sweet investor has finally seen the light of capitalism!" Reuben crowed, reaching for a hug only to be shoved to the ground. "*Oof!* It's okay, there's no need to be shy about it!"

Nacho did a quick check and winced at the idea of releasing the massive windfall.

Chips Guild Stat Sheet
    Total Guild Credits: 57,375
    Total Number of Members: 827
    Guild Leader: Eli "Nacho" Naches

. . .

He was pleasantly taken aback to find they had gained eleven more members since the last time he had checked, but the real surprise was the number of credits that were still accumulating. As much as it pained him to say it, he finally forced the admission out of his mouth. "You're right, Brie."

Nacho grabbed the thousand credit tax he'd gotten from the Barbeque Tunnel bonus and sent all of it back to the members of the Brunch Force. He had some definite ideas on how he wanted to use his credits, but he wanted to get Reuben's and Brie's opinions first.

It was clear—at least to him—that the next step was raising the original Dinner Party to higher levels as fast as they could safely afford to do so. Even with how expensive it was getting to Tier one, the costs would only skyrocket from there. To get from level ten to eleven would be eleven *thousand* credits. Level twelve was seventeen thousand and eight hundred, and so on.

The insane cost was just another reason why people didn't want to spend credits on things like food once they got to higher levels. In his test run, it had been *proven* that it was better to just kill someone, take their credits, and then literally eat them... instead of wasting credits on food. "It's a dog-eat-dog world, but there's no reason to strap meat to your chest and go for a jog."

"What... does that even mean?" Reuben gripped the table and leaned in, entranced by the beautiful phrase he had never heard before.

"It's... you know." Nacho hadn't even realized that he had said the words out loud. "If you're buying food from the store, all you are doing is advertising the fact that you are carrying around a huge amount of credits in order to feed yourself. Someone can just attack you and loot everything you haven't spent. Yeah."

"I think you may need a nap," Brie announced firmly, taking a moment to inspect all of the half-set-up kitchen supplies.

"Oh! You know what I forgot to do? Test out these bad

boys." Reuben made a fist, and his casing clip bracelets glowed in the acid green light of the streetlights. He popped to his feet and jogged over to a wall. As he made a fist, his knuckles glowed silver under his skin, and he sent a straight punch *through* the wall. The rock crumbled, revealing an unhurt hand. "Not only will it let me turn something into ground meat, but it also protects my 'casing' perfectly. So long as I'm actively attacking, I can hit anything and it won't hurt me. My hands are basically indestructible; again, only while attacking. No punching into lava, as that would burn me on the way out, I think. Also, I'm doing a base of fifteen points of damage with each punch."

"That's pretty excellent." Nacho's forehead furrowed as he attempted to do the math on what that attack would look like when it was fully buffed up. He gave up a moment later, silently agreeing with Brie that he might need to call it a day.

"Pretty abyssal-awesome if you ask me. Never thought I could give up my gauntlets, but this is a straight upgrade." Reuben's eyes went blank as he started reading something that only he could see. "Looks like I do fifty percent more damage against food-based monsters? You think that includes the Goat Cheeses? Even if it doesn't, I'm coming for the Costco shelves...!"

"Hot dog!" Nacho loudly called, making both his friends jump. He couldn't hold in his chuckle even for a moment after he saw the shocked expressions on their faces.

"Have you been drinking? *Seriously*, you are ridiculous." Brie shook her head, clearly embarrassed.

"Drinking isn't a thing for me. Like I would intentionally let my guard down and make it easy for the monsters to eat me? Hey, you know what I haven't seen yet?" Nacho motioned for Reuben to sit back down. "Your updated Stat Sheet. You up for sharing?"

"Happy to do that. You want the whole thing? Here." The big guy brushed some rubble off his shoulder as he walked back, and soon Nacho was witnessing the grandeur that was Reuben Colby and his upgraded class.

Reuben Colby
Class: Merchant of Soothing
Level: 10
Experience Points: 14,400 to Level 11!
Current Credits: 2100 (24,515 total Dinner Party pool)

Build Type: Balanced, Instant
Body:

- *Fitness: 18*
- *Metabolic Efficiency: 18*

Mind:

- *Mental Energy: 17*
- *Circuit: 17*

Satiation:

- *Hunger: 100*
- *Thirst: 100*

Total Health Points: 46
Bonus Physical Damage: 9%
Health Regen: 18% Health Regen/minute
Total Mana Pool: 35.5
Bonus Spell Damage: 8.5%
Mana Pool Regen: 17% Mana Regen/minute

Skill Slots (3/4)

- *Healing Hugs (Active) Level 8: 40 Health Points Restored Upon Hugging*

$$Mana\ Cost = 10\%$$
$$Hydration\ Cost = 5\%$$

Metabolic Cost = 0%

- *Positive Vibes (Active) Level 9: Weapon blessing: (applies to entire party, lasts 5 minutes) Adds 18% physical damage*

Mana Cost = 5%
Hydration Cost = 10%
Metabolic Cost = 0%

- *Marketing (Active) Level 9: Able to lure creatures to a location. Impacts up to Level:10*

Mana Cost = 5%
Hydration Cost = 5%
Metabolic Cost = 5%

- *Open slot*

Nacho made approving noises at Reuben's new class name. "All hail the Merchant of Soothing! Please don't start charging to heal us in combat."

"Never even crossed my mind." Reuben shot him a wink. "Until now. Anywho, during my Tier-up, I got a System message about the Ring of Cheese. The Patrons said that I'm too stinky to stop. One of them—they didn't say who—liked the smell of me being hurt."

Brie shook her head. "That sounds so wrong."

"And so!" Reuben brandished the ring. "It's now a Tier *one* Ring of Cheese! I'm a champion of cheese! You could say I rank number one by *being* rank... like number two."

"That is *not* something to brag about," Brie groaned helplessly, knowing that it had been her own choice to say 'I do'.

"That's... your helm *and* your ring got a free upgrade? I thought it was getting counted as a Tierless accessory or something. I don't know what to say." Nacho was way more impressed than he felt was needed. "I guess the Patrons sometimes throw us a little gift, but you can't count on that going forward."

"Heathen!" Reuben wasn't done grandstanding. "The good news doesn't stop there. I still have over two thousand credits, and I'm going to upgrade my Healing Hug because at Tier one… I can heal at range! That's right. I can hug from a distance. I will soon have inescapable hugs that follow wherever I can see you."

"Terrible way to explain that, but okay…" Nacho had been considering their Skills, recognizing a major oversight. "Upgrading Skills isn't that expensive, which gives us a break. It takes two thousand and nine hundred credits to take a Skill from level nine to level nineteen."

"Not expensive, he says." Reuben agreed with a scoff. "From the top of Tier zero, my Skill shoots up like a superhero! Boom; now that my healing is at the peak of Tier one, combat in the future is sure to be fun!"

"From puns to rhyming?" Brie shook her head. "Tiers. Levels. Upgrades. I really am living in one of your video games. Why couldn't we have gone to *my* fantasy world instead of yours?"

"Too much pointless exercise and team sports there," Reuben obliquely stated, nodding along as if someone else had made the point.

Nacho could appreciate her frustration. Their lives were on the line, and the rules of physics had turned out to be more like guidelines. "Let's try to get serious for a minute. We've going to have company down here, and that means I want us all at our most powerful. I'm going to dish out credits to people who need them, and I'm also going to use credits to boost my Cooking Magic to level nineteen. If the trend holds, it'll let me use that from a distance as well. I'll be able to boil pasta from across the room. Ya~ay. Not sure how that's really going to help me, but it's worth the gamble."

"You never know when you'll need to throw that Cooking

Magic around!" Reuben set his Helm of Helming on his head with a grin. "What about your Ingredient Processing?"

"I'm already able to process level nineteen monsters. I'm going to wait until we can survive *meeting* something Tier two before I start to pretend like we could beat and cook one of 'em."

"Good plan," Reuben admitted, though he brightened up immediately. "We can spend that cash on me instead! You know, juice up my Positive Vibes. I'll be able to do it at... I don't know, *longer* range? Whatever it does, we'll have people dishing out more damage. All the people will love me forever and will unanimously vote me in as Guild Leader after you sneeze in their food."

"You forget two things!" Nacho raised a finger and spoke like a villain in a cartoon. "First of all, they'll love me more! My Cooking Magic feeds their bodies *and* their power! *Myahaha!* Second, I already tried to make you Guild Leader, and you said no."

"I'm still happy about that." Reuben shivered at the thought of needing to be *serious* and *responsible*.

Scrubz chose that moment to cross into the courtyard and sink down into a couch, killing further silly conversation by his mere presence. He'd bought a chain to carry around the gauntlets, and he had them thrown over a shoulder like they were boxing gloves. "I heard all that. Not sure anyone will love either of you. Eduardo and I are *trying* to like you, but Nacho... if you really are passing out credits, that'd go a long way to winning me over."

"Depends. What's your Stat Sheet look like? What are your Skills? Your *class*, for abyss' sake?" Nacho felt that his demands were not unreasonable. If he was going to dole out money that was rightfully taxed by the Guild, he needed more information then he felt the other man had been willing to share.

Narrowing his eyes, Scrubz shrugged and allowed a coy smile to play across his face. "How about you show me yours first, if you're gonna force *me* to do it? Lead by example, and all that tripe?"

That made the cook hesitate, but he didn't know why. It was fairly obvious what he could do, as everyone in the group had literally tasted the fruit of his Skills. In the end, though, how could he win over Scrubz and the rest of the Cocktail Party members if he wouldn't trust them first?

"I hate that you just made a convincing argument, and even more that I'm going to go with it." Nacho couldn't help but look at the sneering sandbagger with a hint of newfound respect.

Scrubz snickered and started eagerly reading the new screen that his Guild Leader had shared with him. "Yeah, logic sure has a way of messing with people, don't it?"

CHAPTER TWENTY-FIVE

Nacho realized that his pans were smoking, so he used his Gauntlets of Oven Taming to remove them from the grill before returning to the conversation. "Okay, Bill, since you're looking at my Stat Sheet, let me spend some credits and show you *why* what I'm doing is in all of our best interests. I'm going to raise my Cooking Magic all the way to the current maximum, and then I'm going to upgrade my Small Blades Skill to Tier one. Who knows? At Tier one, I might be able to slice and dice *people* from across the room."

"I'm going by *Scrubz*." The fighter crossed his arms and glared until Nacho rolled his eyes and nodded.

He spent the two thousand and nine hundred credits to get his Cooking Magic to level nineteen; then an additional two hundred credits to boost his Small Blades Skill to level ten. Nacho planned on eventually taking it to level nineteen, but he wasn't in a hurry to spend all their credits—especially not when other people might need the money more. A message distracted him, and he nodded as he looked over what was essentially a direct weapon mastery upgrade.

. . .

Small Blades Skill at Tier 1 bonus skill!

Congratulations on getting your little knife abilities up to Tier 1. You can now use your cutting ability at range! Yes, you can cut things that are six inches away in combat, or when chopping food! Amaze your friends! Be the life of the party. Stand back from blood splatter! The bonuses are amazing! Note: this is a different outcome than processing ingredients. By pulling the Putrid Mana out of a larger chunk, it separates by itself! Technically, it is not cut, it is simply no longer able to attach to the main portion!

Nacho suddenly found himself as interested in his Stat Sheet as Scrubz was, and opened it to see how he had managed to improve.

Eli 'Nacho' Naches
Class: Junior League Chef
Level: 10
Experience Points: 14,400 to Level 11!
Current Credits: 7756

Build Type: Balanced, Delayed
Body:

- *Fitness: 20*
- *Metabolic efficiency: 20*

Mind:

- *Mental energy: 20*
- *Circuit: 20*

Satiation:

- *Hunger: 100*
- *Thirst: 100*

Total Health Points: 50
Bonus Physical Damage: 10%
Health Regen: 20% Health Regen/minute
Total Mana Pool: 40
Bonus Spell Damage: 10%
Mana Pool Regen: 20% Mana Regen/minute

Skill Slots (3/4)

- *Small Blades (Passive) Level 10: 20% bonus damage on all knife attacks.*

Tier 1 Enhancement: Your blades can slice from up to 6 inches away from their edge!

No Mana, Hydration, or Metabolic Cost

- *Ingredient Processing (Active) Level 17: Remove Putrid Mana from monsters up to Level 19.*

Tier 1 Enhancement: Process ingredients from 15 feet away!

Mana Cost = 5%
Hydration Cost = 5%
Metabolic Cost = 5%

- *Cooking Magic (Active) Level 19: Create food that enhances a single stat by 95% of maximum.*

Tier 1 Enhancement: Throw magic into a food item you cooked from 15 feet away!

Mana Cost = 5%
Hydration Cost = 5%
Metabolic Cost = 5%

- *Open slot*

Nacho could think of plenty of new and interesting ways to extend the reach of his blade. It also reminded him that sometimes dodging a *little* was just not enough; you could never be sure what kind of skill your opponent could use to change combat in their favor.

"I think I'm starting to get it." Scrubz' eyes glowed while he perused Nacho's Stat Sheet. "If you do your chicken and biscuits—raising both to at least Uncommon rarity—that's going to give us a hundred and ninety percent boost to one of our stats. With Eduardo using the hammer, and me with the gauntlets… I'll admit it's impressive. You'll make people hit like they're two entire Tiers above their actual level. Three, if you figure out how to make Epic food consistently."

The guy stopped talking, and he seemed upset about something. Brie seemed not to notice, but Reuben caught on immediately. "You okay, Bill-board?"

Scrubz didn't answer right away, ignoring the playful jab. When he did, his voice was bitter. "It's just that build type, and Nacho's stats. I'm… jealous. There. I said it."

He turned to storm away, but Reuben pulled him down onto the couch. "Easy does it. Don't be jealous of *Nacho*. For one, when he kills something, he can't earn credits. Dude can only get it through cooking and selling the food. All those inflated stats? All they are doing is helping him cook for longer periods of time. Lastly, we're here to help *everyone*."

"We are," Brie agreed, though her words came off far colder than Reuben's. Her husband had a level of empathy that she just… didn't. In a lot of ways, Brie saw the Bills and the other disgruntled people as resource sinks; no return on investment from that sort of person for keeping them alive, except as a warm body to bait monsters.

Scrubz gave Nacho a hard, if somewhat nervous, look. "You showed me your Stat Sheet. I'm going to trust you, Nacho."

"Please do." Nacho was more than a little curious at this

point. If Scrubz tried to renege on his agreement, the cook might need to start cutting the man until he folded. Probably wouldn't look too good for a leader to do that.

"I was actively involved in martial arts back before the Juxtaposition, and I got a Generic Martial Arts Skill, along with a passive ability that adds a percentage point of damage per level. It's at level nine, so I'm doing nine percent bonus damage with any kicks and punches. I did pretty well in the Evaluation World, and in the Evaluation Mall, I just bought the simple Warrior class, but I bought three extra Skills." Scrubz scratched his neck, obviously uncomfortable sharing this much information with anyone. "The first one I bought is 'Steel Strike', at level nine. It gives me another percentage on hit, so my attacks are doing nine points each hit."

He looked around to see if that was enough information, but everyone else remained silent so long that Scrubz finally broke down and continued. "I guess my big attack is the Roundhouse Hammer Skill, which doubles my damage for a single hit. It's pretty good, but it takes a lot of Hunger Points. I also have a Billy Block Skill—and I don't know why it's called that. It's my defensive Skill, but I gotta toggle it on and off. It costs Hunger and Thirst per second, but I do damage *and* I block eighteen percent of any attack against me. That's at level nine as well."

"It's called that because your name is *Bill*, no matter what you want to be called out of angst. I bet it's like Abby's Slippery Block," Reuben prodded gently, just enough to keep the conversation flowing. "As to how hard you hit, with the bonus from the gauntlets, you'll be doing ten points per hit, right? That makes you a powerhouse in our group, friend."

"Right," Scrubz stated in a relieved tone. "I'm itching to get my three Skills to Tier one, because then I'll be able to throw punches from a distance while blocking; I'll also be able to throw kicks? Not really sure how that all works, or how far it'll be. But it's going to cost a fortune. We… appreciate you giving us back the thousand. I know we're out here for the good of the guild and all, but you didn't need to do it. You could've just kept it. Still… I'm going to be a couple thousand short."

Nacho closed his eyes and breathed out a light sigh. He should have seen this coming: Bill only came around for two things: handouts or to complain about other people getting handouts. Two thousand credits were sent right away, but he also sent two thousand and nine hundred credits on top of that, some of his own, some from the Dinner Party. "Get to Tier one, but then upgrade all four of your Skills to level nineteen. We need you kicking and punching their hearts out."

"That's right. Just like there's no 'I' in 'team,' there's no 'me' in 'guild'." Reuben held out a double-thumbs up. "Suffice to say, we need you at your best."

Scrubz' face twisted into a more normal shape: a heavy frown. "It's not right. Those are taxes from the guild. I can't take the credits."

Nacho let out a true laugh as the man proved that he wasn't anti-Nacho, he was just anti-big-government. "You are a pain in the meatballs, but you're a good fighter. You're smart, and it seems like you have the best interest of the guild at heart. If we die down here, what good will the credits be? Armor Mountain is secure and in good hands. We have to be successful in this quest, and for that to happen, shut up and upgrade."

The frown faded, slowly replaced on Scrubz' face by an exultant grin. "Well, now, if I do all the upgrades, I'll be unstoppable. I'll be punching at nineteen points of damage. My Roundhouse Hammer will be doing thirty-eight points of damage. That's without Positive Vibes and your Cooking Magic."

"Thank goodness." Brie sighed in happiness at whatever vision was playing out in her mind. "Good. We can put you up front to get beat on like the rest of us. Abby and I are tired of carrying you."

"Let me tell you one thing…" Scrubz turned deadly serious. "I won't let you guys down. I won't. You're taking a chance on me. Maybe I don't even need the Dragon Spear, now that I'm all upgraded. But, uh, I'm going to go buy the levels in private."

Scrubz retreated into the lobby, but Nacho was already focused on other important things. The Dinner Party had thirteen thousand, one hundred and seventy-five credits left among them, which meant they could afford to upgrade four Skills up to level nineteen without tapping into Chips Guild money. He quickly brought his friends in on his mental calculations. "We obviously need to take Reuben's Healing Hugs to Tier one. That's going to be three hundred and forty credits. Then we crank Reuben's Positive Vibes all the way to level nineteen. Then we get all of Brie's Skills up to level nineteen. It's all Brie, all the time, until our tank is absolutely maxed out."

Both of them did a little checking, and their eyes glowed while they accessed the Store. Reuben was the first to blink away the light. "I'll be healing fifty health, and people will be hitting with an extra thirty-eight percentage points of damage thanks to my vibes, man. Gotta love the vibes."

"Let's do this!" Brie grinned like a shark as she realized how hard she would be hitting in the near future. Both of them upgraded their Skills to the max, knowing it was the last time they would be doing anything like this for a long, long time.

It would take hundreds of *thousands* of credits to get to Tier two, and that was when they'd be able to get their Skills up to level twenty. It might take a while, but for the first time... it actually felt like they'd get there.

After the upgrades, Brie shared her Stat Sheet.

Brie McCurdy
Class: Berserker
Tier Class Name: Battle Babe
Level: 10
Experience Points: 14,400 to Level 11!
Current Credits: 3243 (1575 total Dinner Party pool)

Skill Slots (3/4)

- *Athletic Endurance (Passive) Level 19: 38% reduction to hunger loss penalties when using physical skills.*

Tier 1 Enhancement: Eating food considered 'Healthy' will offer an extra portion per three portions.

No Mana, Hydration, or Metabolic Cost

- *Combat Dash (Active) Level 19: 38% Damage on Dash Attacks, 10-meter dash.*

Tier 1 Enhancement: Throw your attack up to 15 feet!

Mana Cost = 0%
Hydration Cost = 0%
Metabolic Cost = 10%

- *Defensive Whirl (Active) Level 19: Spin toward your enemy, auto-blocking up to 10 strikes.*

Tier 1 Enhancement: Throw your Whirl up to 15 feet!

Mana Cost = 0%
Hydration Cost = 0%
Metabolic Cost = 15%

- *Open slot*

Brie was grinning ear to ear. "I can block up to ten attacks simultaneously! No one is going to be able to touch me. I love that thirty-eight percent bonus damage, and I won't get so hungry when I use my skills. Also, *finally* I have a reason not to eat that greasy filth you make. I *demand* healthy food; I can barely stomach the-"

"What's going on with your new Class name?" Reuben was already wincing by the time his question finished leaving his mouth.

"These Patrons..." Brie went completely still, holding her hands out in an attempt to keep her rage internal. "Why aren't *you* the 'Babe of Soothing'? You'd probably *like* that name!"

"No!" Reuben loudly stated, looking around hopefully. "Absolutely not, I'd hate it! Don't tempt the Patrons into making me a name like that next time I Tier up! But seriously, they likely did that to mess with you. Best way to get a better one next time is to give them zero entertainment right now."

Brie took a few deep breaths, flashed a sharp smile, and continued as if she had not been interrupted. "I *do* love that I can throw Combat Dash damage up to fifteen feet, but I'm gonna need to see that one in action to really understand it. But the fact that I can save other people with my Defensive Whirl? At a distance? Awesome."

The group lapsed into silence for a few moments as each person considered how the upgrades were going to impact future battles. Reuben furrowed his brow, an idea seeming to blossom from inside his skull before erupting into the world through his mouth. "Speaking of Skills... when are we going to buy ourselves another Skill? We all have an open slot."

Nacho exhaled slowly. He had known this would come up soon enough, but he hadn't expected it *moments after* they maximized the Skills that they already owned. "Reuben, Skills are tricky. Sometimes you get one you think will be great, but it turns out not to do much, and then you have to spend a bunch of credits to get rid of it. Truth be told, I've been waiting for a Skill Box to show up in a dungeon. Anytime you find one, the System offers up rare and powerful Skills. First person to locate it gets it for way cheaper than anyone else will after them, but everyone else can buy it from then on. Back in my Probability Vision, they were pretty rare at first, but as time passed, more and more people found them. I'd like us to wait."

"Then we wait," Brie agreed easily, knowing that this was a situation his foreknowledge was most likely still heavily useful in.

"But only until we have the credits to buy a new Skill, and keep a free Skill Slot ready for it."

"Maybe we'll find a Skill Box in the UnderFun," Reuben mused aloud.

Personally, Nacho doubted it. He thought they might have to wait a couple years for the Skills Box dungeons to become more plentiful, bu~ut there was no need to tell them that. He left his friends to their excited chatting and decided that he had taken a long enough break.

It was time to get into Active Cooking.

Preparing meals for the mixture of Tiers was a bit more complicated than one Tier had been. It didn't take long for Nacho to learn that it was easier to just make two batches of everything. He started at Tier zero, since there were so many more in the Brunch Force than the Tier ones.

Biscuits, then sausage gravy for both levels. Those were going to pack a punch—he added his Cooking Magic to both after ensuring that the meals were at the Highest quality, and therefore highest Rarity, that he could manage. After breakfast, everyone should be rolling out of the hotel with a one hundred and ninety percent boost to one of their stats.

Nacho finally came to the conclusion that his Pauldrons of Frying were amazing. It didn't matter if he was cooking sausages or eggs, nothing stuck even slightly. Even with the restricted cooking station, he was able to eke out a perfect cooking experience.

As for his new at-range Small Blades ability, it was cool to slice a piece of meat six inches from the initial cut. It also allowed him to slice through thick meat simply by placing his blade atop it. Frankly, if the Skill hadn't granted him a perfect, instinctive way to use it, there was a good chance he would have gutted himself on multiple occasions.

"Ay, Cookie!" Reuben called from across the courtyard where he was comfortably lounging on the couch. "Sending you the upgrade info for Marketing hitting Tier one!"

The message that appeared a moment later wasn't very clear on what the Skill could achieve:

- *Marketing (Active) Level 19: Able to lure creatures to a location. Impacts up to Level: 20. Tier 1 Enhancement: Maximizes the four principles of marketing (Product, Price, Place, and Promotion).*

The nondescript detail gave Nacho pause, but to Reuben's great disappointment, the cook simply got back to work and didn't say anything else about it. Nacho knew that most of the time when the System provided something that didn't have a concrete value to it, the enhancement meant nothing. He didn't want to be the one to tell his friend that his Skill may have just been pointlessly upgraded.

By the time Nacho finished everything necessary, some people had already crashed in the hotel's first floor rooms. While running into UnderFun monsters was inevitable, they were all enjoying real beds and a little break in the meantime.

From his Adirondack in the courtyard, Nacho peered into the distance, noticing a large shape idly flying around some of the underground skyscrapers. He shook his head, reminding himself that the creatures outside were tomorrow's problem, and settled in for a long night of restless sleep.

He was the Guild Leader, and that meant that it was his responsibility to create a feasible plan to explore the entire DKCU and find the Dragon Spear first. He closed his eyes and tried to let his worry fade away. "Shoulda made Reuben take the job. I gotta cook *and* clean up this mess?"

CHAPTER TWENTY-SIX

"Don't go to sleep yet; let's find you a proper bed." Reuben shook Nacho awake just as he had started to doze—potentially deadly in an open area. The cook had no idea what he had been thinking and happily moved inside.

Brie suggested they send their beta and gamma teams out for some reconnaissance, pointing out that they shouldn't bother putting guards at the entrance of the DKCU, since there would be any number of ways to reach the Downtown Under-Fun. Everyone agreed with her, as they had already been informed that she was in charge of combat operations. Her imposing presence and impressive weapon only served to seal that she was, and should remain, in that position.

While they waited for the teams to return, Nacho and the Dinner Party took a trip through the hotel. The entire building felt like a dungeon as they creeped up the stairwell to climb to the second floor without any lights. When they got to the next floor, they opened a door to find a wall of solid limestone. That didn't stop them from trying the next floor, and the next, until they popped a door open and found nicely appointed suites.

The Patrons clearly had complete control over the environment; they hadn't simply thrown a mile of rock over the top of the existing world—the Patrons had decided what sections to keep, and what sections to bury. That explained why Nacho hadn't known about the UnderFun in his Probability Vision: too many variables to account for.

He was itching to get going and find the spear, since they needed to secure their position at the top of the food chain, but Reuben reminded Nacho that he was exhausted. It had been a long day of cooking, fighting, and finding unexplored regions of the Juxtaposition—who knew downtown Kansas City would have become some kind of mythic El Dorado, a bonafide lost city full of treasure?

His friends finally convinced him to grab some sleep while the teams ran their missions, so they picked a two-bedroom suite. The happy married couple took one room, and Nacho collapsed onto the bed in the other as soon as the door shut. The sheets were a little musty, but not terrible. It just felt nice to be on a normal bed again, almost like it had all been a strange dream… he cut that line of thinking as though it was the throat of a CrossHuman.

"Reuben might be on to something. I probably *should* get a real house, with a real bed, and not continue to sleep on a kitchen shelf." He stretched, snuggled his head into a real pillow, and fell into a deep sleep. Unfortunately, since he was asleep, he could only shout internally in frustration as his dreams were invaded once more.

The dream had a certain glow to it, something that his normal dreams didn't have. That meant it was sent by a Patron, so he paid attention. In the vision, he was standing in a shallow river. The summer air was warm, and while there were some monstrous birds winging around in the sky, normal red-winged blackbirds trilled from branches on the shore.

Nacho walked up the stream, picking his way across rocks hidden underneath the dark water. Those rocks sure were uncomfortable—round and hard, always shifting under foot. He pushed his way past several branches to reach a table sitting in the middle of the river. The table was odd, but odder still was the collection of people sitting around it, eating a feast while water gushed around the table legs.

Every one of the dozen diners were wearing sunglasses.

One of them stood, sandwich in hand. It was Arriod, and he wore the katana—that abyssal Sword of Flesh Shearing or whatever it was—sheathed on his back. He slid the sunglasses down his nose so Nacho could see his misshapen pupils, then pointed down with his sandwich.

Nacho somehow knew what the guy wanted him to do. He bent over and reached beneath the water. What he thought had been stones beneath his feet were skulls. The cook recoiled with a disgusted grunt. He'd been walking across a riverbed full of human skulls, which was not something that scared him, but it was most *certainly* unsanitary. That was when he realized that the CrossHumans weren't just eating beef brisket. They were eating human sandwiches absolutely *coated* with Miracle Whip.

"Seriously? *That's* the ingredient you decided you liked best, and you went off-brand? Plus," Nacho jerked upright in his bed, shouting, "that's too much mayo!"

A cursory knock rattled the door, and Reuben busted through it in full combat-ready mode. "Nacho! Where's the mayo? Are you eating a BLT without me?"

"Just a… bad dream." Nacho swung his legs off the bed and shook his head to clear away the nausea. He knew better. The fact that it had all seemed real, but felt completely surreal at the same time, meant that it was a warning. They needed to pick up the pace, or all that would be left of their race was what the CrossHumans were picking out of their teeth at the end of the day.

"That seems like it's completely true," Reuben stated with sarcasm dripping from his tone. "Listen, we just got word that the beta and gamma teams are back. They have some things to report, and it's our turn to go out adventuring. They got a bead on some monsters, some dungeons, and—get this—giant bees. I was like, 'honey, let's go meet Sting', but no one got the reference, so I need you to come out here and laugh at my jokes."

Nacho felt well-rested despite his nightmare vision, so he didn't mind getting up and getting to work. If taking a long nap always meant he was going to be haunted, he saw a large amount of insomnia in his future. The cook soon entered the courtyard to meet up with the rest of the Brunch Force. A few were still healing from battles, indicating that combat had been *recent*. They had all pulled chairs up around the firepit, which was crackling with a happy little fire.

It was chilly in the cavern since they were so deep underground, and the place smelled like wet pavement and other more... *monstrous* fragrances. The wood helped dispel that mustiness—someone must've splurged for Epic pine, because it burned well and had a nice aroma.

There had to be some sort of ventilation, because the smoke from Nacho's grill had found a way out, and the smoke from the fire was sweeping upward and vanishing through various cracks in the stone ceiling far above. After the group was settled, Taye gave them a quick rundown of what he, Kristie, and Abby had found.

"District is overrun. Our patrol took us past Fourteenth Street to the south, to Tenth Street to the north. The west boundary was Broadway, based on some of the buildings we found, and the stone wall that started to the east. We found a disconcerting number of wandering monsters, including Alley Cats—which were more like saber-toothed tigers than kitties. Worse were the Rabid Funnel Cake Dogs, which dripped powdered sugar."

Taye paused to try and remember if he had missed anything, then snapped his fingers as another thought resurfaced. "I'm *ninety* percent certain that the froth is the rabies virus trying to convince us to put it in our mouth willingly, and the dogs looked like deep-fried mongrels. There were also giant pigeons—that wasn't what they were called, but the creatures were too far away for anyone to get a System View on them."

Whatever they were called, Nacho saw it as good news. His knives slowly trailed along a whetstone as he mentally skimmed through his plethora of poultry recipes. Reuben, sitting next to him, was overly pleased to hear about the Rabid Funnel Cake Dogs, since his Sausage Clips of Striking would do fifty percent more damage because the monsters were food-based.

Scrubz led his team over and reported in as well. "We found the source of those giant pigeons you're talking about. They came from the 'Dangerous Dovecote of Devilry'; I think I said that right. It was the city hall building before the Juxtaposition. Another thing… the other side of the convention center, the Kansas City Hotel? Yeah… that's now a dungeon called the 'Hideous Hive of the Bee-hemoth'."

Brie waited for him to be done speaking, then offered her own insight. "We could have found this KC Cesspit place and not even known it. We saw no sign of 'Caelius Apicius'. Maybe we should search for wherever the Plaza ended up? Should be easy to locate, since they had all those fountains shaped like Greek gods or whatever. Point is, there are at least three dungeons within a stone's throw of here, and a *lot* of ground to cover. Those buildings go down as much as they go up, so there are subterranean tunnels connecting most places."

Reuben pushed his leather helmet back on his head to scratch at his temple. "Wouldn't they be *sub*-subterranean tunnels, since we're so deep?"

"*Obviously* that's the correct terminology." Nacho popped up to pace in place as Scrubz scoffed his annoyance at their antics. They had so much work to do and so many places to explore in this strange underground city. Any number of hotels, apartments, the Insomnia Cookies cookie store, a Chipotle's, Bristol's, Cosentino's Market, banks, the big park plaza on Central Street and West thirteenth, and some of the best barbecue in the world…

Reuben's eyes glowed until he blinked the light away. "I read the poem on the Dragon Spear information again. Not much there, but we need something called the 'Ivory Talon', and it seems to have something to do with a dragon. Could it be that Caelius Apicius is guarding the KC Cesspit?"

Nacho hated not knowing, and he was itching to get moving. "Let's have me, Brie, and Reuben go out there and see what we can find. We're rested. We're good."

"I'll go with you," Scrubz demanded more than requested. "I'm not going to sleep, and I want to explore."

"Me too." Eduardo looked like he was trying to cosplay Brie. He stood tall, silver chainmail glittering while the Splatter Mallet rested on his shoulder.

Nacho wanted to argue that they needed sleep, but he knew he wasn't going to win that fight. "Fine. The five of us. We'll just go back out there."

"You should have some spell support." Hazel yawned and waved her hand lazily as they looked at her. "But Hank and I are all tuckered out."

Kristie raised a hand. "I'll go; too excited to sleep, anyway. Can I tell you all about my Skills, so you'll really want me with you? Too late for you to say no! My Sorcery Strike ability has doubled—I'm doing twenty-four damage, and that's without Nacho's Cooking Magic. As a Tier one enhancement, I can create Sorcery Swords, and yes, my magical light blades are pink. Let's see... Death Blossom is even more powerful, doing thirty-six damage in a thirty-foot radius. Thanks to Tier one, I can detonate the Death Blossom at a distance, so I don't have to be in the middle of the action! Also, so I don't hit you all. As much."

Nacho thought it was interesting that Kristie's Tier zero Sorcery Strike had already been a distance attack. Reaching Tier one was all about doing the Skill at a distance, but instead of more distance, now she could... create and wield swords? "I wonder if ranged options get a 'melee' range, and melee gets 'range' when we hit the first Tier?"

"I can't go right now. I'm totally bushed." Taye looked pained at the idea of not going back out into the UnderFun, but Abby slapped him on the back as Reuben talked him down.

"Don't worry, Archer Man. We'll rest up and be out there again before you know it. Let some other people have fun."

Taye sighed and gazed longingly at the building that was the only thing standing between him and a bed. "I guess you're right."

"Time to move." Nacho got to his feet and started walking without waiting for the others to group up; he was excited to get back out there.

It wasn't every day a person got to explore the legendary lost Kansas City.

CHAPTER TWENTY-SEVEN

The Dinner Party, along with the mostly-welcome addition of Scrubz, Eduardo, and Kristie, left through the smashed front doors of the Marriott. They weren't coming back from this mission without at least a clue about either this 'Caelius Apicius' character or the KC Cesspit.

Nacho had left his mobile kitchen backpack behind, as their trek was supposed to be just a quick run through town. He *did* load up his Storage Slots with sacks of treats in case they got pulled into combat, but he had his doubts that people would be happy reaching into a plastic bag and grabbing a scoop of soggy biscuits and gravy mid-fight. "Their loss, really. Hey, Reuben, Have you ever eaten biscuits and gravy out of a plastic bag-"

"Four times, but the third didn't really count," Reuben answered before Nacho had even finished asking. "Couldn't keep it down. Great for sobering up after a little too much fun at the campus parties."

"Oh. My." Brie bit off whatever she had been about to say, breathing heavily and looking away. "I did not need to know that about you. Please don't come too close to me for a day or two."

"See? Everyone said we had no more stories for each other, and they were wrong. How great is that?" Reuben's facts didn't seem to matter to his wife. "It's all good, love! I can hug you from a distance now, remember?"

Once they had reached the remnants of the streets, they took a right and walked down Fourteenth amid the piles of debris and a few monster corpses turning to sludge on the pavement. Nacho couldn't help but feel a bit claustrophobic even though there were seven stories of buildings between the asphalt and the craggy stone ceiling. In this particular area, that was nearly one hundred feet of open space above him... which did absolutely nothing to help with the discomfort that came with being so far underground.

Scrubz pointed a metal-covered finger at a small shop. "Let's hit that convenience store. It's nice to have some of the comforts of home, and a soda sounds good."

"It'll be warm. Probably flat, too," Kristie reminded him as she shined her bracelets into the derelict storefront. It was mostly intact, though the refrigerators and freezers had long since shut off, and anything spoiled had already rotted away or been eaten by some passing creature.

"Looks like you were wrong. Geothermal insulation for the win." Scrubz grabbed a Physician Pepper and threw one to Nacho, then anyone else that raised a hand. The sealed drinks were still fizzy and cold, since the air was cool so far underground. Reuben grabbed a bag of Cheetos and soon was munching happily away. Brie didn't eat anything, though she did take a bottle of water.

"Brie..." Nacho pointed at the bottle, "You're Tier one now. That is about as useful as a bottle of air to you. You might as well have a soda; at least then you get to have your senses tickled."

"Oh. Right."

She sighed and glanced archly at Reuben, who shrugged

and continued licking salty orange-hued flavoring off his fingers. "What? I like the taste; I know they won't do anything for me."

"Just seems wasteful, is all," Brie quietly stated as they walked back to the street. The six of them took a quick tour of the block, and upon confirming that the city hall building was splattered with white droppings, they avoided startling the hundreds of cooing winged monsters that were using it as their dumping grounds.

As the group eased away from the Dovecote of Devilry, an intense *buzzing* filled the air, louder than hundreds of chainsaws working on deforesting the Amazon. They cautiously peeked into the Kansas City Hotel, shuddering at the sight of what could only in the most generous of terms still be called 'bees' inside. A few musk-ox-sized hymenopterans churned the air lazily at the top, where their gargantuan honeycomb filled the top floors of the building. Eduardo winced at the thought of needing to be a frontliner against them. "If those bees are just drones, the queen must be the size of a bus."

"I think those are *bee*-sts, may-bee Bee-hemoths," Reuben commented on the monsters, not even bothering to hide his self-satisfied grin.

"How about we do something productive instead of playing word games? Lady, how did he convince you to marry him?" Kristie stopped them from going further, pointing into the distance as Brie shrugged helplessly at her question. "There's a park on the other side of City Hall. We didn't go there, and there might be an entrance we missed."

"I think we should make new friends. These ones are mean to me," Reuben stage-whispered to Brie. She patted his arm consolingly and tugged him along, ignoring his dramatic pout. The team reversed course and worked their way up to Tenth Street just as a pigeon flew in from the south and dove through a wall that had been smashed out. "*What.* Did you see that? It looked like a normal pigeon, if a pigeon was a bodybuilder fresh from a competition. I hope we don't need to squab-ble with them."

The park they were searching for lay between the back of the city hall and the smooth rock of the cave's northern wall. Kristie led the way with her Bracelets of Brightness illuminating the path. Between that, torches, and necrotic green streetlights, Nacho didn't bother wasting his Firefly Potstickers just to eke out a fraction more visibility.

Kristie shined her bracelet lights on a statue at the south end of the park, a statue that most *certainly* hadn't been around in old earth. The figure wore robes, very regal and medieval, like those of a king—but he was *also* wearing a cowboy hat and boots. His robes were cinched with a belt that had a Texas-shaped buckle. His face was also disturbingly detailed, particu-larly the hooked nose and over-full eyebrows.

The Warlock blinked in shock as she pointed at the statue. "That's it! That's Caelius Apicius, my Patron! This is a good sign."

"Absolutely." Nacho inspected the figure made of pure gold, finding that at the foot of the statue were concrete stairs leading even deeper underground. They carefully crossed the grass to the opening, and Kristie flashed her light down the hole. "Uh, going by the smell... I bet that's the entrance to the KC Cesspit. Looks like we found everything we needed."

Brie strode forward with her black and gold lacrosse stick, one of her glowing lacrosse balls loaded in the net. "Let's see if we get the message when we go in."

She stepped down the stairs without hesitation, followed by the rest of the team. Nacho was in the middle, keeping Firefly Potstickers buzzing around him almost as a nervous reflex. The team descended about halfway until they were finally given a message:

Welcome, Player, to the KC Cesspit of Patron Playfulness! Here you will delve into the secrets of another world! I mean, it's your old world, but different. We've provided you with danger, municipal disasters, and civic fun! The Juxtaposition still believes in bureaucracy; it's the absolute best!

B-b-bonus offer! You can earn a five thousand credit bonus for entering the inner sanctum and surviving! Double your bonus by bringing a friend into the Cesspit's inner sanctum! The more the merrier!

"There's going to be a multi-level marketing meeting down there, I'm sure of it. We should leave." Reuben's tone was too serious for the words that were coming out of his mouth. "If someone tries to make me sell essential oils *one* more time…!"

Nacho, ignoring the man due to being used to these sorts of antics, made sure everyone had their leftover biscuits ready in case they needed the boost to one of their stats. The staircase brought them into the fanciest sewer system imaginable, even if most of the tunnels were the same: a ledge on the right and a channel of water to the left. The ledge didn't have even the smallest speck of dust on it, and the water was perfectly clear. "Not much of a cesspit so far… I'd *love* if it would stay that way."

Every single inch of the wall was decorated with sculptures and friezes, as though every museum in the old world had dumped their supply here. It was also very well-lit, with glass light fixtures on the wall containing the same flickering green magical energy they had seen illuminating the streetlamps above. Easing through the dungeon, they eventually reached larger rooms where whirlpools of fresh water swirled down floor drains.

The passageways split here and there, but they kept going straight as much as they could. Nacho tried to keep track of the passageways, but they all looked so… similar. On his own, he knew that he would have been hopelessly lost by now.

It was *Scrubz*, of all people, that produced a solution. He bought some cheap chalk and marked up the walls as they passed to make sure they could find their way back to the entrance. As unlikely as it seemed, each member of the team was starting to grow a newfound respect for the fistfighting Warrior.

They passed a few stairways that led upward, but Nacho didn't know if leaving now would invalidate the bonus offer. They hadn't come anywhere close to finding any kind of central room, and there were still no signs of any monsters. Eventually, just to make sure everything was staying the way they had left it, the group retraced their steps. Finding their original entrance, they silently agreed to take another tunnel.

It eventually led to what *had* to be the inner sanctum—the hallway was filled with statues, each one sixteen feet high, organized in two rows and facing each other. All of them held spears; a good sign, as they were looking for the Dragon Spear.

Nacho didn't recognize the stone faces at first... all the way until his Firefly Potstickers buzzed around their heads. The New York Yankees cap and toga gave away the fact that one of them was Kronos, and a look at Caelius Apicius in his cowboy hat basically confirmed that all of these were Patrons who had sent their respective followers to hunt for the spear. What would have been a spartan warrior towered above all of them, the main difference between the ancient fighter and this Patron being the fact that he wore a fedora rather than the crested helmet.

The cook advanced ahead of the group to scout and wandered down the room, alert for any changes in danger levels around himself. "This is a grand hallway... and it sure doesn't feel like a sewer. As for those statues, it's clear to me that they're Patrons. They all have spears, but I don't think this is actually the inner sanctum. Nothing has tried to kill us yet, and that's the only reasoning I have on the matter for the moment. Then there's *that*."

He pointed at an archway that led to another hall full of statues, and looked over his shoulder at his team. They nodded their agreement to continue, and Scrubz and Eduardo stepped forward to take point down the aisle between the statues. Brie and Kristie followed close behind them, both ready to hurl their projectiles—magic missile or exploding lacrosse ball of shiny doom.

When the stone figures didn't throw anything, nothing exploded, and no screams of people falling into a trap arose, Nacho and Reuben hurried forward to peer through the archway. The grand hallway beyond was full of more statues carved into the walls, but there was a notable difference: these figures were of normal people, all with quivers on their backs, brandishing bows and arrows. There were grandmothers in dresses, old guys in overalls, kids coming home from baseball practice, middle-aged men wearing vintage War Stars t-shirts with beer bellies hanging over their jeans.

Nacho and the other five people walked through the room ready for those archer statues to attack… but still, nothing happened. Scrubz muttered in a hushed, harsh tone, "This place is starting to creep me out."

At the end of the room waited a solid gold door with symbols orbiting four holes in the wall: four on the top and three on the bottom. The symbols were an odd collection of things: a beehive, a buffalo head, a sword, all the popular elements, as well as what appeared to be the bust of Abraham Lincoln from a rusty penny. The circles could be spun so the symbols aligned over the top of the four holes. The cook stepped forward, his hand reaching for a lever that stuck out right next to the odd door.

"*Nobody touch it!*" Reuben roared as he grabbed Nacho's shirt and hauled him backward. "If the symbols are wrong, we die. I recognize that puzzle: it's just like the one from a game…! Now that it makes sense, we need the Ivory Talon. This is *great*! I know *exactly* what we have to do."

Plink! An arrow rattled off the stone wall next to Nacho's head, striking directly where he would have been standing if Reuben hadn't pulled him back. The group dropped into their combat-ready positions instantly, since they had been on edge the entire time. The statues had started to move, but they had been expecting that.

The archer statues all turned to aim their arrows at the golden puzzle door. Through the archway, in the Patron spear room, statues began moving as well. After a tense wait, the System begrudgingly decided to clue the group in on what was happening.

Well, Player, you came close! Closer than you should be able to, at this Tier. For that, your reward is us trying to kill you!

Bonus objective not completed! Boo-hoo, so sad. You're not in the KC Cesspit's inner sanctum; you're in the pre-sanctums! There are two pre-sanctum halls, since we always say it's better to be pre-pre-prepared. Congrats! This is huge news. Not for you. You don't have what you need to get into the inner sanctum itself, so no bonus for you! Also, you've been marked with the Scarlet Symbol Of Accusatory Trespassing.

That mark isn't good, but you won't know what it is until you get out of this peaceful, very pretty sewage system. Anyway, good job making it to the pre-sanctums. Bad job getting marked as problem children.

We see that one of you is a Satiation Player. That's very interesting. We're choosing you, Cook, because you are a shocking chef, aren't you? Shocking indeed.

Nacho felt both a shiver on his neck and a sinking feeling in his stomach. "What did all of that mean? Is that from the game, too?"

"No~ope." Reuben slammed his fists together and danced to the side as an arrow passed through the space where he had just been standing.

They had no time to figure it out, as things abruptly became even more concerning. Both sets of the statues—the Patrons and the Archers—moved again, stone grinding on stone, sliding closer to the humans. The spear points glowed red, as did the arrows in the bows of the stone statues. Nacho felt a sudden burning on the back of his neck and slapped a hand to the spot. A second later, the spears, bows, and statues returned to normal, non-moving stone, only the arrows no longer displayed arrow points or fletching like normal arrows. No, they looked like shish-kabobs.

Brie shrieked and grabbed at the back of her head, then wheeled and lifted her hair. "What's there?"

"There's… an A?" Nacho's confused response barely managed to leave his mouth before his neck felt like it had likewise lit on fire, and from the pained cries, he wasn't the only one.

Reuben came up behind him. "You got an S, Nacho. It is like we got branded, but they're bright red. Almost like temporary tattoos?"

"Do you mean to tell me that I literally have a *Scarlet Letter* 'A' on the back of my neck?" Brie glared at the statues as though she were trying to figure out whether they would come back to life if she started smashing them. "We will be fixing this, *now*."

They quickly found that they had all received different letters: T, S, S, O, A, and T, which were literally the first letters of the words in 'Scarlet Symbol Of Accusatory Trespassing', though the 'T' had been used twice.

Nacho had no idea why they'd been marked, or what it meant. He'd never heard of players being marked before. This was all completely new territory for him, and it made his past life feel almost like a waste. He tried to shake off that feeling, but he was *furious*.

A second later, another message popped up from the System, and it was clear that it wasn't meant just for them.

Hey there, all you players going for the Dragon Spear! Nacho and the Chips Guild have found a <u>very</u> special door. You better hurry your tushies down to the DKCU if you wanna slam that special door in his face!

*Alert! The six players who are right now standing so close and yet so far away from the Dragon Spear? They've been **marked**! It won't be long before they and you know what that means for them in the near future!*

Good luck, Players, and may your future be delicious!

. . .

"I don't have time for this malarkey." Brie looked around at all the glum faces and put up a brave front on their behalf, tossing her hand up and walking away. "I'm out. Stay fresh, cheese bags."

Silence followed her for a long moment, until Scrubz broke it with a chuckle. "Abyss it, *what*? Where did that even come from?"

"We got together and made catchphrases for ourselves," Reuben explained with as much cheer as he could force into his voice. "It's a proud mark of success, and I highly recommend it."

"Then mine would be… 'death before taxes'?" Scrubz voiced the phrase more as a question than as anything else, and Reuben waved one hand in a see-saw motion.

"That's not *bad*, but it sounds more like you want to revolt against the British than anything else. Keep going, though; you'll find something that fits."

"These symbols on the door… I think they're clues." Nacho brushed his fingers over the inlaid images and considered the three other dungeons they knew of. "The Hive, the Dovecote, and the Hen House of Hana Banana. Out of all of them, it was pretty clear that if we want a claw, we should go after either those huge pigeons, or the hen house. What do you guys think?"

No one had a better solution, so as they retraced their steps, they decided to climb any staircase they found that might offer a closer entrance to their base. Scrubz followed his chalk marks, aiming for a somewhat familiar area, considering what might be above them if they emerged in the wrong location. He finally suggested one that looked just like all the others: a fairly industrial staircase with smooth concrete and a painted railing.

When they reached the top, Scrubz pushed through the waiting door, and they found themselves on the street. Nacho inspected the buildings carefully and confirmed that they'd emerged next to the Yard House restaurant on Thirteenth and Main.

The minute they were all outside, the door slammed shut.

Howdy, Player! We don't want you running back down into the KC Cesspit of Patron Playfulness; at least, not until you've earned a ticket through some serious bloodshed. For now, this door is closed!

The thunderous cacophony of dozens of the dreadful bodybuilder-sized pigeons shook the ground as they came sweeping down on feathery wings. Those were the only fluffy part of the angry birds: the rest of their bodies were bulging with ropy muscles and popping veins.

Even that wasn't enough for the UnderFun. The roided-out pigeons hadn't come alone: a roaring buzz erupted in the air a heart stopping second later. The bees were on their way.

Ever since the Brunch Force had arrived in the DKCU, the monsters hadn't really focused on them, not even when Nacho had cooked up meat, nor when they'd taken over a hotel for a base. Now, the monster birds seemed to be drawn directly to Nacho and his friends.

Almost as if their necks were marked with a bright red letter that acted like monster bait.

CHAPTER TWENTY-EIGHT

Cootie Pigeon
Effective Tier/Level:??
HP:?

The name completely threw Nacho off, as he had expected something like 'Muscle Pigeons', given the fact that the birds looked like refugees from a militant CrossFit class. He was still more confused when one of the birds swooped down and let out a throaty, **Coo!** instead of ripping through his friends with the arm-length claws at the ends of its sinewy legs.

Eduardo swung his hammer, but the air rippled between him and the giant bird and the monster's attack hit him. The tank was instantly surrounded by a dark cloud of biting insects, causing him to let out a shriek of pain as he scrambled to keep them out of his eyes.

Ouch! Someone on your team is on the wrong end of a Debuff! You've caught Cooties! Lose five Health Points per minute unless you can find a way to beat all the biting bugs. Heal your way through the pain, or die from a bad case of lice!

Scrubz stepped up, blasting bees with punches and crushing birds with some truly devastating roundhouse kicks. However, between the boiling honey and the strange bug-filled sonic attacks from the pigeons, Nacho and his people were forced to flee down the street. The air was swarming with massive bees birds alike zeroing in specifically on Nacho.

A man leapt out of nowhere, a sword poised to strike at the sprinting humans. Eduardo, still surrounded by a cloud of biting flies, ran into him—barely managing to stay on his feet—and the insects spread from their original target to the person that was now hidden by bugs and screaming in pain. The Dinner Party didn't slow.

"*Eduardo*! C'mere and hold still! I can heal you from a distance, but you can't move or I'll miss!" Reuben yelled at his screaming teammate. Brie had taken the rear guard, and every time a pigeon *cooed* at her, she whirled and swept the attack away. She held out just long enough for Reuben's healing to land, and then they had to run.

The stalemate could last at most a moment, especially since a pack of dogs down the street started howling, and soon, massive mutts coated in clouds of a white substance appeared and joined the hunt. They didn't have fur; instead, they appeared to have deep-fried skin dusted liberally with powdered sugar. The only thing that stopped the team from being overrun right then was that someone in an unknown group of people shot a flaming arrow at the hounds, and the pack turned to chase after the new intruders.

Nacho led a mad dash into the convention center, but the bees and the pigeons didn't stop, effortlessly smashing through the oversized windows. Brie used their brief disorientation to hurl glowing lacrosse balls that hit like grenades, dealing fifty-three Health Points of damage and blowing dozens of creatures out of the air with every toss. The cook didn't even want to try to follow all of the bonus damage that had gone into making each shot hit like a rocket-propelled grenade, but he credited the Tier one, maxed buffing Skills of himself and Reuben, as well as all of Brie's bonuses working in tandem.

Scrubz had also been vital to their survival, with his heavily boosted Roundhouse Hammer kicks landing for sixty-nine points of sole destruction.

They currently had no shortage of heavy hitters, but there was a veritable *flood* of foes to smack around. Nacho and the other five people in their attack team had all been wounded before they reached the hotel. Reuben had managed to pull Eduardo through, but another well-aimed Cootie attack just might kill them all if they could all spread like this one was.

Eduardo kept babbling about theaters being the only thing that could save him, but Nacho had no idea what that meant. Even though they'd only reached the surface a short time ago, it felt like they'd been in continuous Active Combat for hours—it was like the Barbeque Tunnels all over again. The Scarlet Symbols of Accusatory Trespassing were brutal. The cook risked a glance at Kristie, wincing to see that she was already pale and running low on Mana.

Nacho knew that this was one of their biggest weaknesses— they had to figure out how to refuel Mana while in Active Combat. Reuben could heal them, and they had Nacho's left-over biscuits to keep their Hunger high, but refueling their Mind Players was an issue. "How could we contact Taye and the other people at the Residence Inn?"

"They've gotta know-" Brie was chewing vigorously on his sausage and biscuit combo, as much to keep her buffs up as to deal with her draining Hunger, "-what's going on. They got the message. I'm betting everyone did."

She shrugged and turned to fight off what the System was calling 'Mis-*Bee*-Haves'. The Bumble Dumpers were too wide to fit inside, and thankfully, the pigeons didn't like walking around; no leg days allowed for *these* monsters. They preferred to fly in, blast with their sonic attack, and then watch impassively as the clouds of Cooties killed their target slowly.

Eyes wide and shaking, Scrubz went running toward one of the closed metal doors. "We've got to get away from those things, and I mean now. I saw other people coming. We're in it deep, boy. I'll tell you what; we're close to game over!"

"I saw who that was," Nacho stated darkly. "It was only by pure chance we escaped. Crave couldn't have been expecting that the debuff would be able to jump to another target."

"That was *Crave*?" Reuben gasped in shock. "Yikes, I barely recognized him. He really needs to eat; he's got to be nearly *half* the size he was back in autumn."

"He got shorter?" Eduardo questioned tearfully as he picked bugs out of his ears.

Reuben scowled at the hammer-wielder with a trace of scorn on his face, "Yes. Just as the prophecy foretold."

Nacho ignored the conversation, mind racing. Though he didn't know what their next move should be, it certainly shouldn't be running into dungeons now that they were marked. Brie kept their backs safe while Nacho followed the rest of them through the doors and onto the convention floor. It should've been miles of empty concrete—convention center main halls were huge—only... this one wasn't empty. A ton of booths, but they weren't set up for Planet Comicon.

It seemed more like an egg con. Every booth displayed eggs. Lots and *lots* of eggs, as though the Easter Bunny was going to be the guest of honor. There were eggs of all sizes, shapes, and colors, from tiny pastel blue robin's eggs to massive ostrich eggs covered in sparkles; every last one had been stuffed into comic book boxes and packaged with hay.

Brie was taking on a bunch of bees at the same time, since she could block ten attacks at once. The Mis-Bee-Haves had seventy health each, so with her Combat Dash, she could bash one to death in a single hit if she used all of her juiced-up Skills to the max.

The welcome message hit them as Brie continued to bash the bees, just as her class name had foreshadowed.

Welcome, Player, to The Horrible Hen House of Hana Banana.

We hope you like eggs, because there will be a <u>lot</u> of eggs. Hana Banana is an angry chick, and she has friends in high places. You better bee-lieve it.

Bonus offer! Find the Dim Sum Secret for a reward of 25,000 credits! For every egg you eat, you'll get fifty credits, and we'll <u>double</u> your Mental Energy a short time after eating that first egg. Yum! Think you can eat fifty hard-boiled eggs in an hour? If you can, you'll unlock special treasures that will blow your mind and destroy your bowels!

Brie slammed a door shut and threw herself against it. "We're still in Active Combat. I can't kill all those bees, but I'm liking the looks of this room. I'm starving, and hard-boiled eggs are definitely on the 'healthy food' list. I can eat fewer of them and get a bigger bonus than any of you."

A tremendous roar shook the entire hall, causing a few eggs to fall off shelves and break on the ground. Others cracked and emitted unmistakable growling sounds that slowly grew in strength.

"We need to egg-splore this place as fast as possible, then scramble." Reuben swallowed nervously as he searched for the source of the roar. "Eduardo, let me heal you again. I don't mind being your Physic-hen, and I'll give you a medical eggs-am."

"I'll hold this; you get your Hunger Points under control." Scrubz ran back and braced himself against the door. "Go, Brie! You've gotta be starving. I've been downing the sausage biscuits and trying not to choke, but you've had both hands on your weapon since this started."

"Not quite, but I'm not going to argue with you." Despite the fact that she had likewise fought through the sodden biscuits, Brie didn't hesitate to pull a breakfast sandwich out of a Storage Slot and chew vigorously while Scrubz and Eduardo held the door. Another roar shook the place, and more eggs cracked.

Scratching noises grew closer, scrabbling toward them from nearly every direction. Kristie flashed her bracelet lights around, and Nacho broke out his Firefly Potstickers. Now they had plenty of light, but the booths offered a lot of places for creatures to hide. Between the roaring and the scratching, the tension was terrible. They were down on food, and he figured he'd need to process any eggs he could find, even if they probably shouldn't try eating fifty hardboiled eggs during this adventure. They could always come back.

Once he decided that he needed to get cooking, Nacho was able to calm himself down. Having a set plan always helped with that. "Eggs are eggs... at least I hope."

Scrubz and Eduardo were doing their best to keep the doors closed, but a few hooked legs from the Mis-Bee-Haves threatened to throw the doors wide, or burst right through them. Brie, still chewing, broke the offending legs with a single swipe of Mr. Lacrosse Stick.

Reuben spoke up, all playfulness leeched from his tone. "We either need to go out there and kill those bees to end Active Combat, or we need to make a run for it through the shelves. If we can just manage a few minutes of regular time, Kristie and I can get some of our Mana back. I don't know about you, but a little rest would be egg-celent."

"No more bad yokes!" Kristie laughed a bit too hard at that. "I say we make a run for the egg-spress lane."

Nacho had already brought his skillet and cleaver out and was eyeing the plethora of ingredients just waiting to be sizzled. "I need to start cooking. I want you guys to keep your stats juiced, and you need to-"

"Ha!" Scrubz barked out a laugh. "This is *hilarious*. You

think you're gonna be cooking any time soon? I'm telling you, those pigeons are coming, and they're gonna give us Cooties. Even if *they* don't, that Crave guy had like fifty people in his guild, right? I bet he brought every single one of 'em."

"Everyone stop talking and listen to me." Brie held up one hand, all five of her fingers outstretched. "We'll count down from five. Then we run to try to get away from the bees. We don't really know if the bees will come after us in here. If we can get far enough away from them, that'll end Active combat."

The open ceiling of the building really allowed the roaring monsters to echo well, alongside the scratching of whatever was running around among the tables. Kristie was already walking forward, lighting the way and preparing to run. "There's a good chance that Taye and the rest of them spotted the explosions from Brie's lacrosse stick. More than a better chance. Also, you know the fact that the sky rained down bees and birds means they'll come looking for us. I guarantee it. I agree with Brie. We find our people and hunker down while we recover."

"I admire your optimism." Despite everything looking terrible, Nacho hoped she was right. "We're making a run for it."

"Three, two… *one!*" Brie counted down, and with every word, she dropped a finger. They all sprinted away from the door, and down the main hall of the egg pavilions. The doors were flung open bee-hind them, and the enraged buzzing grew louder… but then something miraculous occurred.

A fight broke out between the invading monster bugs and the highly-territorial bug-eating monster birds. Reuben started cackling as he sprinted, and soon they were alone in the dark. "We did it! *Blood and cheese!*"

Not soon enough, but far before they expected it to happen, the most beautiful words the System could state appeared in their vision.

Well, Player, bravely running away worked. Active Combat is over—for now—but you're stuck in a bad place and low on Mana. You can always buy our very reasonably priced Mana potions to fix that in the future. Shop while you can. Regen away. Hope you have a future. Make it delicious, or whatever.

Nacho threw out his arms to stop everyone before they continued forward and set off a new monster that they weren't expecting. "Hold up! Mana Regen or not, I have to get cooking. Grab hay. Gather eggs. I'll buy wood. We can at least earn some credits, and with more Mental Energy, you'll have a bigger mana pool. Move!"

They had stopped at the intersection of two main paths through the convention space, and so far, they couldn't see or hear any more monsters. Nacho's Potstickers buzzed around in a circle, lighting up the area around them just in case.

Nacho started a fire while the others started picking off-white eggs out of the hay. Upon closer inspection, they resembled the general *shape* of eggs, but who knew what they were actually made of, or what creature had left them there. Scrubz grabbed a pink and blue one and set it down on the floor next to Nacho, while the cook bought a tripod and spit rotisserie set so he could hang his pot helmet over the fire. Unlike Reuben and Kristie, Nacho hadn't been using his Mana, so he had a full forty to work with.

Hey, Cookie, welcome to Active Cooking! No more Store, and kiss your Regens goodbye. Aww, sad face. But look on the bright side. You get eggs! Lots of eggs! Probably isn't good for your cholesterol, but you only live once, right? Unless a necromancer gets you, we guess. Anyway, good luck!

Nacho ignored the nonsense and got out his Coquinaria. He flipped it open to the breakfast section, still finding it hard to believe how beneficial a purchase Colonel White Beard's cookbook had turned out to be. He had a great recipe for never-die hardboiled eggs that involved his all-time favorite ingredients: salt, pepper, and butter.

A squawk echoed around the convention center, and all activity ground to a halt. It was close—too close.

Finally, they caught a glimpse of at least two of the monsters that had been scratching around. In one of the aisles stood a single chicken monster, only it didn't have a chicken head—it had the feet and wings of a chicken, but its head was that of a moray eel. It was soon joined by a tiger-headed chicken who roared a warning. It wasn't the huge roar that had shook the hall, but it was a roar all the same.

Other bizarre chicken-animals joined them, including a shark chicken that gnashed rows and rows of jaggedly sharp teeth. An elephant chicken with trunk and tusks had been combined with the body of a Rhode Island Red. Then, there was the classic buffalo chicken—head of a buffalo and body of a leghorn.

Before they had even realized it, Nacho and his people were surrounded.

The chicken menagerie raced toward them from all sides, talons scraping the concrete, and a cacophony of howls and various trumpeting heralding the assault.

You've been accused of the greatest crime an egg can accuse you of: Poaching!

Back into Active Combat you go, Players!

Nacho had no idea how they were going to get out of this one, but he pulled out his knives and popped his last Kill Basa biscuit into his mouth. He was going to be needed on the front lines of this fight, even if they wouldn't get any credits for his kills. "Need to survive to spend money. Dead men can't shop."

Unbidden, his mind recalled an old proverb—'if you can't stand the heat, get out of the kitchen'. As his feet lightly touched the floor that he was racing across, a wild grin grew on his face.

Whoever had come up with that saying had clearly never met a warrior chef.

CHAPTER TWENTY-NINE

Nacho's helmet was still hanging over the fire, full of water, and he was angry with himself for wasting the wood to get it boiling. It was a magical item that was specifically designed to instantly boil whatever water was put into it. However, that did leave him without headgear, so he would have to fight while keeping his exposed noggin' from getting torn off. Chalk one up in the 'negatives' column of having armor that moonlighted as cooking utensils.

His battle plan coalescing in a flash, the cook's inflated stats allowed him to tear into the strange chimera chickens before anyone except Brie, who sent her attack out with the swiftness of a Berserker and the range of a Mage. One of the monster chickens was sent blasting backward into a stall in a nearly cartoonish fashion, leaving a puff of feathers in an outline where it had stood moments before. Nacho swept down and under another, bringing his blades up as though he were starting a set of overhead press exercises.

The smooth motion, buffs, and Tier one extension to his blades combined to *eviscerate* the beast he had targeted. Its internal organs were swiftly exposed to the open air, and Nacho was coated in Putrid Mana-filled black blood. He didn't let that stop him: this was a target rich environment, and he didn't need to hold back in concern for cashflow anymore.

"Ayy, that little bit of downtime set me right. Positive Vibes, refreshed!" Reuben bellowed as he punched the buffalo chicken in the face. "Let's beat these birds fast. I have a feeling that today is fry-day, and I'm here for it!"

Laughing in sheer exaltation, Nacho brought his cleaver down twice in quick succession onto the head of a rhino chicken with its head lowered to ram him.

Damage Dealt: 22/66.

He deflected the horn with a skillful slap of his skillet, and the bird-beast fell heavily. Dancing out of the way, Nacho pulled up a quick System View on the monster:

Lesser Mammal Hana!
  Effective Tier/Level:??
  HP:?

The only thing that made Nacho grumble at all was the fact that his most potent attacks were still only hitting for twenty-two total damage. After seeing the amount of damage that Brie and Scrubz were doing, it almost felt useless. He was able to shake that feeling off as he sank his blade into a throat and tore it out with a practiced twist that sent a cascade of blood gushing in an artful pattern onto several other enemies. "I can get behind death by a hundred cuts... just need to get used to how many more times I need to hit them. End of the day, they'll still die, and that's what matters. Practice makes better."

Just as he was resigning himself to dealing low but constant damage, he remembered that he still had an upgrade waiting for the HungerCry knives. He'd narrowed his decisions down between Fast Whack and Kitchen WarCry, but he had never committed to one or the other. There was no time like the present, but did he want to double the base damage of his knives?

He blocked a cobra-headed chicken with his skillet just in time to whirl around the feathery wings of another shark chicken. That chomping shark mouth crashed down to rip Nacho's head off, but Brie saved the day. In a flash of black and gold, Brie blasted the creature away by swinging her stick like a golf club, shattering the lower jaw and sending shards up into its brain.

Nacho nodded his thanks as he moved through his ingrained attack patterns, a small portion of his brain considering the math. With a base damage of ten, he'd hit for twenty-five health with a single strike. Double that was fifty–if he dropped his shield and used both knives, he'd be doing a hundred damage with a quick double swipe. Frankly, he was fast enough with his excellent ability to handle his blades on top of his raw stats.

The choice was clear, but Nacho couldn't access the Store if he was in Active Combat or Active Cooking. He'd have to race away into the darkness to get out of combat, but something told him that the boiling helmet-pot meant his proximity to his pots and pans wouldn't matter. If he was baking a pizza in an oven, he was cooking, whether he was in the kitchen or not.

His indecision cost him, and suddenly a wall of feathers took the entirety of his vision. An elephant-head chicken hit him with its trunk, and he took the blow right to his noggin.

Health remaining: 101/126!

. . .

Nacho was surprised to discover how many Health Points he had, but then again, he was getting one hundred and ninety percent of his max of twenty, which added up to a fifty-eight in Fitness. "Cooking Magic is *delightful*."

Kristie had gotten some Mana back during their brief rest and was flinging bright pink missiles into the chest of a zebra-headed chicken. Interestingly, it wasn't using its equine mouth, only its claws. Each missile that tore through the chicken's body as if it were paper was dealing thirty-nine damage, and she could fling two back-to-back... but she was running low on Mana again.

On the plus side, it only took that one-two blast of her Sorcery Strikes to kill the Lesser Mammal Hana.

Reuben was likewise in the thick of things, having waded into battle to put his new sausage clips to the test. His flurry of punches put a shark chicken down, and a surprising number of teeth snapped off and clattered across the floor. Black blood poured out of the dead shark's corpse, and it appeared the Healer was having a ton of fun with his conditionally indestructible hands. A double punch combo was cratering flesh anywhere it landed, his fists hitting for a total of forty-six points with the double strike.

Brie charged into the middle of a chicken attack, whirling so the blows couldn't land, whether it be fang, claw, or rhinoceros horn. She summarily slaughtered any of the chickens that were in range, practically effortlessly even without using her Combat Dash. She tore her way out of the press after her brief stint as an impromptu meat grinder and loaded a ball into Mr. Lacrosse Stick, flinging it over into chickens charging in from the other side.

The resulting explosion scattered the beasts enough to open a path for Eduardo, who was pounding monsters into schnitzel with a yet-unnamed Skill that had him hammering the ground with an area of attack that was able to end the Tier one monsters with a single blast. Each time he used the attack, Nacho could practically *measure* how the man's body drained itself of water, and his stomach looked like it was about to start eating his spine by the third usage.

The ground strike ability dispersed destruction among multiple targets, softening them up for Reuben to go dancing in with his Sausage Clips of Striking. Scrubz moved even faster, his roundhouse blowing the chest out of an angler fish chicken with a scream and a single strike. Scrubz wasn't using the Gauntlets of Monster Destruction's bonuses, only his own Skill. Frankly, the metal gloves were simply providing his knuckles with the barest protection.

Nacho tumbled back into the battle, pressing up on his toes and flinging himself forward with the built-up momentum, his knives held akimbo as he tackled a beast that was about to lacerate Reuben's back. He killed the stegosaur chicken by slamming his cleaver into its neck until he parted the spine, then tucked and used its body as a springboard to reach the next one. "No credits! Only thing I don't like about this class… otherwise, I love it!"

A *hiss* filled the air as the water in his helmet began to boil over, but he didn't have time to worry about the loss of credits he was going to have to accept if the eggs were destroyed. There were plenty more to go around. No, all of his attention was drawn almost forcefully to the Boss Monster that had just come soaring down from the rafters far above them.

It was a chicken-headed chicken, making it seem wildly out of place among these lesser beings that had all been spliced together. The massive fowl was a factor larger than all the others, with feathers that were absurdly fluffy and bright yellow, the color of a perfectly aged banana. One of its huge claws was as yellow as the rest of the body…

But the other talon was a bright white.

"The boss has appeared!" Reuben called above the din of battle, just in case someone had missed its entrance. "Bum, bum, baaah! The plot chickens!"

The chicken queen leapt over the corpses of its comrades,

evaded the weapons of Nacho's friends, and charged straight onto Nacho. "What the-?"

The words had barely left his lips when the Hana Banana's claws ripped into him.

Damage taken: 71/126!

"You piece *of-*" Thirty points of damage were taken per claw that managed to touch him before he could fully evade. As he tried to force himself to his feet through the terrible pain and ignore the gushing lacerations, the Boss bobbed and dipped before spreading its wings and using them to slash into Eduardo and Scrubz at the same time. It had landed in the middle of their group and was about to ruin Nacho's cooking. "You're dead!"

"Call it fowl!" Reuben shouted at Nacho as he kicked the chicken in its comparatively thin legs. "You can't fight a chicken and not say something about fowl!"

The giant chicken squawked and looked at Nacho with rather intelligent eyes. Stifling his growing sense of unease, the cook decided to change tactics. He pulled one of the sticks from his guttering fire and flung it into the booth across the path. The hay burst into flames as he grabbed another stick and went running. Hana Banana let out a shriek, furious that he was frying up her egg babies in their egg booths.

Well, at least he had her attention now. The Boss bird lunged, her beak bashing—but deflecting—off of Nacho's skillet shield as he danced away. He was forced to risk leaving his back exposed, so he ran off with his torch. Hana Banana chased after him for a few booths, but quickly lost interest, turned, and started back to attack the easier targets.

"Oops!" Nacho couldn't let his friends take the brunt of all the monsters *and* the Boss. He grabbed an oversized egg, roughly the size of a football, and smashed it down on the cement. "Oh, no! I sure hope that doesn't happen again; that's *so* unfortunate."

Hana Banana let out a roar, allowing him to finally place the deafening bellow they'd heard when they entered the building. This monster didn't squawk like a chicken; it roared like an angry Tyrannosaurus rex.

Greater Gallinaceous Hana—Hana Banana
  Effective Tier/Level:???
  HP:?

"This… she's a Tier two monster." Nacho felt something drain out of him, and it took him a moment to identify what it was. "Ah. That's what that feels like. I just lost all hope."

Hana Banana came scurrying after him, and the cook started running, even though his motions felt wooden and pointless.

Motion in the distance caught his attention. Bobbing lights flickered through the gap in between the doors they'd come in —had to be either torches or lanterns. He'd left his Firefly Potstickers back at the main fight, and he only had a makeshift torch that was already starting to flame out. Were those bobbing lights a sign of Taye coming to save the day? Or were Crave and his goons coming to help the beasts? No way to tell.

Nacho stored his armor so he could run faster, and whenever Hana paused, he hurled another egg at her or smashed one on the ground. The huge yellow hen *hated* that, and each one he destroyed renewed her efforts in advancing toward him. Most of the eggs went *splat* as he threw them. After the first dozen or so came an unfortunate new surprise: a couple of the shells split in half, and tiny little monsters spilled out. Every egg in the place had the potential to become some kind of Hana, and the team would never run out of monsters unless they were all destroyed.

It was also the only reason he was still alive.

He had been wondering why the Tier two abomination hadn't ripped him apart yet, and the answer had tidily presented itself to him: it was limiting its power and using lighter attacks to avoid accidentally destroying the eggs. "Note to self: do *not* go into a straightaway or open area."

Nacho threw his torch into a booth, and the hay ignited almost instantly. Monster chicks, freshly hatched, squealed in pain as the flames consumed them. Eggs weren't supposed to squeal; they were meant to cook quietly, like the good eggs they were. He slid under a booth and went completely still as the Boss turned to screech at the fire, the covered table breaking its line of sight and causing it to lose him.

A moment later, the screech repeated as the monster realized its quarry had vanished. Nacho was counting on the fact that it wouldn't destroy the booth without knowing for sure that he was under it, and his gamble paid off as the boss turned and sprinted back toward the main fight. Once it was far enough away, he was released from Active Combat and laughed aloud.

In seconds, Nacho spent a thousand credits of guild money on upgrading the HungerCry knives with Kitchen WarCry. He was badly in need of Health and Mana, so he allotted himself a few moments to let the Regens do their work.

Mana was nice, but the Health Regen was critical. He'd taken fifty-five points of damage, which would be a death sentence if his buffed food wore off. At his normal Fitness of twenty, he had a mere fifty health. Luckily, he had a good Health Regen of twenty percent of his total per minute.

After sixty seconds outside of Active Combat, he was at eighty-one out of one hundred and twenty-six. Even if his biscuit wore off, he'd have at least five Health to his name.

Just as a new plan started to form in his mind, Hana Banana was suddenly next to his booth, screeching near the ground in hopes of getting him to reveal himself. He hadn't heard her coming, and the terror that spiked from her proximity to his head almost made him give himself away. He flinched but didn't cry out, understanding that the quick-witted Boss monster had doubled back to try to catch him as he came out of hiding. She took a massive leap over a booth full of sparkly eggs, the flames of the blazing booth casting her in bloody shadows. Around her, newly hatched chicks were growing at astonishing rates until they were man-sized chicken creatures.

The Boss radiated so much Putrid Mana, thanks to being Tier Two, that it was having a direct effect on her spawn. Though the variations in species seemed to depend on the size, shape, and color of the eggs, they'd all hatch just by being close to her. Nacho let out a light groan. "I *hate* Boss monsters that make more mobs for us to fight."

Taking a deep breath, he firmed up his resolve and thrust himself back into action.

Active Combat is back on like donkey song! Good luck, buddy!

He was forced to dodge to the side as Hana speared him with her beak. Luckily, his Skillet of Turtling halved the damage, but practically all of the regenerated health was ripped out of him.

Damage taken: 86/126!

The beak, like the claws, dealt thirty points of chicken pain with each pinpoint strike. If she landed all three of her edged attacks, that would be ninety points of death and destruction. He had no idea how much damage the wings did, but at least it should be blunt damage and not leave bleeding wounds that leeched more health as time passed.

Nacho let his Cry Chef's Knife slide into the palm of his right hand, and his Hunger Cleaver twirled in his left. "I'm going to cut you into chicken bouillon cubes."

Fully armored and moving as erratically as possible to avoid incoming attacks, he hit her with four strikes, each one *thwacking* into flesh for twenty-five points of damage. Nacho couldn't help but scream in excitement, "Yolk's on you, bird! I'm an exorcist, and I'm here to expel all the poultry-geist!"

The hacking of the cleaver was a thing of bloody beauty, while the thrust of his chef's knife was sharper and more precise than a sword could ever hope to achieve. Nacho noticed a little ghostly echo ringing off his blade as it struck six inches sooner than it should have.

Unfortunately… the sad fact was that even with everything he could muster, he wasn't doing enough damage to take her down fast enough to *also* stay alive at the end of the fight. Not with how fast she moved, and the sheer quantity of other monsters coming for him.

Greetings, Player! You are doing some major damage with those upgraded knives now! Too bad for you, Hana Banana regenerates half the damage done to her by magical knives! She had a bad experience with a butcher. You know… us. We had to cut off her yellow leg to give her the Ivory Talon, and we felt bad, so we gave her a little buff. It was the least we could do for her. Better luck next time!

"You dirty *cheaters!*" Nacho howled as he threw himself out of the path of yet another deadly talon. The Patrons didn't reply; they clearly didn't care and wanted him out of the way. "I'm in some serious trouble."

As if in response to his bellow, a familiar knight in black armor stormed forward with a giant black sword. She brought it down on Hana Banana, and the monstrous hen let out a shriek of anger—*anger*, not pain. The blow didn't even break through the giant chicken's skin. Another wave of Hana's monster chicken babies hit the knight from behind while the Boss monster leapt away, racing off into the darkness. To the cook's confusion, it didn't seem as though Hana was heading back to the fire burning in the middle of the convention-center-turned-dungeon.

"Where is she going? Wait…" Nacho had to take a moment to let his rational mind take over. "Kala? What are you doing here?"

The heavily armored Guild Master couldn't answer, far too busy fighting monster chickens. A lizard-headed feathery fiend lurched forward to snap onto her leg, but Nacho interceded by snatching the giant skillet off his back and hurling it right into the beast's open mouth. "I cast iron!"

Damage Dealt: 13/66.

"What-!" Reuben yelled over the din of the fight and the *Do~ong* of the skillet impacting the creature. "That's not a spell! You can't use 'cast iron' like a spell!"

"Watch me!" Nacho cackled as Kala's people rushed in to assist, but they weren't near enough to reach her side before Nacho sped over, grabbed his skillet, and slapped it onto his back. As soon as it magnetized into place, he was sprinting back to the guttering booth fire, not sure if he was about to be attacked by the humans now that the monsters were being held off.

Well, Player, Active Combat is shut off for the moment. Off and on, hot and cold, yes and then no; this is exhausting. Make a choice and end combat properly! Death! Kill or be killed!

"Alexa, silence notifications," Nacho called in annoyance, knowing that wouldn't actually do anything. Still, he was glad to get his Health Regen kicked back on; he was feeling a little dizzy, and that likely meant his sausage biscuit had worn off. A glance to the side confirmed it: he had only a few Health Points remaining. It would take him about five minutes to stumble back to the main fight, which *should* mean he'd be at full health once he was with his people again.

"How did Kala and the Sunrise Brigade find us? Was she working with Crave to get here… how many of her people were with her?" Nacho didn't know the answers to any of the questions that he was asking himself. Still, there was another more important fact that he had forgotten until this moment: with that sword, Kala was doing way more than twenty-three damage per whack, and she hadn't been able to hit the Tier two chicken for real damage either.

"If we can't kill Hana Banana, how are we gonna be able to cut off the Ivory Talon?" Nacho felt at the brand that graced the back of his neck, knowing that the only fate that waited for him if he couldn't breach the inner sanctum of the dungeon was to be continually swarmed by monsters until they finally took him down.

CHAPTER THIRTY

"At least I'm still useful over here." Nacho was pulled back into Active Combat as he closed in on his friends and quadruple-chopped a beetle-headed chicken into pieces. He leapfrogged over a Lesser Hana and landed amidst his people, then pulled the lid off his pot helmet. Thanks to his Gauntlets of Oven Taming, he was able to lift out the eggs without suffering any steam or scalding burns on his hands. He yanked out the last egg just as an inferno of pink energy lit up the convention center and drew a massive amount of attention: Kristie's Death Blossom.

Between Brie, Scrubz, Eduardo, and Reuben, they'd pushed the chicken monsters back far enough to allow an utterly spent Kristie to throw her blast radius in the middle of the cluckers. The result wiped out any wounded chickens, and wounded some more. Unfortunately, the eggs were still hatching, and the monsters were still growing.

Another wave of angry hybrid flesh was already racing toward them.

Reuben crouched down to see if he could help Nacho. "I sure could use some more Mana in my Mana Pool, but we can't get out of Active Combat. Where did you run off to? Don't do that again; we were worried!"

"I had to go buy upgrades to the HungerCry Knives." Nacho was already peeling eggs, finding it nearly impossible, until a flash of inspiration hit and he started cracking them with his knife and sliding the blade between the shells and the whites. "In other news, Hana Banana's a Tier two hen. She's got the Ivory Talon, which we need, but she seems very… attached to it. In other news, both Kala and Crave are in the UnderFun."

"Kala's here? That's crazy!" Reuben was directed back into the fight by Brie just as they heard the roar of Hana Banana from somewhere on the convention center floor. "What's the difference between a Tier one and a Tier two in practical terms, Nacho?"

"Their Mana. If a person or monster hits Tier two, it creates an aura effect." Nacho got the water boiling again, reminding himself just in time that buying wood to heat a self-boiling pot was a waste of credits, shaking his head at himself as he used a swath of Mana to process more eggs and add them to the water.

He slapped down red and yellow plastic Juxtaposition plates for everyone, then added Cooking Magic to his egg dish as he dipped one in soft butter and pressed it into salt and pepper. "You still need to hit for fifteen percent of their health, but the aura is a *big deal*. It almost always provides a specific effect, and in this case, it's the reason the monsters are swarming. When the Boss gets near her eggs, they go from inert breakfast ingredients to full grown monsters in only a few… I *think* minutes, but if she's really close, it only takes a few seconds."

Even if it seemed like overkill to require a recipe, the game logic of the Juxtaposition required recipes for any kind of cooking, which made him even more grateful this one had been quick and easy. He swallowed the first egg whole. It was surprisingly flavorful and kinda perfect, for being a hardboiled egg. Nacho got the prompt to add the bonus to his stats and upped his Mental Energy by ninety-five percent—a huge change from his standard of upping his Fitness—giving himself a total of sixty-eight and a half Mana.

The System was prompt to reveal the results of consuming the egg itself.

Greetings, Player! Aren't these eggs delicious? They were almost more chicken monsters that would've liked nothing more than to rip you apart. However, you're still alive. Are you doing the fifty-egg challenge?
Yes / No

Nacho chose the sane 'no' option.

Booo. Fine. You're no fun. Your Mental Energy is doubled, and you earn fifty credits. Breakfast is the most important meal of the day—normal eggs might not be brain food, but ours have been enhanced with Omega 300,000. That helps your adorable little human brain. Look on the sunny side up; you're getting something nice out of this.

Nacho felt the power hit him, and his thoughts crystalized into perfect clarity. With the boost, he had a Mental Energy of seventy-eight and an expanded pool of one hundred and twenty-seven Mana Points. He'd *never* felt so mystic and power-ful. Better yet, he didn't have to worry about running out of Mana. He could imbue *everything* with his Cooking Magic, and his next dish would provide a nearly two hundred percent bonus. And if that wasn't enough, he could also process as many eggs as he could collect. "Maybe we *should* do the fifty egg challenge."

"Hard boiled eggs while we fight? Choking them down is going to be almost impossible." Brie stated as she came dashing back in, spotting the plate waiting for her. She horked down three eggs, one after another, lubing them up with butter so they would slide down her throat. Hunger satiated and Fitness at a massive peak, she sped back into the battle.

Kristie rotated in next, pale and shaking—using her Death Blossom had drained her like nothing else. She managed to eat one egg. Being a Mind Player, it was all about Mana and Thirst for her, but this dish would also give her a surreal boost to her Mental Energy and Mana. "Oh, *that's* the ticket. I'd used all but one of my mana points, and I just about passed out. Now I have a Mental Energy of *fifty*? That gave me a hundred and twenty-five points remaining in my Mana Pool! I am *Kristie*! Fear the mighty Warlock!"

She slammed a bottle of Tier one Juxta-Ade to help with her Thirst, then turned and casually threw another Death Blossom into an oncoming wave of buffalo chicken. That gave Scrubz and Eduardo enough of a break to swoop back and scarf down three eggs each, then Reuben—though he only ate one egg to send his Mana soaring. The Healer let out a sharp exhale and slapped Nacho on the arm. "Thank *goodness* for your Cooking Magic and this egghead magic. My brain has never liked your cooking more, Nacho."

Reuben stretched out a hand and healed both Scrubz and Brie, restoring some much needed Health. Nacho processed another two dozen eggs, then stuck them into the boiling water. Using his Gauntlets of Oven Taming, he set the pot on the ground and started a timer, only taking a second to eat two more eggs just to get his Hunger Points up. Ingredient Processing and his Cooking Magic had drained him significantly, as both had a Metabolic cost per ingredient and per meal.

"Where's Hana Banana?" he called around the last bit of egg white stuck to the roof of his mouth. "If she isn't here, she's either sitting back and letting her chicks do all the work, or she's trying to eviscerate either Crave or Kala."

Nacho realized that might have been another reason why the Boss didn't seem overly powerful in combat; summoner-type monsters were typically less personally powerful. Instead—like himself— they were intended to boost their allies to greater heights.

A strident *clanking* filled the air, and to his discerning ears, it was the sound of a Death Knight running in full armor from a deadly enemy. Kala staggered into view, the metal protection on her shield arm utterly shredded. She fell to her knees, followed by her father and five of her followers, a relatively even mix of Body and Mind Players. Before long, Myron appeared out of the shadows, bleeding from a nasty head wound.

Nacho saw his timer was approaching completion, so he started plucking eggs out of the hot water and laying them out on a set of slightly-soggy comic books. It was time to address the elephant in the room, and he wasn't thinking about the monsters they had already killed. "Get over here and grab a plate, Kala. I have eggs that'll double your Mental Energy, as well as giving a boost for your Body Players if they want it. Increase your Fitness, and you just might be able to damage Hana Banana."

"The giant chicken." The Death Knight winced as she heaved herself to her feet. "The one with the white claw. We gotta beat that thing?"

"Nah, no white claw; booze is for suckers if you aren't in a safe place," Reuben called back, unable to pass up the opportunity.

"Welcome to the group, and do try to keep up. I'm sorry to need to inform you that we've decided on egg puns instead of alcohol jokes. Reuben, you need to put a credit in the 'out of context puns' jar." Nacho kept his eyes peeled on the humans as he peeled eggs, all while the Healer groaned and played up his suffering and constant draining of funds.

"I don't care what they say; I could use a drink." Kala's father joined the conversation with a wheeze. The older man, outfitted with a chainmail shirt and big steel plates on his boots, was leaning heavily on a nice spear, and he was clearly barely functional at the moment. Even though they were hesitant at first, Kala's people started eating gratefully once she nodded her begrudging approval.

Nacho kept adding Cooking Magic to the eggs and didn't spare any attention for the interlopers. He'd never had so much Mana before, and he found that it was rather nice. Once he'd finished the last of the cooked batch, he briefly turned his focus on Kala, eyeing her as though she were a scorpion poised to strike at any time. "We have to get Hana Banana out in the open. I was able to get her attention by either breaking her eggs on the ground or throwing them at her. We have to get Brie on her, and if *she* can't hit the hen, we need to run the abyss away and try again in a few years."

Kala peeled off her helmet, revealing hair that was a matted tangle of blood and sweat. "If we can retreat to the Green Room—it's a reinforced room where understudies gather for plays and such—we could fight the chickens one at a time. There's a single corridor there, and it would be an easier place to defend. Hey, Nacho… if I killed you, would I get your guild? Is that how it works?"

"You want it?" Nacho smiled a shark's grin back at her. "Let me transfer some credits first. Then you can *try* to do all the killing you want."

"Just trying to make conversation." Kala slowly fell onto her back, and the puddle of blood forming around her sabatons clued Nacho in that she was hurt far worse than she had first let on. "You saved my life back there. With your, um, pan."

"Reuben! Need a heal on aisle five," Nacho shouted toward his friends, never once slowing down his hard-boiled egg production line. "We've got a bleeder!"

"I'll get to it when I *get* to it. I'm a little *busy*!" the Healer shouted back. "Blood and cheese, baby!"

Nacho considered trying to make the Death Knight more comfortable but opted for shrugging and grabbing another egg instead. "How did you guys get here?"

"We were basically following you. *Very* basically. Myron got captured by Crave, so then we followed Crave. We were sure he was following you, and we were right. Last we saw, he was fighting pigeons and bees, so we decided to leave him alone to have fun. When we saw your explosions, we followed you into here: a clear mistake. You guys are Tier one already, huh?"

"That's right." Nacho let everything else go unspoken. Kala and her people *had* made the wrong choice by following them into this horror show. "How many are you?"

"There were a dozen of us, but we lost half of them right off the bat. Giant chicken went through our group even before her creepy chicks found us." Kala winced from the pain and the memory. "We have a couple hundred in our guild hall, and we didn't think we'd need them all for this quest. We should've brought them."

"No. If you had brought more Tier zeros, you'd have just been bringing along a larger group of burdens that you clearly have no way of protecting," Nacho informed her succinctly, only stopping as she gasped and her eyelids fluttered. Kala obviously didn't have long, and she probably had a nasty bleeding debuff. It was clear Reuben couldn't get away from the fight without help, so the cook dropped his egg with a long-suffering grumble and rejoined combat. After he took Reuben's place on the front line, the big guy nodded and dropped back to pass out Health like he was a candy-thrower in a parade. "I'm too nice to outsiders."

Moments after the others were stable, Reuben returned and put his fist through the head of a wolf-chicken.

"I could use another egg!" Brie called out with a nervous chuckle in her voice. "I'm in danger."

"Dry yoke and all?" Nacho couldn't help but needle his favorite Berserker a bit as he sped back to the fire and scooped up a plate. "Kala, get your people to start smashing eggs, as many as you can, then start burning down the booths. We have to draw Hana Banana in so Brie can take her down."

"You want us to fight… the eggs?" The old Kala was back, helmet in place and attitude right along with it. "I'm not going to break eggs while you people steal all the credits. No way!"

"Fine!" Nacho snorted a laugh. "*You* hold off the chickens, and *we'll* break the eggs."

"Kala, stop it." Myron rushed over—clearly *not* being held captive by Crave—short sword and dagger dripping with fresh blood. "He's right. We have to break the eggs. Anytime the big yellow chicken runs by, the eggs grow into monsters. But how are we going to do enough fast enough to get their attention-"

"Allow me to demonstrate my preferred method of killing eggs." Nacho grabbed a stick from his fire and threw it end-over-end into a booth, the hay and shredded comic books igniting in an instant. "Demonstration is complete."

As he went back to boiling eggs, he had to shake his head at the action. Here they were in an epic battle, and he was working on making the perfect hard-boiled snack. He thought back to the Evaluation Mall and all the trash talk the Patrons had done. "'Being a cook will be so boring', they said. 'Oh, you'll be stuck in the kitchen,' they told me. Uh huh. Lies, abyssal lies!"

Nacho couldn't keep the work up much longer: even with his monster bonuses and the eggs he was continuing to eat, he was running out of resources. He would be forced to get back into the thick of combat soon. Meanwhile, Kala was finally figuring things out. She took her father and Myron to go egg smashing, and the destruction brought Hana Banana right to them.

The Greater Gallinaceous Hana sped forward on her huge yellow and white claws, both deadly and ready to take his flesh off everyone's bones. She was heading right for Nacho, and time seemed to slow in his mind.

At that moment, Brie went Combat Dashing into the furiously squawking chicken and slammed her lacrosse mallet against its beak. A tremendous *crack* echoed through the cement hall, and the Hana Banana clucked the most agonized cluck there ever had been.

"She has *four hundred* and twenty-five Health!" Brie shouted with grim intent. "I can hit her, but this is going to be a rough fight. I need anyone that can help keep her distracted to *do it*."

"Rough fight?" Reuben called while punching a goat-headed chicken. "Story of our lives. Who can hit for sixty-four damage?"

"I can!" Scrubz turned on a dime and launched himself at the chicken-headed chicken, planning to engage it in fisticuffs. Brie was hitting for a max damage of seventy-two, and Scrubz could do sixty-nine, which meant the pair should be able to bring the chicken monster down with around six strikes if they were able to keep it in position.

Nacho tossed Scrubz an egg, and the Warrior shoved the whole thing into his mouth. He managed to get it down—dry yoke and all—and sent a roundhouse kick into Hana Banana's already cracked beak; causing the damage in the bony appendage to spread.

Hana Banana *screamed* and tried to rip Scrubz into shreds by hopping in the air and slashing her lethal talons toward his face in retaliation, but then Brie was there, spinning and protecting him with her Defensive Whirl. Mr. Lacrosse Stick swung around into the feathery chest, sending massive feathers puffing into the air as they were torn from the skin.

The giant chicken turned to run, but Brie wasn't about to let that happen. She caught the yellow leg with an exploding ball, and the bird was unceremoniously tossed into a burning booth.

With Hana Banana pinned down, fewer chickens were spawning to attack the groups, but both guilds were still fighting for their lives. Kristie's bracelets and the Firefly Potstickers provided the Brunch Force with a minimum of light, but shadows were still abundant.

Kala staggered and fell to her knees with a clatter, dropping onto her side. Myron let out what almost sounded like an annoyed grunt, then followed the trend—out like a light. A moment later, Kala's father joined both his daughter and Myron on the floor.

Nacho didn't know what was going on, his head only jerking up to look at them *after* they fell. Brie spun her stick and finished smashing Hana Banana's beak off, and the severed bone went sliding across the floor as the chicken wailed in agony.

Scrubz danced up, spun on one foot, and landed his other foot *into* Hana Banana's head, breaking her surprisingly-fragile neck. The chicken-headed chicken was finally dead, and in the following moments, the lesser Hana of various shapes, sizes, and biologies all fell to the floor, squawking piteously. Without their mistress's life-enhancing presence, they seemed to have collectively lost the will to live.

Nacho held his skillet and cleaver ready as his eyes tried to find the villain in the shadows. "People dropping to the ground, asleep, mid-combat? On your guard! Watch for-"

Scrubz raised a steel fist and screamed his victory. "Yes! I *finally* see why you had me max out my class and roundhouse skill."

Brie was breathing hard as she took off her helmet. "Me too, Scrubz."

"*Guys*! Ambush!" Nacho shouted in warning. "Watch out for-"

Letting out a choked gasp, Scrubz gaped down at the slender blade of a black sword emerging from his chest. He weakly coughed up a thin stream of blood and smiled. "Still alive enough to transfer every credit I have to the Chips Guild. Ha. Joke's on you…"

He slid to the floor as all of the gear that had been in his Storage Slots burst into existence around his body in a haphazard pile, revealing Richard Crave, who kicked the fresh corpse in irritation and wiped his sword—stained with Scrubz's blood—on the dead man's sleeve to clean it off.

"Does *every* person in your guild have to be a massive pain in the neck?"

CHAPTER THIRTY-ONE

When someone died in the Juxtaposition, whatever was in their Storage Slot appeared, but it seemed that Scrubz had been traveling lightly. A pillow fell to the floor off the low pile, followed by a blanket. A plate of Nacho's pancakes clattered off the shattered tile, along with a bottle of Epic Tier one maple syrup. That was it.

It was a terribly sad sight for Nacho.

A flaming arrow—part fantasy fire arrow and part concussion grenade—arched through the convention center and exploded in the middle of Nacho's guild members, sending them staggering away. Richard Crave was in the house, and he had brought friends.

The Final Victory's Greatmace Warrior came charging into the melee and slammed his giant weapon into Brie, who went rolling across the floor even though she blocked the massive attack. Reuben ran forward with a challenging shout, clearly planning to punch the flavor off the bruiser's tongue, but Rizzo slid out of the shadows and slashed the Healer's legs as he passed.

Reuben went down hard as the other dregs of Crave's organization, wounded, torn up, and mightily displeased, closed in with bows, crossbows, and spells ready for flinging.

One small bonus was that Red Suzy Blacke's exploding arrow had woken up the people who'd been sleeping, but Crave's people already had everyone under the tip of their sword, arrow, or spear.

It was clear that if anyone moved, they'd die.

Tears streamed down Eduardo's face as he slowly raised his arms in surrender. He and Scrubz had been close, and Nacho was struck by how influential the man had been, even if they hadn't seen eye-to-eye during their time together. Crave wiped his sword off on Scrubz's body once more, kicked the dead man's face, then slid the blade into a shaft of wood until it *clicked* and took on the appearance of a simple cane once more. He eyed the cook coolly and stated a simple fact. "Nacho, I'm going to kill you. Don't take it personally; you killed my people first."

"Your taste in minions sucks, and they needed to die." Reuben tried to get up, but Rizzo knocked off his leather helm, grabbed him by his hair, and placed a dagger to his throat.

The killer whispered almost soothingly, "*Easy*, friend. We want the Ivory Talon, and we want your boss. If you don't fight, you'll get through this. Otherwise, I'm going to have my buddy Battalion paint the floor with your girlfriend's brain."

Brie had struggled to her feet, but the Greatmace guy kicked her back down. Nacho could see that the Berserker must've used up every one of her Hunger Points to take out Hana Banana, because she wasn't Defensive Whirling or Combat Dashing to get away from the mountainous brute.

Even though he hated the outcome, Nacho had to admit to himself that he was impressed. Crave must've waited *incredibly* patiently before deciding to strike. The cook slowly replaced his Skillet of Turtling on his back and sheathed his cleaver with a flourish. He picked up the last of the eggs and started to peel it, as though what was happening didn't bother him one whit.

"Howdy, Dick Crave. Can I finish cooking lunch before you kill me? Just about done over here."

"Oh *no* you aren't. Cook *fifty* of those eggs. I'll eat them all. There's a bonus offer, right?" Crave strolled over and grabbed the dead Hana Banana, trying to drag the monster closer to the campfire but failing. The beast easily weighed over a ton. After a couple of tugs, the Guild Master shrugged and dropped the wing, turning his attention back to Nacho.

There was no Health or Mana coming back to them: they were still officially in Active Combat with Crave and his Final Victory guild. Nacho cursed lightly at the fact that the Patrons weren't going to go easy on them. He kept his expression blank as the rival Guild Master used an overhead chop of a fallen sword to cut off the Hana Banana's white claw. The albino limb wasn't the only thing that fell from the Boss, though Nacho was the only one to notice—everyone else was busy reading the message that had been broadcast to every person on the Starter World.

Dragon Spear Update!

Hello, Players! Richard Crave, of the Final Victory Guild, has found the Ivory Talon! He's come a long way, and he just might be taking down two other guilds at the same time. We'll keep the AKC posted! As for you, Mr. Nibbles, you may want to consider moving slightly faster, if that's something that interests you! You and the Walking Freds are going to miss out on all the Dragon Spear fun, sir!

Nacho had heard of the Walking Freds during the Probability Vision, but he'd been fairly certain they were just Juxtaposition gossip. If this 'Nibbles' was real, it was almost guaranteed that he was another *highly* concerning threat. Especially if the *Patrons* were calling him 'Mister' and 'sir', instead of some throwaway insulting title. He had *never* heard them sound respectful to a person, and it was downright chilling.

SEWER SKEWERS

Crave held the Ivory Talon aloft and let the cheers of his guild wash over him. "Looks like we got the key to our futures!"

Nacho wasn't feeling too great at that moment, what with his impending murder looming over his head. Crave had really put a damper on his day. The cook bent and rolled his freshly peeled egg in the butter, salt, and pepper mixture, then stood tall. "I'll need fifty eggs, Richard. You need me to process out the Putrid Mana, so you can't kill me just yet. Perhaps we use this time to talk, and maybe set some terms?"

The entire time he addressed the Assassin, he made sure to keep his eyes off the monster drop. Crave pointed at one of the booths that hadn't been destroyed or burned. "Cutthroat Charlie, Ranger Jim, go collect the smallest eggs you can find. The Patrons didn't say it had to be chicken eggs."

"Oh no. There goes my master plan," Nacho stated dryly as he held up the egg.

"That a fact?" Crave walked over to him, knuckles white from the death grip he had on his sword cane. "You have some kind of 'master plan', Doritos? You going to egg salad us to death? You gonna devil my eggs?"

That made Nacho chuckle in mild appreciation. "I must seem pretty odd. All of your warriors are here, surrounding us, threatening us—me, I should say. Have you thought about what happens if you kill me, Crave? The other Chips aren't going to be happy. Shouldn't you be offering a merger? We're close to a thousand members, and that *juicy* bonus. How many are you up to? Not a thousand, I'm betting."

"None of your business." Crave took the egg from Nacho's hand. "This is magic food, right?"

"Right you are. Chock full of Cooking Magic. You wouldn't want to spoil your appetite; you have fifty eggs to eat, right?" Nacho glanced up and met Reuben's eyes. His gaze shifted to Brie, who was up on one knee, leaning on her lacrosse stick. Blood dripped off the side of her face and onto the floor. Before she could fight again, she'd need healing and food.

Kala sat on her Death Knight helmet to Nacho's right,

327

holding her head in her hands and looking completely defeated. One of Crave's Mind Players stood behind her with red energy sparkling off his hand. Nacho could tell that the man was *hoping* Kala would make a move so he could implant spellfire into her skull. Myron wasn't in any better of a situation, as Red Suzy Blacke had an arrow nocked and ready to sizzle through his head.

Crave smashed the peeled egg into Nacho's hand, leaving behind greasy, seasoned paste. "Here's the deal, tortilla breath. After what you did, there's no way I can trust you. You're powerful, though the new armor makes you look ridiculous. How can a Guild Master be respected when he looks like a garage sale?"

"I'm a Guild *Leader*, not a Master. Hear that, enemy guild? There was always the option not to be controlled by your Master, but he would have needed to trust that you wouldn't betray him. Hard for a betrayer to trust other people." Nacho slurped down the egg mush from his hand, and his bonus Mana points were gone. He added the new egg Cooking Magic to Fitness and felt his body grow *dense* with coiled power. "Crave, I gotta ask… is it the happy oven mitt gloves? I didn't get to choose the color, you know. The Patrons love that bright red and yellow. Are you part bull, and you just hate the red?"

Nacho knew they weren't getting out of this without a fight, and it would be tricky at best. They'd all have to strike at the same time, and he only had one egg left, which had already been smeared with butter and seasoned before Crave had dropped in. He bent and picked it up from the garish Juxtaposition plate, holding the greasy food in his fingers. "I guess it doesn't matter, Dick, though I'm pretty sure if you try to kill me, my friends and Kala are going to kill you right back. In fact, I would count on it."

"Kala is a friend?" Crave's eyes narrowed, and a tight smile crossed his lips. "*Is* she now?"

"Kala, we're friends," Nacho called to the Death Knight. "Tell him."

She scoffed and shook her head. "I've hated you since the first time I met you. No, we're not friends. You *did* save my life, so I owe you... something. It's not nearly enough to make me go up against Crave, not even if he tries to kill you."

"Not friends," Crave affirmed as his grin turned wicked. Nacho hid his own smile; there was a glint in Kala's eyes that told a different story. The fact that he'd saved her life meant a lot to her. More than that, it was the fact that Brie and Scrubz had been able to hit Hana Banana when she hadn't... all thanks to *his* cooking. The ability to give people power went a long way when trying to make friends.

"Oh, hey! Any chance your guild knows you killed your wife in cold blood?" Nacho loudly questioned the Assassin in an almost conversational way. Crave had insisted he hadn't, that she'd died five minutes into the Juxtaposition when they'd appeared off I-70. But Nacho had heard the whole story from Crave himself, when he'd had a little too much Epic wine to drink. "Hard to build a guild based on trust when you'd do that to a person that was *that* close to you."

All color drained out of the Final Victory Guild Master's face, and he whipped his blade, ready to end Nacho in the next instant. "How d... how *dare* you? I would *never* have hurt Tiffany."

"Fair, fair." Nacho shrugged as though conceding the point. "I should have said 'you didn't even bother trying to save her'. That's more accurate, anyway. When that monster pulled her into that cave... well, you just looked the other way. I just feel it's important that your guild should know that about you, so they don't make the mistake of trusting that you'd ever try to save anyone but yourself."

"Shut your face-hole!" Red Suzy snarled. "We've *all* done things that we wished we didn't have to do. If something like that actually *did* happen, Crave had his reasons!"

Nacho chuckled a little. "Yeah, his reasons were simple. Either he was afraid, or he didn't like Tiffany very much.

Divorce is free and easy these days, isn't it? Just gotta… look the other way for a few seconds."

Crave stepped close, towering over Nacho. His voice was a strangled whisper that barely reached the cook, "How do you know about Tiffany and the cave? How *could* you know?"

"You talk to your Patron… well, so do I. I know a *lot* about you, Dick. In another life, we would have been friends. All the way until you killed me."

Crave grabbed him, and that was all the distraction Nacho needed to toss Brie the last egg with an underhand throw. She caught it and stuffed the whole thing into her mouth. At the same time, Reuben reached out with a glowing hand. That glow touched Brie, healing the wound on her head. The extra Health Points helped, and the egg would be a quarter portion, which would at least give her the ability to Defensive Whirl.

The Guild Master flung his cane sword forward in an attempt to drive the point into Nacho's chest, but the Wok of Blocking easily turned the blow. The thin blade did drive into the cook's side, which didn't feel good… but between the armor and his Tier one bonus, the blade didn't even break his skin.

A look of shock filled Crave's face, but rage quickly took over as he snarled in Nacho's face. "You're going to die!"

"Maybe, Dick. But not today, and not by you." Nacho grabbed the Assassin's wrists and started to *squeeze*, earning a scream of pain as his nearly-forty points in Fitness—thanks to his food buffs—allowed him to practically *powder* the bones.

Out of the corner of his eye, Nacho saw Kala's father throw himself at the Mind Player holding his daughter captive. Red Suzy Blacke turned and fired her arrow into the older man, generating an explosion of flame. Nacho winced even as he realized that he had just been handed a massive boon: the old dude wasn't going to survive that, and Nacho wasn't to blame. The cook had been the one to kill Kala's father in the Probability Vision, which had eventually led to his own death. This time, things were playing out *far* differently.

Much more in his favor, as dark as that thought was.

Rizzo tried to cut Reuben's throat, but an arrow sprouted from the killer's back, one Nacho recognized. The cavalry had come in the form of their amazing teen archer decked out in his Robbin' Hoodie armor. A purple spell grenade hit near where Brie and Battalion had faced off, and an instant later, a lacrosse ball exploded next to the skewered Rizzo and Reuben, knocking them both to the floor.

Abby popped up and slammed her staff into Crave's head, sending the man staggering back, unable to use his hands.

"*How?*" was all Crave could sputter as he gaped at the cook in undiluted horror. In response, Nacho pulled off his skillet and smacked the Guild Master in the face, sending him tumbling rear-over-teakettle.

Damage Dealt: 33/46.

"I have an answer," Nacho told the man that was near-death from the single hit, "but you're not going to like it. Those eggs are *really* good. You should've had one."

Kala leapt up with a scream, hacking her huge sword into Red Suzy with blind fury. It was far too late to save her father, but his murderer was right in front of her. Suzy might have been tough enough to survive one cut, but not two—but Kala didn't get another chance to attack.

Everyone exploded into maximum violence, the room filling with complete pandemonium in an instant.

Nacho dropped his skillet and drew his knives, stepping forward with a sense of purpose. "Two swipes of my HungerCry blades will put an end to this."

However, the Assassin was quick with his magical feather, which he was holding in his mouth.

"Crave-!" Nacho's eyes rolled up into his head, and he went down, fast asleep.

CHAPTER THIRTY-TWO

He awoke to bees, *lots* of bees—both the Mis-Bee-Haves and the Bumble Dumpers. Active Cooking was officially over, but his team was still smack dab in the middle of combat. Something new had appeared, furiously buzzing down from a big gaping hole in the roof. Somehow, the bees must've gnawed through the ceiling, and the opening allowed their queen, the Beehemoth, to swoop down.

That giant insect thing *had* to be a Tier two. Nacho couldn't get a good look, but it was strange and waspish, with far too many appendages. Reuben scooped up the woozy Nacho and started running after Kala. Somehow, the Death Knight knew the location of a place called 'the Green Room' and was leading them to the more defensible space. Nacho struggled out of his friend's grasp and stumbled back to Hana Banana's body. He collapsed next to the feathery heap and grabbed the monster drop, only then allowing Reuben to help him stagger along.

"Whatcha got there?" Reuben questioned with his characteristic joviality.

"Not sure," Nacho stated shortly as they loped after the

others. They were being cautious; thankfully the eggs weren't cracking open, now that Hana Banana was dead, but the stink of the place was vile, and they stumbled on a couple of dead Buffalo Chicken that hadn't started to liquify yet. Brie and Abby, bringing up the rear, had the presence of mind to drag the bison-headed poultry up a couple of floors and haul them along the Green Room.

The Warrior and Berserker slammed and locked the door behind them, only for the killer bees to hit it with a thud and angry *buzz* in almost the same moment.

No one spoke for a long time.

The first sound came from Kala breaking down, sobbing for her lost father.

Eduardo joined her in weeping, and Nacho looked him over, doing a double take when he realized that the bugs that had been infesting him all this time from the sonic pigeon attacks were littering the ground around him, dead. Reuben had been constantly forced to heal the man throughout combat, else he would have been chewed to pieces within minutes. "How-?"

The cook paused and bit his tongue, realizing that it was not the time for questions. Their losses had been terrible, but the dead were already dead. Crave had the Ivory Talon, and he also knew about the golden puzzle door. If they didn't stop the Guild Master, he was going to have a weapon in his hands that would enable him to kill not only them, but *anyone* who wouldn't submit to what was sure to be the start of a tyrannical rule.

No matter what happened, they had to heal up and get out there.

What Kala had called the 'Green Room' was just a concrete square area with industrial carpet covering the floor, a few rickety tables, and several mismatched folding chairs. Nacho, like everyone else in the room, waited for the end of Active Combat... but it appeared that the message wasn't coming. The angry buzzing just beyond the barrier keeping them safe *might* be the issue, but it was upsetting to be considered in 'active' combat while they were all just sitting around.

To the cook's great annoyance—though he fully understood why—Kala spent the first few minutes incoherently mourning over her father. They needed to make a plan, and it was highly unlikely that she would agree to anything they wanted unless she had a say. In her current state of nearly catatonic grief, that wasn't possible. Nacho counted the others in the room and realized that only a handful of her people were left alive. The remaining members of the Chips Guild had grouped around the tables, trying to catch their breath and adjust their mindset.

His eye alighted on a stairwell at one end of the room, and he rushed over to find that it dropped down a few floors. It seemed unlikely the steps would lead to the KC Cesspit, but they had a built-in option for egress. That more than anything filled Nacho with relief. "Thank goodness for the old-world fire code. Everyone, we're going to be able to get out of here! I know it's hard, but try to keep it together until we are *actually* in a safe location."

To his surprise, it was Kala that got moving first. Clutching her Death Knight helmet, she dried her tears and attempted to take over: an admirable emotional swing. "Form up, group! We're going to heal up, get Mana back, and then we're going to run out there and fight our way through those bees. I'm not a fan of the Chips Guild, but we'll work together to kill Crave and every *last one* of his Final Victory monsters pretending to be humans! Every. Last. One. Of. Them."

Nacho let her talk. Even though he did not agree with everything she was saying, he had something very important to consider. Specifically, he needed to read over the monster drop that he had retrieved from the slain Boss. When he activated the item, which looked like a silver feather with golden edges, it shifted into a three-by-five index card. Scanning over it, he realized that it had become a recipe for Honey Buffalo Chicken Shish Kabobs. "That's an... interesting drop. I wonder if it's important for the success of this mission?"

When Kala ran out of breath from elaborating on what they were going to do to their fellow humans—which took a disturbingly long time—Nacho opened his mouth to offer a better plan… one that *wasn't* tantamount to suicide.

Eduardo beat him to it, thin rivulets of blood still trickling down his body from everywhere the sedulous lice had been tearing into him. "Yeah, we're going to destroy them all, Kala. For Scrubz, man."

"No," Reuben firmly stated. "At the end, he proved himself, and we were friends. I don't think he resented the fact that he chose to be with us anymore. To me—and I hope this is the same for all of you… *Bill* was someone I respect. Deeply, and truly."

Congratulations, Player! Active Combat is over! Well, that was a close one for most of you. Our condolences to your guild members. In lieu of flowers, we'll give the Chips Guild fifty credits and the Sunrise Brigade fifty-one credits. We really liked Kala's father. What was his name? Can't remember, but we liked him.

Kala went on a new rant about getting a measly fifty-one credits for her father getting detonated from the inside and the Patrons pretending not to know his name. All Nacho could do was tune her out.

Once his Mana Regen topped off, he did a little shopping for ingredients, then dove right back into Active Cooking. He wasted no time in removing the Putrid Mana from the two Buffalo Chickens in preparation for using them in his new recipe. After he'd butchered the meat, he stuck it into an unused Storage Slot. He paused dinner production to focus on making a generous batch of his peanut butter balls—the only recipe he could whip up without needing to heat anything.

He was even able to purchase all the ingredients from the system, so he decided to make two different batches for the different Tiers, since the cost-to-benefit ratio made it worth his time to separate them out. Of course he planned to imbue both sets of treats with his Cooking Magic, but he wasn't about to waste *credits*.

When she saw him fiddling around with peanut butter ratios, Kala stormed over looking like she was about to take a swing at him. "What in the name of all the semi-sweet Patrons are you *doing*?"

"Making peanut butter balls; they'll be ready in a minute. Had to buy a bowl. Heads up: the System forces me to charge you, otherwise I'd give you them free of charge. Sorry about your dad."

"You… you can't just feed us and assume everything is fine!" Kala wiped angry tears off her face with her wrist, leaving a smear of blood across her cheeks. "Fifty-one credits… why aren't you fighting me about running out there? You clearly disagree. I could tell by the look on your face."

Kristie quietly took the lead. "We're hoping the stairs in the back lead down to the KC Cesspit, which would take us to the inner sanctum's golden puzzle door. That's where Crave is heading. If I'm guessing correctly, Nacho thinks that we will be able to cut him off even if we take the time that we need to prepare."

Nacho merely nodded as he rolled his hands back and forth in smooth motions, not wasting any effort as he dropped a completed ball and started forming another.

"We can't go out there." That fact seemed to *dawn* on Eduardo in lieu of him making the connection logically. "We're marked. At least… Bill was. So I *can* go out there."

He'd replaced his crying with raging, but Kala ignored him as she furrowed her brow and took a fresh grip on her huge sword. "I'll take my people and go the normal way, right through the center of anything that gets in our way. Tell us how to get into the KC Cesspit."

Brie barked out a scathing mimicry of a laugh. "So you can kill Crave, grab the Ivory Talon, and get the Dragon Spear? It's not happening, Kala. Our way or nothing."

"That's right!" Abby agreed with gusto, sending a bit of

side-eye at the grimacing Death Knight. "You're going to follow our lead, Kala. We have the power, and we have the Cooking Magic. It's delicious and nutritious, full of superstitious!"

"If you *think* that I am going to listen to *you-*" Kala broke into a full bellow as they all devolved into yelling at each other, and in an instant, chaos flooded the room.

"Nah." Nacho calmly collected his cooking equipment, crossed over to the steps, and started down. He felt terrible for Scrubz. He shook his head. Whoops... they were calling him Bill again, after Reuben's impassioned words. It was strange that Kala's father was killed as well. It was almost as though the Juxtaposition had fixed events in time that the Patrons *wanted* to make happen. Or was it all chance and chaos? Nacho couldn't decide which was worse: having the entire universe out to get him at a specific moment in time, or having a chance to live... then dying no matter what, just because the people around him were so nightmarish.

He went down to the first landing, his Firefly Potstickers *buzzing* around to ensure that nothing crept out of the darkness to catch him unawares. He could still hear the yelling, but it was less intense, and he could easily sprint up the stairs in case someone called for him.

Dropping back into the smooth, practiced rhythm for his personal catharsis, Nacho rolled all of the Tier zero peanut butter balls and stored them on one tray until the mixture was completely finished, then got to work making his Tier one snacks. He needed to clear his head, but his thoughts were screaming in his skull as loudly as the argument one floor up.

"Crave has the Ivory Talon, and he knew about the inner sanctum's golden puzzle door... how? Probably because his Patron had told him about it, or it was part of the information package he got for betting his entire guild on winning," Nacho muttered sullenly, completely ignoring the fact that his Patron was trying to help him in a similar manner. "Dirty cheater... clearly, Fourtuna's helping him. Then there was that thing with Hana Banana being resistant to magic knives?

That was blatant favoritism and an attempt to off me, I just *know* it."

It could have been that the Patrons were furious at Kronos for giving Nacho the Probability Vision, which had allowed him to become a Common Cook. Or it could just have been the fact that he *was* a Satiation player, and Kronos being his Patron had nothing to do with it. The Patrons truly seemed to hate anything that would impact their desires for bloodshed and violence, especially when Humanity was doing it to themselves.

Nacho heaved out a sigh. He shouldn't feel bad about Bill. Players died. It was part of the Juxtaposition. The game was terrible, unfair, and there was no changing it. Yet at the minimum, losing Bill and the Ivory Talon in one fell swoop had infuriated Nacho like nothing else ever could. Beyond the fact that he was down a friend and effective teammate, Bill had been one of his main detractors. Nacho had worked hard to sway the obstinate man to his side, and with him gone, the cook was likely going to need to deal with a new opposition leader that might not come around to Team Dinner Party being in full control.

He heard footsteps as his thoughts slowed, and he expected that Reuben had come to talk to him. Instead, Taye came shuffling down with the hood of his Robbin' Hoodie armor thrown back. Nacho eyed him, then nodded at a stair. "Sit down. Can I get you something to eat?"

"Not sure." Taye sat with the end of his bow resting on the floor between his legs. "That arguing up there got to me. Kala hasn't changed a bit. She's the same old power-hungry control freak. It's weird... she wants power and will do *anything* to get it. I was offered all the power I could take, and I didn't want it. It's ironic."

Nacho held out a treat with an apologetic smile. "Can I offer you a peanut butter ball in this trying time?"

Taye winced even though he took one. "That's a reference to a meme of some kind, isn't it? It's cringy to see old people-"

"You watch your mouth; I'm nowhere *near* old." Nacho

waved at his magnificent self. "Look at this strapping young body, wiry muscles, and debonair good looks."

"You're not helping. What college student says 'debonair'? It's like you're an old man in your head, and it's freaky." Taye sighed as he ran out of tiny insults, missing the spastic twitching on Nacho's face as the cook held off on spilling his own secrets. "Even though I'm down on Hunger Points, I just don't want to eat. For a second there, I thought Kala would join us, but then she went right back to being... *Kala*."

"She has her own issues, for sure. We all do." Nacho shrugged as Taye met his gaze and nodded seriously. The cook narrowed his eyes. "Don't look at me like that; I'm right as rain over here. You know... when I saved her life back there, and when she saw what Brie and Bill could do, she changed her tune real fast. You need to remember, she's just lost her dad and she's under a huge amount of stress. Her people are looking to her for answers while the leader of the most powerful guild on this planet makes peanut butter balls and whistles like nothing could ever phase him."

"This is weird." Taye chuckled even while speaking his mind. "*You*, standing up for Kala? Never thought I'd see the day."

Silence surrounded them for a few moments, aside from the slight *swish* of batter being rolled back and forth into a shapely shape. Nacho had braced his *Aria* open and was casually browsing recipes between balls, searching for another option that people could easily swallow that could turn his round snack into a square meal. "I bet you thought about leaving people on their own and going off to succeed privately when the Juxtaposition first hit. It couldn't have been easy to have Kala breathing down your neck, let alone so many other people doubting the advice you were giving them."

Taye nodded and tapped his bow on the concrete step. "You *bet* I thought about leaving. It would've been... just so much easier to do everything on my own. But it would've been harder too, in a way. I mean, being alone when the world is ending is worse than being with people, unless they're *all* jerks. They weren't. Abby was supportive, Kristie was nice, and Mayor Dan and Iron Becky were like clueless parents trying to understand the game their new kid was playing. It was kinda nice."

Both of them chuckled. Mayor Dan was good with people, but the gaming elements eluded him just like changing the manifold in an engine eluded Nacho. The cook didn't know what else to say—having used the *entirety* of his empathy in this conversation already—so he just reached over and patted Taye's leather-armored leg. He realized too late that his hands were still goopy from rolling balls. "Uh, I got your armor dirty. Sorry."

Taye laughed self-deprecatingly. "No point in keeping it clean; it's going to get bloody anyway. Sorry I was starting to lose it there for a minute."

Nacho patted the archer again, this time intentionally smearing more peanut butter on him. With a chuckle, Taye grabbed a ball and bounced it off Nacho's face in retaliation, though he still caught it and gulped it down. They all knew better than to waste food. "It's funny... I sometimes like the Juxtaposition, especially after upgrading. I kind of like it a lot. But at times like this... bleh."

More footsteps resounded down the stairwell from above, and both men went silent as Reuben came tromping down to join them with his leather helmet in his hands. His Sausage Clips of Striking jingled merrily as the Healer casually stated, "Breaking news: I'm pretty sure that Abby is going to bash Kala's brains in. Also, Myron completely creeps me out. There are a few cool people who just don't want to die... and I gotta tell you, they're looking at the Chips Guild with hardcore envy in their eyes. Betcha we could get a couple of them to join our side."

"You're forgetting that the contracts are magically binding. They can't jump ship unless Kala lets them. We *all* know that isn't happening." Nacho finished the last of the Tier one treats and felt better, as well as more prepared for going back to dealing with people. "I think I have a plan for your wife, Reuben—something she can eat without choking in combat—but I need to buy a new recipe."

"All we need to do is win, Nacho." Reuben shrugged and started back up the stairs. "Then we get an entire year to show them that our way is better. Magically binding and everything."

Nacho regarded the face of his best friend and felt a deep sense of gratitude. They still weren't out of trouble yet, and winning seemed like a longshot, but the simple fact that he, Reuben, and Brie were all breathing? That solitary fact gave Nacho some much-needed courage. His mind drifted back to the recipe problem. "I could buy yogurt and strawberry jelly, but I need a third ingredient. What could it be?"

Some purposeful searching in the Store yielded exactly what he needed. A single recipe, Tier one. While it would be pricey, it was *perfect*. He ordered it and the required ingredients, then went back into Active Cooking to whip it up while Reuben and Taye had already retreated a flight of stairs above him, still slowly climbing.

With a satisfied smile, the cook loaded up the sweet yogurt mixture into plastic cups and stowed them away into his Storage Slots. He'd just finished when the stairwell echoed with Abby's roar, "Get out of my way, Brie! I'm going to knock that armored emo witch into an early grave!"

Only, Abby hadn't said 'witch'.

"Better get up here," Taye called worriedly. "I'm *so* glad I'm not the one that has to be in charge of telling them to calm down."

"No one is ever going to be forced into the task of telling a group of armed ladies to 'calm down'." Reuben patted Taye's head. "You might be able to survive monsters, but you have a *lot* to learn about not dying in a 'safe' area… like your own house."

The three of them laughed, then speeded up the stairs when they heard metal clash against metal. Nacho zipped past them to lead the way, cursing under his breath.

CHAPTER THIRTY-THREE

As their heads popped above floor level, all three of the men blanched and ran to intervene. Reuben pulled Brie back and whispered furiously in her ear, while Taye tackled Abby and wrestled her to the floor.

Kala slammed her helmet on and gripped her sword in both hands, taking a deep inhale as though she were about to command her forces to attack. Nacho flipped through the air in a flashy maneuver, landing between the factions and shouting for attention. "Everybody *stop*! Before you do anything rash, let me explain that I've found a new recipe for the ultimate in quick combat snacks! It's called Life Hack Yogurt: plain Greek yogurt, strawberry jelly, and cottage cheese!"

"Kill th…" Kala's voice stuttered to a stop as she processed what Nacho had said, then thundered, "You… that sounds *disgusting*!"

Abby guffawed from her position on the ground, glaring hatefully at the Death Knight. "See how little *you* know, Kala. That's an old weightlifter's recipe. Not enough protein in your basic yogurt, so you add cottage cheese to get you there."

"It's practically a liquid!" Brie's eyes lit up as her attention shifted hungrily to the cup. "Yes! Hey! Cups are fine, but we should put that stuff in a tube. We could basically make it like Gogurt. A quarter portion of nutrients I could swallow down with a single breath to get fed and gain bonuses? Ahh... *yes*, please! Why didn't you start with this instead of pocket pancakes?"

"Everyone is welcome to make a suggestion on better ideas *before* I have them," Nacho stated blandly as he handed her a cup. "Otherwise you're just complaining about the fact that I came up with it first and are therefore showcasing your ignorance. Twice. Now, we all need to get out of here, and we *must* get along."

The grinding of the bees chewing through cement was getting louder, and once attention was called to it, everyone involved in the fight backed down with guilty expressions. Nacho passed the Life Hack yogurt around to his team, and even though Kala snarled as she gulped down her cup before rage-eating a peanut butter ball, she seemed far less shaky after eating. "Fine. We're healthy, we have food to deal with our Satiation levels, and we have water from the Store. Let's get out there and kick some bee butt!"

From the sound of it, a million of the Mis-Bee-Haves were waiting out there. They also needed to account for the Bumble Dumpers, and finally the queen bee herself. Concrete began to crumble around the doorframe—Nacho had to assume they hadn't gone for the metal, as chewing through steel was probably more difficult than chewing through concrete. Kala's people wearily regarded the wall, seeming to resign themselves to the fact that their Guild Master was leading them on a suicide mission.

"You sucked down that yogurt like it disappointed you." Nacho shook his head firmly as she tried to figure out if he was insulting her. "I'm not going to sugar coat this free advice, because you'd probably eat that, too. Charging into a swarm of bees that *absolutely* have a Tier two with them is a terrible idea. If you try to *force* your people to go out there, knowing what's waiting on the other side… I will do everything I can to kill you just so that they have a chance at living. I won't stand by and watch you mistreat them to that level."

The Death Knight froze stock-still, taking deep breaths as she contemplated attacking or backing down. Her sword wavered, then slowly slid to the side. "You have a better idea?"

"There's a staircase, and it might lead down into the tunnels or outside," Nacho calmly reminded her as he waved at the point of egress.

"Why did…? I thought you went down the staircase already and had to come back. Isn't it blocked?" Kala pointed the hilt of her sword at him as Nacho shook his head clearly, so there would be no misinterpretation. The Death Knight cleared her throat and grunted. "Oh. I thought you… look, my bad, okay? I was going to lead us out in a blaze of glory because I thought we were just waiting to die in this killbox. Obviously we should explore the stairs first."

"Let's not forget the point of this quest: getting the Dragon Spear. That is the main objective, second only to making sure that *Crave* doesn't get it." Reuben started to herd everyone down the steps, pausing to point at Eduardo, who'd collected the Gauntlets of Monster Destruction from Bill's corpse. "If you're going to use my gauntlets, great. Otherwise, we should see if someone else has the skill to use them."

"You're giving out free weapons?" One of Kala's people, a dark, skinny guy with black hair, raised his hand. "I have an actual boxing skill!"

"You're at Tier zero?" Nacho questioned absently.

The guy nodded, so Eduardo stomped over and slammed the gauntlets into the guy's chest. "I'm Eduardo. These were *Bill's*. We called him Scrubz, or Young Bill. He was my friend, and if you turn out to be a crappy person, I'll hunt you down and cut your hands off."

"Um. Hello there. I'm Ahmed. If I can, I'll rename the gauntlets to Bill's Gauntlets in his honor. Any monster I kill, I'll think of him," the brawler stated slowly as he pulled the gauntlets away from Eduardo's crushing grip. He slid them on and laughed in astonishment. "The Patrons heard me! They're now called 'Young Bill's Gauntlets of Monster Bashing'. I'll even do an extra point of damage if I yell, 'For Bill!' before I attack."

Nacho, as well as the others that he could see, actually felt touched by that gesture. It was a rare moment when the Patrons decided to do a properly nice thing. Reuben kept on herding folks toward the stairs, keeping the moment from stretching. "Come *on*, people. We've got to get moving. I know you're all abuzz with ideas, but If you don't hurry, you will be *buzzing* with bees killing you. Yes, not my best joke, but I *really* don't want to be penetrated by a stinger longer than my arm."

At the bottom of the stairs, the collective teams joyfully discovered a concrete hallway that led to the outside of the building. Further exploration indicated the possibility of revealing a path into the KC Cesspit from the convention center proper, but the concrete raining down the stairwell from the bees' destruction of the wall above informed them that they didn't have the time to figure it out.

Nacho turned around to face his people in the corridor. He had his skillet on his back, Reuban had retrieved his pot and dropped it on Nacho's head, and the cook was officially ready for whatever battle might materialize. He slowly chewed a peanut butter ball, then chased it down with a cup of his strawberry Life Hack yogurt. The slurry went down pretty quickly, though the chunky cottage cheese texture was going to take a bit to get used to.

He promptly added the bonuses to his Fitness, since he was planning on being on the front lines of combat the rest of his night. Taking a breath to center himself, Nacho addressed the two guilds. "When we get out there, we're going to run to the Yard House restaurant down the street. I can almost guarantee that we'll find a doorway nearby that will lead us down into the sewers; the stairs we found in the cesspit were labeled. Keep in mind, five of us are marked, but we can use that to our advantage. The monsters will focus on us, and you can hit them in the rear."

Myron tittered, only for Kala to silence him with the *squeak* of her helmet as she turned to give him a dead stare. Reuben ignored the byplay and doubled down on the immaturity. "That's right. Blast them right in the butt! You know what we should do? Start a new raid group. The Posterior Patrol? Thoughts?"

Brie didn't acknowledge her husband except to add, "Joining our party isn't a bad idea. Kala. We're the Brunch Force. Don't mind the name, it's a... we have a food thing going on. Don't ask."

Kala didn't respond right away. Nacho figured it would be a fight, and that she'd want *them* to join *her* party. A pleasant surprise occurred as a defeated sigh leaked out of the Death Knight's helmet. "*Fine*. We'll join your Brunch Force. How about we rename it the Lunch Bunch?"

"Maybe next time, if we decide to downgrade our naming conventions even further. Like... if we take a bunch of blows to the head." Brie kept her voice even. "Just join the Brunch Force."

"Hold your human treadmills there, Brie. For the record, Lunch Bunch is really good." No one could tell if Reuben was trying to soothe things over, or if he genuinely believed that it was a good name.

"Human... treadmill?" The Death Knight's voice was on the edge of breaking, clearly unsure whether they were making fun of her.

"Can't hold your horses; they turn into monsters if you don't do it right," Reuben informed her earnestly.

"Let's just join them, Kala. Before we get more of... whatever this is," Ahmed called, banging his fists together. An instant later, several *pings* rang from the System as Kala and her people joined the Brunch Force.

Nacho peeked outside of the building and confirmed that the coast was clear. At first. As soon as his head poked past the stone, the mark on his neck lit up, and big bee bodies lifted off the convention center, angry about something they didn't understand. He withdrew inside, and they returned to swarming through the hole in the roof.

Steeling himself for combat, Nacho sprinted in full armor toward the Yard House, followed by the others as closely as possible. Thanks to his *massive* Fitness, Nacho reached cover under a copse of trees to the north of the convention center and was forced to wait for more than a dozen seconds until the last of the group finally caught up.

There was enough dead foliage and branches to hide them, and it seemed that the mark on his neck produced some kind of line-of-sight signal. The cook took a quick head count, finding that they had about twenty people all told. Nacho thought about sending someone back to the Residence Inn to call in the rest of the Brunch Force, but they didn't have the time. They couldn't spare a single person, and frankly… most of the others would only be a burden against the Tier one monsters, and bait at best against the Tier twos. Worse, Crave might already be at the inner sanctum's golden puzzle door.

Nacho and the Brunch Force had just reached their target street when the *cooing* started. After the first call, there was suddenly a *whole* lotta cooing going on. A slow glance upward revealed that endless flocks of pigeons had perched on the rooftops, flexing their weirdly muscled wings and stretching the tendons on their necks. They were staring directly at Nacho and the Brunch Force.

The cook kept his knives sheathed, as he had a plan to help in other ways. He started to call out directions, only for Brie to take charge—as was her right as field commander. "If you have a projectile weapon, concentrate on one bird at a time. Take them out before they can get close, since we want to avoid their Cootie attacks. Abby, the pigeons will concentrate on me, since I'm marked. I'll take point, and when they swoop in, you pluck their tail feathers."

Ahmed ran forward with his gauntlets raised. "I can block

an attack if I don't punch. I'll block, punch, then block again. Put me where I'm needed."

Kala also shoved her way to the front. "My armor should keep me safe."

"It *won't*. They attack with a damage-over-time debuff that hops to anyone else that gets too close. Eduardo got hit with it and... actually, how *did* you get rid of it? It had something to do with the Green Room, right?" Nacho released a growl of frustration when the meaty man merely shrugged in confusion. "Everyone with the Scarlet Symbol of Accusatory Trespassing will stand with Brie. That's me, Reuben, Eduardo, and Kristie. The rest of you get back and attack while they focus on us."

"I know how he got rid of the Cootie debuff! Tell you later!" Reuben paused for a moment to mutter into Nacho's ear as he ran over to the people who would be attacking from a distance. Spreading his arms wide, he incanted, "Positive Vibes for everyone!"

The glow on his hands flashed outward, rippling across their troops. Reuben ran back to Brie and activated his buff again, as there were too many people for him to get all at once. With a nod from Brie, Hazel opened combat by hurling her purple grenade magic. Feathers, screeches of pain, and bursting magenta projectiles filled the air.

Taye followed up with an exploding arrow as Kristie used her pink missiles to sizzle one of the pigeons out of the air with a perfect shot. It gave out a *squawk* of surprise and fell to the ground... then exploded. The cook could only stare in shock; even if they'd had the time, Nacho wouldn't have been able to process a single ounce of meat from that particular pigeon puddle.

Brie joined in the fun by whipping a lacrosse ball upward like a trebuchet, the concussive force of the explosion taking out a pigeon easily. Everyone smiled when they learned what they could accomplish when their stats had been juiced like snack time at a daycare center.

The grin melted off Nacho's face as five pigeons landed at

once and opened their beaks, targeting him with a collective sonic attack. The air wavered in front of their beaks, and the biting bugs appeared out of nothing.

"Sorry, bird. Can't accept that debuff. I've got this, Nacho!" Brie rushed forward, and the Cootie Attack was spun away, all the creepy-crawlies being dispersed by the hurricane of power. Kala, Ahmed, and Abby hit the five birds from behind, and the road became a slaughterhouse. The Berserker twirled her weapon, winked at Reuben, and made a 'V' with her fingers. "Stay fresh, cheese bags."

Bird after bird was sniped out of the air by Taye, the Archer coolly ignoring dangerous situations in order to reach hearts and minds with sharpened metal. He drew so much aggro that the flock tried to rush him from behind, and Brie was forced to Combat Dash and *crack* her stick into the face of one of the frontline pigeons.

In the blink of an eye, she smoothly transitioned into a Defensive Whirl, and the sonic *coo* hit her weapon, only to be dissipated. She laughed as savagely as only a Berserker could. As her ferocious exhilaration echoed off the buildings, she was *moving* once more, and another bird got Mr. Lacrosse Stick slammed into its gizzard.

Nacho knew they couldn't get pinned down. He spun across the alleyway as some of the birds dove too close to the ground, his cleaver making short work of anything unfortunate enough to gain his ire. As he flourished his knives to remove the putrid blood coating them, he led the charge to safety with a command of, "Follow me! Everyone to the Yard House; we'll hold them off there! Taye, Kristie, Hazel, get to that door—be ready to give us some cover fire!"

Kala hacked into a pigeon, refusing to retreat even though more of the parasite-spreading buggy birds were on the way. Nacho noticed her when he turned to make sure he was being followed, and had to force himself not to leave her there to be felled. "Kala! Follow the plan! You've done well so far, but now you *run*!"

"Stop telling me-! *Ow!*" the Death Knight roared as she took a hit that sent her tumbling. She didn't bother to see what had attacked, merely turning the momentum into a roll back to her feet, then a shaky run.

From there, it was a race to the stairwell.

The good news was that the pigeons ignored Kala and the rest of the Brunch Force as they ran down the street. That was the *only* good news, as those marked by the Scarlet Symbol of Accusatory Trespassing were forced to dodge a whole *host* of contagious *coos* as the pigeons exclusively targeted them.

One bird got too close, only to vanish without even a chance to squawk in surprise as the Berserker's weapon cratered its chest cavity. Brie sucked down a red and yellow cup of the Life Hack yogurt. "Move forward! *I'll* hold them off."

A light show of Hazel's purple grenades erupted into being overhead, followed closely by Kristie's pink missiles and Taye's explosive arrows.

It was barely enough... but it *was* enough.

The Brunch Force made it to the stairwell and hurriedly started their descent into the KC Cesspit of Patron Playfulness. As the last person moved into cover, Brie used the last of her Hunger Points to dash over in a flashy blur of chainmail.

Nacho escorted her inside, then slammed the door and locked it to the beautiful noise of a cacophonous *cooing*. The birds were not happy that they had been locked out, and the cook could only laugh as he stepped away and let the barrier block off the birds. "They might have muscles, but opening a door with your feet isn't easy."

The birdcalls slowly petered out, and the pigeons drifted off when it became clear that their meal ticket wasn't returning. It took a few minutes, but the System finally let them know that Active Combat was over, and they all started to heal.

"I never thought I'd be so grateful to descend into a sewer, but after all the stuff we've faced up there, this 'cesspit' is a breath of fresh air." Reuben took a deep breath, then slowly let it out. "Literally. The sewers smell better than the buggy birds, for *sure*. Also... I pulled a monster drop."

Nacho's attention snapped to the Healer's hands, curiosity and excitement in his eyes, only to freeze in confusion when he saw that his friend was holding up a small stack of feathers. "What... ah... what are they?"

"I'm not going to use them here, since they are consumable items," Reuben explained excitedly, "but all we have to do is stick the sharp end in the ground, then lay down in the air above it. Essentially, it allows us to sleep as comfortably as though we are in a deluxe feather bed, but in reality, we will just be floating in midair! This would have been a game changer at sleepovers when I was a teenager."

Utility items were always nice, but frankly the cook was a little annoyed that Reuben had decided to get all excited about them at this moment. There were far more pressing things that demanded their attention.

"Right; listen up, everyone. All we have to do now is run to the inner sanctum's puzzle door and ambush Crave." Nacho was hoping that the opposing guild was still wandering cluelessly around. "We know where we're going, so they can't have beaten us to the inner sanctum, right?"

"Only one way to find out." Kala grimly hefted her blade and started walking. "Hurry up, *cook*. I have revenge to serve."

"I'm told that's a dish best served cold?" Reuben called over, his voice echoing in the sewers. "Nacho, check your recipes?"

"Now's not the time, sweets." Brie gave her husband a peck on the cheek in passing. "Good work up there. We didn't lose a single person."

"Oh... *you*." Reuben blushed furiously as he tried to hide his sudden massive grin. He winked at Nacho as they started following the chalk markings that Bill had left to guide them toward the inner sanctum. "Blood and cheese, y'all."

CHAPTER THIRTY-FOUR

As they progressed through the tunnels, they kept their eyes peeled for any signs of other people, but the nearly identical paths refused to divulge any secrets. As soon as Nacho had that thought, he realized that he needed to get an answer to the pigeon problem. "Reuben, you said you know how the Cootie attack was finally defeated?"

"Yes! Right, so… it *was* the fact that he went into the Green Room. That by itself fixed the issue," Reuben stated instantly, then scanned the group to see if anyone understood from only that much context. "Nothing? Alright, listen. What is a Green Room for?"

"It's where the understudies in a play or concert go to wait and see if they'll be needed for the event." Kala broke into the conversation, clearly wanting this information as well. "I was in one of those things all the time."

"Uh-huh. Eduardo! What did the debuff tell you when you got it?" Reuben prodded the Warrior, who was completely taken aback that he had been put on the spot.

"It said… that I needed to kill all the bugs at once or find my way into something like a theater or concert hall to get rid of the debuff." He looked around helplessly, trying to understand what was going on. "I didn't, though, so I don't know what happened."

"Perfect. Allow me to elucidate on your behalf." Reuben cleared his throat and met the eye of everyone that was waiting on his answer. "You were hit by a pigeon's sonic attack, which deals damage over time and spreads to anyone else that gets too close. The bugs are real, but they can't be grabbed. That's okay, because you didn't need to grab them in the Green Room. They couldn't get off the floor or the walls after they were drawn to those surfaces."

"Right..." Eduardo, just like everyone else, couldn't see where the explanation was going. "How does going into the Green Room solve my problem?"

"We didn't *need* to grab them or kill them. They couldn't get off the *surfaces* in there." Reuben waved his hands in a 'come on' gesture. "Really, guys? We didn't need to pull them off of you because as soon as they got near the surfaces... the *acoustics* got rid of them. The *coo... sticks*. Pigeons. Sonic attacks. A-coo-*sticks* to the walls."

From that point forward, until they were approaching the outer rooms, no one would speak to Reuben, no matter how hard he tried.

"The worst part is, you know he's right," Brie confided in Kala, who angrily nodded her agreement. "Why couldn't the end of the world be a zombie apocalypse instead?"

"Listen up, Brunch Force," Nacho called as soon as they could see statues, "it looks like we've beaten Crave to the pre-sanctum rooms. But... just in case we didn't, be ready. Watch your back as we go through. Rear guard, we're counting on you."

The group grimly nodded and took a step into the room. The *thwack* of an arrow releasing greeted their entrance, and Nacho threw himself to the ground—barely dodging the quarrel that exploded in the chest of the person behind him, one of Kala's people, who was immediately slain.

Myron, also near Nacho, stared down at his chest, and in a grotesque mimicry of Bill's death, found the blood-covered tip of a slender sword sticking out of his chest. It pulled back with a *squelch*, and just like that... Nacho had no more need to worry about what Myron might do in the future: he'd been killed by the sword cane in a single hit.

Crave slipped into a shadow and reappeared across the room to throw more backstabs at the Brunch Force. "Limited teleportation? That means... no! *Everyone*, attack!"

Shadow teleportation was a cheap trick that Nacho had used back in the day, but there was one specific requirement that was terrifying to Nacho. If Crave could use that Skill, it meant that he had found a way to get to Tier two. Nacho spread out his glowing potstickers, eradicating every bit of darkness he could. Stopping Crave with dumplings seemed ridiculous, but in a battle, a smart fighter used every weapon they could.

Taye answered Nacho's call to action with his own exploding arrow, but Red Suzy melted it in midair with a flash of Flame Fingers. The payload exploded and blew the arms off one of the Patron statues, sending the gigantic spear crashing to the ground as the whole structure creaked. Dust boiled throughout the room, and suddenly Nacho could hardly see a thing. Even though Crave needed the darkness of shadows—not the obscurity of dust—the cook kept his head on a swivel, knives ready to strike, and *never* stopped moving.

Abby went sliding across the floor, leveled by the mace-wielding tank from Final Victory, Battalion. He'd nearly taken her head off with a cheap shot, and Kala stormed over to engage the armored bruiser in retaliation, only to be blasted to the ground by blue magic missiles and crossbow bolts.

Kala's guild member, the crossbow guy whose name no one could ever remember, simultaneously caught a flaming arrow in the neck and a blue spell to the chest. Just like that, there was no more need to try to remember the crossbow guy's name.

"Positive Vibes! Pull together; we can do this! Blood and

cheese!" Reuben blustered while raising his hands, and the entire Brunch Force glowed. Their Healer rushed forward with his fists up, punching his way through the crowd toward Crave. Before he could manage to get too far, Rizzo appeared out of the murkiness and tried to impale him, but Kristie's pink bolts cut through the weaselly man's leather armor. The thief swore and reversed course without hesitation to disappear back into the smoke and shadows.

Crave vanished into the shadows as well. Nacho and his people were well and truly surrounded in Downtown Backstab. Being in that room was like taking a stroll down Crime Alley while chuckling about how much cash they were carrying.

"Everyone down a Life Hack and form up on me!" Nacho called out as he threw his back against a statue, cleaver raised and skillet shield covering his arm. Just as he got into position, one of Crave's goons rushed him with a two-handed battle axe and a war cry.

Nacho deflected the blow on his shield, but for some reason, blood sprayed from his chest.

Health remaining: 35/50!

Nacho swung at the guy and struck him twice in the chest, but his cleaver went right through the strange man. It had been an illusion, and the goon's real body flickered into sight about two feet to the right. That big axe whacked Nacho again.

Damage taken: 20/50! We're fixin' you up a pretty hole in the ground!

"Hazel! I need you to shove a grenade down this guy's throat!" Nacho directed as he swung around wildly, hoping to catch the illusionist by pure chance.

"Coming, boss!" A purple explosion knocked both the goon and his illusory self to the floor, where he was perfectly placed to take the Splatter Mallet that Eduardo brought down on his spine to end him.

The cook thought about going for another of Crave's people, but they *needed* to get out of the smoke and dust and form a skirmish line in a well-lit place. His thoughts coalesced rapidly: if Crave was in front of them, he couldn't use his devastating backstab abilities. That did not pan out as he had hoped it would.

Nacho flinched as Eduardo screamed, a flaming arrow bristling out of his stomach. The Warrior survived the blast, but he dropped his hammer and someone kicked it away from him. Crave's sword appeared out of nowhere and sent him to the ground in pieces.

A dark chuckle echoed from seemingly all around them as Crave teleported away and repositioned himself.

More of Kala's people were killed. Abby was already on the floor, eerily motionless.

Brie popped a peanut butter ball and washed it down with the strawberry Life Hack yogurt but kept up her Combat Dashing. By speeding around, she couldn't get hit by a backstabber. She drove Mr. Lacrosse Stick into Battalion with a grunt of pure focus, and he stumbled back and coughed up a mouthful of blood. Unfortunately, the enormous bruiser didn't go down, swinging his mace and catching Brie's helmet at an angle to send it soaring off her head. Sanguine fluid splashed down her face, but she wasn't about to stop.

"Get to the archway!" Nacho organized the survivors as well as possible. "There are bright, magical torches in it, and there's safety in the light!"

"I'm heading that way!" Reuben called out just as a loud *bra~ap* echoed from his ring, and the stink of cheese filled the room. "*Ow!* I'm getting tired of all this backstabbing! It's ironic *and* painful!"

Having lost sight of Crave, Nacho knew better than to hesitate. He swung his Skillet of Turtling onto his back, and a sword point screeched off the metal just as it magnetized into place. "My skillet just saved me from death… I'll have to thank it by cooking bacon later! No! Survive! If we *win*, I'll find and make bacon!"

Not as many people were able to put aside the existential horror of what was happening and join in on any kind of gallows humor, but the situation being as it was… Nacho could let it go for now. Reuben made it to the archway and winced when he looked at his friend. "Hate to say it, Nacho, but you look terrible. You need a heal?"

"Eventually, but I have no debuffs. Prioritize Brie first, then Abby needs you the most." Nacho inspected his wounds, which were gaping and unpleasant, but none were actively bleeding and making him lose health. "Game logic is a strange thing, isn't it?"

"On it!" Reuben flung out his hands, wrapping himself up. "Hugging you from a distance, sweets! Now… I can't get a line on Abby, the dust is…"

Nacho and Reuben had their backs to each other as they carefully scanned the area. Hazel and Taye joined them, Hazel acting as the archer's shieldmaiden. If she started throwing indiscriminate grenades, she'd wind up hurting their own people. Kristie made it to the archway next, though she dived back into the scrum instead of finding succor, her silhouette highlighted by pink missiles whenever she got a bead on someone. Taye's arrows were fired with the intent to kill, and he was using his *massive* damage arrows.

The billowing dust parted in cloudy swirls as Brie dashed over to the archway. Abby, Kala, and Eduardo were down if not dead, leaving only Brie as their heavy damage dealer. Just as she joined the group, a flaming arrow zipped out of the dust and exploded in their midst.

Someone else pelted them with boulders, practically making it rain rocks—a clear sign of an Earth Mage in the opposing guild. A stone banged off Nacho's pot, and the Helm of Boiling barely managed to save his life.

Health remaining: 10/50! If you're seeing this, you should be fighting instead of reading!

Nacho wolfed down a peanut butter ball and followed it with a power yogurt chaser, devoting the boost to his Fitness to grant him a slew of extra health to play with. He couldn't even remember when the last boost had worn off, but that had been *way* too close. A quick check showed he had jumped up to a total of eighty-eight Health Points. Even with being down forty, he now had over half his health remaining instead of knocking on death's door.

For a moment, the cook couldn't understand why *this* fight was so different. Why they were losing, and frankly getting *whooped*. Then he put the pieces together. "Crave didn't just upgrade himself; he leveled his people as well. That would have cost… millions of credits. I guess Crave can use everything his guild collects without any fear of reprisal, but *how* did he get so many, so fast? He must have used almost everything that hundreds of people had collected on *himself* before we got here. Not… alright, it is surprising, but I feel like it *shouldn't* be."

The floor buckled, statues fell, and Nacho pushed his people out of the archway as his honed senses told him that they needed to *move*. Reuben and Brie dragged Hazel and Kristie against a wall, behind one of the only statues of the patrons left —Kronos in his toga and his Yankees baseball cap. That felt like a good omen to Nacho, and now they had a position about twenty feet from the archway that was relatively concealed by the dust, smoke, and ash hanging in the air. They kept their backs to the wall, and Nacho's glowing potstickers buzzed around them, preventing shadows from forming nearby.

"You're in my corner, and I should stay in *your* corner,"

Nacho murmured softly as he realized that Kronos had given him a hint to survival the last time they had talked. With light back in his eyes, he tried to give his people hope. "No shadows, no shadow teleportation. Stay close…"

Taye stepped forward, out in the open, drawing a bead on someone, then paused to use Eagle Aim. The minute he let the arrow fly, Battalion's mace appeared out of the mess and smacked Taye in the face. Their Archer went down, and Battalion laughed as he dragged Taye by the foot to the edge of the archway.

Trying to keep the desperation out of his voice, Nacho called out, "Crave! It's not us you want! The Dragon Spear is *right there*, isn't it?"

The dust slowly settled, the sounds of combat fading to nothing. Nacho scanned the haze for everything he could see, breathing a sigh of relief when he saw that Kristie was still alive, her pink hair nearly gray from the smoke and ash. Hazel lay next to her, barely conscious, though all the color had drained from her face. Nacho felt sick to his stomach when he realized that her husband, Hank, likely hadn't survived the fight.

They'd seen Battalion take Taye's body. The entire fight had been a massacre. Even so, the Chips Guild—with a *tish* of help from the Sunrise Brigade—hadn't done too bad, all things considered.

Crave was left with only his three best fighters—Suzy, Rizzo, and Battalion—as well as one last guy in chainmail pants and a ring-mail shirt, who was breathing hard and struggling for air. Judging by the soft body he had managed to keep even after months of near-starvation, the last person was a spellcaster.

The five remaining guild members of the Final Victory stood under the archway. Battalion rested one bulky metal shoe on Taye's body. The man heaving for breath lifted his hand, his fists glowed, and the wounds on Crave and his goons healed over.

"Not something you need to worry about. We *are* going to

get the Dragon Spear," Crave calmly informed them. "But I think it's clear that we win. Let's you and I talk terms of your surrender. I'm thinking *absolute* surrender, you empty your guild vault, and then join my guild at the lowest rank."

Nacho wasn't going about to get chatty and give away whatever bargaining power they had. Instead he weighed his odds of success in a direct fight. Crave had four people, as did Nacho, so it would be five against five.

The silence stretched, and Crave didn't approve. "Doritos, are you listening?"

Keeping his voice low, Nacho motioned for the others to try to ease into position. "Kristie, Hazel, how are your Mana levels?"

From the bleak expression on their faces, it was clear they were out. Reuben made a face and shook his head. "As always, we can eat to hit people during combat, but we can't eat to improve our Mana situation."

Crave wasn't going to wait long, and he had Taye as a hostage. "Last chance, Doritos. Battalion is getting *impatient*. There's this special skull-crushing thing he does; it's truly a beautiful work of art. If you don't want to see it, you need to give up now."

Nacho had a large bonus to his total Health for the moment, as did Brie, who was even topped off, thanks to Reuben. The Healer didn't look too good, so Nacho decided that any plan he made needed to limit his friend's involvement. Brie had a cup of the Life Hack yogurt at her lips and was sucking down the cottage cheese and strawberries to max out her Hunger Points. Knowing her, she was gearing up for an attack. Nacho considered that, thinking that perhaps she could Combat Dash over, then Defensive Whirl to save herself from the initial attack, but by then... Taye would be dead.

The cook took a deep breath, adjusted his pot helmet, raised his skillet shield, and crept forward until he was standing in the middle of the room. "Okay, Crave. No need for any more murder. Look at him... Taye is just a kid. Let him go, and we'll get out of here. You can have the Dragon Spear."

"How *gracious* of you to *give* us what we've earned already." Battalion let his mace drop onto Taye's inert body, and the archer let out a wheezing cry.

Crave grinned contemptuously at Nacho. He'd taken some damage, he was dusty, and yet… that melonhead looked like he was at home. "I'm estimating that your Mind Players are out of Mana. They won't be thirsty, because water, even Tier one water, is relatively cheap. Your Body Players have your Healer and your snacks to keep them going. Which means… you trying to buy time, Doritos? That's an expensive purchase. It'll cost you your little friend here, for starters."

Nacho shrugged easily and waved his hand at the downed teen. "The thought occurred to me; I decided against it. I just want Taye."

"You won't find any time here." Battalion lifted and dropped his mace on Taye, letting out a chuckle at the *crunch* and whimper that resulted. "Every time I hurt this kid, it guarantees that Active Combat keeps going. No one gets Health or Mana Regen, but how long will he last, do you think?"

Crave sheathed his sword back into his cane, casually pulling the Ivory Talon from his Storage Slot. "I know you want your Archer. How old is he? Fifteen? He couldn't even have his driver's license yet."

Brie stepped forward, stick raised and glowing ball loaded. "Nacho is offering you a deal. Take it, or I will kill you and every last one of your people. Though I might keep that Healer alive; I could use a spare to kick around."

The fleshy Healer turned a few shades whiter.

It seemed like Crave didn't know if he wanted to scoff at the threat or leer at her in victory. "You wouldn't sacrifice the kid. Besides, I have the Ivory Talon. I've won."

Brie was about to turn on her speed, Nacho could see it in her eyes. She was going to smash in Battalion's face. She could, because she'd been eating, and she had the Hunger Points and massive Fitness boost. Battalion had to be low on Hunger Points, and he wouldn't be able to block her attacks. The Berserker could wipe them out. Maybe not by herself, but Reuben and Nacho could help. But… if they attacked, that was the end for Taye.

"Stop." Nacho's hand shot out, and he grabbed her shoulder to lock her in place. As the dust settled, he had noticed something that changed *everything*. It had started as little things, one being the archer statues of regular people in the room. The shape of the arrows, the symbols in the circles around the door… everything clicked.

The mob drop from Hana Banana: the recipe for Honey Buffalo Chicken Skewers. That was the answer.

"Brie," Nacho turned to face her, taking his eyes off the enemy to drive his point home. All he could do was hope that his eyes showcased that he had a plan. "Crave is right. He won. Stand down."

CHAPTER THIRTY-FIVE

"Stand… down?" Brie turned and slowly met his eyes. "Nacho, what are you doing?"

"Brie." Nacho stared intently into her horrified face. "We lost. They out-level and out-Tier us. We don't want to risk Taye, and they're going to win one way or another. We'll back up, and… *try* to run."

He was communicating with her with all of his might. They'd known each other for a long time—they were best friends. Abyss it all, after everything they had been through, she should be able to read his mind.

"Nacho's right." Reuben approached and drew her back, giving her a huge wink when his face was turned away from their opponents. "Come on; he knows what he's doing."

Battalion barked out a derisive laugh. "Charlie, come over here and take over. Kick the Archer every now and again so the system can't mess with us by dropping combat. You up for that?"

Charlie—the previously unnamed Healer—crept forward and gave Taye a tentative kick, looking guilty as all get-out, but it was enough.

"Keep an eye on them." Crave tapped the Ivory Talon against his thigh and pointed his cane at them. "I accept your surrender, Doritos. I'll tell you now, I know you're playing games, but we'll be ready if you don't follow through. Make no mistake, we will *annihilate* you."

Red Suzy kept her bow ready, a bloodstained arrow nocked, one she'd fired and collected from someone's corpse. Rizzo had disappeared, and Nacho knew he could be anywhere in the room. Battalion stood as eye-catchingly as possible with his huge mace on his shoulder. "Don't worry, boss. I'll keep an eye on 'em. Get the weapon, so there's no way they can fight back."

Crave swiveled on a heel and entered the Earthling-statue Archer hall like he owned it. He paused. "There's the message from the System. Look at that: I'll be getting the bonus for bringing so many 'friends'. Love that they're counting you in the equation. I'm pretty sure the Patrons are pleased that I'm the one who's completing this quest."

The Guild Master walked up to the door, cackling as he turned the circles until the top symbol was a cloak, the middle circle was a feather, and the bottom circle was a sword.

He had chosen an Assassin's symbols, perfectly aligned for him to walk away with the prize.

"See? My Patron said he wasn't sure if things would line up for me, but it's pretty abyssal clear that I was destined to open this door and claim the Dragon Spear. It's finally time for Richard Johnson Crave to shine! Final Victory is officially the most powerful guild! This is me winning, Doritos... this is me winning."

Crave tried to turn the claw to the left, frowning as nothing happened. "Huh. Locks always open counter-clockwise...?"

Battalion threw a look over his shoulder. "Charlie, kick the guy again."

The enemy Healer awkwardly slammed his foot into Taye even as he winced. "Sorry, kid."

"You know what I always say... something that goes double for deadly doors in the middle of a dungeon..." Nacho took a step back, a quick hand motion pushing Brie and Reuben to do the same as they glanced at him with a question in their eyes. A cryptic smile started to spread across his lips.

Crave cranked it to the right, "Let's try that again. Me... winning!"

Every statue let loose their arrows. None of the bolts had fletching like normal arrows; no, they'd been altered when Nacho had first entered the room, right after the Patrons referenced his Satiation Player class in their cryptic message. Those statues—everything from the elementary school girl in braids, to the old man with his pants pulled up above his waist, to the severe woman with her hair in a hard bun—unleashed their missiles. As soon as the projectiles were airborne, they shifted from stone to metal.

Nacho watched everything happen, exactly as he had expected. The statues weren't firing arrows. They were firing shish-kabob skewers. The metal brochettes flashed through the air, finding Battalion first and piercing his armor. He went from tank to hedgehog before the Ivory Talon had even finished turning, before anyone else even had time to notice that there was an issue.

Red Suzy Blacke was impaled from every direction, and one skewer hit her bowstring, releasing an arrow that flashed off to join the shish-kabob barrage.

Rizzo fell out of a shadow, filled with metal shafts.

Crave remained standing for a long few seconds, but ever so slowly slipped to his knees. His armor might as well have been cardboard, and he had taken the brunt of the skewers. Inch by slumping inch, the pin cushioned Assassin fell face-first into the door.

"Practice makes better." Nacho finally finished his thought, nodding grimly as the stench of death wafted over them. "I just figured I'd let someone *else* do the practicing this time around. Messing around with trapped puzzle doors was never my forte."

The statues reloaded, pulling extra skewers out of the very ground. Stone cracked as the figures pulled their bows back, then everything went still. A heartbeat later, everything that had been stashed in the Storage Slots of the dead players appeared on the floor around them. In a flash, the most powerful members of the Final Victory were reduced to gore: nothing but loot drops surrounding too many bloody heaps.

Taye and Charlie the Healer had been under the archway, and to everyone's great relief, both were unharmed.

"Can't breathe. Can't breathe... can't..." the rival Healer dropped to his knees, then caught himself on his hands as he gasped for air that just wouldn't come. He flopped to the stone floor, choking on nothing, and the group stared as he writhed around.

Brie frowned and reached out to poke him with her weapon. "Is this some kind of trick or trap?"

Reuben walked over and knelt next to Charlie. "It's okay, guy. You're okay; we're not going to kill you unless you give us a reason to do it. We *might* kick you a bit, but that's just for petty revenge."

"Reuben!" Brie scolded him in a shocked tone.

"Just kidding." Reuben glanced up and shrugged. "I think he's having a panic attack. I don't think he was cursed or anything. My first thought was that a curse had been placed on the entire guild to ensure that they would die if Crave died."

Charlie nodded, though it wasn't too obvious, thanks to his eyes rolling wildly in their sockets. "Panic. Attack. I'm also... I was... only one left alive?"

He went back to hyperventilating, and the noise was starting to annoy Nacho. The cook walked over, straddled the thrashing man's chest, and gently choked him out, using his massive Fitness to ignore the weak attempts to slap him away. As soon as Charlie went limp, Nacho stood, let out a cheerful exhalation, then strode past his horrified teammates into the archer room.

"Sometimes I forget that you're a little more... *direct* than we remember you to be." Reuben chuckled nervously, his eyes on the now-unconscious man. "Then you go and do something like *that,* and it very clearly reminds me not to… I don't know, pop out and shout 'boo' at you?"

Everyone that had stepped forward to peek into the room practically tripped over themselves to squeeze past the archway as Nacho strolled toward the door that had just killed a Tier two human without issue.

The cook barely took notice of the 'Active Combat ended' notice, and only paused when he heard Reuben cast Healing Hugs, causing their Archer to groan and sit up. Taye's scratchy voice crossed the space, and Nacho let out a sigh of relief at the young man's words. "I feel terrible."

"You gotta be alive to feel anything," Brie commented, slapping him on the shoulder and pulling the teen to his feet. "Go rest over there for a few."

Only a few of the Brunch Force managed to get on their feet. Abby and Kala had made it, as well as—miraculously—Eduardo. The cook had no idea how that had happened; the man had literally been cut in half. After giving it a moment's thought, he could only shrug and say the words that went along with every other absolutely illogical thing that happened in this strange world. "Weird game logic."

Hazel let out a strangled cry and scrambled to her fallen husband's corpse. The heartbroken wife dropped to her knees next to Hank, and Nacho's heart forced him to feel a terrible pang of sympathy. "Urgh… thought I had managed to get to the point where that kind of emotion died before it could impact me. Being in charge of people is making me soft again."

Nacho *glared* at the golden puzzle door, pretty sure he knew how to open it. But… "Perhaps other things should come first."

In a move that would have been completely uncharacteristic for his past life, he turned back and went to sit with Hazel, doing what he could to comfort her while his internal monologue called him an idiot for not taking the time to consolidate his power. Every survivor knelt around her. Well, all except for Kala, who began the sordid task of collecting her dead, only pausing over Myron's body.

After staring at the lifeless form of her closest friend for a few moments, the Death Knight clenched her fists, walked to the archway, and spat into the room. "I'm *glad* you're dead, Dick. I'm just sad I didn't get to do it myself... Hey! Who here has fire magic? I want to burn that body until there's not even *dust* that can be used to remember him!"

There was no answer. Everyone was grieving in their own way. Taye's tears made tracks down through the dust on his face. Reuben was hugging anyone that needed a hug—healing or no—and Brie and Nacho were watching everyone else with a few feet between them.

Neither of them wanted to be caught up in a hug, no matter how many times Reuben gave them helpless glances.

Charlie was awake again, and he was healing, but he still looked pale. That only grew worse as he met Nacho's gaze, and his mouth started opening and closing. He tried to speak several times, and even though it seemed that he could talk clearly again, Nacho wasn't interested in what he had to say. "Before you start panicking again, let me remind you that I haven't run out of my ability to choke you out just because we aren't in combat."

Hazel wiped away her tears with sharp motions, then managed to get to her feet. "We're taking his body home. But... let's finish this. Nacho, how did you know? How could you *possibly* know that Crave would mess up the puzzle? If he had gotten that weapon, and he was Tier two... there was nothing you could have done to stop him from becoming the ruling tyrant of humanity. That was a huge risk, unless you *knew* he'd get it wrong."

Nacho could only point to the skewers. "Those changed when I entered the room the first time. I think the whole puzzle hinged upon what kind of player reached the door first. I'm a Satiation Player, and I believe I have the right recipe to whip up a solution for getting into that room. Besides, cloak, feather, and sword? That's a bad combo; you're basically *begging* to get back-stabbed."

Hazel sniffled and nodded, trying to put on a brave face. "You better go and win that spear."

"Uh, we'll stay out here, bucko." Abby forced a smile, though it looked ghastly.

Eduardo was silent, likely still getting over the shock of being *bisected* and coming back from it without any issue. Reuben locked arms with Nacho and started skipping. "It's you and me, buddy. If *you* get shish-kabobbed, *I* get shish-kabobbed."

"Brie makes it three." The Berserker escorted them into the room with far less cheer than Reuben managed. "At least if we get it wrong, we'll be fancy cheeses."

"What? I don't-" Reuben started, only for Brie to shake her head and gesture forward.

"Fancy cheeses are served on toothpicks, right?"

"You... you were making a *joke*!" Reuben pushed Nacho out of the way and swept her into a hug, tossing her back and forth. "Even when this could go horribly wrong? I *knew* I loved you!"

Nacho took a few moments to scoop some of Crave's corpse-sludge out of the way, just enough that he wouldn't step in it while moving the huge circles. Reuben bravely reached into the mess and retrieved Crave's Sleeping Feather in what was left of its holster from under the dead guy's arm. "Look at this! How did it survive that barrage? This is way too powerful to just leave laying around-"

The Sleeping Feather burst into flames, and Reuben tossed it with a yelp of surprise. The feather turned to ashes before it hit the stone floor, and the Healer seemed utterly crestfallen. Nacho tried to make his friend feel better. "At least you got a free upgrade on your Ring of Cheese."

Reuben sighed and rolled his shoulders. "The Patrons giveth, and the Patrons taketh away."

The rest of the Brunch Force used the wait to collect and divide up the magic items of the Final Victory that had popped out of Storage Slots. While his friends looted the bodies, Nacho got out his *Aria*. He leafed hurriedly through the pages full of intricate writing until he found the recipe. "This was a drop from Hana Banana. But even without this, I would've already thought that the chicken wing, the honeycomb, and the bottle of hot sauce symbols would've matched me. I just wouldn't have known what order to set them up in."

Nacho swallowed hard, a sudden thought shaking his confidence. His two best friends, who—in his mind—he had been sent through time to save, had almost not survived the first serious ambush they had found themselves in. His leadership, or lack thereof, had nearly cost him everything. A handful of lives had already been lost because of him, but if he ever needed to add those two to the list…

He shook off the intrusive thoughts and sucked in a deep breath. "We survived. We made it. Don't borrow trouble that doesn't exist."

Nacho focused on the door, turning the top circle to the chicken wing, the next circle to the honeycomb, and then the final one to the bottle of hot sauce. Hoping that he was right, he inserted the Ivory Talon into the lock. He felt himself sweating lightly. If he got even one wrong, he'd wind up on the floor with Crave and the gang. "The only positive thing is: if I got it wrong… I'll never know! Ha…"

Taye called from the archway. "We believe in you completely, Nacho! You got this!"

"Completely, eh? I notice that you're not stepping into the room, bucko," Abby gruffly pointed out.

The Archer's cheeks turned as pink as Kristie's hair. "Someone has to stay alive—I mean, if anything bad happens to Nacho. Which shouldn't happen. Because, you know, he's awesome."

Reuben loudly gave Nacho a command. "Come on, dude. Just turn that talon clockwise, and it's 'winner, winner, chicken dinner'. Dra~agon Spear. Dragon Spear. Dragon Spear!"

The others took up the chant as Reuben built up the tension. Even Kala raised an armored thumb. Nacho couldn't hold back for a single second after that, turning the key, hearing the door *click*, and bracing for pain. Instead… the symbols glowed and the entire door radiated energy before swinging open noiselessly.

"We did—*bleh*!" Nacho immediately clutched his nose as a smell hit him, the perfume of a porta potty after an August weekend at Lake Alcoholism.

Reuben grunted in actual pain. "Oh, celestials. I think we found what puts the 'cess' in 'cesspit'."

Brie was silent for a beat, then slammed on her helmet to hide her face. "If there's a dragon with food poisoning in there, I'm Combat Dashing the other way. Just saying… I will *not* be fighting anything that the Patrons came up with that is involved in a potty humor pun."

"Noted." Nacho summoned his glowing potstickers and sent them buzzing into the darkness beyond the door. A room made from crumbling red brick slowly grew more visible. It wasn't very big, and the interior was rather plain. A layer of smelly dirt covered the floor. Inside the center of the small chamber sat a cylinder, about five feet wide, eight feet long, and six feet tall. The smell seemed to be emitting from the cylinder, judging by the practically cartoonish waves of stink wafting in the air above it.

The cylinder bore no other embellishment than a hatch, hinges, and a handle.

Nacho crunched across the pungent, coarse dirt and took hold of the handle, steeling himself before wrenching it open.

The smell worsened considerably. Inside the plain metal box lay a thick layer of muck, but floating above the black filth was a Spear, rotating slightly in midair. The shaft had been crafted from a beautiful red-tinged wood, polished to a bright mahogany. Glowing golden filigree ran the length of the wood, and the spearhead was a dark sanguine metal—almost black—outlined in gold.

After how clean the dungeon had been, the crumbling brick, the nasty dirt, and the old-Earth metal cylinder seemed completely out of place. Even more disorienting was the fact that there were no heroic statues, nor any statues at all; just metal and murk. Abby eventually crossed the room, along with Kala, Kristie, and Taye. Eduardo and Hazel had stayed with Hank's body, which Nacho agreed was appropriate.

Abby poked at the spear with her staff. "That right there is a septic tank. Probably suitable for a small house with only a couple of people. That's old technology, too. They're doing amazing things with septic tanks, or they *were*, back on Earth. Leech fields, floats, valves—your basic eco-friendly wastewater management system."

Nacho had no idea how they were going to get that Dragon Spear out of the septic tank. There was absolutely no way he was going to crawl into that death trap. Charlie eased forward with a length of rope, already tying a knot. "Here. We can, you know, grab it with this. Rope is super useful. You guys aren't going to kill me… I'm helpful, right?"

"Charlie is the man!" Reuben strode forward and slapped the guy on the back. "Look at this old-school gamer with fifty feet of rope. Also, no, you're totally free to go. We wouldn't have hurt you either way; that's not our jam."

Charlie handed the rope to Nacho with shaking hands, clearly not trusting Reuben fully. The cook tossed the makeshift lariat over the spearhead and eased the rope behind the spear-head before pulling it taut on the shaft. Although the spear was floating above the muck and had not been embedded in the grossness, it somehow still felt like pulling a stick out of sludge,

Nacho drew the spear out of the septic tank inch by inch, then carefully grabbed it.

The minute he touched the wood, the System went crazy.

Greetings, All Players Everywhere in the AKC!

The Dragon Spear has been found! Yes, the Dragon Spear has been claimed by none other than Eli 'Nacho' Naches, leader of the Chips Guild. He has won the hearts and minds of so many, and not only do we think

that the Sunrise Brigade is going to join the Chips during their Guild Master's tenure, but the Final Victory Guild is now his to command!

Congratulations, big winner! Everyone else lost, and their wager is now yours. As we promised , winner take all!

The messages didn't end there, turning slightly more ominous.

Listen up people! Nacho and the Chips Guild are the big winners. That means no more mark of the Scarlet Symbol of Accusatory Trespassing for those who invaded the inner sanctum without the Ivory Talon. Now, that's enough about that! No more special attention where we tell everyone how amazing you're doing.

You get the bonus points for finding the KC Cesspit's inner sanctum, stinky friends! That's five thousand credits for finding the smelly sanctum and surviving. Nacho brought nine friends with him—Reuben, Brie, Kala, Charles, Hazel, Eduardo, Taye, Kristie, and Abigail! That's an additional forty-five thousand credits!

We'll also throw in an extra 50K of credits for an even 100K. Just kidding! We're only giving you your thousand-person guild bonus since The Final Victory guild submitted to your rule while we were sending this. Calculating everything out, the Chips guild has a total windfall of... 550,000 credits after all bets are also accounted for!

Minor note (and you really shouldn't worry about this too much): you've put yourselves on the CrossHumans' radar in a big way. Their entire planet now knows that the place to be on your Starter World is the AKC. It's not London. It's not France. It's not in Thailand's underpants! It's right there!

Good luck fighting the CrossHumans!

Arriod has his sword, but you have the spear. That's good, right?

May your futures be delicious.

. . .

The massive influx of credits was excellent, but the surprises didn't end there. As he watched on in growing horror, the spear in his hands fell apart... collapsing into a dozen metal skewers with polished wooden ends. Shape-wise, they were identical to the skewers that had killed Crave, only about five times as long.

"Yes! We didn't win *one* lousy Dragon Spear!" Reuben raised a fist and whooped. "We won a *dozen* Sewer Skewers!"

A new System message flashed across Nacho's field of vision.

Sewer Skewers? Love that name; we updated the item from 'Dragon Skewers' to 'Sewer Skewers'! What can the Sewer Skewers do? Let us get out the bullet points! Boom.
Each skewer:

- *Is a Tierless Weapon that anyone can use—as long as that 'anyone' is a Satiation Player.*
- *Will hit any monster, of any Tier, regardless of their Putrid Mana protection.*
- *Does a base damage of 25 Health Points in the hands of someone who knows what they are doing. These are not easy weapons to wield. They are **skewers**, not spears. There's a reason ancient warriors used Javelins and not cooking utensils in battle.*
- *So long as you have at least one of the Skewers in your possession and you are registered as their owner, you can recall all of them over the course of a minute at the cost of half your Mana pool.*
- *For every Sewer Skewer embedded in a single enemy, deal 10% additional damage with remaining Sewer Skewers.*
- *Will cook up something really scrumptious... fifty percent of the time. They work one hundred percent of the time to cook meat well. If we need to state it in plain language: half the time, the meal will be upgraded by one Rarity level. NOTE:*

Results may vary wildly based on the skill of the Satiation Player. Trash is still trash.
- *Releases a constant fume that attracts rats of all Tiers when in range. This is the weapon that has cooked their genus for all of human's history, and they hold a grudge.*
- *Deals 100% more damage to all Tiers of Rats.*

Nacho wasn't sure what all of the details meant, but he'd figure it out later. What he did understand was already amazing enough, especially the ability to automatically increase the Rarity of whatever he was cooking. Being able to create Epic food would allow him to provide another stack of buffs when people ate it. "These are great for me, but it says they might attract rats?"

"I mean… okay? I'm kinda shuddering at the thought of seeing rats every time I'm around you, but I can manage," Brie stated as they prepared to leave.

All of them were hoping that it would be smooth sailing through the KC Sewers. Without the Scarlet Symbol of Accusatory Trespassing, they would no longer have every monster around gunning for them. They'd finish plundering the bodies of the Final Victory, make preparations for their own dead, and then hightail it out of there.

Nacho fished the skewers out of what he kept calling 'mud' that covered the ground. It wasn't mud. Taking a deep breath, he promised himself that he was going to buy some Epic industrial-strength soap and clean them an embarrassing number of times in boiling water before ever using them to cook.

Weapons collected, enemies defeated, Health and Mana at full, the heartsore yet triumphant group started toward home.

One last thing before you leave the cesspit, Player! A fun little surprise we've been keeping back: the monsters of this dungeon!

. . .

They got as far as the archway to the pre-sanctum before sounds began echoing through the tunnels of the cesspit. Scratching, squeaking, a multitude of monsters closing in on their location. Reuben eyed Nacho sideways, shaking his head as he gestured at the new weapons. "Might attract 'some' rats, huh? You know Brie will make you pay for this."

"That's what it says!" Nacho defensively held his skewers closer, trying to figure out a better way of carrying them around than simply wearing a jingling stack of sharpened metal rods on his belt. He settled on keeping them in a Storage Slot, though it felt like a waste if he'd have to abandon the meat that was being stored there.

"At least you'll get some practice with the new weapons," Brie stated reluctantly.

Her observation gave Nacho pause, and he stared down at the unwieldy weapons, then recalled his heavily boosted Fitness stat. "That's a good point. I *do* need some practice. Give me some space, and only help me if I really need it."

"What are you…?" Reuben called nervously, his thought trailing off as Nacho launched forward and took the fight to the incoming dungeon monsters.

The cook braced a skewer in each hand, and only his practice in dealing with horrible situations allowed him to keep his grip on them as the dungeon monsters came into view. Not a single one of the creatures was below Tier one, but luckily, he only found a single one of them at Tier two, and it was waiting at the back of the wave of monsters, its beady little eyes locked on him in patient hunting mode.

Every moment of the ensuing battle was brutal, and Nacho was forced to rely on his inflated stats to bull his way through the murderous rodents. He attempted to fight with his usual finesse, but slashing attacks simply didn't work with this type of weapon, and he was forced to readjust his strategy time and again.

He found that the weapons worked extremely well as rapiers, insofar as parrying and reducing damage, while keeping his enemies at a distance. In terms of actually using them as a tool to implement pain, he found that they resembled punch daggers. The grip was a little wrong, but so long as he could maintain his angle of attack, they entered flesh in a very similar way. As soon as he was able to associate his new weapons with ones that he was fairly proficient with, the tide of the battle turned nearly instantly.

In the first wave, he had been pushed back relentlessly, but now he was dancing around the corridor, slamming skewers into bodies, then pulling fresh ones out of his Storage Slots without slowing down even slightly. When he was down to a single skewer, he whirled around and slapped a level seventeen rat in the face with his cast iron pan—before jamming the sharpened rod into its body and leaving it there. "Hold on to that for a moment for me, would you?"

Jumping backward and using the momentum to tuck into a barrel roll, Nacho sprang into wild motion, racing to his defeated enemies and pulling skewers out until he had collected what he considered to be enough of them. His hands full, he sprang back to the still-alive, still-furious rat that was waiting for him, and started poking it with his skewers until it finally succumbed to its wounds.

"I'm going to cook you after I win-" Breathing heavily, but only from sheer adrenaline, Nacho stared down at the Tier two rat and prepared himself mentally. It was going to be the first time that he was taking on a creature this strong by himself, let alone expecting to win. Fully psyched up, he cried out his nearly sinister taunt, "-so I get to taste victory *twice!*"

EPILOGUE

"I don't care how 'trustworthy' you'll be as a guild member. *We'll* control the credits." Nacho's eyebrow twitched as Kala balked at his flat denial of the last in a long string of demands for joining her guild to the Chips. "The Chips will control the credits. I'll cook, you'll eat. Together, we'll figure out how to beat the CrossHumans. You need to remember that it's not just monsters we'll be fighting, but beings that can think and plan as well as we can, and who actively want to destroy us. With the CrossHumans, it's total war. That's going to drive the other guilds to us anyway, even if the food situation doesn't do it first."

Kala flinched away at the venom in his words. Something about bearing witness to one single person taking down an entire swarm of Tier one rats, followed by essentially nailing a Tier two version to the wall with ten different skewers before driving one through its heart—laughing the entire time—had given her a *vastly* different attitude when dealing with the easygoing cook she had met so many months ago. "You're serious. That wasn't just another joke I didn't understand from the Patrons? The CrossHumans are real? Intelligent humanoid aliens from another world, pitted against us in a battle to the death?"

"I'm afraid so." Nacho nodded darkly. They had finished up down in the UnderFun and had almost fought their way back to the surface once more. It was not his favorite thing in the world to break his focus from his surroundings, especially in a dungeon, but everyone had known that asking her to be quiet until they were in a safe location was never going to work. Unfortunately, that meant that ending negotiations with her for her guild members was incredibly important for their long-term survival.

Nacho steeled himself and started sharing what little information he had. "The timeline has been accelerated, and Arriod —their leader—won't be what he would've been three years from now, even with the sword. We have a chance, which is something we need to take now, before things go as wrong as I *know* they can. If we're going to do that… we have to work together."

Kala finally found a smile, though it was a shadow of its usual brightness. "Good thing Final Victory already handed you their guild. Still, I can't imagine that guild is going to rally behind you."

"Luckily for us, they don't *need* to rally. Crave was the Guild *Master*, and they're bound by the deal he made on their behalf. Until Nacho gives them an option to get out, he can *force* them to do whatever he wants." Reuben lifted his mug. "To greedy killers who will sign away leadership at the drop of a hat for a *tiny* chance at success! You know, on that note, you could talk to the remnants of Final Victory and see who would want to live in Jalapeño Town. I'm sure you'll click with a few of those people; that's where we're going to house everyone that's a little too… *spicy* to enjoy the polite society we've built on Armor Mountain."

Kala didn't look at Nacho, keeping her eyes on Reuben. He'd won her over, and anyone could read the trust on her face. Nacho made a note to keep Brie from 'accidentally' giving the

Death Knight a permanent makeover if she tried to make a move on the charismatic man. "Even after I left, after I threatened you, and we almost killed each other... you'd still let me have Jalapeño Town?"

"*Have?*" Nacho shook his head with a wry smile. "You'll be placed in charge of it, but you're still going to be answerable to the Chips Guild."

She nodded without a hint of reluctance, her inner passion shining through. "I'll try not to be as difficult as... well, you know how I've been. Losing my father, Myron, some friends... this has been hard for me to take. However, I still have good people, and you're right. We're stronger together. I don't mind not being the final say anymore; I just want to have a voice. I've had it taken away before, and... I guess I'm afraid it will happen again."

"Doesn't hurt that Nacho can keep your people fed." Reuben put out a hand, and the two shook while Brie watched the interaction blandly. *Very* blandly. "We're looking forward to saving the world with you."

They were approaching the fetid waterfall that poured down the circular stairs to the surface when Taye called out to the cook. "Nacho! You'll want to come and see this... I think someone left us a message?"

Nacho hurried through the group and stopped at a blank wall. It was a rough painting done in a black pigment, depicting a dozen figures wearing sunglasses standing over the bodies of people with comically round pupils.

One of the figures standing above the dead humans was a man with a curved sword—a katana. He wasn't wearing sunglasses, and his eyes weren't round.

They were crosses.

Nacho felt a shiver at the back of neck. A cold sweat dripped down his sides as memories tried to take over and keep him afraid. He shoved the thoughts down, remembering that he wasn't the same person he had been the last time they had fought... and neither was Arriod. "Let's get home. We have a war to win."

"Don't be so glum, Nacho. All of us believe in you." Brie pulled her friend in for an awkward side-hug. "We all saw what you did to those rats, and we'll follow you to the abyss and back again, twice. If those CrossHumans have made the *very* unwise decision to come after us, I think that all you'll need to do is give them a taste of your Sewer Skewers."

ABOUT DAKOTA KROUT

Dakota Krout, a heartwarmingly clever author known for weaving fun, punny, and clean humor into his LitRPG fantasy novels, brings joy and laughter to readers through his best-selling series: including Cooking With Disaster, Divine Dungeon, Completionist Chronicles, and Full Murderhobo! His work, celebrated for its wit and charm, earned him a spot as one of Audible's top 5 fantasy picks in 2017, alongside a top 5 bestseller rank that was featured on the New York Times.

Drawing upon his experiences in the Army, Dakota expertly crafts vast, imaginative worlds with intricate systems that captivate and delight. His background in programming and information technology not only infuses his writing with a distinct, logical flair; but also fuels his innovative spirit in managing his publishing company, Mountaindale Press. These unique perspectives shine through in his stories, making him beloved by fans of all ages who seek a wholesome and humorous escape.

Dakota's journey in publishing has been filled with gratefulness, and a deep desire to continue bringing smiles and laughter to his readers. "I hope you Read Every Book With A Smile!" - Dakota Krout

Connect with Dakota:
MountaindalePress.com

Patreon.com/DakotaKrout
Facebook.com/DakotaKrout
Twitter.com/DakotaKrout
Discord.gg/mdp

ABOUT MOUNTAINDALE PRESS

Dakota and Danielle Krout, a husband and wife team, strive to create as well as publish excellent fantasy and science fiction novels. Self-publishing *The Divine Dungeon: Dungeon Born* in 2016 transformed their careers from Dakota's military and programming background and Danielle's Ph.D. in pharmacology to President and CEO, respectively, of a small press. Their goal is to share their success with other authors and provide captivating fiction to readers with the purpose of solidifying Mountaindale Press as the place 'Where Fantasy Transforms Reality.'

Connect with Mountaindale Press:
MountaindalePress.com
Facebook.com/MountaindalePress
Twitter.com/_Mountaindale
Instagram.com/MountaindalePress

MOUNTAINDALE PRESS TITLES
GameLit and LitRPG

The Completionist Chronicles,
Cooking with Disaster,
The Divine Dungeon,
Full Murderhobo, and
Year of the Sword by Dakota Krout

A Touch of Power by Jay Boyce

Red Mage and
Farming Livia by Xander Boyce

Ether Collapse and
Ether Flows by Ryan DeBruyn

Unbound by Nicoli Gonnella

Threads of Fate by Michael Head

Lion's Lineage by Rohan Hublikar and Dakota Krout

Wolfman Warlock by James Hunter and Dakota Krout

Axe Druid,
Mephisto's Magic Online, and
High Table Hijinks by Christopher Johns

Dragon Core Chronicles by Lars Machmüller

Pixel Dust and
Necrotic Apocalypse by David Petrie

Viceroy's Pride and
Tower of Somnus by Cale Plamann

Henchman by Carl Stubblefield

Artorian's Archives by Dennis Vanderkerken and Dakota Krout

Made in United States
Troutdale, OR
07/02/2024

20988790R00239